One Winter's Sunrise

KANDY SHEPHERD

ALISON ROBERTS

BARBARA HANNAY

MILLS & BOON

Published in Great Britain 2018
by Mills & Boon, an imprint of HarperCollins*Publishers*
1 London Bridge Street, London, SE1 9GF

ISBN: 978-0-263-26844-7

MIX
Paper from responsible sources
FSC™ C007454

This book is produced from independently certified FSC™ paper to ensure responsible forest management.

For more information visit: www.harpercollins.co.uk/green

Printed and bound in Spain
by CPI, Barcelona

GIFT-WRAPPED IN HER WEDDING DRESS

KANDY SHEPHERD

To all my Christmas magazine colleagues, in particular Helen, Adriana and Jane—
the magic of the season lives on!

CHAPTER ONE

So HE'D GOT on the wrong side of the media. Again. Dominic's words, twisted out of all recognition, were all over newspapers, television and social media.

Billionaire businessman Dominic Hunt refuses to sleep out with other CEOs in charity event for homeless.

Dominic slammed his fist on his desk so hard the pain juddered all the way up his arm. He hadn't *refused* to support the charity in their Christmas appeal, just refused the invitation to publicly bed down for the night in a cardboard box on the forecourt of the Sydney Opera House. His donation to the worthy cause had been significant—but anonymous. *Why wasn't that enough?*

He buried his head in his hands. For a harrowing time in his life there had been no choice for him but to sleep rough for real, a cardboard box his only bed. He couldn't go there again—not even for a charity stunt, no matter how worthy. There could be no explanation—he would not share the secrets of his past. *Ever.*

With a sick feeling of dread he continued to read onscreen the highlights of the recent flurry of negative press about him and his company, thoughtfully compiled in a report by his Director of Marketing.

Predictably, the reporters had then gone on to rehash his well-known aversion to Christmas. Again he'd been misquoted. It was true he loathed the whole idea of celebrating Christmas. But not for the reasons the media had so fancifully contrived. Not because he was a *Scrooge.* How he hated that label and the erroneous aspersions that he didn't ever give to charity. Despaired that he was included in a round-up of Australia's Multi-Million-Dollar Misers. *It couldn't be further from the truth.*

He strongly believed that giving money to worthy causes should be conducted in private—not for public acclaim. But this time he couldn't ignore the name-calling and innuendo. He was near to closing a game-changing deal on a joint venture with a family-owned American corporation run by a man with a strict moral code that included obvious displays of philanthropy.

Dominic could not be seen to be a Scrooge. He had to publicly prove that he was not a miser. But he did not want to reveal the extent of his charitable support because to do so would blow away the smokescreen he had carefully constructed over his past.

He'd been in a bind. Until his marketing director had suggested he would attract positive press if he opened his harbourside home for a lavish fund-raising event for charity. 'Get your name in the newspaper for the right reasons,' he had been advised.

Dominic hated the idea of his privacy being invaded but he had reluctantly agreed. He wanted the joint venture to happen. If a party was what it took, he was prepared to put his qualms aside and commit to it.

The party would be too big an event for it to be organised in-house. His marketing people had got outside companies involved. Trouble was the three so-called 'party planners' he'd been sent so far had been incompetent and he'd shown them the door within minutes of meeting. Now there was a fourth. He glanced down at the eye-catching card on the desk in front of him. Andrea Newman from a company called Party Queens—*No party too big or too small* the card boasted.

Party Queens. It was an interesting choice for a business name. Not nearly as stitched up as the other companies that had pitched for this business. But did it have the gravitas required? After all, this event could be the deciding factor in a deal that would extend his business interests internationally.

He glanced at his watch. This morning he was working from his home office. Ms Newman was due to meet with him right now, here at his house where the party was to take place. Despite the attention-grabbing name of the business, he had no reason to expect Party Planner Number Four to be any more impressive than the other three he'd sent packing. But he would give her twenty minutes—that was only fair and he made a point of always being fair.

On cue, the doorbell rang. Punctuality, at least, was a point in Andrea Newman's favour. He headed down the wide marble stairs to the front door.

His first impression of the woman who stood on his porch was that she was attractive, not in a conventionally pretty way but something rather more interesting—an angular face framed by a tangle of streaked blonde hair, a wide generous mouth, unusual green eyes. So attractive he found himself looking at her for a moment longer than was required to sum up a possible contractor. And the almost imperceptible curve of her mouth let him know she'd noticed.

'Good morning, Mr Hunt—Andie Newman from Party Queens,' she said. 'Thank you for the pass code that got me through the gate. Your security is formidable, like an eastern suburbs fortress.' Was that a hint of challenge underscoring her warm, husky voice? If so, he wasn't going to bite.

'The pass code expires after one use, Ms Newman,' he said, not attempting to hide a note of warning. The three party planners before her were never going to get a new pass code. But none of them had been remotely like her—in looks or manner.

She was tall and wore a boldly patterned skirt of some silky fine fabric that fell below her knees in uneven layers, topped by a snug-fitting rust-coloured jacket and high heeled shoes that laced all the way up her calf. A soft leather satchel was slung casually across her shoulder. She presented as smart but more unconventional than the corporate dark suits and rigid briefcases of the other three—whose ideas had been as pedestrian as their appearances.

'Andie,' she replied and started to say something else about his security system. But, as she did, a sudden gust of balmy spring breeze whipped up her skirt, revealing long slender legs and a tantalising hint of red underwear. Dominic tried to do the gentlemanly thing and look elsewhere—difficult when she was standing so near to him and her legs were so attention-worthy.

'Oh,' she gasped, and fought with the skirt to hold it down, but no sooner did she get the front of the skirt in place, the back whipped upwards and she had to twist around to hold it down. The back view of her legs was equally as impressive as the front. He balled his hands into fists by his sides so he did not give into the temptation to help her with the flyaway fabric.

She flushed high on elegant cheekbones, blonde hair tousled around her face, and laughed a husky, uninhibited laugh as she battled to preserve her modesty. The breeze died down as quickly as it had sprung up and her skirt floated back into place. Still, he noticed she continued to keep it in check with a hand on her thigh.

'That's made a wonderful first impression, hasn't it?' she said, looking up at him with a rueful smile. For a long moment their eyes connected and he was the first to look away. *She was beautiful.*

As she spoke, the breeze gave a final last sigh that ruffled her hair across her face. Dominic wasn't a fanciful man, but it seemed as though the wind was ushering her into his house.

'There are worse ways of making an impression,' he said gruffly. 'I'm interested to see what you follow up with.'

Andie wasn't sure what to reply. She stood at the threshold of Dominic Hunt's multi-million-dollar mansion and knew for the first time in her career she was in serious danger of losing the professional cool in which she took such pride.

Not because of the incident with the wind and her skirt. Or because she was awestruck by the magnificence of the house and the postcard-worthy panorama of Sydney Harbour that stretched out in front of it. No. It was the man who towered above her who was making her feel so inordinately flustered. Too tongue-tied to come back with a quick quip or clever retort.

'Th…thank you,' she managed to stutter as she pushed the breeze-swept hair back from across her face.

During her career as a stylist for both magazines and advertising agencies, and now as a party planner, she had acquired the reputation of being able to manage difficult people. Which was why her two partners in their fledgling business had voted for her to be the one to deal with Dominic Hunt. Party Queens desperately needed a high-profile booking like this to help them get established. Winning it was now on her shoulders.

She had come to his mansion forewarned that he could be a demanding client. The gossip was that he had been scathing to three other planners from other companies much bigger than theirs before giving them the boot. Then there was his wider reputation as a Scrooge—a man who did not share his multitude of money with others less fortunate. He was everything she did not admire in a person.

Despite that, she been blithely confident Dominic Hunt wouldn't be more than she could handle. Until he had answered that door. Her reaction to him had her stupefied.

She had seen the photos, watched the interviews of the billionaire businessman, had recognised he was good-looking in a dark, brooding way. But no amount of research had prepared her for the pulse-raising reality of this man—tall, broad-shouldered, powerful muscles apparent even in his sleek tailored grey suit. He wasn't pretty-boy handsome. Not with that strong jaw, the crooked nose that looked as though it had been broken by a viciously aimed punch, the full, sensual mouth with the faded white scar on the corner, the spiky black hair. And then there was the almost palpable emanation of power.

She had to call on every bit of her professional savvy to ignore the warm flush that rose up her neck and onto her cheeks, the way her heart thudded into unwilling awareness of Dominic Hunt, not as a client but as a man.

She could not allow that to happen. This job was too important to her and her friends in their new business. *Anyway, dark and brooding wasn't her type.* Her ideal man was sensitive and sunny-natured, like her first lost love, for whom she felt she would always grieve.

She extended her hand, willing it to stay steady, and forced a smile. 'Mr Hunt, let's start again. Andie Newman from Party Queens.'

His grip in return was firm and warm and he nodded acknowledgement of her greeting. If a mere handshake could send shivers of awareness through her, she could be in trouble here.

Keep it businesslike. She took a deep breath, tilted back her head to meet his gaze full-on. 'I believe I'm the fourth party planner you've seen and I don't want there to be a fifth. I should be the person to plan your event.'

If he was surprised at her boldness, it didn't show in his scrutiny; his grey eyes remained cool and assessing.

'You'd better come inside and convince me why that should be the case,' he said. Even his voice was attractive—deep and measured and utterly masculine.

'I welcome the opportunity,' she said in the most confident voice she could muster.

She followed him into the entrance hall of the restored nineteen-twenties house, all dark stained wood floors and cream marble. A grand central marble staircase with wrought-iron balustrades split into two sides to climb to the next floor. This wasn't the first grand home she'd been in during the course of her work but it was so impressive she had to suppress an impulse to gawk.

'Wow,' she said, looking around her, forgetting all about how disconcerted Dominic Hunt made her feel. 'The staircase. It's amazing. I can just see a choir there, with a chorister on each step greeting your guests with Christmas carols as they step into the house.' Her thoughts raced ahead of her. Choristers' robes in red and white? Each chorister holding a scrolled parchment printed with the words to the carol? What about the music? A string quartet? A harpsichord?

'What do you mean?' he said, breaking into her reverie.

Andie blinked to bring herself back to earth and turned to look up at him. She smiled. 'Sorry. I'm getting ahead of myself. It was just an idea. Of course I realise I still need to convince you I'm the right person for your job.'

'I meant about the Christmas carols.'

So he would be that kind of pernickety client, pressing her for details before they'd even decided on the bigger picture. Did she need to spell out the message of 'Deck the Halls with Boughs of Holly'?

She shook her head in a don't-worry-about-it way. 'It was just a top-of-mind thought. But a choir would be an amazing use of the staircase. Maybe a children's choir. Get your guests into the Christmas spirit straight away, without being too cheesy about it.'

'It isn't going to be a Christmas party.' He virtually spat the word *Christmas*.

'But a party in December? I thought—'

He frowned and she could see where his reputation came from as his thick brows drew together and his eyes darkened. 'Truth be told, I don't want a party here at all. But it's a necessary evil—necessary to my business, that is.'

'Really?' she said, struggling not to jump in and say the wrong thing. A client who didn't actually want a party? This she hadn't anticipated. Her certainty that she knew how to handle this situation—this man—started to seep away.

She gritted her teeth, forced her voice to sound as conciliatory as possible. 'I understood from your brief that you wanted a big event benefiting a charity in the weeks leading up to Christmas on a date that will give you maximum publicity.'

'All that,' he said. 'Except it's not to be a Christmas party. Just a party that happens to be held around that time.'

Difficult and demanding didn't begin to describe this. But had she been guilty of assuming December translated into Christmas? Had it actually stated that in the brief? She didn't think she'd misread it.

She drew in a calming breath. 'There seems to have been a misunderstanding and I apologise for that,' she said. 'I have the official briefing from your marketing department here.' She patted her satchel. 'But I'd rather hear your thoughts, your ideas for the event in your own words.

A successful party plan comes from the heart. Can we sit down and discuss this?'

He looked pointedly at his watch. Her heart sank to the level of the first lacing on her shoes. She did not want to be the fourth party planner he fired before she'd even started her pitch. 'I'll give you ten minutes,' he said.

He led her into a living room that ran across the entire front of the house and looked out to the blue waters of the harbour and its icons of the Sydney Harbour Bridge and the Opera House. Glass doors opened out to a large terrace. *A perfect summer party terrace.*

Immediately she recognised the work of one of Sydney's most fashionable high-end interior designers—a guy who only worked with budgets that started with six zeros after them. The room worked neutral tones and metallics in a nod to the art deco era of the original house. The result was masculine but very, very stylish.

What an awesome space for a party. But she forced thoughts of the party out of her head. She had ten minutes to win this business. Ten minutes to convince Dominic Hunt she was the one he needed.

CHAPTER TWO

DOMINIC SAT ANDIE NEWMAN down on the higher of the two sofas that faced each other over the marble coffee table—the sofa he usually chose to give himself the advantage. He had no need to impress her with his greater height and bulk—she was tall, but he was so much taller than her even as he sat on the lower seat. Besides, the way she positioned herself with shoulders back and spine straight made him think she wouldn't let herself be intimidated by him or by anyone else. *Think again.* The way she crossed and uncrossed those long legs revealed she was more nervous than she cared to let on.

He leaned back in his sofa, pulled out her business card from the inside breast pocket of his suit jacket and held it between finger and thumb. 'Tell me about Party Queens. This seems like a very new, shiny card.'

'Brand new. We've only been in business for three months.'

'We?'

'My two business partners, Eliza Dunne and Gemma Harper. We all worked on a magazine together before we started our own business.'

He narrowed his eyes. 'Now you're "party queens"?' He used his fingers to enclose the two words with quote marks. 'I don't see the connection.'

'We always were party queens—even when we were working on the magazine.' He quirked an eyebrow and she paused. He noticed she quirked an eyebrow too, in unconscious imitation of his action. 'Not in that way.' She tried to backtrack, then smiled. 'Well, maybe somewhat in that way. Between us we've certainly done our share of partying. But then you have to actually enjoy a party to organise one; don't you agree?'

'It's not something I've given thought to,' he said. Business-wise, it could be a point either for her or against her.

Parties had never been high on his agenda—even after his money had opened so many doors for him. Whether he'd been sleeping rough in an abandoned building project in the most dangerous part of Brisbane or hobnobbing with decision makers in Sydney, he'd felt he'd never quite fitted in. So he did the minimum socialising required for his business. 'You were a journalist?' he asked, more than a little intrigued by her.

She shook her head. 'My background is in interior design but when a glitch in the economy meant the company I worked for went bust, I ended up as an interiors editor on a lifestyle magazine. I put together shoots for interiors and products and I loved it. Eliza and Gemma worked on the same magazine, Gemma as the food editor and Eliza on the publishing side. Six months ago we were told out of the blue that the magazine was closing and we had all lost our jobs.'

'That must have been a shock,' he said.

When he'd first started selling real estate at the age of eighteen he'd lived in terror he'd lose his job. Underlying all his success was always still that fear—which was why he was so driven to keep his business growing and thriving. Without money, without a home, he could slide back into being Nick Hunt of 'no fixed abode' rather than Dominic Hunt of Vaucluse, one of the most exclusive addresses in Australia.

'It shouldn't have come as a shock,' she said. 'Magazines close all the time in publishing—it's an occupational hazard. But when it actually happened, when *again* one minute I had a job and the next I didn't, it was…soul-destroying.'

'I'm sorry,' he said.

She shrugged. 'I soon picked myself up.'

He narrowed his eyes. 'It's quite a jump from a magazine job to a party planning business.' Her lack of relevant experience could mean Party Planner Number Four would go the way of the other three. He was surprised at how disappointed that made him feel.

'It might seem that way, but hear me out,' she said, a determined glint in her eye. If one of the other planners had said that, he would have looked pointedly at his watch. This one, he was prepared to listen to—he was actually interested in her story.

'We had to clear our desks immediately and were marched out of the offices by security guards. Shell-shocked, we all retired to a café and thought about what we'd do. The magazine's deputy editor asked could we organise her sister's eighteenth birthday party. At first we said no, thinking she was joking. But then we thought about it. A big magazine shoot that involves themes and food and props is quite a production. We'd also sometimes organise magazine functions for advertisers. We realised that between us we knew a heck of a lot about planning parties.'

'As opposed to enjoying them,' he said.

'That's right,' she said with a smile that seemed reminiscent of past parties enjoyed. 'Between the three of us we had so many skills we could utilise.'

'Can you elaborate on that?'

She held up a slender index finger, her nails tipped with orange polish. 'One, I'm the ideas and visuals person—creative, great with themes and props and highly organised with follow-through.' A second finger went up.

'Two, Gemma trained as a chef and is an amazing food person—food is one of the most important aspects of a good party, whether cooking it yourself or knowing which chefs to engage.'

She had a little trouble getting the third finger to stay straight and swapped it to her pinkie. 'Then, three, Eliza has her head completely around finances and contracts and sales and is also quite the wine buff.'

'So you decided to go into business together?' Her entrepreneurial spirit appealed to him.

She shook her head so her large multi-hoop gold earrings clinked. 'Not then. Not yet. We agreed to do the eighteenth party while we looked for other jobs and freelanced for magazines and ad agencies.'

'How did it work out?' He thought about his eighteenth birthday. It had gone totally unmarked by any celebration —except his own jubilation that he was legally an adult and could never now be recalled to the hell his home had become. It had also marked the age he could be tried as an adult if he had skated too close to the law—though by that time his street-fighting days were behind him.

'There were a few glitches, of course, but overall it was a great success. The girl went to a posh private school and both girls and parents loved the girly shoe theme we organised. One eighteenth led to another and soon we had other parents clamouring for us to do their kids' parties.'

'Is there much money in parties for kids?' He didn't have to ask all these questions but he was curious. Curious about her as much as anything.

Her eyebrows rose. 'You're kidding, right? We're talking wealthy families on the eastern suburbs and north shore. We're talking one-upmanship.' He enjoyed the play of expressions across her face, the way she gesticulated with her hands as she spoke. 'Heck, we've done a four-year-old's party on a budget of thousands.'

'All that money for a four-year-old?' He didn't have anything to do with kids except through his anonymous charity work. Had given up on his dream he would ever have children of his own. In fact, he was totally out of touch with family life.

'You'd better believe it,' she said.

He was warming to Andie Newman—how could any red-blooded male not?—but he wanted to ensure she was experienced enough to make his event work. All eyes would be on it as up until now he'd been notoriously private. If he threw a party, it had better be a good party. Better than good.

'So when did you actually go into business?'

'We were asked to do more and more parties. Grown-up parties too. Thirtieths and fortieths, even a ninetieth. It snowballed. Yet we still saw it as a stopgap thing although people suggested we make it a full-time business.'

'A very high percentage of small businesses go bust in the first year,' he couldn't help but warn.

She pulled a face that told him she didn't take offence. 'We were very aware of that. Eliza is the profit and loss spreadsheet maven. But then a public relations company I worked freelance for asked us to do corporate parties and product launches. The work was rolling in. We began to think we should make it official and form our own company.'

'A brave move.' He'd made brave moves in his time—and most of them had paid off. He gave her credit for initiative.

She leaned forward towards him. This close he could appreciate how lovely her eyes were. He didn't think he had ever before met anyone with genuine green eyes. 'We've leased premises in the industrial area of Alexandria and we're firing. But I have to be honest with you—we haven't done anything with potentially such a profile as your party.

We want it. We need it. And because we want it to so much we'll pull out every stop to make it a success.'

Party Planner Number Four clocked up more credit for her honesty. He tapped the card on the edge of his hand. 'You've got the enthusiasm; do you have the expertise? Can you assure me you can do my job and do it superlatively well?'

Those remarkable green eyes were unblinking. 'Yes. Absolutely. Undoubtedly. There might only be three of us, but between us we have a zillion contacts in Sydney—chefs, decorators, florists, musicians, waiting staff. If we can't do it ourselves we can pull in the right people who can. And none of us is afraid of the hard work a party this size would entail. We would welcome the challenge.'

He realised she was now sitting on the edge of the sofa, her hands clasped together and her foot crossed over her ankle was jiggling. She really did want this job—wanted it badly.

Dominic hadn't got where he was without a fine-tuned instinct for people. Instincts honed first on the streets where trusting the wrong person could have been fatal and then in the cut-throat business of high-end real estate and property development. His antennae were telling him Andie Newman would be able to deliver—and that he would enjoy working with her.

Trouble was, while he thought she might be the right person for the job, he found her very attractive and would like to ask her out. And he couldn't do both. He *never* dated staff or suppliers. He'd made that mistake with his ex-wife—he would not make it again. Hire Andie Newman and he was more than halfway convinced he would get a good party planner. Not hire her and he could ask her on a date. But he needed this event to work—and for that the planning had to be in the best possible hands. He was torn.

'I like your enthusiasm,' he said. 'But I'd be taking

a risk by working with a company that is in many ways still…unproven.'

Her voice rose marginally—she probably didn't notice but to him it betrayed her anxiety to impress. 'We have a file overflowing with references from happy clients. But before you come to any decisions let's talk about what you're expecting from us. The worst thing that can happen is for a client to get an unhappy surprise because we've got the brief wrong.'

She pulled out a folder from her satchel. He liked that it echoed the design of her business card. That showed an attention to detail. The chaos of his early life had made him appreciate planning and order. He recognised his company logo on the printout page she took from the folder and quickly perused.

'So tell me,' she said, when she'd finished reading it. 'I'm puzzled. Despite this briefing document stating the party is to be "A high-profile Christmas event to attract favourable publicity for Dominic Hunt" you still insist it's not to reference Christmas in any way. Which is correct?'

Andie regretted the words almost as soon as they'd escaped from her mouth. She hadn't meant to confront Dominic Hunt or put him on the spot. Certainly she hadn't wanted to get him offside. But the briefing had been ambiguous and she felt she had to clarify it if she was to secure this job for Party Queens.

She needed their business to succeed—never again did she want to be at the mercy of the whims of a corporate employer. To have a job one day and then suddenly not the next day was too traumatising after that huge personal change of direction she'd had forced upon her five years ago. But she could have put her question with more subtlety.

He didn't reply. The silence that hung between them became more uncomfortable by the second. His face tightened with an emotion she couldn't read. Anger? Sorrow? Regret? Whatever it was, the effect was so powerful she had to force herself not to reach over and put her hand on his arm to comfort him, maybe even hug him. And that would be a mistake. Even more of a mistake than her ill-advised question had been.

She cringed that she had somehow prompted the unleashing of thoughts that were so obviously painful for him. Then braced herself to be booted out on to the same scrapheap as the three party planners who had preceded her.

Finally he spoke, as if the words were being dragged out of him. 'The brief was incorrect. Christmas has some… difficult memories attached to it for me. I don't celebrate the season. Please just leave it at that.' For a long moment his gaze held hers and she saw the anguish recede.

Andie realised she had been holding her breath and she let it out with a slow sigh of relief, amazed he hadn't shown her the door.

'Of…of course,' she murmured, almost gagging with gratitude that she was to be given a second chance. And she couldn't deny that she wanted that chance. Not just for the job but—she could not deny it—the opportunity to see more of this undoubtedly interesting man.

There was something deeper here, some private pain, that she did not understand. But it would be bad-mannered prying to ask any further questions.

She didn't know much about his personal life. Just that he was considered a catch—rich, handsome, successful. *Though not her type, of course.* He lived here alone, she understood, in this street in Vaucluse where house prices started in the double digit millions. Wasn't there a bitter divorce in his background—an aggrieved ex-wife, a public battle for ownership of the house? She'd have to look it up. If she were to win this job—and she understood that it was still a big *if*—she needed to get a grasp on how this man ticked.

'Okay, so that's sorted—no Christmas,' she said, aiming to sound briskly efficient without any nod to the anguish she had read at the back of his eyes. 'Now I know what you *don't* want for your party, let's talk about what you *do* want. I'd like to hear in your words what you expect from this party. Then I can give you my ideas based on your thoughts.'

The party proposals she had hoped to discuss had been based on Christmas; she would have to do some rapid thinking.

Dominic Hunt got up from the sofa and started to pace. He was so tall, his shoulders so broad, he dominated even the large, high-ceilinged room. Andie found herself wondering about his obviously once broken nose—who had thrown the first punch? She got up, not to pace alongside him but to be closer to his level. She did not feel intimidated by him but she could see how he could be intimidating.

'The other planners babbled on about how important it was to invite A-list and B-list celebrities to get publicity. I don't give a damn about celebrities and I can't see how that's the right kind of publicity.'

Andie paused, not sure what to say, only knowing she had to be careful not to *babble on*. 'I can organise the party, but the guest list is up to you and your people.'

He stopped his pacing, stepped closer. 'But do you agree with me?'

Was this a test question? Answer incorrectly and that scrapheap beckoned? As always, she could only be honest. 'I do agree with you. It's my understanding that this party is aimed at…at image repair.'

'You mean repair to my image as a miserly Scrooge who hoards all his money for himself?'

She swallowed a gasp at the bitterness of his words, then looked up at him to see not the anger she expected but a kind of manly bewilderment that surprised her.

'I mightn't have put it quite like that, but yes," she said. 'You do have that reputation and I understand you want to demonstrate it's not so. And yes, I think the presence of a whole lot of freeloading so-called celebrities who run the gamut from the A to the Z list and have nothing to do with the charities you want to be seen to be supporting might not help. But you *are* more likely to get coverage in the social pages if they attend.'

He frowned. 'Is there such a thing as a Z-list celebrity?'

She laughed. 'If there isn't, there should be. Maybe I made it up.'

'You did say you were creative,' he said. He smiled—the first real smile she'd seen from him. It transformed his face, like the sun coming out from behind a dark storm cloud, unleashing an unexpected charm. Her heartbeat tripped into double time like it had the first moment she'd seen him. Why? Why this inexplicable reaction to a man she should dislike for his meanness and greed?

She made a show of looking around her to disguise her consternation. Tamed the sudden shakiness in her voice into a businesslike tone. 'How many magazines or lifestyle programmes have featured this house?' she asked.

'None. They never will,' he said.

'Good,' she said. 'The house is both magnificent and unknown. I reckon even your neighbours would be willing to cough up a sizeable donation just to see inside.' In her mind's eye she could see the house transformed into a glittering party paradise. 'The era of the house is nineteen-twenties, right?'

'Yes,' he said. 'It was originally built for a wealthy wool merchant.'

She thought some more. 'Why not an extravagant

Great Gatsby twenties-style party with a silver and white theme—that gives a nod to the festive season—and a strictly curated guest list? Guests would have to dress in silver or white. Or both. Make it very exclusive, an invitation to be sought after. The phones of Sydney's social set would be set humming to see who got one or not.' Her eyes half shut as her mind bombarded her with images. 'Maybe a masked party. Yes. Amazing silver and white masks. Bejewelled and befeathered. Fabulous masks that could be auctioned off at some stage for your chosen charity.'

'Auctioned?'

Her eyes flew open and she had to orientate herself back into the reality of the empty room that she had just been envisioning filled with elegant partygoers. Sometimes when her creativity was firing she felt almost in a trance. Then it was her turn to frown. How could a Sydney billionaire be such a party innocent?

Even she, who didn't move in the circles of society that attended lavish fund-raising functions, knew about the auctions. The competitive bidding could probably be seen as the same kind of one-upmanship as the spending of thousands on a toddler's party. 'I believe it's usual to have a fund-raising auction at these occasions. Not just the masks, of course. Other donated items. Something really big to up the amount of dollars for your charity.' She paused. 'You're a property developer, aren't you?'

He nodded. 'Among other interests.'

'Maybe you could donate an apartment? There'd be some frenzied bidding for that from people hoping for a bargain. And you would look generous.'

His mouth turned down in an expression of distaste. 'I'm not sure that's in keeping with the image I want to… to reinvent.'

Privately she agreed with him—why couldn't people just donate without expecting a lavish party in return? But she kept her views to herself. Creating those lavish parties was her job now.

'That's up to you and your people. The guest list and the auction, I mean. But the party? That's my domain. Do you like the idea of the twenties theme to suit the house?' In her heart she still longed for the choristers on the staircase. Maybe it would have to be a jazz band on the steps. That could work. Not quite the same romanticism and spirit as Christmas, but it would be a spectacular way to greet guests.

'I like it,' he said slowly.

She forced herself not to panic, not to bombard him with a multitude of alternatives. 'If not that idea, I have lots of others. I would welcome the opportunity to present them to you.'

He glanced at his watch and she realised she had been there for much longer than the ten-minute pitch he'd allowed. Surely that was a good sign.

'I'll schedule in another meeting with you tomorrow afternoon,' he said.

'You mean a second interview?' she asked, fingers crossed behind her back.

'No. A brainstorming session. You've got the job, Ms Newman.'

It was only as, jubilant, she made her way to the door—conscious of his eyes on her back—that she wondered at the presence of a note of regret in Dominic Hunt's voice.

CHAPTER THREE

TRY AS SHE MIGHT, Andie couldn't get excited about the nineteen-twenties theme she had envisaged for Dominic Hunt's party. It would be lavish and glamorous and she would enjoy every moment of planning such a visually splendid event. Such a party would be a spangled feather in Party Queens' cap. But it seemed somehow *wrong.*

The feeling niggled at her. How could something so extravagant, so limited to those who could afford the substantial donation that would be the cost of entrance make Dominic Hunt look less miserly? Even if he offered an apartment for auction—and there was no such thing as a cheap apartment in Sydney—and raised a lot of money, wouldn't it be a wealthy person who benefited? Might he appear to be a Scrooge hanging out with other rich people who might or might not also be Scrooges? Somehow, it reeked of...well, there was no other word but hypocrisy.

It wasn't her place to be critical—the media-attention-grabbing party was his marketing people's idea. Her job was to plan the party and make it as memorable and spectacular as possible. But she resolved to bring up her reservations in the brainstorming meeting with him. *If she dared.*

She knew it would be a fine line to tread—she did not want to risk losing the job for Party Queens—but she felt she had to give her opinion. After that she would just keep her mouth shut and concentrate on making his event the most memorable on the December social calendar.

She dressed with care for the meeting, which was again at his Vaucluse mansion. *An outfit that posed no danger of showing off her underwear.* Slim white trousers, a white top, a string of outsize turquoise beads, silver sandals that strapped around her ankles. At the magazine she'd made friends with the fashion editor and still had access to sample sales and special deals. She felt her wardrobe could hold its own in whatever company she found herself in—even on millionaire row.

'I didn't risk wearing that skirt,' she blurted out to Dominic Hunt as he let her into the house. 'Even though there doesn't appear to be any wind about.'

Mentally she slammed her hand against her forehead. What a dumb top-of-mind remark to make to a client. But he still made her nervous. Try as she might, she couldn't shake that ever-present awareness of how attractive he was.

His eyes flickered momentarily to her legs. 'Shame,' he said in that deep, testosterone-edged voice that thrilled through her.

Was he flirting with her?

'It…it was a lovely skirt,' she said. 'Just…just rather badly behaved.' How much had he seen when her skirt had flown up over her thighs?

'I liked it very much,' he said.

'The prettiness of its fabric or my skirt's bad behaviour?'

She held his cool grey gaze for a second longer than she should.

'Both,' he said.

She took a deep breath and tilted her chin upward. 'I'll take that as a compliment,' she said with a smile she hoped radiated aplomb. 'Thank you, Mr Hunt.'

'Dominic,' he said.

'Dominic,' she repeated, liking the sound of his name on her lips. 'And thank you again for this opportunity to plan your party.' *Bring it back to business.*

In truth, she would have liked to tell him how good he looked in his superbly tailored dark suit and dark shirt but she knew her voice would come out all choked up. Because it wasn't the Italian elegance of his suit that she found herself admiring. It was the powerful, perfectly proportioned male body that inhabited it. And she didn't want to reveal even a hint of that. *He was a client.*

He nodded in acknowledgement of her words. 'Come through to the back,' he said. 'You can see how the rooms might work for the party.'

She followed him through where the grand staircase split—a choir really would be amazing ranged on the steps—over pristine marble floors to a high-ceilinged room so large their footsteps echoed as they walked into the centre of it. Furnished minimally in shades of white, it looked ready for a high-end photo shoot. Arched windows and a wall of folding doors opened through to an elegant art deco style swimming pool and then to a formal garden planted with palm trees and rows of budding blue agapanthus.

For a long moment Andie simply absorbed the splendour of the room. 'What a magnificent space,' she said finally. 'Was it originally a ballroom?'

'Yes. Apparently the wool merchant liked to entertain in grand style. But it wasn't suited for modern living, which is why I opened it up through to the terrace when I remodelled the house.'

'You did an awesome job,' she said. In her mind's eye she could see flappers in glittering dresses trimmed with feathers and fringing, and men in dapper suits doing the Charleston. Then had to blink, not sure if she was imagining what the room had once been or how she'd like it to be for Dominic's party.

'The people who work for me did an excellent job,' he said.

'As an interior designer I give them full marks,' she said. She had gone to university with Dominic's designer. She just might get in touch with him, seeking inside gossip into what made Dominic Hunt tick.

She looked around her. 'Where's the kitchen? Gemma will shoot me if I go back without reporting to her on the cooking facilities.'

'Through here.'

Andie followed him through to an adjoining vast state-of-the-art kitchen, gleaming in white marble and stainless steel. The style was sleek and modern but paid homage to the vintage of the house. She breathed out a sigh of relief and pleasure. A kitchen like this would make catering for hundreds of guests so much easier. Not that the food was her department. Gemma kept that under her control. 'It's a superb kitchen. Do you cook?'

Was Dominic the kind of guy who ate out every night and whose refrigerator contained only cartons of beer? Or the kind who excelled at cooking and liked to show off his skills to a breathlessly admiring female audience?

'I can look after myself,' he said shortly. 'That includes cooking.'

That figured. After yesterday's meeting she had done some research into Dominic Hunt—though there wasn't much information dating back further than a few years. Along with his comments about celebrating Christmas being a waste of space, he'd also been quoted as saying he would never marry again. From the media accounts, his marriage in his mid-twenties had been short, tumultuous and public, thanks to his ex-wife's penchant for spilling the details to the gossip columns.

'The kitchen and its position will be perfect for the caterers,' she said. 'Gemma will be delighted.'

'Good,' he said.

'You must love this house.' She could not help a wistful note from edging her voice. As an interior designer she knew only too well how much the remodelling would have cost. Never in a million years would she live in a house like this. He was only a few years older than her—thirty-two to her twenty-eight—yet it was as if they came from different planets.

He shrugged those impressively broad shoulders. 'It's a spectacular house. But it's just a house. I never get attached to places.'

Or people?

Her online research had showed him snapped by paparazzi with a number of long-legged beauties—but no woman more than once or twice. *What did it matter to her?*

She patted her satchel. *Back to business.* 'I've come prepared for brainstorming,' she said. 'Have you had any thoughts about the nineteen-twenties theme I suggested?'

'I've thought,' he said. He paused. 'I've thought about it a lot.'

His tone of voice didn't give her cause for confidence. 'You...like it? You don't like it? Because if you don't I have lots of other ideas that would work as well. I—'

He put up his right hand to halt her—large, well sculpted, with knuckles that looked as if they'd sustained scrapes over the years. His well-spoken accent and obvious wealth suggested injuries sustained from boxing or rugby at a private school; the tightly leashed power in those muscles, that strong jaw, gave thought to injuries sustained in something perhaps more visceral.

'It's a wonderful idea for a party,' he said. 'Perfect for this house. Kudos to you, Ms Party Queen.'

'Thank you.' She made a mock curtsy and was pleased when he smiled. *How handsome he was without that scowl.* 'However, is that a "but" I hear coming on?'

He pivoted on his heel so he faced out to the pool, gleaming blue and pristine in the afternoon sun of a late-spring day in mid-November. His back view was impressive, broad shoulders tapering to a tight, muscular rear end. Then he turned back to face her. 'It's more than one "but",' he said. 'The party, the guest list, the—'

'The pointlessness of it all?' she ventured.

He furrowed his brow. 'What makes you say that?'

She found herself twisting the turquoise beads on her necklace between her finger and thumb. Her business partners would be furious with her if she lost Party Queens this high-profile job because she said what she *wanted* to say rather than what she *should* say.

'This party is all about improving your image, right? To make a statement that you're not the…the Scrooge people think you are.'

The fierce scowl was back. 'I'd rather you didn't use the word Scrooge.'

'Okay,' she said immediately. But she would find it difficult to stop *thinking* it. 'I'll try again: that you're not a…a person lacking in the spirit of giving.'

'That doesn't sound much better.' She couldn't have imagined his scowl could have got any darker but it did. 'The party is meant to be a public display of something I would rather be kept private.'

'So…you give privately to charity?'

'Of course I do but it's not your or anyone else's business.'

Personally, she would be glad if he wasn't as tight-fisted as his reputation decreed. But this was about more than what she felt. She could not back down. 'If that's how you feel, tell me again why you're doing this.'

He paused. 'If I share with you the reason why I agreed to holding this party, it's not to leave this room.'

'Of course,' she said. A party planner had to be discreet. It was astounding what family secrets got aired in the planning of a party. She leaned closer, close enough to notice that he must be a twice-a-day-shave guy. *Lots of testosterone, all right.*

'I've got a big joint venture in the United States on the point of being signed. My potential business partner, Walter Burton, is the head of a family company and he is committed to public displays of philanthropy. It would go better with me if I was seen to be the same.'

Andie made a motion with her fingers of zipping her lips shut. 'I…I understand,' she said. Disappointment shafted through her. *So he really was a Scrooge.*

She'd found herself wanting Dominic to be someone better than he was reputed to be. But the party, while purporting to be a charity event, was simply a smart business ploy. More about greed than good-heartedness.

'Now you can see why it's so important,' he said.

Should she say what she thought? The scrapheap of discarded party planners beckoned again. She could imagine her silver-sandal-clad foot kicking feebly from the top of it and hoped it would be a soft landing.

She took a deep steadying breath. 'Cynical journalists might have a field-day with the hypocrisy of a Scrooge—*sorry!*—trying to turn over a new gilded leaf in such an obvious and staged way.'

To her surprise, something like relief relaxed the tense lines of his face. 'That's what I thought too.'

'You…you did?'

'I could see the whole thing backfiring and me no better off in terms of reputation. Possibly worse.'

If she didn't stop twisting her necklace it would break and scatter her beads all over the marble floor. 'So—help me out here. We're back to you not wanting a party?'

She'd talked him out of the big, glitzy event Party Queens really needed. Andie cringed at the prospect of the combined wrath of Gemma and Eliza when she went back to their headquarters with the contract that was sitting in her satchel waiting for his signature still unsigned.

'You know I don't.' *Thank heaven.* 'But maybe a different kind of event,' he said.

'Like…handing over a giant facsimile cheque to a charity?' Which would be doing her right out of a job.

'Where's the good PR in that?'

'In fact it could look even more cynical than the party.'

'Correct.'

He paced a few long strides away from her and then back. 'I'm good at turning one dollar into lots of dollars. That's my skill. Not planning parties. But surely I can get the kind of publicity my marketing department wants, impress my prospective business partner and actually help some less advantaged people along the way?'

She resisted the urge to high-five him. 'To tell you the truth, I couldn't sleep last night for thinking that exact same thing.' *Was it wise to have admitted that?*

'Me too,' he said. 'I tossed and turned all night.'

A sudden vision of him in a huge billionaire's bed, all tangled in the sheets wearing nothing but…well nothing but a billionaire's birthday suit, flashed through her mind and sizzled through her body. *Not my type. Not my type.* She had to repeat it like a mantra.

She willed her heartbeat to slow and hoped he took the flush on her cheekbones for enthusiasm. 'So we're singing from the same hymn sheet. Did you have any thoughts on solving your dilemma?'

'That's where you come in; you're the party expert.'

She hesitated. 'During my sleepless night, I did think of something. But you might not like it.'

'Try me,' he said, eyes narrowed.

'It's out of the ball park,' she warned.

'I'm all for that,' he said.

She flung up her hands in front of her face to act as a shield. 'It…it involves Christmas.'

He blanched under the smooth olive of his tan. 'I told you—'

His mouth set in a grim line, his hands balled into fists by his sides. Should she leave well enough alone? After all, he had said the festive season had difficult associations for him. 'What is it that you hate so much about Christmas?' she asked. She'd always been one to dive straight into the deep end.

'I don't *hate* Christmas.' He cursed under his breath. 'I'm misquoted once and the media repeat it over and over.'

'But—'

He put up his hand to halt her. 'I don't have to justify anything to you. But let me give you three good reasons why I don't choose to celebrate Christmas and all the razzmatazz that goes with it.'

'Fire away,' she said, thinking it wasn't appropriate for her to counter with three things she adored about the festive season. This wasn't a debate. It was a business brainstorming.

'First—the weather is all wrong,' he said. 'It's hot when it should be cold. A *proper* Christmas is a northern hemisphere Christmas—snow, not sand.'

Not true, she thought. For a born-and-bred Australian like her, Christmas was all about the long, hot sticky days of summer. Cicadas chirruping in the warm air as the family walked to a midnight church service. Lunch outdoors, preferably around a pool or at the beach. Then it struck her—Dominic had a distinct trace of an English accent. That might explain his aversion to festivities Down Under style. But something still didn't seem quite right. His words sounded…too practised, as if he'd recited them a hundred times before.

He continued, warming to his point as she wondered

about the subtext to his spiel. 'Then there's the fact that the whole thing is over-commercialised to the point of being ludicrous. I saw Christmas stuff festooning the shops in September.'

She almost expected him to snarl a Scrooge-like *Bah! Humbug!* but he obviously restrained himself.

'You have a point,' she said. 'And carols piped through shopping malls in October? So annoying.'

'Quite right,' he said. 'This whole obsession with extended Christmas celebrations, it…it…makes people who don't celebrate it—for one reason or another—feel…feel excluded.'

His words faltered and he looked away in the direction of the pool but not before she'd seen the bleakness in his eyes. She realised those last words hadn't been rehearsed. That he might be regretting them. Again she had that inane urge to comfort him—without knowing why he needed comforting.

She knew she had to take this carefully. 'Yes,' she said slowly. 'I know what you mean.' That first Christmas without Anthony had been the bleakest imaginable. And each year after she had thought about him and the emptiness in her heart he had left behind him. But she would not share that with this man; it was far too personal. And nothing to do with the general discussion about Christmas.

His mouth twisted. 'Do you?'

She forced her voice to sound cheerful and impersonal. Her ongoing sadness over Anthony was deeply private. 'Not me personally. I love Christmas. I'm lucky enough to come from a big family—one of five kids. I have two older brothers and a sister and a younger sister. Christmas with our extended family was always—still is—a special time of the year. But my parents knew that wasn't the case for everyone. Every year we shared our celebration with children who weren't as fortunate as we were.'

'Charity cases, you mean,' he said, his voice hard-edged with something she couldn't identify.

'In the truest sense of the word,' she said. 'We didn't query them being there. It meant more kids to play with on Christmas Day. It didn't even enter our heads that there would be fewer presents for us so they could have presents too. Two of them moved in with us as long-term foster kids. When I say I'm from five, I really mean from seven. Only that's too confusing to explain.'

He gave a sound that seemed a cross between a grunt and a cynical snort.

She shrugged, inexplicably hurt by his reaction. 'You might think it goody-two-shoes-ish but that's the way my family are, and I love them for it,' she said, her voice stiff and more than a touch defensive.

'Not at all,' he said. 'I think it…it sounds wonderful. You were very lucky to grow up in a family like that.' With the implication being he hadn't?

'I know, and I'm thankful. And my parents' strong sense of community didn't do us any harm. In fact those Christmas Days my family shared with others got me thinking. It was what kept me up last night. I had an idea.'

'Fire away,' he said.

She channelled all her optimism and enthusiasm to make her voice sound convincing to Sydney's most notorious Scrooge. 'Wouldn't it be wonderful if you opened this beautiful home on Christmas Day for a big lunch party for children and families who do it hard on Christmas Day? Not as a gimmick. Not as a stunt. As a genuine act of hospitality and sharing the true spirit of Christmas.'

CHAPTER FOUR

DOMINIC STARED AT Andie in disbelief. Hadn't she heard a word he'd said about his views on Christmas? She looked up at him, her eyes bright with enthusiasm but backlit by wariness. 'Please, just consider my proposal,' she said. 'That's all I ask.' He could easily fire her for straying so far from the brief and she must know it—yet that didn't stop her. Her tenacity was to be admired.

Maybe she had a point. No matter what she or anyone else thought, he was not a Scrooge or a hypocrite. To make a holiday that could never be happy for him happy for others had genuine appeal. He was aware Christmas *was* a special time for a huge percentage of the population. It was just too painful for him to want to do anything but lock himself away with a bottle of bourbon from Christmas Eve to Boxing Day.

Deep from within, he dredged memories of his first Christmas away from home. Aged seventeen, he'd been living in an underground car park beneath an abandoned shopping centre project. His companions had been a ragtag collection of other runaways, addicts, criminals and people who'd lost all hope of a better life. Someone had stolen a branch of a pine tree from somewhere and decorated it with scavenged scraps of glittery paper. They'd all stood around it and sung carols with varying degrees of sobriety. Only he had stood aloof.

Now, he reached out to where Andie was twisting her

necklace so tightly it was in danger of snapping. Gently, he disengaged her hand and freed the string of beads. Fought the temptation to hold her hand for any longer than was necessary—slender and warm in his own much bigger hand. Today her nails were painted turquoise. And, as he'd noticed the day before, her fingers were free of any rings.

'Your idea could have merit,' he said, stepping back from her. Back from her beautiful interesting face, her intelligent eyes, the subtle spicy-sweet scent of her. 'Come and sit outside by the pool and we can talk it over.'

Her face flushed with relief at his response and he realised again what spunk it had taken for her to propose something so radical. He was grateful to whoever had sent Party Planner Number Four his way. Andie was gorgeous, smart and not the slightest in awe of him and his money, which was refreshing. His only regret was that he could not both employ her and date her.

He hadn't told the complete truth about why he'd been unable to sleep the night before. Thoughts of her had been churning through his head as much as concerns about the party. He had never felt so instantly attracted to a woman. Ever. If they had met under other circumstances he would have asked her out by now.

'I really think it could work,' she said as she walked with him through the doors and out to the pool area.

For a heart-halting second he thought Andie had tuned into his private thoughts—that she thought dating her could work. *Never.* He'd met his ex-wife, Tara, when she'd worked for his company, with disastrous consequences. The whole marriage had, in fact, been disastrous—based on lies and deception. He wouldn't make that mistake again—even for this intriguing woman.

But of course Andie was talking about her party proposal in businesslike tones. 'You could generate the right kind of publicity—both for your potential business partner and in general,' she said as he settled her into one of the white outdoor armchairs that had cost a small fortune because of its vintage styling.

'While at the same time directly benefiting people who do it tough on the so-called Big Day,' he said as he took the chair next to her.

'Exactly,' she said with her wide, generous smile. When she smiled like that it made him want to make her do it again, just for the pleasure of seeing her face light up. *Not a good idea.*

Her chair was in the shade of one of the mature palm trees he'd had helicoptered in for the landscaping but the sun was dancing off the aqua surface of the pool. He was disappointed when she reached into her satchel, pulled out a pair of tortoiseshell-rimmed sunglasses and donned them against the glare. They looked 'vintage' too. In fact, in her white clothes and turquoise necklace, she looked as if she belonged here.

'In principal, I don't mind your idea,' he said. 'In fact I find it more acceptable than the other.'

Her smile was edged with relief. 'I can't tell you how pleased that makes me.'

'Would the lunch have to be on actual Christmas Day?' he said.

'You could hold it on Christmas Eve or the week leading up to Christmas. In terms of organisation, that would be easier. But none of those peripheral days is as lonely and miserable as Christmas Day can be if you're one…one of the excluded ones,' she said. 'My foster sister told me that.'

The way she was looking at him, even with those too-perceptive green eyes shaded from his view, made him think she was beginning to suspect he had a deeply personal reason for his anti-Christmas stance.

He'd only ever shared that reason with one woman—Melody, the girl who'd first captivated, then shredded, his teenage heart back in that car park squat. By the time Christmas had loomed in the first year of his marriage to Tara, he'd known he'd never be sharing secrets with her. But there was something disarming about Andie that seemed to invite confidences—something he had to stand guard against. She might not be what she seemed—and he had learned the painful lesson not to trust his first impressions when it came to beautiful women.

'I guess any other day doesn't have the same impact,' he reluctantly agreed, not sure he would be able to face the festivities. Did he actually have to be present on the day? Might it not be enough to provide the house and the meal? No. To achieve his goal, he knew his presence would be necessary. Much as he would hate every minute of it.

'Maybe your marketing people will have other ideas,' she said. 'But I think opening your home on the actual December twenty-five to give people who really need it a slap-up feast would be a marvellous antidote to your Scrooge...sorry, *miser*...I mean *cheap* reputation.' She pulled a face. 'Sorry. I didn't actually mean any of those things.'

Why did it sting so much more coming from her? 'Of course you did. So does everyone else. People who have no idea of what and where I might give without wanting any fanfare.' The main reason he wanted to secure the joint venture was to ensure his big project in Brisbane would continue to be funded long after his lifetime.

She looked shamefaced. 'I'm sorry.'

He hated that people like Andie thought he was stingy. Any remaining reservations he might hold about the party had to go. He needed to take action before this unfair reputation become so deeply entrenched he'd never free himself from it. 'Let's hope the seasonal name-calling eases if I go ahead with the lunch.'

She held up a finger in warning. 'It wouldn't appease everyone. Those cynical journalists might not be easily swayed.'

He scowled. 'I can't please everyone.' But he found himself, irrationally, wanting to please *her.*

'It might help if you followed through with a visible, ongoing relationship with a charity. If the media could see…could see…'

Her eyes narrowed in concentration. He waited for the end of her sentence but it wasn't forthcoming. 'See what?'

'Sorry,' she said, shaking her head as if bringing herself back to earth. 'My thoughts tend to run faster than my words sometimes when I'm deep in the creative zone.'

'I get it,' he said, though he wasn't sure what the hell being in the creative zone meant.

'I meant your critics might relent if they could see your gesture was genuine.'

He scowled. 'But it *will* be genuine.'

'You know it and I know it but they might see it as just another publicity gimmick.' Her eyes narrowed again and he gave her time to think. 'What if you didn't actually seek publicity for this day? You know—no invitations or press releases. Let the details leak. Tantalise the media.'

'For a designer, you seem to know a lot about publicity,' he said.

She shrugged. 'When you work in magazines you pick up a lot about both seeking and giving publicity. But your marketing people would have their own ideas, I'm sure.'

'I should talk it over with them,' he said.

'As it's only six weeks until Christmas, and this would be a big event to pull together, may I suggest there's not a lot of discussion time left?'

'You're right. I know. But it's a big deal.' So much bigger for him personally than she realised.

'You're seriously considering going ahead with it?'

He so much preferred it to the Z-list celebrity party. 'Yes. Let's do it.'

She clapped her hands together. 'I'm so glad. We can make it a real dream-come-true for your guests.'

'What about you and your business partners? You'd have to work on Christmas Day.'

'Speaking for me, I'd be fine with working. True spirit of Christmas and all that. I'll have to speak to Gemma and Eliza, but I think they'd be behind it too.' Securing Dominic Hunt's business for Party Queens was too important for them to refuse.

'What about caterers and so on?' he asked.

'The hospitality industry works three hundred and sixty-five days a year. It shouldn't be a problem. There are also people who don't celebrate Christmas as part of their culture who are very happy to work—especially for holiday pay rates. You don't have to worry about all that—that's our job.'

'And the guests? How would we recruit them?' He was about to say he could talk to people in Brisbane, where he was heavily involved in a homeless charity, but stopped himself. That was too connected to the secret part of his life he had no desire to share.

'I know the perfect person to help—my older sister, Hannah, is a social worker. She would know exactly which charities to liaise with. I think she would be excited to be involved.'

It was her. *Andie.* He would not be considering this direction if it wasn't for her. The big glitzy party had seemed so wrong. She made him see what could be right.

'Could we set up a meeting with your sister?' he asked.

'I can do better than that,' she said with a triumphant toss of her head that set her oversized earrings swaying. 'Every Wednesday night is open house dinner at my parents' house. Whoever of my siblings can make it comes.

Sometimes grandparents and cousins too. I know Hannah will be there tonight and I'm planning to go too. Why don't you come along?'

'To your family dinner?' His first thought was to say no. Nothing much intimidated him—but meeting people's families was near the top of the list.

'Family is an elastic term for the Newmans. Friends, waifs and strays are always welcome at the table.'

What category would he be placed under? His memory of being a real-life stray made him wince. Friend? Strictly speaking, if circumstances were different, he'd want to be more than friends with Andie. Would connecting with her family create an intimacy he might later come to regret?

He looked down at his watch. Thought about his plan to return to the office.

'We need to get things moving,' she prompted.

'I would like to meet your sister tonight.'

Her wide smile lit her eyes. 'I have a really good feeling about this.'

'Do you always go on your feelings?' he asked.

She took off her sunglasses so he was treated to the directness of her gaze. 'All the time. Don't you?'

If he acted on his feelings he would be insisting they go to dinner, just the two of them. He would be taking her in his arms. Tasting her lovely mouth. Touching. Exploring. *But that wouldn't happen.*

He trusted his instincts when it came to business. But trusting his feelings when it came to women had only led to bitterness, betrayal and the kind of pain he never wanted to expose himself to again.

No to feeling. *Yes* to pleasant relationships that mutually fulfilled desires and were efficiently terminated before emotions ever became part of it. And with none of the complications that came with still having to work with that person. Besides, he suspected the short-term liaison that was all he had to offer would not be acceptable to Andie. She had *for ever* written all over her.

Now it was her turn to look at her watch. 'I'll call my mother to confirm you'll be joining us for dinner. How about I swing by and pick you up at around six?'

He thought about his four o'clock meeting. 'That's early for dinner.'

'Not when there are kids involved.'

'Kids?'

'I have a niece and two nephews. One of the nephews belongs to Hannah. He will almost certainly be there, along with his cousins.'

Dominic wasn't sure exactly what he was letting himself in for. One thing was for certain—he couldn't have seen himself going to a family dinner with any of Party Planners Numbers One to Three. And he suspected he might be in for more than one surprise from gorgeous Party Planner Number Four.

Andie got up from the chair. Smoothed down her white trousers. They were nothing as revealing as her flyaway skirt but made no secret of her slender shape.

'By the way, I'm apologising in advance for my car.'

He frowned. 'Why apologise?'

'I glimpsed your awesome sports car in the garage as I came in yesterday. You might find my hand-me-down hatchback a bit of a comedown.'

He frowned. 'I didn't come into this world behind the wheel of an expensive European sports car. I'm sure your hatchback will be perfectly fine.'

Just how did she see him? His public image—Scrooge, miser, rich guy—was so at odds with the person he knew himself to be. That he wanted her to know. But he could not reveal himself to her without uncovering secrets he would rather leave buried deep in his past.

CHAPTER FIVE

DOMINIC HAD FACED down some fears in his time. But the prospect of being paraded before Andie's large family ranked as one of the most fearsome. As Andie pulled up her hatchback—old but in good condition and nothing to be ashamed of—in front of her parents' home in the northern suburb of Willoughby, sweat prickled on his forehead and his hands felt clammy. How the hell had he got himself into this?

She turned off the engine, took out the keys, unclipped her seat belt and smoothed down the legs of her sleek, very sexy leather trousers. But she made no effort to get out of the car. She turned her head towards him. 'Before we go inside to meet my family I… I need to tell you something first. Something…something about me.'

Why did she look so serious, sombre even? 'Sure, fire away,' he said.

'I've told them you're a client. That there is absolutely nothing personal between us.'

'Of course,' he said.

Strange how at the same time he could be relieved and yet offended by her categorical denial that there ever could be anything *personal* between them.

Now a hint of a smile crept to the corners of her mouth. 'The thing is…they won't believe me. You're good-looking, you're smart and you're personable.'

'That's nice of you to say that,' he said. He noticed she hadn't added that he was rich to his list of attributes.

'You know it's true,' she said. 'My family are determined I should have a man in my life and have become the most inveterate of matchmakers. I expect they'll pounce on you. It could get embarrassing.'

'You're single?' He welcomed the excuse to ask.

'Yes. I...I've been single for a long time. Oh, I date. But I haven't found anyone special since...since...' She twisted right around in the car seat to fully face him. She clasped her hands together on her lap, then started to twist them without seeming to realise she was doing it. 'You need to know this before we go inside.' The hint of a smile had completely dissipated.

'If you think so,' he said. She was twenty-eight and single. What was the big deal here?

'I met Anthony on my first day of university. We were inseparable from the word go. There was no doubt we would spend our lives together.'

Dominic braced himself for the story of a nasty break-up. Infidelity? Betrayal? A jerk in disguise as a nice guy? He was prepared to make polite noises in response. He knew all about betrayal. But a *quid pro quo* exchange over relationships gone wrong was not something he ever wanted to waste time on with Andie or anyone else.

'It ended?' he said, making a terse contribution only because it was expected.

'He died.'

Two words stated so baldly but with such a wealth of pain behind them. Dominic felt as if he'd been punched in the chest. Nothing he said could be an adequate response. 'Andie, I'm sorry,' was all he could manage.

'It was five years ago. He was twenty-three. He...he went out for an early-morning surf and didn't come back.' He could hear the effort it took for her to keep her tone even.

He knew about people who didn't come back. Goodbyes left unsaid. Personal tragedy. That particular kind of pain. 'Did he…? Did you—?'

'He…he washed up two days later.' She closed her eyes as if against an unbearable image.

'What happened?' He didn't want her to think he was interrogating her on something so sensitive, but he wanted to find out.

'Head injury. An accident. The doctors couldn't be sure exactly how it happened. A rock? His board? A sandbank? We'll never know.'

'Thank you for telling me.' He felt unable to say anything else.

'Better for you to know than not to know when you're about to meet the family. Just in case someone says something that might put you on the spot.'

She heaved a sigh that seemed to signal she had said what she felt she had to say and that there would be no further confidences. Why should there be? *He was just a client.* Something prompted him to want to ask—was she over the loss? Had she moved on? But it was not his place. Client and contractor—that was all they could be to each other. Besides, could anyone *ever* get over loss like that?

'You needed to be in the picture.' She went to open her door. 'Now, let's go in—Hannah is looking forward to meeting you. As I predicted, she's very excited about getting involved.'

Her family's home was a comfortable older-style house set in a chaotic garden in a suburb where values had rocketed in recent years. In the car on the way over, Andie had told him she had lived in this house since she was a baby. All her siblings had. He envied her that certainty, that security.

'Hellooo!' she called ahead of her. 'We're here.'

He followed her down a wide hallway, the walls crammed with framed photographs. They ranged from old-fashioned sepia wedding photos, dating from pre-Second World War, to posed studio shots of cherubic babies. Again he found himself envying her—he had only a handful of family photos to cherish.

At a quick glance he found two of Andie—one in a green checked school uniform with her hair in plaits and that familiar grin showing off a gap in her front teeth; another as a teenager in a flowing pink formal dress. A third caught his eye—an older Andie in a bikini, arm in arm with a tall blond guy in board shorts who was looking down at her with open adoration. The same guy was with her in the next photo, only this time they were playing guitars and singing together. Dominic couldn't bear to do more than glance at them, aware of the tragedy that had followed.

Just before they reached the end of the corridor, Andie stopped and took a step towards him. She stood so close he breathed in her scent—something vaguely oriental, warm and sensual. She leaned up to whisper into his ear and her hair tickled his neck. He had to close his eyes to force himself from reacting to her closeness.

'The clan can be a bit overwhelming *en masse*,' she said. 'I won't introduce you to everyone by name; it would be unfair to expect you to remember all of them. My mother is Jennifer, my father is Ray. Hannah's husband is Paul.'

'I appreciate that,' he said, tugging at his collar that suddenly seemed too tight. As an only child, he'd always found meeting other people's families intimidating.

Andie gave him a reassuring smile. 'With the Newman family, what you see is what you get. They're all good people who will take you as they find you. We might even get some volunteers to help on Christmas Day out of this.'

The corridor opened out into a spacious open-plan family room. At some time in the last twenty years the parents had obviously added a new extension. It looked dated now but solid—warm and comfortable and welcoming. Delicious aromas emanated from the farmhouse-style kitchen in the northern corner. He sniffed and Andie smiled. 'My mother's lasagne—wait until you taste it.'

She announced him with an encompassing wave of her arm. 'Everyone, this is Dominic. He's a very important new client so please make him welcome. And yes, I know he's gorgeous but it's strictly business between us.'

That was met with laughter and a chorus of 'Hi, Dominic!' and 'Welcome!' Andie then briefly explained to them about the party and Hannah's likely role in it.

There were so many of them. Andie's introduction had guaranteed all eyes were on him. About ten people, including kids, were ranged around the room, sitting in comfortable-looking sofas or around a large trestle table.

Each face came into focus as the adults greeted him with warm smiles. It wasn't difficult to tell who was related—Andie's smile was a strong family marker that originated with her father, a tall, thin man with a vigorous handshake. Her mother's smile was different but equally welcoming as she headed his way from the kitchen, wiping her hands on her apron before she greeted him. Three young children playing on the floor looked up, then kept on playing with their toys. A big black dog with a greying muzzle, lying stretched out near the kids, lifted his head, then thumped his tail in greeting.

Andie's sister Hannah and her husband, Paul, paused in their job of setting the large trestle table to say hello. His experience with social workers in his past had been good—a social worker had pretty much saved his life—and he was not disappointed by Hannah's kind eyes in a gentle face.

'I straight away know of several families who are facing a very grim Christmas indeed,' she said. 'Your generous gesture would make an immense difference to them.'

Andie caught his eye and smiled. Instinctively, he knew she had steered him in the right direction towards her sister. If all Andie's ideas for his party were as good as this one, he could face the Christmas Day he dreaded with more confidence than he might have expected.

Andie's policy of glaring down any family member who dared to even hint at dating possibilities with Dominic was working. Except for her younger sister, Bea, who could not resist hissing, 'He's hot,' at any opportunity, from passing the salad to refilling her water glass. Then, when Andie didn't bite, Bea added, 'If you don't want him, hand him over to me.' Thankfully, Dominic remained oblivious to the whispered exchanges.

Her family had, unwittingly or not, sat Dominic in the same place at the table where Anthony had sat at these gatherings. *Andie and Ant—always together.* She doubted it was on purpose. Dominic needed to sit between Hannah and her and so it had just happened.

In the years since he'd died, no man had come anywhere near to replacing Anthony in her heart. How could they? Anthony and she had been two halves of the same soul, she sometimes thought. Maybe she would never be able to love anyone else. *But she was lonely.* The kind of loneliness that work, friends, family could not displace.

In the months after Anthony's death her parents had left Anthony's customary seat empty out of respect. Unable to bear the emptiness that emphasised his absence, she had stopped coming to the family dinners until her mother had realised the pain it was causing. From then on, one of her brothers always occupied Anthony's chair.

Now she told herself she was okay with Dominic sitting there. He was only a client, with no claim to any place in her heart. Bringing him along tonight had worked out well—one of those spur-of-the-moment decisions she mightn't have made if she'd given it more thought.

Dominic and Hannah had spent a lot of time talking—but he'd managed to chat with everyone else there too. They were obviously charmed by him. That was okay too. *She* was charmed by him. Tonight she was seeing a side of him, as he interacted with her family, that she might never have seen in everyday business dealings.

Her sister was right. *Dominic was hot.* And Andie was only too aware of it. She was surprised at the fierce urge of possessiveness that swept over her at the thought of 'handing over' Dominic to anyone else. Her sister could find her own hot guy.

Even at the dinner table, when her back was angled away from him to talk to her brother on her other side, she was aware of Dominic. His scent had already become familiar—citrus-sharp yet warm and very masculine. Her ears were tuned into the sound of his voice—no matter where he was in the room. Her body was on constant alert to that attraction, which had been instant and only continued to grow with further contact. On their way in, in the corridor, when she'd drawn close to whisper so her family would not overhear, she'd felt light-headed from the proximity to him.

It had been five years now since Anthony had gone—the same length of time they'd been together. She would never forget him but that terrible grief and anguish she had felt at first had eventually mellowed to a grudging acceptance. She realised she had stopped dreaming about him.

People talked about once-in-a-lifetime love. She'd thought she'd found it at the age of eighteen—and a cruel fate had snatched him away from her. Was there to be only one great love for her?

Deep in her heart, she didn't want to believe that. Surely there would be someone for her again? She didn't want to be alone. One day she wanted marriage, a family. She'd been looking for someone like Anthony—and had been constantly disappointed in the men she'd gone out with. But was it a mistake to keep on looking for a man like her teenage soulmate?

Thoughts of Dominic were constantly invading her mind. He was so different from Anthony there could be no comparison. Anthony had been blond and lean, laidback and funny, always quick with a joke, creative and musical. From what she knew of Dominic, he was quite the opposite. She'd dismissed him as not for her. But her body's reaction kept contradicting her mind's stonewalling. How could she be so certain he was Mr Wrong?

Dessert was being served—spring berries and homemade vanilla bean ice cream—and she turned to Dominic at the precise moment he turned to her. Their eyes connected and held and she knew without the need for words that he was happy with her decision to bring him here.

'Your family is wonderful,' he said in a low undertone.

'I think so,' she said, pleased. 'What about you? Do you come from a large family?'

A shadow darkened his eyes. He shook his head. 'Only child.'

She smiled. 'We must seem overwhelming.'

'In a good way,' he said. 'You're very lucky.'

'I know.' Of course she and her siblings had had the usual squabbles and disagreements throughout their childhood and adolescence. She, as number four, had had to fight for her place. But as adults they all got on as friends as well as brothers and sisters. She couldn't have got through the loss of Anthony without her family's support.

'The kids are cute,' he said. 'So well behaved.'

Her nephews, Timothy and Will, and her niece, Caitlin,

were together down the other end of the table under the watchful eye of their grandmother. 'They're really good kids,' she agreed. 'I adore them.'

'Little Timothy seems quite…delicate,' Dominic said, obviously choosing his words carefully. 'But I notice his older cousin looks after him.'

A wave of sadness for Hannah and Paul's little son overwhelmed her. 'They're actually the same age,' she said. 'Both five years old. Timothy just looks as though he's three.'

'I guess I don't know much about kids,' Dominic said, shifting uncomfortably in his chair.

She lowered her voice. 'Sadly, little Timothy has some kind of rare growth disorder, an endocrine imbalance. That's why he's so small.'

Dominic answered in a lowered voice. 'Can it be treated?'

'Only with a new treatment that isn't yet subsidised by the public health system. Even for private treatment, he's on a waiting list.' It was the reason why she drove an old car, why Bea had moved back home to save on rent, why the whole family was pulling together to raise the exorbitant amount of money required for tiny Timothy's private treatment.

But she would not tell Dominic that. While she might be wildly attracted to him, she still had no reason to think he was other than the Scrooge of his reputation. A man who had to be forced into a public display of charity to broker a multi-million-dollar business deal. Not for one moment did she want him to think she might be angling for financial help for Timothy.

'It's all under control,' she said as she passed him a bowl of raspberries.

'I'm glad to hear that,' he said, helping himself to the berries and then the ice cream. 'Thank you for inviting me tonight and for introducing me to Hannah. The next step is for you and your business partners to come in to my headquarters for a meeting with my marketing people. Can the three of you make it on Friday?'

CHAPTER SIX

ANDIE AND HER two business partners, Gemma and Eliza, settled themselves in a small waiting room off the main reception area of Dominic's very plush offices in Circular Quay. She and her fellow Party Queens had just come out of the Friday meeting with Dominic, his marketing people and senior executives in the boardroom and were waiting for Dominic to hear his feedback.

Situated on Sydney Cove, at the northern end of the CBD, the area was not just one of the most popular harbourside tourist precincts in Sydney—it was also home to the most prestigious office buildings. Even in this small room, floor-to-ceiling glass walls gave a magnificent close view of the Sydney Harbour Bridge and a luxury cruise liner in dock.

Andie couldn't help thinking the office was an ideal habitat for a billionaire Scrooge. Then she backtracked on the thought. That might not be fair. He hated the term and she felt vaguely disloyal even thinking it. Dominic was now totally committed to the Christmas Day feast for underprivileged families and had just approved a more than generous budget. She was beginning to wonder if his protestation that he was *not* a Scrooge had some truth in it. And then there was his gift to her mother to consider.

As she pondered the significance of that, she realised her thoughts had been filled with nothing much but Dominic since the day she'd met him. Last night he had even invaded her dreams—in a very passionate encounter that made her blush at the hazy dream memory of it. *Did he kiss like that in real life?*

It was with an effort that she forced her thoughts back to business.

'How do you guys think it went?' she asked the other two. 'My vote is for really well.' She felt jubilant and buoyant—Dominic's team had embraced her idea with more enthusiasm than she could ever have anticipated.

'Considering the meeting was meant to go from ten to eleven and here it is, nearly midday, yes, I think you could say that,' said Eliza with a big smile splitting her face.

'Of course that could have had something to do with Gemma's superb macadamia shortbread and those delectable fruit mince pies,' said Andie.

'Yes,' said Gemma with a pleased smile. 'I thought I could describe until I was blue in the face what I wanted to serve for the lunch, but they'd only know by tasting it.'

Party Queens' foodie partner had not only come up with a detailed menu for Dominic's Christmas Day lunch, but she'd also brought along freshly baked samples of items from her proposed menus. At the end of the meeting only a few crumbs had remained on the boardroom's fine china plates. Andie had caught Dominic's eye as he finished his second pastry and knew it had been an inspired idea. The Christmas star shaped serviettes she had brought along had also worked to keep the meeting focused on the theme of traditional with a twist.

'I think they were all-round impressed,' said Eliza. 'We three worked our collective socks off to get our presentations so detailed and professional in such a short time. Andie, all the images and samples you prepared to show the decorations and table settings looked amazing—I got excited at how fabulous it's going to look.'

'I loved the idea of the goody bags for all the guests too,' said Gemma. 'You really thought of everything.'

'While we're doing some mutual backslapping I'm giving yours a hearty slap, Eliza,' said Andie. 'Their finance guy couldn't fault your detailed costings and timelines.'

Eliza rubbed her hands together in exaggerated glee. 'And I'm sure we're going to get more party bookings from them. One of the senior marketing people mentioned her daughter was getting married next year and asked me did we do weddings.'

'Well done, Party Queens,' said Andie. 'Now that the contract is signed and the basic plan approved I feel I can relax.' Her partners had no idea of how tight it had been to get Dominic across the line for the change from glitz and glamour to more humble with heart.

She and her two friends discreetly high-fived each other. The room was somewhat of a goldfish bowl and none of them wanted to look less than professional to any of Dominic's staff who might be walking by.

Eliza leaned in to within whispering distance of Andie and Gemma. 'Dominic Hunt was a surprise,' she said in an undertone. 'I thought he'd be arrogant and overbearing. Instead, I found myself actually liking him.'

'Me too,' said Gemma. 'Not to mention he's so handsome. I could hardly keep my eyes off him. And that voice.' She mimed a shiver of delight.

'But *he* couldn't keep his eyes off Andie,' said Eliza. 'You'd be wasting your time there, Gemma.'

Had he? Been unable to keep his eyes off her? Andie's Dominic radar had been on full alert all through the meeting. Again she'd that uncanny experience of knowing exactly where he was in the room even when her back was turned. Of hearing his voice through the chatter of others. She'd caught his eye one too many times to feel comfortable. Especially with the remnants of that dream lingering in her mind. She'd had to force herself not to let her gaze linger on his mouth.

'Really, Andie?' said Gemma. 'Has he asked you out?'

'Nothing like that,' Andie said.

Eliza nodded thoughtfully. 'But you like him. Not in the way I liked him. I mean you *really* like him.'

Andie had no intention of admitting anything to anyone. She forced her voice to sound cool, impartial—though she doubted she would fool shrewd Eliza. 'Like you, I was surprised at how easy he is to get on with and how professional he is—even earlier this week when I switched the whole concept of his party into something he had never envisaged.' That overwhelming attraction was just physical—nothing more.

'And you totally didn't get how hot he was?' said Gemma. 'Don't expect me to believe that for one moment.'

Eliza rolled her eyes at Andie. 'I know what's coming next. *He's not your type*. How many times have I heard you say that when you either refuse a date or dump a guy before you've even had a chance to get to know him?'

Andie paused. 'Maybe that's true. Maybe that's why I'm still single. I'm beginning to wonder if I really know what *is* my type now.'

Her friendships with Gemma and Eliza dated from after she'd lost Anthony. They'd been sympathetic, but never really got why she had been so determined to try and find another man cast in the same mould as her first love. That her first love had been so perfect she'd felt her best chance of happiness would be with someone like Anthony.

Trouble was, they'd broken the mould when they'd made Anthony. Maybe she just hadn't been ready. Maybe she'd been subconsciously avoiding any man who might challenge her. Or might force her to look at why she'd put her heart on hold for so long. *Dominic would be a challenge in every way.* The thought both excited and scared her.

Eliza shook her head. 'It's irrelevant anyway,' she said. 'It would be most unwise for you to start anything with Dominic Hunt. His party is a big, important job for us and we don't have much time to organise it. It could get very messy if you started dating the client. Especially when I've never known you to stay with anyone for more than two weeks.'

'In my eagerness to get you fixed up with a handsome rich guy, I hadn't thought of that,' said Gemma. 'Imagine if you broke up with the billionaire client right in the middle of the countdown to the event. Could get awkward.'

'It's not going to happen, girls,' Andie said. 'I won't lie and say I don't think he's really attractive. But that's as far as it goes.' Thinking of last night's very intimate dream, she crossed her fingers behind her back.

'This is a huge party for us to pull together so quickly. We've got other jobs to get sorted as well. I can't afford to get…distracted.' How she actually stopped herself from getting distracted by Dominic was another matter altogether.

'I agree,' said Eliza. 'Eyes off the client. Okay?'

Andie smiled. 'I'll try,' she said. 'Seriously, though, it's really important for Dominic that this party works. He's got a lot riding on it. And it's really important for us. As you say, Eliza, more work could come from this. Not just weddings and private parties. But why not his company's business functions too? We have to think big.'

Gemma giggled. 'Big? Mr Hunt is way too big for me anyway. He's so tall. And all those muscles. His face is handsome but kind of tough too, don't you think?'

'Shh,' hissed Eliza, putting her finger to her lips. 'He's coming.'

Andie screwed up her eyes for a moment. How mortifying if he'd caught them gossiping about him. She'd been just about to say he wasn't too big for her to handle.

Along with the other two, she looked up and straightened her shoulders as Dominic strode towards them. In his dark charcoal suit he looked every inch the billionaire businessman. And, yes, very big.

She caught her breath at how handsome he looked. At the same time she caught his eye. And got the distinct impression that, of the three women in the room, she was the only one he really saw.

Did Andie get more and more beautiful every time he saw her? Dominic wondered. Or was it just the more he got to know her, the more he liked and admired her?

He had been impressed by her engaging and professional manner in the boardroom—the more so because he was aware she'd had such a short time to prepare her presentation. Her two business partners had been impressive too. It took a lot to win over his hard-nosed marketing people but, as a team, Party Queens had bowled them over.

The three women got up from their seats as he approached. Andie, tall and elegant in a deceptively simple caramel-coloured short dress—businesslike but with a snug fit that showed off her curves. Her sensational legs seemed to go on for ever to end in sky-high leopard-skin-print stilettos. He got it. She wanted to look businesslike but also let it be known who was the creative mind behind Party Queens. It worked.

Gemma—shorter, curvier, with auburn hair—and sophisticated, dark-haired Eliza were strikingly attractive too. They had a glint in their eyes and humour in their smiles that made him believe they could enjoy a party as well as plan them. But, in his eyes, Andie outshone them. Would any other woman ever be able to beat her? It was disturbing that a woman who he had known for such a short time could have made such an impression on him.

He addressed all three, while being hyper aware of

Andie as he did so. Her hair pulled back in a loose knot that fell in soft tendrils around her face, her mouth slicked with coral gloss, those remarkable green eyes. 'As I'm sure you're aware,' he began, 'my marketing team is delighted at both the concept for the party and the way you plan to implement the concept to the timeline. They're confident the event will meet and exceed the target we've set for reputation management and positive media engagement.'

It sounded like jargon and he knew it. But how else could he translate the only real aim of the party: to make him look less the penny-pincher and more the philanthropist?

'We're very pleased to be working with such a professional team,' said Eliza, the business brains of the partnership. But all three were business savvy in their own way, he'd realised through the meeting.

'Thank you,' he said. He glanced at his watch. 'The meeting ran so late it's almost lunchtime. I'm extending an invitation to lunch for all of you,' he said. 'Not that restaurants around here, excellent as they are, could match the standard of your cooking, Gemma.'

'Thank you,' said Gemma, looking pleased. 'But I'm afraid I have an appointment elsewhere.'

'Me too, and I'm running late,' said Eliza. 'But we couldn't possibly let you lunch alone, Mr Hunt, could we, Andie?'

Andie flushed high on those elegant cheekbones. 'Of course not. I'd be delighted to join Dominic for lunch.'

Her chin tilted upwards and he imagined her friends might later be berated for landing her in this on her own. Not that he minded. The other women were delightful, but lunch one-on-one with Andie was his preferred option.

'There are a few details of the plan I need to finalise with Dominic anyway,' she said to her friends.

Dominic shook hands with Gemma and Eliza and they

headed towards the elevators. He turned to Andie. 'Thank you for coming to lunch with me,' he said.

She smiled. 'Be warned, I'm starving. I was up at the crack of dawn finalising those mood boards for the presentation.'

'They were brilliant. There's only one thing I'd like to see changed. I didn't want to mention it in the meeting as it's my personal opinion and I didn't want to have to debate it.'

She frowned, puzzled rather than worried, he thought. 'Yes?'

He put his full authority behind his voice—he would not explain his reasons. Ever. 'The Christmas tree. The big one you have planned for next to the staircase. I don't want it.'

'Sure,' she said, obviously still puzzled. 'I thought it would be wonderful to have the tree where it's the first thing the guests see, but I totally understand if you don't want it there. We can put the Christmas tree elsewhere. The living room. Even in the area near where we'll be eating. Wherever you suggest.'

He hadn't expected this to be easy—he knew everyone would expect to see a decorated tree on Christmas Day. 'You misunderstood me. I mean I don't want a Christmas tree anywhere. No tree at all in my house.'

She paused. He could almost see her internal debate reflected in the slight crease between her eyebrows, the barely visible pursing of her lips. But then she obviously thought it was not worth the battle. 'Okay,' she said with a shrug of her slender shoulders. 'No tree.'

'Thank you,' he said, relieved he wasn't going to have to further assert his authority. At this time of year, Christmas trees were appearing all over the place. He avoided them when he could. But he would never have a tree in his home—a constant reminder of the pain and loss and guilt associated with the festive season.

They walked together to the elevator. When it arrived, there were two other people in it. They got out two floors below. Then Dominic was alone in the confined space of the elevator, aware of Andie's closeness, her warm scent. What was it? Sandalwood? Something exotic and sensual. He had the craziest impulse to hold her closer so he could nuzzle into the softness of her throat, the better to breathe it in.

He clenched his fists beside him and moved as far as he could away from her so his shoulder hit the wall of the elevator. That would be insanity. And probably not the best timing when he'd just quashed her Christmas tree display.

But she wouldn't be Andie if she didn't persevere. 'Not even miniature trees on the lunch table?' she asked.

'No trees,' he said.

She sighed. 'Okay, the client has spoken. No Christmas tree.'

The elevator came to the ground floor. He lightly placed his hand at the small of her back to steer her in the direction of the best exit for the restaurant. Bad idea. Touching Andie even in this casual manner just made him want to touch her more.

'But you're happy with the rest of the plan?' she said as they walked side by side towards the restaurant, dodging the busy Sydney lunchtime crush as they did.

'Very happy. Except you can totally discard the marketing director's suggestion I dress up as Santa Claus.'

She laughed. 'Did you notice I wrote it down but didn't take the suggestion any further?' Her eyes narrowed as she looked him up and down in mock inspection. 'Though it's actually a nice idea. If you change your mind—'

'No,' he said.

'That's what I thought,' she said, that delightful smile dancing around the corners of her mouth.

'You know it's been a stretch for me to agree to a Christmas party at all. You won't ever see me as Santa.'

'What if the marketing director himself could be convinced to play Santa Claus?' she said thoughtfully. 'He volunteered to help out on the day.'

'This whole party thing was Rob Cratchit's idea so that might be most appropriate. Take it as an order from his boss.'

'I'll send him an email and say it's your suggestion,' she said with a wicked grin. 'He's quite well padded and would make a wonderful Santa—no pillow down the front of his jacket required.'

'Don't mention that in the email or all hell will break loose,' he said.

'Don't worry; I can be subtle when I want to,' she said, that grin still dancing in her eyes as they neared the restaurant.

In Dominic's experience, some restaurants were sited well and had a good fit-out; others had excellent food. In this case, his favourite place to eat near the office had both—a spectacular site on the top of a heritage listed building right near the water and a superlative menu.

There had been no need to book—a table was always there for him when he wanted one, no matter how long the waiting list for bookings.

An attentive waiter settled Andie into a seat facing the view of Sydney Harbour. 'I've always wanted to eat at this restaurant,' she said, looking around her.

'Maybe we should have our meetings here in future?'

'Good idea,' she said. 'Though I'll have to do a detailed site inspection of your house very soon. We could fit in a meeting then, perhaps?'

'I might not be able to be there,' he said. 'I have a series of appointments in other states over the next two weeks. Any meetings with you might have to be via the Internet.'

Was that disappointment he saw cloud her eyes. 'That's a shame. I—'

'My assistant will help you with access and the security code,' he said. He wished he could cancel some of the meetings, but that was not possible. Perhaps it was for the best. The more time he spent with Andie, the more he wanted to break his rules and ask her on a date. But those rules were there for good reason.

'As you know, we have a tight timeline to work to,' she said. 'The more we get done early the better, to allow for the inevitable last-minute dramas.'

'I have every confidence in you that it will go to plan.'

'Me too,' she said with another of those endearing grins. 'I've organised so many Christmas room sets and table settings for magazine and advertising clients. You have to get creative to come up with something different each year. This is easier in a way.'

'But surely there must be a continuity?' he asked, curious even though Christmas was his least favourite topic of conversation.

'Some people don't want to go past traditional red and green and that's okay,' she said. 'I've done an entire room themed purple and the client was delighted. Silver and gold is always popular in Australia, when Christmas is likely to be sweltering—it seems to feel cooler somehow. But—'

The waiter came to take their orders. They'd been too busy talking to look at the menu. Quickly they discussed their favourites before they ordered: barramundi with prawns and asparagus for him; tandoori roasted ocean trout with cucumber salsa for her and an heirloom tomato salad to share. They each passed on wine and chose mineral water. 'Because it's a working day,' they both said at the exact time and laughed. *It felt like a date.* He could not let his thoughts stray that way. Because he liked the idea too much.

'You haven't explained the continuity of Christmas,' he said, bringing the conversation back to the party.

'It's nothing to do with the baubles and the tinsel and everything to do with the feeling,' she said with obvious enthusiasm. 'Anticipation, delight, joy. For some it's about religious observance, spirituality and new life; others about sharing and generosity. If you can get people feeling the emotion, then it doesn't really matter if the tree is decorated in pink and purple or red and green.'

How about misery and fear and pain? Those were his memories of Christmas. 'I see your point,' he said.

'I intend to make sure your party is richly imbued with that kind of Christmas spirit. Hannah told me some of the kids who will be coming would be unlikely to have a celebration meal or a present and certainly not both if it wasn't for your generosity.'

'I met with Hannah yesterday; she mentioned how important it will be for the families we're inviting. She seems to think the party will do a powerful lot of good. Your sister told me how special Christmas is in your family.' It was an effort for him to speak about Christmas in a normal tone of voice. But he seemed to be succeeding.

'Oh, yes,' said Andie. 'Heaven help anyone who might want to celebrate it with their in-laws or anywhere else but my parents' house.'

'Your mother's a marvellous cook.'

'True, but Christmas is well and truly my dad's day. My mother is allowed to do the baking and she does that months in advance. On the day, he cooks a traditional meal—turkey, ham, roast beef, the lot. He's got favourite recipes he's refined over the years and no one would dare suggest anything different.'

Did she realise how lucky she was? How envious he felt when he thought about how empty his life had been of the kind of family love she'd been gifted with. He'd used to think he could start his own family, his own traditions, but his ex-wife had disabused him of that particular dream. It involved trust and trust was not a thing that came easily to him. Not when it came to women. 'I can't imagine you would want to change a tradition.'

'If truth be told, we'd be furious if he wanted to change one little thing,' she said, her voice warm with affection for her father. *She knew.*

He could see where she got her confidence from—that rock-solid security of a loving, supportive family. But now he knew she'd been tempered by tragedy too. He wanted to know more about how she had dealt with the loss of her boyfriend. But not until it was appropriate to ask.

'What about you, Dominic—did you celebrate Christmas with your family?' she asked.

This never got easier—which was why he chose not to revisit it too often. 'My parents died when I was eleven,' he said.

'Oh, I'm so sorry,' she said with warm compassion in her eyes. 'What a tragedy.' She paused. 'You were so young, an only child...who looked after you?'

'We lived in England, in a village in Norfolk. My father was English, my mother Australian. My mother's sister was staying with us at the time my parents died. She took me straight back with her to Australia.' It was difficult to keep his voice matter of fact, not to betray the pain the memories evoked, even after all this time.

'What? Just wrenched you away from your home?' She paused. 'I'm sorry. That wasn't my call to say that. You were lucky you had family. Did your aunt have children?'

'No, it was just the two of us,' he said and left it at that. There was so much more he could say about the toxic relationship with his aunt but that was part of his past he'd rather was left buried.

Wrenched. That was how it had been. Away from everything familiar. Away from his grandparents, whom he didn't see again until he had the wherewithal to get himself back to the UK as an adult. Away from the dog he'd adored. Desperately lonely and not allowed to grieve, thrust back down in Brisbane, in the intense heat, straight into the strategic battleground that was high school in a foreign country. To a woman who had no idea how to love a child, though she had tried in her own warped way.

'I'd prefer not to talk about it,' he said. 'I'm all grown up now and don't angst about the past.' Except when it was dark and lonely and he couldn't sleep and he wondered if he was fated to live alone without love.

'I understand,' she said. But how could she?

She paused to leave a silence he did not feel able to fill.

'Talking about my family,' she finally said, 'you're my mother's new number one favourite person.'

Touched by not only her words but her effort to draw him in some way into her family circle, he smiled. 'And why is that?'

'Seriously, she really liked you at dinner on Wednesday night. But then, when you had flowers delivered the next day, she was over the moon. Especially at the note that said she cooked the best lasagne you'd ever tasted.'

'I'm glad she liked them. And it was true about the lasagne.' Home-made anything was rarely on the menu for him so he had appreciated it.

'How did you know pink was her favourite colour in flowers?'

'I noticed the flowers she'd planted in her garden.'

'But you only saw the garden so briefly.'

'I'm observant,' he said.

'But the icing on the cake was the voucher for dinner for two at their local bistro.'

'She mentioned she liked their food when we were talking,' he said.

'You're a thoughtful guy, aren't you?' she said, tilting her head to the side.

'Some don't think so,' he said, unable to keep the bitterness from his voice.

She lowered her voice to barely a whisper so he had to lean across the table to hear her, so close their heads were touching. Anyone who was watching would think they *were* on a date.

She placed her hand on his arm in a gesture of comfort which touched him. 'Don't worry. The party should change all that. I really liked Rob's idea that no media would be invited to the party. That journalists would have to volunteer to help on the day if they wanted to see what it was all about.'

'And no photographers allowed, to preserve our guests' privacy. I liked that too.'

'I really have a good feeling about it,' she said. She lifted her hand off his arm and he felt bereft of her touch.

He nodded. If it were up to him, if he didn't *have* to go ahead with the party, he'd cancel it at a moment's notice. Maybe there was a touch of Scrooge in him after all.

But he didn't want Andie to think that of him. Not for a moment.

He hadn't proved to be a good judge of women. His errors in judgement went right back to his aunt—he'd loved her when she was his fun auntie from Australia. She'd turned out to be a very different person. Then there'd been Melody—sweet, doomed Melody. At seventeen he'd been a man in body but a boy still in heart. He'd been gutted at her betrayal, too damn wet behind the ears to realise a teenage boy's love could never be enough for an addict. Then how could he have been sucked in by Tara? His ex-wife was a redhead like Melody, tiny and delicate. But her frail exterior hid an avaricious, dishonest heart and she had lied to him about something so fundamental to their marriage that he could never forgive her.

Now there was Andie. He didn't trust his feelings when he'd made such disastrous calls before. *'What you see is what you get,'* she'd said about her family.

Could he trust himself to judge that Andie was what she appeared to be?

He reined in his errant thoughts—he only needed to trust Andie to deliver him the party he needed to improve his public image. Anything personal was not going to happen.

CHAPTER SEVEN

'ANDIE, I NEED to see you.' Dominic's voice on her smartphone was harsh in its urgency. It was eight a.m. and Andie had not been expecting a call from him. He'd been away more than a week on business and she'd mainly communicated with him by text and email—and only then if it was something that needed his approval for the party. The last time she'd seen him was the Friday they'd had lunch together. The strictly business lunch that had somehow felt more like a date. But she couldn't let herself think like that.

'Sure,' she said. 'I just have to—'

'Now. Please. Where do you live?'

Startled at his tone, she gave him the address of the apartment in a converted warehouse in the inner western suburb of Newtown she shared with two old schoolfriends. Her friends had both already left for work. Andie had planned on a day finalising prop hire and purchase for Dominic's party before she started work for a tuxedo-and-tiara-themed twenty-first birthday party.

She quickly changed into skinny denim jeans and a simple loose-knit cream top that laced with leather ties at the neckline. Decided on her favourite leopard-print stilettos over flats. And make-up. And her favourite sandalwood and jasmine perfume. What the heck—her heart was racing at the thought of seeing him. She didn't want to seem as though she were trying too hard—but then again she didn't want to be caught out in sweats.

When Dominic arrived she was shocked to see he didn't look *his* sartorial best. In fact he looked downright dishevelled. His black hair seemed as if he'd used his fingers for a comb and his dark stubble was one step away from a beard. He was wearing black jeans, a dark grey T-shirt and had a black leather jacket slung over his shoulders. Immediately he owned the high-ceilinged room, a space that overwhelmed men of lesser stature, with the casual athleticism of his stance, the power of his body with its air of tightly coiled energy.

'Are you alone?' he asked.

'Yes,' she said. *Yes!*

Her first thought was that he looked hotter than ever—so hot she had to catch her breath. This Dominic set her pulse racing even more than executive Dominic in his made-to-measure Italian suits.

Her second thought was that he seemed stressed—his mouth set in a grim line, his eyes red-rimmed and darkly shadowed. 'Are you okay?' she asked.

'I've come straight from the airport. I just flew in from Perth.' Perth was on the other side of Australia—a six-hour flight. 'I cut short my trip.'

'But are you okay?' She forced her voice to sound calm and measured, not wanting him to realise how she was reacting to his untamed good looks. Her heart thudded with awareness that they were alone in the apartment.

With the kind of friendly working relationship they had now established, it would be quite in order to greet him with a light kiss on his beard-roughened cheek. But she wouldn't dare. She might not be able to resist sliding her mouth across his cheek to his mouth and turning it into a very different kind of kiss. And that wouldn't do.

'I'm fine. I've just…been presented with…with a dilemma,' Dominic said.

'Coffee might help,' she said.

'Please.'

'Breakfast? I have—'

'Just coffee.'

But Andie knew that sometimes men who said they didn't want anything to eat needed food. And that their mood could improve immeasurably when they ate something. Not that she'd been in the habit of sharing breakfast with a man. Not since… She forced her mind back to the present and away from memories of breakfasts with Anthony on a sun-soaked veranda. Her memories of him were lit with sunshine and happiness.

Dominic dragged out a chair and slumped down at her kitchen table while she prepared him coffee. *Why was he here?* She turned to see him with his elbows on the tabletop, resting his head on his hands. Tired? Defeated? Something seemed to have put a massive dent in his usual self-assured confidence.

She slid a mug of coffee in front of him. 'I assumed black but here's frothed milk and sugar if you want.'

'Black is what I need,' he said. He put both hands around the mug and took it to his mouth.

Without a word, she put a thick chunk of fresh fruit bread, studded with figs and apricots, from her favourite baker in King Street in front of him. Then a dish of cream cheese and a knife. 'Food might help,' she said.

He put down his coffee, gave her a weary imitation of his usual glower and went to pick up the bread. 'Let me,' she said and spread it with cream cheese.

What was it about this man that made her want to comfort and care for him? He was a thirty-two-year-old billionaire, for heaven's sake. Tough, self-sufficient. Wealthier than she could even begin to imagine. And yet she sometimes detected an air of vulnerability about him that wrenched at her. A sense of something broken. But it was not up to her to try and fix him. He ate the fruit bread in two bites. 'More?' she asked.

He nodded. 'It's good,' he said.

Andie had to be honest with herself. She wanted to comfort him, yes. She enjoyed his company. But it was more than that. She couldn't deny that compelling physical attraction. He sat at her kitchen table, his leather jacket slung on the back of the chair. His tanned arms were sculpted with muscle, his T-shirt moulded ripped pecs and abs. With his rough-hewn face, he looked so utterly *male.*

Desire, so long unfamiliar, thrilled through her. She wanted to kiss him and feel those strong arms around her, his hands on her body. *She wanted more than kisses.* What was it about this not-my-type man who had aroused her interest from the moment she'd first met him?

When he'd eaten two more slices of fruit bread, he pushed his plate away and leaned back in his seat. His sigh was weary and heartfelt. 'Thank you,' he said. 'I didn't realise I was hungry.'

She slipped into the chair opposite him and nursed her own cooling cup of coffee to stop the impulse to reach over and take his hand. 'Are you able to tell me about your dilemma?' she asked, genuinely concerned.

He raked his hands through his hair. 'My ex-wife is causing trouble. Again.'

In her research into Dominic, Andie had seen photos of Tara Hunt—she still went by his name—a petite, pale-skinned redhead in designer clothes and an over-abundance of jewellery.

'I'm sorry,' she said, deciding on caution in her reaction. 'Do you want to tell me about it?' Was that why he wanted to see her? To cry on her shoulder about his ex-wife? Dominic didn't seem like a crying-on-shoulders kind of guy.

He went to drink more coffee, to find his mug was

nearly empty. He drained the last drops. 'You make good coffee,' he said appreciatively.

'I worked as a barista when I was a student,' she said.

She and Anthony had both worked in hospitality, saving for vacation backpacker trips to Indonesia and Thailand. It seemed so long ago now, those days when she took it for granted they had a long, happy future stretched out ahead of them. They'd been saving for a trip to Eastern Europe when he'd died.

She took Dominic's mug from him, got up, refilled it, brought it back to the table and sat down again. He drank from it and put it down.

Dominic leaned across the table to bring him closer to her. 'Can I trust you, Andie?' he asked in that deep, resonant voice. His intense grey gaze met hers and held it.

'Of course,' she said without hesitation.

He sat back in his chair. 'I know you're friends with journalists, so I have to be sure what I might talk to you about today won't go any further.' The way he said it didn't sound offensive; in fact it made her feel privileged that he would consider her trustworthy. Not to mention curious about what he might reveal.

'I assure you, you can trust me,' she said.

'Thank you,' he said. 'Tara found out about my impending deal with Walter Burton and is doing her best to derail it.'

Andie frowned. 'How can she do that?'

'Before I married Tara, she worked for my company in the accounts department. She made it her business to find out everything she could about the way I ran things. I didn't know, but once I started dating her she used that knowledge to make trouble, hiding behind the shield of our relationship. None of my staff dared tell me.'

'Not good,' Andie said, wanting to express in no uncertain terms what she thought of his ex, yet not wanting to get into a bitching session about her.

'You're right about that,' he said. 'It's why I now never date employees.'

His gaze met hers again and held it for a long moment. Was there a message in there for her? If she wasn't a contractor, would he ask her out? If she hadn't promised her partners to stay away from him, would she suggest a date?

'That policy makes…sense,' she said. What about after Christmas, when she and Dominic would no longer be connected by business? Could they date then? A sudden yearning for that to happen surprised her with its intensity. *She wanted him.*

'It gets worse,' he continued. 'A former employee started his own business in competition with me—' Andie went to protest but Dominic put up his hand. 'It happens; that's legit,' he said. 'But what happened afterwards wasn't. After our marriage broke up, Tara used her knowledge of how my company worked to help him.'

Andie couldn't help her gasp of outrage. 'Did her…her betrayal work?'

'She gave him the information. That didn't mean he knew how to use it. But now I've just discovered she's working with him in a last-minute rival bid for the joint venture with Walter Burton.'

Andie shook her head in disbelief. 'Why?' Her research had shown her Tara Hunt had ended up with a massive divorce settlement from Dominic. Per day of their short marriage, she had walked away with an incredible number of dollars.

Dominic shrugged. 'Revenge. Spite. Who knows what else?'

'Surely Walter Burton won't be swayed by that kind of underhand behaviour?'

'Traditional values are important to Walter Burton. We

know that. That's why we're holding the party to negate the popular opinion of me as a Scrooge.'

'So what does your ex-wife have to do with the deal?'

Dominic sighed, a great weary sigh that made Andie want to put comforting arms around him. She'd sensed from the get-go he was a private person. He obviously hated talking about this. Once more, she wondered why he had chosen to.

He drew those dark brows together in a scowl. 'Again she's raked over the coals of our disastrous marriage and talked to her media buddies. Now she's claiming I was unfaithful—which is a big fat lie. According to her, I'm a womaniser, a player and a complete and utter bastard. She dragged out my old quote that I will never marry again and claims it's because I'm incapable of settling with one woman. It's on one of the big Internet gossip sites and will be all over the weekend newspapers.' He cursed under his breath.

Andie could see the shadow of old hurts on his face. He had once loved his ex enough to marry her. A betrayal like this must be painful, no matter how much time had elapsed. She had no such angst behind her. She knew Anthony had been loyal to her, as she had been to him. *First love.* Sometimes she wondered if they might have grown apart if he'd lived. Some of their friends who had dated as teenagers had split when they got older. But she dismissed those thoughts as disloyal to his memory.

Andie shook her head at Dominic's revelations about his ex—it got worse and worse. 'That's horrible—but can't you just ignore it?'

'I would ignore it, but she's made sure Walter Burton has seen all her spurious allegations set out as truth.'

Andie frowned. 'Surely your personal life is none of Mr Burton's business? Especially when it's not true.' She believed Dominic implicitly—why, she wasn't completely sure. Trust went both ways.

'He might think it's true. The *"bed-hopping billionaire"*,' the article calls me.' Dominic growled with wounded outrage. 'That might be enough for Burton to reconsider doing business with me.'

Andie had to put her hand over her mouth to hide her smile at the description.

But Dominic noticed and scowled. 'I know it sounds ludicrous, but to a moralistic family man like Walter Burton it makes me sound immoral and not the kind of guy he wants to do business with.'

'Why do you care so much about the deal with Mr Burton? If you have to pretend to be someone you're not, how can it be worth it?'

'You mean I should pretend *not* to be a bed-hopping billionaire?'

'You must admit the headline has a certain ring to it,' Andie said, losing her battle to keep a straight face.

That forced a reluctant grin from him. 'A tag like that might be very difficult to live down.'

'Is…is it true? Are you a bed-hopping guy?' She held her breath for his reply.

'No. Of course I've had girlfriends since my divorce. Serial monogamy, I think they call it. But nothing like what this scurrilous interview with my ex claims.'

Andie let out her breath on a sigh of relief. 'But do you actually need to pursue this deal if it's becoming so difficult? You're already very wealthy.'

Dominic's mouth set in a grim line. 'I'm not going to bore you with my personal history. But home life with my aunt was less than ideal. I finished high school and got out. I'd tried to run away before and she'd dragged me back. This time she let me go. I ended up homeless, living in a squat. At seventeen I saw inexplicably awful things a boy that age should never see. I never again want to be without money and have nowhere to live. That's all I intend to say about that.' He nodded to her. 'And I trust you not to repeat it.'

'Of course,' she said, rocked by his revelations, aching to know more. *Dominic Hunt was a street kid?* Not boring. There was so much more about his life than he was saying. She thought again about his scarred knuckles and broken nose. There had been nothing about his past in her online trawling. She hoped he might tell her more. It seemed he was far more complex than he appeared. Which only made him more attractive.

'My best friend and first business partner, Jake Marlow, is also in with me on this,' he said. 'He wants it as much as I do, for his own reasons I'm not at liberty to share.'

'Okay,' she said slowly. 'So we're working on the party to negate the Scr…uh…the other reputation, to get Mr Burton on board. What do you intend to do about the bed-hopper one?'

'When Burton contacted me I told him that it was all scuttlebutt and I was engaged to be married.'

She couldn't help a gasp. 'You're engaged?' She felt suddenly stricken. 'Engaged to who?'

'I'm not engaged. I'm not even dating anyone.'

'Then why…?' she said.

He groaned. 'Panic. Fear. Survival. A gut reaction like I used to have back in that squat. When you woke up, terrified, in your cardboard box to find some older guy burrowing through your backpack and you told him you had nothing worth stealing even though there was five dollars folded tiny between your toes in your sock. If that money was stolen, you didn't eat.'

'So you lied to Mr Burton?'

'As I said, a panic reaction. But it gets worse.' Again he raked his fingers through his hair. 'Burton said he was flying in to Sydney in two weeks' time to meet with both me and the other guy. He wants to be introduced to my fiancée.'

Andie paused, stunned at what Dominic had done, appalled that he had lied. 'What will you do?'

Again he leaned towards her over the table. 'I want you to be my fiancée, Andie.'

CHAPTER EIGHT

DOMINIC WATCHED ANDIE'S reactions flit across her face—shock and indignation followed by disappointment. In him? He braced himself—certain she was going to say *no*.

'Arc you serious?' she finally said, her hands flat down on the table in front of her.

'Very,' he said, gritting his teeth. He'd been an idiot to get himself into a mess like this. *Panic.* He shouldn't have given in to panic in that phone call with Walter Burton. He hadn't let panic or fear rule him for a long time.

Andie tilted her head to one side and frowned. 'You want me to *marry* you? We hardly know each other.'

Marriage? Who was talking about marriage? 'No. Just to *pretend*—' Whatever he said wasn't going to sound good. 'Pretend to be my fiancée. Until after the Christmas party.'

Andic shook her head in disbelief. 'To pretend to be engaged to you? To lie? No! I can't believe you asked me to…to even think of such a thing. I'm a party planner, not a…a…the type of person who would agree to that.'

She looked at him as though she'd never seen him before. And that maybe she didn't like what she saw. Dominic swallowed hard—he didn't like the feeling her expression gave him. She pushed herself up from the chair and walked away from the table, her body rigid with disapproval. He was very aware she wanted to distance herself from him. He didn't like that either. It had seemed so intimate, drinking coffee and eating breakfast at her table. And he *had* liked that.

He swivelled in his chair to face her. 'It was a stupid thing to do, I know that,' he said. He had spent the entire flight back from Perth regretting his impulsive action. 'But it's done.'

She turned around, glared at him. 'Then I suggest you undo it.'

'By admitting I lied?'

She shrugged. 'Tell Mr Burton your fiancée dumped you.'

'As if that would fly.'

'You think it's beyond belief that a woman would ever dump you?'

'I didn't say that.' Though it was true. Since it had ended with Melody, he had always been the one to end a relationship. 'It would seem too…sudden.'

'Just like the sudden engagement?'

'It wouldn't denote…stability.'

'You're right about that.' She crossed her arms in front of her chest—totally unaware that the action pushed up her breasts into an enticing cleavage in the V-necked top she wore. 'It's a crazy idea.'

'I'm not denying that,' he growled. He didn't need to have his mistake pointed out to him. 'But I'm asking you to help me out.'

'Why me? Find someone else. I'm sure there would be no shortage of candidates.'

'But it makes sense for my fiancée to be you.' He could be doggedly persistent when he wanted to be.

He unfolded himself from the too-small chair at the kitchen table. Most chairs were too small for him. He took a step towards her, only for her to take a step back from him. 'Andie. Please.'

Her hair had fallen across her face and she tossed it back. 'Why? We're just client and contractor.'

'Is that all it is between us?'

'Of course it is.' But she wouldn't meet his gaze and he felt triumphant. *So she felt it too.* That attraction that had flashed between them from the get-go.

'When I opened the door to the beautiful woman with the misbehaving skirt—' that got a grudging smile from her '—I thought it could be more than just a business arrangement. But you know now why I don't date anyone hired by the company.'

'And Party Queens has a policy of not mixing business with...with pleasure.' Her voice got huskier on the last words.

He looked her direct in the face, pinning her with his gaze. 'If it ever happened, it would be pleasure all the way, Andie, I think we both know that.' She hadn't quite cleared her face of a wisp of flyaway hair. He reached down and gently smoothed it back behind her ear.

She trembled under his touch. A blush travelled up her throat to stain her cheeks. 'I've never even thought about it, the...the *pleasure,* I mean,' she said.

She wouldn't blush like that if she hadn't. Or flutter her hands to the leather laces of her neckline. *Now who was lying?*

She took a deep breath and he tried to keep his gaze from the resulting further exposure of her cleavage. 'I don't want to be involved in this mad scheme in any way,' she said. 'Except to add your pretend fiancée—when you find one—to the Christmas party guest list.'

'I'm afraid you're already involved.'

She frowned. 'What do you mean?'

Dominic took the few steps necessary back to his chair and took out his smartphone from the inside pocket of his leather jacket. He scrolled through, then handed it to Andie.

She stared at the screen. 'But this is me. *Us*.'

The photo she was staring at was of him and her at a restaurant table. They were leaning towards each other, looking into each other's faces, Andie's hand on his arm.

'At the restaurant in Circular Quay, the day of the Friday meeting,' she said.

'Yes,' he said. The business lunch that had felt like a date. In this photo, it *looked* like a date.

She shook her head, bewildered. 'Who took it?'

'Some opportunistic person with a smartphone, I expect. Maybe a trouble-making friend of Tara's. Who knows?'

She looked back down at the screen, did some scrolling of her own. He waited for her to notice the words that accompanied the image on the gossip site.

Her eyes widened in horror. 'Did you see this?' She read out the heading. *'"Is This the Bed-Hopping Billionaire's New Conquest?"'* She swore under her breath—the first time he had heard her do so.

'I'm sorry. Of course I had no idea this was happening. But, in light of it, you can see why it makes sense that my fake fiancée should be you.'

She shook her head. 'No. It doesn't make any sense. That was a business lunch. Not the…the romantic rendezvous it appears to be in the picture.'

'You know that. I know that. But the way they've cropped the photo, that's exactly what it seems. Announce an engagement and suddenly the picture would make a whole lot of sense. Good sense.'

Her green eyes narrowed. 'This photo doesn't bother me. It will blow over. We're both single. Who even cares?'

He'd been stunned to see the expression in his eyes as he'd looked into her face in the photo. It had looked as if he wanted to have her for dessert. Had she noticed? No wonder the gossip site had drawn a conclusion of romantic intrigue.

'If you're so indifferent, why not help me out?' he said. 'Be my fake fiancée, just until after Christmas.'

'Christmas is nearly a month away. Twenty-five days, to be precise. For twenty-five days I'd have to pretend to be your fiancée?'

'So you're considering it? Because we've already been "outed", so to speak, it wouldn't come out of the blue. It would be believable.'

'Huh! We've only known each other for two weeks. Who would believe it?'

'People get married on less acquaintance,' he said.

'Not people like me,' she said.

'You don't think anyone would believe you could be smitten by me in that time? I think I'm offended.'

'Of course not,' she said. 'I…I believe many women would be smitten by you. You're handsome, intelligent—'

'And personable, yes, you said. Though I bet you don't think I'm so personable right now.'

She glared at him, though there was a lilt to the corners of her mouth that made it seem like she might want to smile. 'You could be right about that.'

'Now to you—gorgeous, sexy, smart Andie Newman.' Her blush deepened as he sounded each adjective. 'People would certainly believe I could be instantly smitten with such a woman,' he said. 'In fact they'd think I was clever getting a ring on your finger so quickly.'

That flustered her. 'Th…thank you. I…I'm flattered. But it wouldn't seem authentic. We'd have to pretend so much. It would be such deception.'

With any other woman, he'd be waiting for her to ask: *What's in it for me?* Not Andie. He doubted the thought of a reward for her participation had even entered her head. He would have to entice her with an offer she couldn't refuse. And save the big gun to sway her from her final refusal.

'So you're going to say "yes"?'

She shook her head vehemently. 'No. I'm not. It wouldn't be right.'

'What's the harm? You'd be helping me out.'

She spun on her heel away from him and he faced her back view, her tensely hunched shoulders, for a long moment before she turned back to confront him. 'Can't you see it makes a mockery of…of a man and a woman committing to each other? To spending their lives together in a loving union? That's what getting engaged is all about. Not sealing a business deal.'

He closed his eyes at the emotion in her voice, the blurring of her words with choking pain. Under his breath he cursed fluently. Because, from any moral point of view, she was absolutely right.

'Were you engaged to…to Anthony?' he asked.

Her eyes when she lifted them to him glistened with the sheen of unshed tears. 'Not officially. But we had our future planned, even the names of our kids chosen. That's why I know promising to marry someone isn't something you do lightly. And not…not for a scam. Do you understand?'

Of course he did. He'd once been idealistic about love and marriage and sharing his life with that one special woman. But he couldn't admit it. Or that he'd become cynical that that kind of love would ever exist for him. Too much rode on this deal. Including his integrity.

'But this isn't really getting engaged,' he said. 'It's just …a limited agreement.'

Slowly she shook her head. 'I can't help you,' she said. 'Sorry.'

Dominic braced himself. He'd had to be ruthless at times to get where he'd got. To overcome the disadvantages of his youth. *To win.*

'What if by agreeing to be my fake fiancée you were helping someone else?' he said.

She frowned. 'Like who? Helping Walter Burton to make even more billions? I honestly can't say I like the sound of that guy, linking business to people's private lives. He sounds like a hypocrite, for one thing—you know, rich men and eyes of needles and all that. I'm not lying for him.'

'Not Walter Burton. I mean your nephew Timothy.' The little boy was his big gun.

'What do you mean, Timothy?'

Dominic fired his shot. 'Agree to be my fake fiancée and I will pay for all of Timothy's medical treatment—both immediate and ongoing. No limits. Hannah tells me there's a clinic in the United States that's at the forefront of research into treatment for his condition.'

Andie stared at him. 'You've spoken to Hannah? You've told Hannah about this? That you'll pay for Timothy if I agree to—'

He put up his hand. 'Not true.'

'But you—'

'I met with Hannah the day after the dinner with your family to talk about her helping me recruit the families for the party. At that meeting—out of interest—I asked her to tell me more about Timothy. She told me about the American treatment. I offered *then* to pay all the treatment—airfares and accommodation included.'

The colour rushed back into Andie's cheeks. 'That... that was extraordinarily generous of you. What did Hannah say?'

'She refused.'

'Of course she would. She hardly knows you. A Newman wouldn't accept charity. Although I might have tried to convince her.'

'Maybe you could convince her now. If Hannah thought

I was going to be part of the family—her brother-in-law, in fact—she could hardly refuse to accept, could she? And isn't it the sooner the better for Timothy's treatment?'

Andie stared at Dominic for a very long moment, too shocked to speak. 'Th…that's coercion. Coercion of the most insidious kind,' she finally managed to choke out.

A whole lot more words she couldn't express also tumbled around in her brain. Ruthless. Conniving. Heartless. And yet…he'd offered to help Timothy well before the fake fiancée thing. *Not a Scrooge after all.* She'd thought she'd been getting to know him—but Dominic Hunt was more of a mystery to her than ever.

He drew his dark brows together. 'Coercion? I wouldn't go that far. But I did offer to help Timothy without any strings attached. Hannah refused. This way, she might accept. And your nephew will get the help he needs. I see it as a win-win scenario.'

Andie realised she was twisting the leather thronging that laced together the front of her top and stopped it. Nothing in her life had equipped her to make this kind of decision. 'You're really putting me on the spot here. Asking me to lie and be someone I'm not—'

'Someone you're not? How does that work? You'd still be Andie.'

She found it difficult to meet his direct, confronting gaze. Those observant grey eyes seemed to see more than she wanted him to. 'You're asking me to pretend to be… to pretend to be a woman in love. When…when I'm not.' She'd only ever been in love once—and she didn't want to trawl back in her memories to try and relive that feeling—love lost hurt way too much. She did have feelings for Dominic beyond the employer/contractor relationship—but they were more of the other 'l' word—lust rather than love.

His eyes seemed to darken. 'I suppose I am.'

'And you too,' she said. 'You would have to pretend to be in love with...with me. And it would have to look darn authentic to be convincing.'

This was why she was prevaricating. As soon as he'd mentioned Timothy, she knew she would have little choice but to agree. If it had been any other blackmailing billionaire she would probably have said "yes" straight away—living a lie for a month would be worth it for Timothy to get the treatment her family's combined resources couldn't afford.

But not *this* man. How could she blithely *pretend* to be in love with a man she wanted as much as she wanted him? It would be some kind of torture.

'I see,' he said. Had he seriously not thought this through?

'We would be playing with big emotions, here, Dominic. And other people would be affected too. My family thinks you hung the moon. They'd be delighted if we dated—a sudden engagement would both shock and worry them. At some stage I would have to introduce you to Anthony's parents—they would be happy for me and want to meet you.'

'I see where you're going,' he said, raking his hand through his hair once more in a gesture that was becoming familiar.

She narrowed her eyes. 'And yet...would it all be worth it for Hannah to accept your help for Timothy?' She put up her hand to stop him from replying. 'I'm thinking out loud here.'

'And helping me achieve something I really want.'

There must be something more behind his drive to get this American deal. She hoped she'd discover it one day, sooner rather than later. It might help her understand him.

'You've backed me into a corner here, Dominic, and I can't say I appreciate it. How can I say "no" to such an incredible opportunity for Timothy?'

'Does that mean your answer is "yes"?'

She tilted her chin upwards—determined not to capitulate too readily to something about which she still had serious doubts. 'That's an unusual way to put it, Dominic—rather like you've made me a genuine proposal.'

Dominic pulled a face but it didn't dull the glint of triumph in his eyes. He thought he'd won. But she was determined to get something out of this deal for herself too.

Andie had no doubt if she asked for recompense—money, gifts—he'd give it to her. Dominic was getting what he wanted. Timothy would be getting what he so desperately needed. But what about *her*?

She wasn't interested in jewellery or fancy shopping. What she wanted was *him.* She wanted to kiss him, she wanted to hold him and she very much wanted to make love with him. Not for fake—for real.

There was a very good chance this arrangement would end in tears—her tears. But if she agreed to a fake engagement with this man, who attracted her like no other, she wanted what a fiancée might be expected to have—*him.* She thought, with a little shiver of desire, about what he'd said: *pleasure all the way.* She would be fine with that.

'Would it help if I made it sound like a genuine proposal?' he said, obviously bemused.

That hurt. Because the way he spoke made it sound as if there was no way he would ever make a genuine proposal to her. Not that she wanted that—heck, she hardly knew the guy. But it put her on warning. *Let's be honest,* she thought. She wanted him in her bed. But she also wanted to make darn sure she didn't get hurt. This was just a business deal to him—nothing personal involved.

'Do it,' she said, pointing to the floor. 'The full down-on-bended-knee thing.'

'Seriously?' he said, dark brows raised.

'Yes,' she said imperiously.

He grinned. 'Okay.'

The tall, black denim-clad hunk obediently knelt down on one knee, took her left hand in both of his and looked up into her face. 'Andie, will you do me the honour of becoming my fake fiancée?' he intoned in that deep, so-sexy voice.

Looking down at his roughly handsome face, Andie didn't know whether to laugh or cry. 'Yes, I accept your proposal,' she said in a voice that wasn't quite steady.

Dominic squeezed her hand hard as relief flooded his face. He got up from bended knee and for a moment she thought he might kiss her.

'But there are conditions,' she said, pulling away and letting go of his hand.

CHAPTER NINE

ANDIE ALMOST LAUGHED out loud at Dominic's perplexed expression. He was most likely used to calling the shots—in both business and his relationships. 'Conditions?' he asked.

'Yes, conditions,' she said firmly. 'Come on over to the sofa and I'll run through the list with you. I need to sit down; these heels aren't good for pacing in.' The polished concrete floor was all about looks rather than comfort.

'Do I have any choice about these "conditions"?' he grumbled.

'I think you'll see the sense in them,' she said. This was not going to go all his way. There was danger in this game she'd been coerced into playing and she wanted to make sure she and her loved ones were not going to get hurt by it.

She led him over to the red leather modular sofa in the living area. The apartment in an old converted factory warehouse was owned by one of her roommates and had been furnished stylishly with Andie's help. She flopped down on the sofa, kicked off the leopard stilettos that landed in an animal print clash on the zebra-patterned floor rug, and patted the seat next to her.

As Dominic sat down, his muscular thighs brushed against hers and she caught her breath until he settled at a not-quite-touching distance from her, his arm resting on the back of the sofa behind her. She had to close her eyes momentarily to deal with the rush of awareness from his already familiar scent, the sheer maleness of him in such close proximity.

'I'm interested to hear what you say,' he said, angling his powerful body towards her. He must work out a lot to have a chest like that. She couldn't help but wonder what it would feel like to splay her hands against those hard muscles, to press her body against his.

But it appeared he was having no such sensual thoughts about *her.* She noticed he gave a surreptitious glance to his watch.

'Hey, no continually checking on the clock,' she said. 'You have to give time to an engagement. Especially a make-believe one, if we're to make it believable. Not to mention your fake fiancée just might feel a tad insulted.'

She made her voice light but she meant every word of it. She had agreed to play her role in this charade and was now committed to making it work.

'Fair enough,' he said with a lazy half-smile. 'Is that one of your conditions?'

'Not one on its own as such, but it will fit into the others.'

'Okay, hit me with the conditions.' He feinted a boxer's defence that made her smile.

'Condition Number One,' she said, holding up the index finger of her left hand. 'Hannah never knows the truth—not now, not ever—that our engagement is a sham,' she said. 'In fact, none of my family is *ever* to know the truth.'

'Good strategy,' said Dominic. 'In fact, I'd extend that. *No one* should ever know. Both business partners and friends.'

'Agreed,' she said. It would be difficult to go through with this without confiding in a friend but it had to be that way. *No one must know how deeply attracted she was to him.* She didn't want anyone's pity when she and Dominic went their separate ways.

'Otherwise, the fallout from people discovering they'd been deceived could be considerable,' he said. 'What's next?'

She held up her middle finger. 'Condition Number Two—a plausible story. We need to explain why we got engaged so quickly. So start thinking…'

'Couldn't we just have fallen for each other straight away?'

Andie was taken aback. She hadn't expected anything that romantic from Dominic Hunt. 'You mean like "love at first sight"?'

'Exactly.'

'Would that be believable?'

He shook his head in mock indignation. 'Again you continue to insult me…'

'I didn't mean…' She'd certainly felt *something* for him at first sight. Sitting next to him on this sofa, she was feeling it all over again. But it wasn't *love*—she knew only too well what it was like to love. To love and to lose the man she loved in such a cruel way. Truth be told, she wasn't sure she wanted to love again. It hurt too much to lose that love.

'I don't like the lying aspect of this any more than you do,' he said. He removed his arm from the back of the sofa so he could lean closer to her, both hands resting on his knees. 'Why not stick to the truth as much as possible? You came to organise my party. I was instantly smitten, wooed you and won you.'

'And I was a complete walkover,' she said dryly.

'So we change it—you made me work very hard to win you.'

'In two weeks—and you away for one of them?' she said. 'Good in principle. But we might have to fudge the timeline a little.'

'It can happen,' he said. 'Love at first sight, I mean. My

parents…apparently they fell for each other on day one and were married within mere months of meeting. Or so my aunt told me.'

His eyes darkened and she remembered he'd only been eleven years old when left an orphan. If she'd lost her parents at that age, her world would have collapsed around her—as no doubt his had. But he was obviously trying to revive a happy memory of his parents.

'How lovely—a real-life romance. Did they meet in Australia or England?'

'London. They were both schoolteachers; my mother was living in England. She came to his school as a temporary mathematics teacher; he taught chemistry.'

Andie decided not to risk a feeble joke about their meeting being explosive. Not when the parents' love story had ended in tragedy. 'No wonder you're clever then, with such smart parents.'

'Yes,' he said, making the word sound like an end-of-story punctuation mark. She knew only too well what it was like not to want to pursue a conversation about a lost loved one.

'So we have a precedent for love at first sight in your family,' she said. 'I…I fell for Anthony straight away too. So for both of us an…an instant attraction—if not *love*—could be feasible.' Instant and ongoing for her—but he was not to know that.

That Dominic had talked about his parents surprised her. For her, thinking about Anthony—as always—brought a tug of pain to her heart but this time also a reminder of the insincerity of this venture with Dominic. She knew what real commitment should feel like. But for Timothy to get that vital treatment she was prepared to compromise on her principles.

'Love at first sight it is,' he said.

'*Attraction* at first sight,' she corrected him.

'Surely it would had to have led to love for us to get engaged,' he said.

'True,' she conceded. He tossed around concepts of love and commitment as if they were concepts with which to barter, not deep, abiding emotions between two people who cared enough about each other to pledge a lifetime together. *Till death us do part.* She could never think of that part of a marriage ceremony without breaking down. She shouldn't be thinking of it now.

'Next condition?' he said.

She skipped her ring finger, which she had trouble keeping upright, and went straight for her pinkie. 'Condition Number Three: no dating other people—for the duration of the engagement, that is.'

'I'm on board with that one,' he said without hesitation.

'Me too,' she said. She hadn't even thought about any man but Dominic since the moment she'd met him, so that was not likely to be a hardship.

He sat here next to her in jeans and T-shirt like a regular thirty-two-year-old guy—not a secretive billionaire who had involved her in a scheme to deceive family and friends to help him make even more money. If he were just your everyday handsome hunk she would make her interest in him known. But her attraction went beyond his good looks and muscles to the complex man she sensed below his confident exterior. She had seen only intriguing hints of those hidden depths—she wanted to discover more.

Andie's thumb went up next. 'Resolution Number Four: I dump you, not the other way around. When this comes to an end, that is.'

'Agreed—and I'll be a gentleman about it. But I ask you not to sell your story. I don't want to wake up one morning to the headline *"My Six Weeks with Scrooge"*.'

He could actually *joke* about being a Scrooge—Dominic had come a long way.

'Of course,' she said. 'I promise not to say *"I Hopped Out of the Billionaire's Bed"* either. Seriously, I would never talk to the media. You can be reassured of that.'

'No tacky headlines, just a simple civilised break-up to be handled by you,' he said.

They both fell silent for a moment. Did he feel stricken by the same melancholy she did at the thought of the imagined break-up of a fake engagement? And she couldn't help thinking she'd like a chance to hop *into* his bed before she hopped *out* of it.

'On to Condition Number Five,' she said, holding up all five fingers as she could not make her ring finger stand on its own. 'We have to get to know each other. So we don't get caught out on stuff we would be expected to know about each other if we were truly…committing to a life together.'

How different this fake relationship would be to a real relationship—getting to know each other over shared experiences, shared laughter, shared tears, long lazy mornings in bed…

Dominic sank down further into the sofa, his broad shoulders hunched inward. 'Yup.' It was more a grunt than a word.

'You don't sound keen to converse?'

'What sort of things?' he said with obvious reluctance. Not for the first time, she had a sense of secrets deeply held.

'For one thing, I need to know more about your marriage and how it ended.' And more about his time on the streets. And about that broken nose and scarred knuckles. And why he had let people believe he was a Scrooge when he so obviously wasn't. Strictly speaking, she probably didn't *need* to know all that about him for a fake engagement. Fact was, she *wanted* to know it.

'I guess I can talk to you about my marriage,' he said,

still not sounding convinced. 'But there are things about my life that I would rather remain private.'

What things? 'Just so long as I'm not made a fool of at some stage down the track by not knowing something a real fiancée would have known.'

'Fine,' he grunted in a response that didn't give her much confidence. She ached to know more about him. And yet there was that shadow she sensed. She wouldn't push for simple curiosity's sake.

'As far as I'm concerned, my life's pretty much an open book,' she said, in an effort to encourage him to open up about his life—or past, to be more specific. 'Just ask what you need to know about me and I'll do my best to answer honestly.'

Was any person's life truly an open book? Like anyone else, she had doubts and anxieties and dumb things she'd done that she'd regretted, but nothing lurked that she thought could hinder an engagement. No one would criticise her for finding love again after five years. In truth, she knew they would be glad for her. So would Anthony.

She remembered one day, lying together on the beach. *'I would die if I lost you,'* she'd said to Anthony.

'Don't say that,' he'd said. *'If anything happened to me, I'd want you to find another guy. But why are we talking like this? We're both going to live until we're a hundred.'*

'Why not schedule in a question-and-answer session?' Dominic said.

She pulled her thoughts back to the present. 'Good idea,' she said. 'Excellent idea, in fact.'

Dominic rolled his eyes in response.

'Oh,' she said. 'You weren't serious. I…I was.'

'No, you're right. I guess there's no room for spontaneity in a fake engagement.' It was a wonder he could get the words out when his tongue was so firmly in his cheek. 'A question-and-answer session it is. At a time to be determined.'

'Good idea,' she said, feeling disconcerted. Was all this just a game to him?

'Are there any more conditions to come?' he asked. 'You're all out of fingers on one hand, by the way.'

'There is one more very important condition to come—and may I remind you I do have ten fingers—but first I want to hear if there's anything you want to add.'

She actually had two more conditions, but the final condition she could not share with him: *that she could not fall for him*. She couldn't deal with the fallout in terms of pain if she were foolish enough to let down the guard on her heart.

Andie's beautiful green eyes had sparkled with good humour in spite of the awkward position he had put her into. *Coerced* her into. But now her eyes seemed to dim and Dominic wondered if she was being completely honest about being an 'open book'.

Ironically, he already knew more about Andie, the fake fiancée, than he'd known about Tara when he'd got engaged to her for real. His ex-wife had kept her true nature under wraps until well after she'd got the wedding band on her finger. *What you see is what you get.* He so wanted to believe that about Andie.

'My condition? You have to wear a ring,' he said. 'I want to get you an engagement ring straight away. Today. Once Tara sees that she'll know it's serious. And the press will too. Not to mention a symbol for when we meet with Walter Burton.'

She shrugged. 'Okay, you get me a ring.'

'You don't want to choose it yourself?' He was taken aback. Tara had been so avaricious about jewellery.

'No. I would find it…sad. Distressing. The day I choose

my engagement ring is the day I get engaged for real. To me, the ring should be a symbol of a true commitment, not a…a prop for a charade. But I agree—I should wear one as a visible sign of commitment.'

'I'll organise it then,' he said. He had no idea why he should be disappointed at her lack of enthusiasm. She was absolutely right—the ring would be a prop. But it would also play a role in keeping it believable. 'What size ring do you wear?'

'I haven't a clue,' she said. She held up her right hand to show the collection of tiny fine silver rings on her slender fingers. Her nails were painted cream today. 'I bought these at a market and just tried them on until I found rings that fitted.' She slid off the ring from the third finger of her right hand. 'This should do the trick.' She handed it to him. It was still warm with her body heat and he held it on his palm for a moment before pocketing it.

'What style of engagement ring would you like?' he asked.

Again she shrugged. 'You choose. It's honestly not important to me.'

A hefty carat solitaire diamond would be appropriate—one that would give her a good resale value when she went to sell it after this was all over.

'Did you choose your ex-wife's engagement ring?' Andie asked.

He scowled at the reminder that he had once got engaged for real.

Andie pulled one of her endearing faces. 'Sorry. I guess that's a sensitive issue. I know we'll come to all that in our question-and-answer session. I'm just curious.'

'She chose it herself. All I had to do was pay for it.' That alone should have alerted him to what the marriage was all about—giving her access to his money and the lifestyle it bought.

'That wasn't very…romantic,' Andie said.

'There was nothing romantic about my marriage. Shall I tell you about it now and get all that out of the way?'

'If you feel comfortable with it,' she said.

'Comfortable is never a word I would relate to that time of my life,' he said. 'It was a series of mistakes.'

'If you're ready to tell me, I'm ready to listen.' He thought about how Andie had read his mood so accurately earlier this morning—giving him breakfast when he hadn't even been aware himself that he was hungry. She was thoughtful. And kind. Kindness wasn't an attribute he had much encountered in the women he had met.

'The first mistake I made with Tara was that she reminded me of someone else—a girl I'd met when I was living in the squat. Someone frail and sweet with similar colouring—someone I'd wanted to care for and look after.' It still hurt to think of Melody. Andie didn't need to know about her.

'And the second mistake?' Andie asked, seeming to understand he didn't want to speak further about Melody. She leaned forward as if she didn't want to miss a word.

'I believed her when she said she wanted children.'

'You wanted children?'

'As soon as possible. Tara said she did too.'

Andie frowned. 'But she didn't?'

Even now, bitterness rose in his throat. 'After we'd been married a year and nothing had happened, I suggested we see a doctor. Tara put it off and put it off. I thought it was because she didn't want to admit to failure. It was quite by accident that I discovered all the time I thought we'd been trying to conceive, she'd been on the contraceptive pill.'

Andie screwed up her face in an expression of disbelief and distaste. 'That's unbelievable.'

'When I confronted her, she laughed.' He relived the horror of discovering his ex-wife's treachery and the realisation she didn't have it in her to love. Not him. Certainly not a child. Fortunately, she hadn't been clever enough to understand the sub-clauses in the pre-nuptial agreement and divorce had been relatively straightforward.

'You had a lucky escape,' Andie said.

'That's why I never want to marry again. How could I ever trust another woman after that?'

'I understand you would feel that way,' she said. 'But not every woman would be like her. Me…my sisters, my friends. I don't know anyone who would behave with such dishonesty. Don't write off all women because of one.'

Trouble was, his wealth attracted women like Tara.

He was about to try and explain that to Andie when her phone started to sound out a bar of classical music.

She got up from the sofa and headed for the kitchen countertop to pick it up. 'Gemma,' she mouthed to him. 'I'd better take it.'

He nodded, grateful for the reprieve. Tara's treachery had got him into this fake engagement scenario with Andie, who was being such a good sport about the whole thing. He did not want to waste another word, or indeed thought, on his ex. Again, he thanked whatever providence had sent Andie into his life—Andie who was the opposite of Tara in every way.

He couldn't help but overhear Andie as she chatted to Gemma. 'Yes, yes, I saw it. We were having lunch after the meeting that Friday. Yes, it does look romantic. No, I didn't know anyone took a photo.'

Andie waved him over to her. 'Shall I tell her?' she mouthed.

He gave her the thumbs-up. 'Yes,' he mouthed back as he got up. There was no intention of keeping this 'engagement' secret. He walked over closer to Andie, who was standing there in bare feet, looking more beautiful in jeans than any other woman would look in a ball gown.

'Actually, Gemma, I…haven't been completely honest with you. I…uh…we…well, Dominic and I hit it off from the moment we first saw each other.'

Andie looked to Dominic and he nodded—she was doing well.

She listened to Gemma, then spoke again. 'Yes. We are…romantically involved. In fact…well…we're engaged.' She held the phone out from her ear and even Dominic could hear the excited squeals coming from Gemma.

When the squeals had subsided, Andie spoke again. 'Yes. It is sudden. I know that. But…well…you see I've learned that you have to grab your chance at happiness when you can. I…I've had it snatched away from me before.' She paused as she listened. 'Yes, that's it. I didn't want to wait. Neither did he. Gemma, I'd appreciate it if you didn't tell anyone just yet. Eliza? Well, okay, you can tell Eliza. I'd just like to tell my family first. What was that? Yes, I'll tell him.' She shut down her phone.

'So it's out,' he said.

'Yes,' she said. 'No denying it now.'

'What did Gemma ask you to tell me?'

She looked up at him. 'That she hoped you knew what a lucky guy you are to…to catch me.'

He looked down at her. 'I know very well how lucky I am. You're wonderful in every way and I appreciate what you're doing to help me.'

For a long moment he looked down into her face—still, serious, even sombre without her usual animated expression. Her eyes were full of something he couldn't put a name to. But not, he hoped, regret.

'Thank you, Andie.'

He stepped closer. For a long moment her gaze met his and held it. He saw wariness but he also saw the stirrings of what he could only read as invitation. To kiss his pretend fiancée would probably be a mistake. But it was a mistake he badly wanted to make.

He lifted his hand to her face, brushed first the smooth skin of her cheek and then the warm softness of her lips with the back of his knuckles. She stilled. Her lips parted under his touch and he could feel the tremor that ran through her body. He dropped his hand to her shoulder, then dipped his head and claimed her mouth in a firm gentle kiss. She murmured her surprise and pleasure as she kissed him back.

CHAPTER TEN

DOMINIC WAS KISSING her and it was more wonderful than Andie ever could have imagined. His firm, sensuous mouth was sure and certain on hers and she welcomed the intimate caress, the nudging of his tongue against the seam of her lips as she opened her mouth to his. His beard growth scratched her face but it was a pleasurable kind of pain. *The man knew how to kiss.*

But as he kissed her and she kissed him back she was shocked by the sudden explosion of chemistry between them that turned something gentle into something urgent and demanding. She wound her arms around his neck to bring him closer in a wild tangle of tongues and lips as she pressed herself against his hard muscular chest. He tasted of coffee and hot male and desire. Passion this instant, this insistent was a surprise.

But it was too soon.

She knew she wanted him. But she hadn't realised until now just how *much* she wanted him. And how careful she would have to be to guard her heart. Because these thrilling kisses told her that intimate contact with Dominic Hunt might just become an addiction she would find very difficult to live without. To him, this pretend engagement was a business ploy that might also develop into an entertaining game on the side. *She did not want to be a fake fiancée with benefits.*

When it came down to it, while she had dated over the

last few years, her only serious relationship had been with a boy who had adored her, and whom she had loved with all her heart. Not a man like Dominic, who had sworn off marriage and viewed commitment so lightly he could pretend to be engaged. Her common sense urged her to stop but her body wanted more, more, more of him.

With a great effort she broke away from the kiss. Her heart was pounding in triple time, her breath coming in painful gasps. She took a deep steadying breath. And then another.

'That…that was a great start on Condition Number Six,' she managed to choke out.

Dominic towered over her; his breath came in ragged gasps. He looked so darkly sensual, her heart seemed to flip right over in her chest. 'What?' he demanded. 'Stopping when we'd just started?'

'No. I…I mean the actual kiss.'

He put his hand on her shoulder, lightly stroking her in a caress that ignited shivers of delight all through her.

'So tell me about your sixth condition,' he said, his deep voice with a broken edge to it as he struggled to control his breathing.

'Condition Number Six is that we…we have to look the part.'

He frowned. 'And that means…?'

'I mean we have to act like a genuine couple. To seem to other people as if we're…we're crazy about each other. Because it would have to be…something very powerful between us for us to get engaged so quickly. In…real life, I mean.'

She found it difficult to meet his eyes. 'I was going to say we needed to get physical. And we just did…get physical. So we…uh…know that there's chemistry between us. And that…that it works.'

He dropped his hand from her shoulder to tilt her chin

upwards with his finger so she was forced to meet his gaze. 'There was never any doubt about that.'

His words thrummed through her body. That sexual attraction had been there for her the first time she'd met him. *Had he felt it too?*

'So the sixth condition is somewhat superfluous,' she said, her voice racing as she tried to ignore the hunger for him his kiss had ignited. 'I think we might be okay, there. You know, holding hands, arms around each other. Appropriate Public Displays of Affection.' It was an effort to force herself to sound matter of fact.

'This just got to be my favourite of all your conditions,' he said slowly, his eyes narrowing in a way she found incredibly sexy. 'Shall we practise some more?'

Her traitorous body wrestled down her hopelessly outmatched common sense. 'Why not?' she murmured, desperate to be in his arms again. He pulled her close and their body contact made her aware he wanted her as much as she wanted him. She sighed as she pressed her mouth to his.

Then her phone sang out its ringtone of a piano sonata.

'Leave it,' growled Dominic.

She ignored the musical tone until it stopped. But it had brought her back to reality. There was nothing she wanted more than to take Dominic by the hand and lead him up the stairs to her bedroom. She intended to have him before this contract between them came to an end.

But that intuition she usually trusted screamed at her that to make love with him on the first day of their fake engagement would be a mistake. It would change the dynamic of their relationship to something she did not feel confident of being able to handle.

No sooner had the ringtone stopped than it started again.

Andie untangled herself from Dominic's embrace and

stepped right back from him, back from the seductive reach of his muscular arms.

'I…I have to take this,' she said.

She answered the phone but had to rest against the kitchen countertop to support knees that had gone shaky and weak. Dominic leaned back against the wall opposite her and crossed his arms against his powerful chest. His muscles flexed as he did so and she had to force herself to concentrate on the phone call.

'Yes, Eliza, it's true. I know—it must have been a surprise to you. A party?' Andie looked up to Dominic and shook her head. He nodded. She spoke to Eliza. 'No. We don't want an engagement party. Yes, I know we're party queens and it's what we do.' She rolled her eyes at Dominic and, to her relief, he smiled. 'The Christmas party is more than enough to handle at the moment,' she said to Eliza.

We. She and Dominic were a couple now. A fake couple. It would take some getting used to. So would handling the physical attraction between them.

'The wedding?' Eliza's question about the timing of the wedding flustered her. 'We…we…uh…next year some time. Yes, I know next year is only next month. The wedding won't be next month, that's for sure.' *The* wedding—wouldn't a loved-up fiancée have said *our* wedding?

She finished the call to Eliza and realised her hands were clammy. 'This is not going to be easy,' she said to Dominic.

'I never thought it would be,' he said. Was there a double meaning there?

'I have no experience in this kind of deception. The first thing Eliza asked me was when are we getting married. She put me on the spot. I…I struggled to find an answer.'

He nodded slowly. 'I suggest we say we've decided on a long engagement. That we're committed but want to use the engagement time to get to know each other better.'

'That sounds good,' she said.

The deceptive words came so easily to him while she was so flustered she could scarcely think. She realised how hopelessly mismatched they were: he was more experienced, wealthier, from a completely different background. And so willing to lie.

And yet... That kiss had only confirmed how much she wanted him.

Her phone rang out again. 'Why do I get the feeling this phone will go all day long?' she said, a note of irritation underscoring her voice. She looked on the caller ID. 'It's my fashion editor friend, Karen. I knew Gemma wouldn't be able to stop at Eliza,' she told Dominic as she answered it.

The first part of the conversation was pretty much a repeat of the conversation she'd had with Gemma. But then Karen asked should she start scouting around for her wedding dress. Karen hunted down bargain-priced clothes for her; of course she'd want to help her with a wedding. 'My wedding dress? We…uh…haven't set a date for the wedding yet. Yes, I suppose it's never too early to think about the dress. Simple? Vintage inspired? Gorgeous shoes?' She laughed and hoped Karen didn't pick up on the shrill edge to her laughter. 'You know my taste only too well, Karen. A veil? A modest lace veil? Okay. Yes. I'll leave it to you. Thank you.'

'Your friends move fast,' Dominic said when she'd disconnected the call.

'They're so thrilled for me. After…after…well, you know. My past.' Her past of genuine love, unsullied by lies and deception.

'Of course,' he said.

She couldn't bring herself to say anything about the kisses they'd shared. It wasn't the kind of thing she found easy to talk about. Neither, it appeared, did he.

He glanced down at his watch. The action drew her attention to his hands. She noticed again how attractive they were, with long strong fingers. And thought how she would like to feel them on her body. Stroking. Caressing. Exploring. *She had to stop this.*

'I know I'm breaking the terms of one of your conditions,' he said. 'But I do have to get to the office. There are cancelled meetings in other states to reschedule and staff who need to talk to me.'

'And I've got to finalise the furniture hire for the Christmas party. With two hundred people for lunch, we need more tables and chairs. It's sobering, to have all those families in need on Christmas Day.'

'Hannah assures me it's the tip of a tragic iceberg,' said Dominic.

They both paused for a long moment before she spoke. 'I also have to work on a tiaras-and-tuxedos-themed twenty-first party. Ironic, isn't it, after what we've just been saying?' But organising parties was her job and brought not only employment to her and her partners but also the caterers, the waiting staff and everyone else involved.

'I didn't think twenty-first parties were important any more, with eighteen the legal age of adulthood,' Dominic said.

'They're still very popular. This lovely girl turning twenty-one still lives at home with her parents and has three more years of university still ahead of her to become a veterinarian. I have to organise tiaras for her dogs.'

'Wh...what?' he spluttered. 'Did you say you're putting a tiara on a *dog*?'

'Her dogs are very important to her; they'll be honoured guests at the party.'

He scowled. 'I like dogs but that's ridiculous.'

'We're getting more and more bookings for dog parties.

A doggy birthday boy or girl invites their doggy friends. They're quite a thing. And getting as competitive as the kids' parties. Of course it's a learning curve for a party planner—considering doggy bathroom habits, for one thing.'

'That is the stupidest—'

Andie put up her hand. 'Don't be too quick to judge. The doggy parties are really about making the humans happy—I doubt the dogs could care less. Frivolity can be fun. Eliza and I have laid bets on how many boys will arrive wearing tiaras to the vet student's twenty-first.'

She had to smile at his bah-humbug expression.

'By the time I was twenty-one, I had established a career in real estate and had my first million in sight.'

That interested her. 'I'd love to know about—'

He cut her off. 'Let's save that for the question-and-answer session, shall we?'

'Which will start…?'

'This afternoon. Can you come to my place?'

'Sure. It doesn't hurt to visit the party site as many times as I can.'

'Only this time you'll be coming to collect your engagement ring.'

'Of…of course.' She had forgotten about that. In a way, she dreaded it. 'And to find out more about you, fake fiancé. We have to be really well briefed to face my family tomorrow evening.'

She and Anthony had joked that by the time they'd paid off their student loans all they'd be able to afford for an engagement ring would be a ring pull from a can of soft drink. The ring pull would have had so much more meaning than this cynical exercise.

She felt suddenly subdued at the thought of deceiving her family. Her friends were used to the ups and downs of dating. A few weeks down the track, they'd take a broken engagement in their stride. If those kisses were anything to go by, she might be more than a tad upset when her time with Dominic came to an end. She pummelled back down to somewhere deep inside her the shred of hope that perhaps something real could happen between them after the engagement charade was done.

'When will you tell your parents?' Dominic asked.

'Today. They'd be hurt beyond belief if they found out from someone else.'

'And you'll talk to Hannah about Timothy?'

'At the family dinner. We should speak to her and Paul together.'

'I hope she won't be too difficult to convince. I really want to help that little boy.'

'I know,' she said, thinking of how grateful her family would be to him. How glad she was she'd agreed to all this for her tiny nephew's sake. But what about Dominic's family? This shouldn't be all about hers. 'What about your aunt? Do we need to tell her?'

The shutters came slamming down. 'No. She's out of the picture.'

The way he said it let her know not to ask more. Not now anyway.

Dominic shrugged on his leather jacket in preparation to go. She stared, dumbstruck, feasting her eyes on him. *He was so hot.* She still felt awkward after their passionate kissing session. Should she reach up and kiss him on the cheek?

While she was making up her mind, he pulled her close for a brief, exciting kiss on her mouth. She doubted there could be any other type of kiss but exciting from Dominic. 'Happy to fulfil Condition Number Six at any time,' he said, very seriously.

She smiled, the tension between them immediately dissipated. But she wasn't ready to say goodbye just yet.

'Before you go…' She picked up her smartphone again. 'The first thing my friends who don't know you will want to see is a photo of my surprise new fiancé.'

He ran his hand over his unshaven chin. 'Like this? Can't it wait?'

'I like your face like that. It's hot. No need to shave on my behalf.' Without thinking, she put her fingers up to her cheek, where there was probably stubble rash. *His kiss had felt so good.*

'If you say so,' he said, looking pleased.

'Just lean against the door there,' she said. 'Look cool.'

He slouched against the door and sent her a smouldering look. The wave of want that crashed through her made her nearly drop the phone. 'Do I look *cool*?' he said in a self-mocking tone. 'I thought you liked *hot*?'

'You know exactly what I mean.' She was discovering a light-hearted side to Dominic she liked very much.

Their gazes met and they both burst into laughter. He looked even more gorgeous when he laughed, perfect teeth white in his tanned face, and she immediately captured a few more images of him. Who would recognise this good-humoured hunk in jeans and leather jacket as the billionaire Scrooge of legend?

'What about a selfie of us together?' she asked. 'In the interests of authenticity,' she hastily added.

Bad idea. She stood next to him, aware of every centimetre of body contact, and held her phone out in front of them. She felt more self-conscious than she could ever remember feeling. He pulled her in so their faces were close together. She smiled and clicked, and as she clicked again he kissed her on the cheek.

'That will be cute,' she said.

'Another?' he asked. This time he kissed her on the mouth. *Click. Click. Click.* And then she forgot to click.

After he had left, Andie spent more minutes than she should scrolling through the photos on her phone. *No one would know they were faking it.*

CHAPTER ELEVEN

DOMINIC NOW KNEW more about diamond engagement rings than even a guy who was genuinely engaged to be married needed to know. He'd thought he could just march into Sydney's most exclusive jewellery store and hand over an investment-sized price for a big chunk of diamond. Not so.

The sales guy—rather, *executive consultant*—who had greeted him and ushered him into a private room had taken the purchase very seriously. He'd hit Dominic with a barrage of questions. It was unfortunate that the lady was unable to be there because it was very important the ring would suit her personality. What were the lady's favourite colours? What style of clothes did she favour? Her colouring?

'Were you able to answer the questions?' Andie asked, her lips curving into her delightful smile.

She had just arrived at his house. After she'd taken some measurements in the old ballroom, he had taken her out to sit in the white Hollywood-style chairs by the pool. Again, she looked as if she belonged. She wore a natural-coloured linen dress with her hair piled up and a scarf twisted and tied right from the base of her neck to the top of her head. It could have looked drab and old-fashioned but, on her, with her vintage sunglasses and orange lipstick, it looked just right.

Last time she'd been there he'd been so caught up with her he hadn't thought to ask her would she like a drink.

He didn't want a live-in housekeeper—he valued his privacy too much—but his daily housekeeper had been this morning and the refrigerator was well stocked. He'd carried a selection of cool drinks out to the poolside table between their two chairs.

'You're finding this story amusing, aren't you?' he said, picking up his iced tea.

She took off her sunglasses. 'Absolutely. I had no idea the rigmarole involved in buying an engagement ring.'

'Me neither. I thought I'd just march in, point out a diamond ring and pay for it.' This was a first for him.

'Me too,' said Andie. 'I thought that's what guys did when they bought a ring.'

'Oh, no. First of all, I'd done completely the wrong thing in not having you with me. He was too discreet to ask where you were, so I didn't have to come up with a creative story to explain your absence.'

'One less lie required anyway,' she said with a twist of her lovely mouth. 'Go on with the story—I'm fascinated.'

'Apparently, the done thing is to have a bespoke ring—like the business suits I have made to measure.'

'A bespoke ring? Who knew?' she said, her eyes dancing.

'Instead, I had to choose from their ready-to-wear couture pieces.'

'I had no idea such a thing existed,' she said with obvious delight. *Her smile.* It made him feel what he'd thought he'd never feel again, made him want what he'd thought he'd never want.

'You should have been there,' he said. 'You would have had fun.' He'd spent the entire time in the jewellery store wishing she'd been by his side. He could imagine her suppressing giggles as the consultant had run through his over-the-top sales pitch.

'Perhaps,' she said, but her eyes dimmed. 'You know

my reasons for not wanting to get involved in the purchase. Anyway, what did you tell them about my—' she made quote marks in the air with her fingers '—"personal style"? That must have put you on the spot?'

'I told the consultant about your misbehaving skirt—only I didn't call it that, of course. I told him about your shoes that laced up your calves. I told him about your turquoise necklace and your outsized earrings. I told him about your leopard-print shoes and your white trousers.'

Andie's eyes widened. 'You remember all that about what I wear?'

'I did say I was observant,' he said.

Ask him to remember what Party Planners Numbers One to Three had been wearing for their interviews and he would scarcely recall it. But he remembered every detail about her since that errant breeze at his front door had blown Andie into his life.

At the jewellery store, once he'd relaxed into the conversation with the consultant, Dominic had also told him how Andie was smart and creative and a touch unconventional and had the most beautiful smile and a husky, engaging laugh. 'This is a lucky lady,' the guy had said. 'You must love her very much.'

That had thrown Dominic. 'Yes,' he'd muttered. *Love* could not enter into this. He did not want Andie to get hurt. And hurt wasn't on his personal agenda either. He didn't think he had it in him to love. To give love you had to be loved—and genuine love was not something that had been part of his life.

'So… I'm curious,' said Andie. What kind of ring did you—did I—end up with?'

'Not the classic solitaire I would have chosen. The guy said you'd find it boring.'

'Of course I wouldn't have found it boring,' she said not very convincingly.

'Why do I not believe you?' he said.

'Stop teasing me and show me the darn ring,' she said.

Dominic took out the small, leather, case from his inside suit jacket pocket. 'I hope you like it,' he said. *He wanted her to like it.* He didn't know why it was suddenly so important that she did.

He opened the case and held it out for Andie to see. Her eyes widened and she caught her breath. 'It…it's exquisite,' she said.

'Is it something you think you could wear?' he asked.

'Oh, yes,' she said. 'I love it.'

'It's called a halo set ring,' he said. 'The ring of little diamonds that surround the big central diamond is the halo. And the very narrow split band—again set with small diamonds—is apparently very fashionable.'

'That diamond is enormous,' she said, drawing back. 'I'd be nervous to wear it.'

'I got it well insured,' he said.

'Good,' she said. 'If I lost it, I'd be paying you back for the rest of my life and probably still be in debt.'

'The ring is yours, Andie.'

'I know, for the duration,' she said. 'I promise to look after it.' She crossed her heart.

'You misunderstand. The ring is yours to keep after… after all this has come to an end.'

She frowned and shook her head vehemently. 'No. That wasn't part of the deal. Timothy's treatment was the deal. I give this ring back to you when…when I dump you.'

'We'll see about that,' he said, not wanting to get into an argument with her. As far as he was concerned, this ring was *hers*. She could keep it or sell it or give it away—he never wanted it back. 'Now, shouldn't I be getting that diamond on your finger?'

He was surprised to find his hand wasn't steady as he took the ring out of its hinged case. It glittered and sparkled as the afternoon sunlight danced off the multi-cut facets of the diamonds. 'Hold out your hand,' he said.

'No', she said, again shaking her head. 'Give it to me and I'll put it on myself. This isn't a real engagement and I don't want to jinx myself. When I get engaged for real, my real fiancé will put my ring on my wedding finger.'

Again, Dominic felt disappointed. Against all reason. He wanted to put the ring on her finger. But he understood why he shouldn't. He felt a pang of regret that he most likely would never again be anyone's 'real fiancé'—and a pang of what he recognised as envy for the man who would win Andie's heart for real.

He put the ring back in its case. 'You do want to get married one day?'

He wasn't sure if she was still in love with the memory of her first boyfriend—and that no man would be able to live up to that frozen-in-time ideal. Melody had been his first love—but he certainly held no romanticised memories of her.

'Of course I do. I want to get married and have a family. I…I… It took me a long time to get over the loss of my dreams of a life with Anthony. I couldn't see myself with anyone but him. But that was five years ago. Now… I think I'm ready to move on.'

Dominic had to clear his throat to speak. 'Okay, I see your point. Better put on the ring yourself,' he said.

Tentatively, she lifted the ring from where it nestled in the velvet lining of its case. 'I'm terrified I'll drop it and it will fall into the pool.' She laughed nervously as she slid it on to the third finger of her left hand. 'There—it's on.' She held out her hand, fingers splayed to better display the ring. 'It's a perfect fit,' she said. 'You did well.'

'It looks good on you,' he said.

'That sales guy knew his stuff,' she said. 'I can't stop looking at it. It's the most beautiful ring I've ever seen.'

She looked up at him. 'I still have my doubts about the wisdom of this charade. But I will enjoy wearing this magnificent piece of jewellery. Thank you for choosing something so perfect.'

'Thank you for helping me out with this crazy scheme,' he said. The scheme that had seemed crazy the moment he'd proposed it and which got crazier and crazier as it went along. But it was important he sealed that deal with Walter Burton. And was it such a bad thing to have to spend so much time with Andie?

Andie took a deep breath to try and clear her head of the conflicting emotions aroused by wearing the exquisite ring that sat so perfectly on her finger. *The ring pull would have been so much more valuable.* This enormous diamond with its many surrounding tiny diamonds symbolised not love and commitment but the you-scratch-my-back-and-I'll-scratch-yours deal between her and Dominic.

Still, she couldn't help wondering how he could have chosen a ring so absolutely *her.*

'I've been thinking about our getting-to-know-each-other session,' she said. 'Why don't we each ask the other three questions?'

'Short and to the point,' he said with obvious relief.

'Or longer, as needs might be. I want to be the best fake fiancée I can. No way do I want to be caught out on something important I should know about you. I didn't like the feeling this morning when I froze as Karen questioned me about our wedding plans.'

Dominic drank from his iced tea. To give himself time to think? Or plan evasive action? 'I see where you're going. Let's see if we can make it work.'

Andie settled back in the chair. She didn't know whether to be disappointed or relieved there was a small table between her and Dominic. She would not be averse to his thigh nudged against hers—at the same time, it would undoubtedly be distracting. 'Okay. I'll start. My Question Number One is: How did you get from street kid to billionaire?'

Dominic took his time to put his glass back down on the table. 'Before I reply, let's get one thing straight.' His gaze was direct. 'My answers are for you and you alone. What I tell you is to go no further.'

'Agreed,' she said, meeting his gaze full-on. 'Can we get another thing straight? You can trust me.'

'Just so long as we know where we stand.'

'I'm surprised you're not making me sign a contract.' She said the words half in jest but the expression that flashed across his face in response made her pause. She sat forward in her seat. 'You thought about a contract, didn't you?'

With Dominic back in his immaculate dark business suit, clean-shaven, hair perfectly groomed, she didn't feel as confident with him as she had this morning.

'I did think of a contract and quickly dismissed it,' he said. 'I do trust you, Andie.'

Surely he must be aware that she would not jeopardise Timothy's treatment in any way? 'I'm glad to hear that, Dominic, because this won't work if we don't trust each other—it goes both ways. Let's start. C'mon—answer my question.'

He still didn't answer. She waited, aware of the palm leaves above rustling in the same slight breeze that ruffled the aquamarine surface of the pool, the distant barking of a neighbour's dog.

'You know I hate this?' he said finally.

'I kind of get that,' she said. 'But I couldn't "marry" a man whose past remained a dark secret to me.'

Even after the question-and-answer session, she suspected big chunks of his past might remain a secret from her. Maybe from anyone.

He dragged in a deep breath as if to prepare himself for something unpleasant. 'As I have already mentioned, at age seventeen, I was homeless. I was living in an underground car park on the site of an abandoned shopping centre project in one of the roughest areas of Brisbane. The buildings had only got to the foundation stage. The car park was…well, you can imagine what an underground car park that had never been completed was like. It was a labyrinth of unfinished service areas and elevator shafts. No lights, pools of water whenever it rained, riddled with rats and cockroaches.'

'And human vermin too, I'll bet.' Andie shuddered. 'What a scary place for a teenager to be living—and dangerous.'

He had come from such a dark place. She could gush with sympathy and pity. But she knew instinctively that was not what he wanted to hear. Show how deeply moved she was at the thought of seventeen-year-old Dominic living such a perilous life and he would clam up. And she wanted to hear more.

Dominic's eyes assumed a dark, faraway look as though he was going back somewhere in his mind he had no desire to revisit. 'It was dangerous and smelly and seemed like hell. But it was also somewhere safer to sleep than on the actual streets. Darkness meant shadows you could hide in, and feel safe even if it was only an illusion of safety.'

She reached out and took the glass from his hand; he seemed unaware he was gripping it so tightly he might break it. 'Your home life must have been kind of hellish too for you to have preferred that over living with your aunt.'

'Hell? You could say that.' The grim set of his mouth let her know that no more would be forthcoming on that subject.

'Your life on the streets must have been…terrifying.'

'I toughened up pretty quick. One thing I had in my favour was I was big—the same height I am now and strong from playing football at school. It was a rough-around-the-edges kind of school, and I'd had my share of sorting out bullies there.' He raised his fists into a fighting position in a gesture she thought was unconscious.

So scratch the elite private school. She realised now that Dominic was a self-made man. And his story of triumph over adversity fascinated her. 'So you could defend yourself against thugs and…and predators.'

Her heart went out to him. At seventeen she'd had all the security of a loving family and comfortable home. But she knew first-hand from her foster sisters that not all young people were that fortunate. It seemed that the young Dominic had started off with loving parents and a secure life but had spiralled downwards from then on. What the heck was wrong with the aunt to have let that happen?

She reached over the table and trailed her fingers across his scarred knuckles. 'That's how you got these?' It was amazing the familiarity a fake engagement allowed.

'I got in a lot of fights,' he said.

'And this?' She traced the fine scar at the side of his mouth.

'Another fight,' he said.

She dropped her hands to her sides, again overwhelmed by that urge to comfort him. 'You were angry and frightened.'

He shifted uncomfortably in his seat. 'All that.'

'But then you ended up with this.' She waved her hand to encompass the immaculate art deco pool, the expensively landscaped gardens, the superb house. It was an oasis of beauty and luxury.

'My fighting brought me to the attention of the police. I was charged with assault,' he said bluntly.

She'd thought his tough exterior was for real—had sensed the undercurrents of suppressed rage.

'Believe me, the other guy deserved it,' he said with an expression of grim satisfaction. 'He was drug-dealing scum.'

'What happened? With the police, I mean.' He'd been seventeen—still a kid. All she'd been fighting at that age was schoolgirl drama.

'I got lucky. The first piece of luck was that I was under eighteen and not charged as an adult. The second piece of luck was I was referred to a government social worker—Jim, his name was. Poor man, having to deal with the sullen, unhappy kid I was then couldn't have been easy. Jim was truly one of the good guys—still is. He won my confidence and got me away from that squat, to the guidance of another social worker friend of his down the Queensland Gold Coast.'

'Sun, surf and sand,' she said. She knew it sounded flippant but Dominic would not want her to pity his young self.

'And a booming real estate market. The social worker down there was a good guy too. He got me a job as a gofer in a real estate agency. I was paid a pittance but it was a start and I liked it there. To cut a long story short, I was soon promoted to the sales team. I discovered I was good at selling the lifestyle dream, not just the number of bedrooms and bathrooms. I became adept at gauging what was important to the client.'

'Because you were observant,' she said. And tough and resilient and utterly admirable.

'That's important. Especially when I realised the role the woman played in a residential sale. Win her over and you more than likely closed the sale.'

Andie could see how those good looks, along with intuition and charm and the toughness to back it up, could have accelerated him ahead. 'Fascinating. And incredible how you've kept all the details away from the public. Surely people must have tried to research you, would have wanted to know your story?'

'As a juvenile, my record is sealed. I've never spoken about it. It's a time of my life I want well behind me. Without Jim the social worker, I might have gone the other way.'

'You mean you could have ended up as a violent thug or a drug dealer? I don't believe that for a second.'

He shrugged those broad street-fighter shoulders. 'I appreciate your faith in me. But, like so many of my fellow runaways, I could so easily have ended up…broken.'

Andie struggled to find an answer to that. 'It…it's a testament to your strength of character that you didn't.'

'If you say,' he said. But he looked pleased. 'Once I'd made enough money to have my own place and a car—nowhere as good as your hatchback, I might add—I started university part-time. I got lucky again.'

'You passed with honours?' She hadn't seen a university degree anywhere in her research on him but there was no harm in asking.

'No. I soon realised I knew more about making money and how business operated than some of the teachers in my commerce degree. I dropped out after eighteen months. But in a statistics class I met Jake Marlow. He was a brilliant, misunderstood geek. Socially, I still considered myself an outcast. We became friends.'

'And business partners, you said.' He was four years older than she was, and yet had lived a lifetime more. And had overcome terrible odds to get where he had.

'He was playing with the concept of ground-breaking online business software tools but no bank would loan him the money to develop them. I was riding high on commissions. We set up a partnership. I put in the money he needed. I could smell my first million.'

'Let me guess—it was an amazing success?'

'That software is used by thousands of businesses around the world to manage their digital workflow. We made a lot of money very quickly. Jake is still developing successful new software.' His obvious pride in his friend warmed his words.

'And you're still business partners.'

He nodded. 'The success of our venture gave me the investment dollars I needed to also spin off into my own separate business developing undervalued homemaker centres. We call them bulky goods centres—furnishing, white goods, electricals.'

'I guess the Gold Coast got too small for you.' That part she'd been able to research.

'I moved to Sydney. You know the rest.'

In silence she drank her mineral water with lime, he finished his iced tea. He'd given her a lot to think about. Was that anger that had driven him resolved? Or could it still be bubbling under the surface, ready to erupt?

He angled himself to look more directly at her. 'Now it's your turn to answer my question, Andie,' he said. 'How did you get over the death of your…of Anthony?'

She hadn't been expecting that and it hit her hard. But he'd dug deep. She had to too. 'I… I don't know that I will ever be able to forget the shock of it. One minute he was there, the next minute gone. I… I was as good as a widow, before I'd had the chance to be a bride.'

Dominic nodded, as if he understood. Of course he'd lost his parents.

'We were staying the weekend at his parents' beach house at Whale Beach. Ant got up very early, left a note to say he'd gone surfing, kissed me—I was asleep but awake enough to know he was going out—and then he was gone. Of course I blamed myself for not going with him. Then I was angry he'd gone out by himself.'

'Understandably,' he said and she thought again how he

seemed to see more than other people. She had no deep, dark secrets. But, if she did, she felt he'd burrow down to them without her even realising it.

'After Anthony died, I became terrified of the sea. I hated the waves—blamed them for taking him from me, which I know was all kinds of irrational. Then one day I went to the beach by myself and sat on the sand. I remember hugging my knees as I watched a teenage boy, tall and blond like Anthony, ride a wave all the way into the shore, saw the exultation on his face, the sheer joy he felt at being one with the wave.'

'If this is bringing back hurtful memories, you don't have to go any further.'

'I'm okay… When someone close dies, you look for a sign from them—I learned I wasn't alone in that when I had counselling. That boy on his board was like a message from Anthony. He died doing something he truly loved. I ran into the surf and felt somehow connected to him. It was a healing experience, a turning point in my recovery from grief.'

'That's a powerful story,' Dominic said.

'The point of it is, it's five years since he died and of course I've moved on. Anyone who might wonder if my past could affect our fake future can be assured of that. Anthony was part of my youth; we grew up together. In some ways I'm the person I am because of those happy years behind me. But I want happy years ahead of me too. I've dated. I just haven't met the right person.'

For the first time she wondered if she could feel more for Dominic than physical attraction. For a boy who had been through what he had and yet come through as the kind of man who offered to pay for a little boy's medical treatment? Who was more willing to open his house to disadvantaged people than celebrities? There was so much more to Dominic than she ever could have imagined—and the more she found out about him the more she liked about him.

And then there were those kisses she had not been able to stop thinking about—and yearning for more.

'I appreciate you telling me,' he said.

She poured herself another long, cool mineral water. Offered to pour one for Dominic, but he declined.

'On to my next question,' she said. 'It's about your family. Do you have family other than your aunt? My mother will certainly want to know because she's already writing the guest list for the wedding.'

'You told your mother about the engagement?'

'She couldn't be more delighted. In fact…well…she got quite tearful.' Andie had never felt more hypocritical than the moment she realised her mother was crying tears of joy for her.

'That's a relief,' he said.

'You could put it that way. I didn't realise quite how concerned they were about me being…lonely. Not that I am lonely, by the way—I have really good friends.' But it was not the same as having a special someone.

'I'm beginning to see that,' he said. 'I'm surprised we've been able to have this long a conversation without your phone going off.'

'That's because I switched it off,' she said. 'There'll probably be a million messages when I switch it back on.'

'So your mother didn't question our…haste?'

'No. And any guilt I felt about pulling the wool over her eyes I forced firmly to the back of my mind. Timothy getting the treatment he needs is way more important to my family than me finding a man.' She looked at him. 'So now—the guest list, your family?'

'My aunt and my mother were the only family each other had. So there is no Australian family.'

'Your aunt has…has passed away?' There was something awkward here that she didn't feel comfortable probing. But they were—supposedly—planning to get married. It made sense for her to know something of his family.

'She's in the best of residential care, paid for by me. That's all I want to say about her.'

'Okay,' she said, shaken by the closed look on his face.

'I have family in the UK but no one close since my grandparents died.'

'So no guests from your side of the family for our imaginary wedding?'

'That's right. And I consider the subject closed. In fact, I've had a gutful of talking about this stuff.'

'Me too,' she said. Hearing about his difficult youth, remembering her early loss was making her feel down. 'I reckon we know enough about each other now to be able to field any questions that are thrown at us. After all, we're not pretending to have known each other for long.'

She got up from her chair, walked to the edge of the pool, knelt at the edge and swished her hand through the water. 'This is such a nice pool. Do you use it much?'

'Most days I swim,' he said, standing behind her. 'There's a gym at the back of the cabana too.'

She imagined him working out in his gym, then plunging into the pool, muscles pumped, spearing through the water in not many clothes, maybe in *no* clothes.

Stop it!

She got up, wishing she could dive in right now to cool herself down. 'Do you like my idea to hire some lifeguards so the guests can swim on Christmas Day?'

'It's a good one.'

'And you're okay with putting a new swimsuit and towel in each of the children's goody bags? Hannah pointed out that some of the kids might not have a swimsuit.'

'I meant to talk to you about that,' he said. Surely he wasn't going to query the cost of the kids' gifts? She would be intensely disappointed if he did. 'I want to buy each of the adults a new swimsuit too; they might not have one either,' he said. 'I don't want anyone feeling excluded for any reason we can avoid.'

She looked up at him. 'You're not really a Scrooge, are you?'

'No,' he said.

'I don't think people are going to be calling you that for much longer. Certainly not if I've got anything to do with it.'

'But not a word about my past.'

'That's understood,' she said, making a my-lips-are-sealed zipping motion over her mouth. 'Though I think you might find people would admire you for having overcome it.'

The alarm on her watch buzzed. 'I'm running late,' she said. 'I didn't realise we'd been talking for so long.'

'You have an appointment? I was going to suggest dinner.'

'No can do, I'm afraid.' Her first impulse was to cancel her plans, to jump at the opportunity to be with Dominic. But she would not put her life on hold for the fake engagement.

'I have a hot date with a group of girlfriends. It's our first Tuesday of the month movie club. We see a movie and then go to dinner. We're supposed to discuss the movie but we mainly catch up on the gossip.' She held out her hand, where the diamond flashed on the third finger of her left hand. 'I suspect this baby is going to be the main topic of conversation.'

She made to go but, before she could, Dominic had pulled her close for a kiss that left not a scrap of lipstick on her mouth and her hair falling out of its knot.

It was the kind of kiss she could get used to.

CHAPTER TWELVE

ANDIE SAT AT her desk in the Party Queens' headquarters. 'Headquarters' was rather a grand term for their premises. It comprised an industrial kitchen where Gemma could do her thing; a workroom used for making props; a storage area; and an area loosely termed an office, where she and her two partners squeezed in their desks.

To say they were frantically busy would be an understatement. The weeks leading up to Christmas and New Year were the busiest time of the year for established party planners. For a new company like Party Queens to be so busy was gratifying. But it was the months after the end of the long Aussie summer vacation they had to worry about for advance bookings. Business brain, Eliza, was very good at reminding them of that.

Andie's top priority was Dominic's Christmas party. Actually, it was no longer just his party. As his fiancée, she had officially become co-host. But that didn't mean she wasn't flat-out with other bookings, including a Christmas Eve party for the parents of their first eighteenth party girl. Andie wanted to pull out all the stops for the people who'd given Party Queens their very first job. And then there was the business of being Dominic's fake fiancée—almost a job on its own.

Andie had been 'engaged' to Dominic for ten days and so far so good. She'd been amazed that no one had seriously queried the speed at which she had met, fallen in love with and agreed to marry a man she had known for less than a month.

The swooning sighs of 'love at first sight' and 'how romantic' from her girlfriends she understood, not so much the delight from her pragmatic father and the tears of joy from her mother. She hardly knew Dominic and yet they were prepared to believe she would commit her life to him?

Of course it was because her family and friends had been worried about her, wanted her to be happy, had been concerned she had grieved for Anthony for too long.

'Your dad and I are pleased for you, sweetheart, we really are,' her mother had said. 'We were worried you were so fearful about loving someone again in case you lost them, that you wouldn't let yourself fall in love again,' she'd continued. 'But Dominic is so strong, so right for you; I guess he just broke through those barriers you'd spent so long putting up. And I understand you didn't want to waste time when you knew what it was like to have a future snatched away from you.'

Really? She'd put up *barriers*? She'd just been trying to find someone worthy of stepping into Anthony's shoes. Now she'd found a man who had big boots of his own and would never walk in another man's shadow. *But he wasn't really hers.*

'You put us off the scent by telling us Dominic wasn't your type,' Gemma had said accusingly. Gemma, who was already showing her ideas for a fabulous wedding cake she planned to bake and decorate for her when the time came. Andie felt bad going through images of multi-tiered pastel creations with Gemma, knowing the cake was never going to happen.

Condition Number One, that she and Dominic didn't *ever* tell *anyone* about the deception, seemed now like a very good idea. To hear that their engagement had been a cold-blooded business arrangement was never going to go down well with all these people wishing them well.

At last Wednesday's family dinner, Dominic had been joyfully welcomed into the Newman family. 'I'm glad you saw sense about how hot he was,' her sister Bea had said, hugging her. 'And as for that amazing rock on your finger… Does Dominic have a brother? No? Well, can you find me someone just like him, please?'

But every bit of deception was all worth it for Timothy. After the family dinner, Andie and Dominic had drawn Hannah and Paul aside. Now that Dominic was to be part of the family—or so they thought—her sister and her husband didn't take much convincing to accept Dominic's offer of paying all Timothy's medical expenses.

Dominic's only condition was that they kept him posted on their tiny son's progress. 'Of course we will,' Hannah had said, 'but Andie will keep you updated and you'll see Timothy at family functions. You'll always be an important part of his life.' And the little boy had more chance of a better life, thanks to Dominic's generosity.

Later, Hannah had hugged her sister tight. 'You've got yourself a good man, Andie, a very, very good man.'

'I know,' said Andie, choked up and cringing inside. She was going to have to come up with an excellent reason to explain why she 'dumped' Dominic when his need for the fake engagement was over.

There had only been one awkward moment at the dinner. Her parents wanted to put an announcement of the engagement in the newspaper. 'Old-fashioned, I know, but it's the right thing to do,' her mother had said.

She'd then wanted to know what Dominic's middle name was for the announcement. Apparently full names were required, Andrea Jane Newman was engaged to Dominic *who*?

She had looked at Dominic, eyes widened by panic.

She should have known that detail about the man she was supposedly going to marry.

Dominic had quickly stepped in. 'I've kept quiet about my middle name because I don't like it very much,' he'd said. 'It's Hugo. Dominic Hugo Hunt.'

Of course everyone had greeted that announcement with cries of how much they loved the name Hugo. 'You could call your first son Hugo,' Bea had suggested.

That was when Andie had decided it was time to go home. She felt so low at deceiving everyone, she felt she could slink out of the house at ankle level. If it wasn't for Timothy, she would slide that outsize diamond off her finger and put an end to this whole deception.

Dominic had laughed the baby comment off—and made no further mention of it. He'd wanted a baby with his first wife—how did he feel about children now?

Her family was now expecting babies from her and Dominic. She had not anticipated having to handle that expectation. But of course, since then, the image of a dear little boy with black spiky hair and grey eyes kept popping into her mind. A little boy who would be fiercely loved and never have to face the hardships his father had endured.

She banished the bordering on insane thoughts to the area of her brain reserved for impossible dreams. Instead, she concentrated on confirming the delivery date of two hundred and ten—the ten for contingencies—small red-and-white-striped hand-knitted Christmas stockings for Dominic's party. They would sit in the centre of each place setting and contain all the cutlery required by that person for the meal.

She had decided on a simple red-and-white theme, aimed squarely at pleasing children as well as the inner child of the adults. Tables would be set up in the ballroom for a sit-down meal served from a buffet. She wanted it to be as magical and memorable as a Christmas lunch in the home of a billionaire should be—but without being intimidating.

Gemma had planned fabulous cakes, shaped and frosted like an outsize white candle and actually containing a tea light, to be the centrepiece of each table. Whimsical Santa-themed cupcakes would sit at each place with the name of the guest piped on the top. There would be glass bowls of candy canes and masses of Australian Christmas bush with its tiny red flowers as well as bowls of fat red cherries.

Andie would have loved to handle all the decorations herself but it was too big a job. She'd hired one of her favourite stylists to coordinate all the decorations. Jeremy was highly creative and she trusted his skills implicitly. And, importantly, he'd been happy to work on Christmas Day.

She'd been careful not to discuss anything too 'Christmassy' with Dominic, aware of his feelings about the festive season. He still hadn't shared with her just why he hated it so much; she wondered if he ever would. There was some deep pain there, going right back to his childhood, she suspected.

The alarm on her computer flashed a warning at her the same time the alarm on her watch buzzed. Not that she needed any prompts to alert her that she was seeing Dominic this evening.

He had been in meetings with Walter Burton all afternoon. Andie was to join them for dinner. At her suggestion, the meal was to be at Dominic's house. Andie felt that a man like Walter might prefer to experience home-style hospitality; he must be sick of hotels and restaurants. Not that Dominic's house was exactly the epitome of cosy, but it was elegant and beautiful and completely lacking in any brash, vulgar display of wealth.

A table set on the terrace at the front of the house facing the harbour. A chef to prepare the meal. A skilled waiter to serve them. All organised by Party Queens with a menu devised by Gemma. Eliza had, as a matter of course, checked with Walter's personal assistant as to the tycoon's personal dietary requirements.

Then there would be Andie, on her best fiancée behaviour. After all, Mr Burton's preference for doing business with a married man was the reason behind the fake engagement.

Not that she had any problem pretending to be an attentive fiancée. That part of the role came only too easily. Her heartbeat accelerated just at the thought of seeing Dominic this evening. He'd been away in different states on business and she'd only seen him a few times since the family dinner. She checked her watch again. There was plenty of time to get home to Newtown and then over to Vaucluse before the guest of honour arrived.

Dominic had been in Queensland on business and only flown back into Sydney last night. He'd met Walter Burton from a very early flight from the US this morning. After an afternoon of satisfactory meetings, Dominic had taken him back to his hotel. The American businessman would then make his own way to Vaucluse for the crucial dinner with Dominic and Andie.

As soon as he let himself in through the front door of the house Dominic sensed a difference. There was a subtle air of expectation, of warmth. The chef and his assistant were in the kitchen and, if enticing aromas had anything to do with it, dinner was under way. Arrangements of exotic orchids were discreetly arranged throughout the house. That was thanks to Andie.

It was all thanks to Andie. He would have felt uncomfortable hosting Walter Burton in his house if it weren't for her. He would have taken him to an upscale restaurant, which would have been nice but not the same. The older man had been very pleased at the thought of being invited to Dominic's home.

And now here she was, heading towards him from the terrace at the eastern end of the house where they would dine. He caught his breath at how beautiful she looked in a body-hugging cream top and matching long skirt that wrapped across the front and revealed, as she walked, tantalising glimpses of long slender legs and high heeled ankle-strap sandals. Her hair was up, but tousled strands fell around her face. Her only jewellery was her engagement ring. With her simple elegance, again she looked as if she belonged in this house.

'You're home,' she said in that husky voice, already so familiar.

Home. That was the difference in his house this evening. *Andie's presence made it a home.* And he had not felt he'd had a real home for a long time.

But Andie and her team were temporary hired help—she the lead actress in a play put on for the benefit of a visiting businessman. *This was all just for show.*

Because of Walter Burton, because there were strangers in the house, they had to play their roles—he the doting fiancé and she his betrothed.

Andie came close, smiling, raised her face for his kiss. Was that too for show? Or because she was genuinely glad to see him? At the touch of her lips, hunger for her instantly ignited. He closed his eyes as he breathed in her sweet, spicy scent, not wanting to let her go.

A waiter passed by on his way to the outdoor terrace, with a tray of wine glasses.

'I've missed you,' Andie murmured. For the waiter's benefit or for Dominic's? She sounded convincing but he couldn't be sure.

'Me too—missed you, I mean,' he said stiffly, self-consciously.

That was the trouble with this deception he had initiated. It was only too easy to get caught between a false intimacy and an intimacy that could possibly be real. Or could it? He broke away from her, stepped back.

'Is this another misbehaving skirt?' he asked.

He resisted the urge to run his hand over the curve of her hip. It would be an appropriate action for a fiancé but stepping over the boundaries of his agreement with Andie. Kisses were okay—their public displays of affection had to look authentic. Caresses of a more intimate nature, on the other hand, were *not* okay.

She laughed. 'No breeze tonight so we'll never know.' She lowered her voice. 'Is there anything else you need to brief me about before Mr Burton arrives? I've read through the background information you gave me. I think I'm up to speed on what a fiancée interested in her future husband's work would most likely know.'

'Good,' he said. 'I have every faith you won't let me down. If you're not sure of anything, just keep quiet and I'll cover for you. Not that I think I'll have to do that.'

'Fingers crossed I do you proud,' she said.

Walter Burton arrived punctually—Dominic would have been surprised if he hadn't. The more time he spent with his prospective joint venture partner, the more impressed he was by his acumen and professionalism. *He really wanted this deal.*

Andie greeted the older man with warmth and charm. Straight away he could see Walter was impressed.

She led him to the front terrace where the elegantly set round table—the right size for a friendly yet business orientated meal—had been placed against a backdrop of Sydney Harbour, sparkling blue in the light of the long summer evening. As they edged towards the longest day on December the twenty-second, it did not get dark until after nine p.m.

Christmas should be cold and dark and frosty. He pushed the painful thought away. Dwelling on the past was not appropriate here, not when an important deal hung in the balance.

Andie was immediately taken with Walter Burton. In his mid-sixties and of chunky build, his silver hair and close-trimmed silver beard gave him an avuncular appearance. His pale blue eyes actually sparkled and she had to keep reminding herself that he could not be as genial as he appeared and be such a successful tycoon.

But his attitude to philanthropy was the reason she was here, organising the party, pretending to be Dominic's betrothed. He espoused the view that making as much money as you could was a fine aim—so long as you remembered to share it with those who had less. 'It's a social responsibility,' he said.

Dominic had done nothing but agree with him. There was not a trace of Scrooge in anything he said. Andie had begun to believe the tag was purely a media invention.

Walter—he insisted she drop the 'Mr Burton'—seemed genuinely keen to hear all the details of the Christmas party. He was particularly interested when she told him Dominic had actively sought to dampen press interest. That had, as intended, flamed media interest. They already had two journalists volunteer to help out on that day—quite an achievement considering most people wanted to spend it with their families or close friends.

Several times during the meal, Andie squeezed Dominic's hand under the table—as a private signal that she thought the evening was going well. His smile in return let her know he thought so too. The fiancée fraud appeared to be doing the trick.

The waiter had just cleared the main course when Walter sat back in his chair, relaxed, well fed and praising the excellent food. Andie felt she and Dominic could also finally relax from the knife-edge of tension required to impress the American without revealing the truth of their relationship.

So Walter's next conversational gambit seemed to come from out of the blue. 'Of course you understand the plight of your Christmas Day guests, Dominic, as you've come from Struggle Street yourself,' he said. 'Yet you do your utmost to hide it.'

Dominic seemed shocked into silence. Andie watched in alarm as he blanched under his tan and gripped the edge of the table so his knuckles showed white. 'I'm not sure what you mean,' he said at last.

Walter's shrewd eyes narrowed. 'You've covered your tracks well, but I have a policy of never doing business with someone I haven't fully researched. I know about young Nick Hunt and the trouble he got into.'

Dominic seemed to go even paler. 'You mean the assault charge? Even though it never went to court. Even though I was a juvenile and there should be no record of it. How did you—?'

'Never mind how I found out. But I also discovered how much Dominic Hunt has given back to the world in which he had to fight to survive.' Walter looked to Andie. 'I guess you don't know about this, my dear.'

'Dominic has told me about his past,' she said cautiously. She sat at the edge of her seat, feeling trapped by uncertainty, terrified of saying the wrong thing, not wanting to reveal her ignorance of anything important. 'I also know how very generous he is.'

'Generous to the point that he funds a centre to help troubled young people in Brisbane.' Andie couldn't help a gasp of surprise that revealed her total lack of knowledge. 'He hasn't told you about his Underground Help Centre?' Walter didn't wait for her to answer. 'It provides safe emergency accommodation, health care, counselling, rehab—all funded by your fiancé. Altogether a most admirable venture.'

Why had Dominic let everyone think he was a Scrooge?

'You've done your research well, Walter,' Dominic said. 'Yes, I haven't yet told Andie about the centre. I wanted to take her to Brisbane and show her the work we do there.'

'I'll look forward to that, darling,' she said, not having to fake her admiration for him.

Dominic addressed both her and Walter. 'When I started to make serious money, I bought the abandoned shopping centre site where I'd sought refuge as a troubled runaway and redeveloped it. But part of the site was always going to be for the Underground Help Centre that I founded. I recruited Jim, the social worker who had helped me, to head it up for me.'

Andie felt she would burst with pride in him. Pride and something even more heartfelt. He must hate having to reveal himself like this.

Walter leaned towards Dominic. 'You're a self-made man and I admire that,' he said. 'You're sharing the wealth you acquired by your own hard work and initiative and I admire that too. What I don't understand, Dominic, is why you keep all this such a big secret. There's nothing to be ashamed of in having pulled yourself up by your bootstraps.'

'I'm not ashamed of anything I've done,' Dominic said. 'But I didn't want my past to affect my future success. Especially, I didn't want it to rub off on my business partner, Jake Marlow.'

Andie felt as if she was floundering. Dominic had briefed her on business aspects she might be expected to know about tonight, but nothing about this. She could only do what she felt was right. Without hesitation, she reached out and took his hand so they stood united.

'People can be very judgemental,' she said to Walter. 'And the media seem to be particularly unfair to Dominic. I'm incredibly proud of him and support his reasons for wanting to keep what he does in Brisbane private. To talk about that terrible time is to relive it, over and over again. From what Dominic has told me, living it once would be more than enough for anyone.'

Dominic squeezed her hand back, hard, and his eyes were warm with gratitude. Gratitude and perhaps—just perhaps—something more? 'I can't stop the nightmares of being back there,' he said. 'But I can avoid talking about it and bringing those times back to life.'

Andie angled herself to face Walter full-on. She was finding it difficult to keep her voice steady. 'If people knew about the centre they'd find out about his living rough and the assault charge. People who don't know him might judge him unfairly. At the same time, I'd love more people to know how generous and kind he actually is and—' She'd probably said enough.

Walter chuckled. 'Another thing he's done right is his choice of fiancée.'

Dominic reached over to kiss her lightly on the lips. 'I concur, Walter,' he said. Was it part of the act or did he really mean it?

'Th...thank you,' stuttered Andie. She added Walter to the list of people who would be disappointed when she dumped Dominic.

'I'm afraid I can't say the same for your choice of first wife,' Walter said.

Dominic visibly tensed. 'What do you mean?'

'I met with her and your former employee this morning. He's an impressive guy, though not someone I feel I want to do business with. But your ex-wife made it clear she would do anything—and I stress *anything*—to seal the deal. She suggested that to me—happily married for more than forty years and who has never even looked at another woman.'

Dominic made a sound of utter disgust but nothing more. Andie thought more of him that he didn't say anything to disparage Tara, appalling though her behaviour had been. Dominic had more dignity.

'The upshot of this is, Dominic, that you are exactly the kind of guy I want to do business with. You and your delightful wife-to-be. You make a great team.'

Dominic reached over to take Andie's hand again. 'Thank you, Walter. Thank you from us both.'

Andie smiled with lips that were aching from all her false smiles and nodded her thanks. The fake engagement had done exactly what it was intended to. She should be jubilant for Dominic's sake. But that also meant there would soon be no need to carry on with it. And that made her feel miserable. *She wasn't doing a very good job of guarding her heart.*

When Andie said goodnight to Dominic, she clung to him for a moment longer than was necessary. Playing wife-to-be for the evening had made her start to wish a real relationship with Dominic could perhaps one day be on the cards.

Perhaps it was a good thing she wouldn't see Dominic again until Christmas Eve. He had to fly out to Minneapolis to finalise details with Walter, leaving her to handle the countdown to the Christmas party. And trying not to think too much about what had to happen after Christmas, when her 'engagement' would come to an end.

CHAPTER THIRTEEN

IT WAS MIDDAY on Christmas Eve and as Andie pushed open the door into Dominic's house she felt as if she was stepping into a nightmare. The staircase railings were decorated as elegantly as she'd hoped, with tiny lights and white silk cord. The wreath on the door was superb. But dominating the marble entrance hall was an enormous Christmas tree, beautifully decorated with baubles and ornaments and winking with tiny lights. She stared at it in shocked disbelief. *What the heck was that doing there?*

When she said it out loud she didn't say *heck* and she didn't say it quietly.

Her stylist Jeremy's assistant had been rearranging baubles on the lower branches of the tree. She jumped at Andie's outburst and a silver bauble smashed on to the marble floor. Calmly, very calmly, Andie asked the girl where Jeremy was. The girl scuttled out to get him.

Throughout all the Christmas party arrangements, through all the fake fiancée dramas, Andie had kept her cool. Now she was in serious danger of losing it. She had planned this party in meticulous detail. Of all the things that could go wrong, it would have to be this—Dominic would think she had deliberately defied his specific demand. And she didn't want him thinking badly of her.

Jeremy came into the room with a swathe of wide red ribbons draped over his outstretched arm. Andie recognised them as the ones to be looped and tied into extravagant bows on the back of the two hundred chairs in the ballroom.

She had to grit her teeth to stop herself from exploding. 'Why is there a Christmas tree in here?' Her heart was racing with such panic she had to put her hand on her chest to try and slow it.

'Because this entrance space cried out for one. How can you have a Christmas party without a tree?' Jeremy said. 'I thought you'd made a mistake and left it off the brief. Doesn't it look fabulous?'

'It does indeed look fabulous. Except the client specifically said *no tree.*' She could hear her voice rising and took a deep breath to calm herself.

How had she let this happen? Maybe she should have written *NO CHRISTMAS TREE* in bold capitals on every page of the briefing document. She'd arrived here very early this morning to let the decorating crew in and to receive final deliveries of the extra furniture. Jeremy had assured her that all was on track. And it was—except for this darn tree.

'But why?' asked Jeremy. 'It seems crazy not to have a tree.'

Crazy? Maybe. She had no idea why—because Dominic, for all his talk with Walter Burton over dinner that night that had seemed so genuine, still refused to let her in on the events in his past he held so tightly to himself. He'd drip-fed some of the details but she felt there was something major linked to Christmas he would not share. It made her feel excluded—put firmly in her place as no one important in his life. And she wanted to be important to him. She swallowed hard. *Had she really just admitted that to herself?*

'The client actually has a thing against Christmas trees,' she said. 'You might even call it a phobia. For heaven's sake, Jeremy, why didn't you call me before you put this up?' Her mouth was dry and her hands felt clammy at the thought of Dominic's reaction if he saw the tree.

'I'm sorry,' said Jeremy, crestfallen. 'You didn't specify not to include a tree in the decorations. I was just using my initiative.'

On other jobs she'd worked with Jeremy she'd told him to think for himself and not bother her with constant calls, so she couldn't be *too* cranky with him. Creative people could be tricky to manage—and Jeremy's work was superb. The tree was, in fact, perfect for the spot where he'd placed it.

She took a step back to fully appraise its impact. The tree looked spectacular, dressed in silver with highlights of red, in keeping with her overall colour scheme. She sighed her pleasure at its magnificence. This perfect tree would make a breathtaking first impression for the guests tomorrow. To the children it would seem to be the entrance to a magical world. It spoke of tradition, of hope, of generosity. Everything they were trying to achieve with this party. It would make Dominic look good.

The beautiful tree was beginning to work its magic on her. Surely it would on Dominic too? He'd come such a long way since that first day, when he'd been so vehemently anti everything Christmas. *Christmas was not Christmas without a tree.*

She took a series of deep, calming breaths. Dominic should at least have the chance to see the tree in place. To see how wonderful it looked there. Maybe the sight of this tree would go some way towards healing those hidden deep wounds he refused to acknowledge.

She turned to Jeremy, the decision firm in her mind. 'We'll leave it. You've done such a good job on the tree, it would be a real shame to have to take it down.'

'What about the client?'

'He's a client but he's also my fiancé.' The lie threatened to choke her but she was getting more adept at spinning falsehoods. 'Leave him to me. In the meantime, let me give you a hand with placing the final few ornaments on the lower branches,' she said. She was wearing work clothes—jeans, sneakers and a loose white shirt. She rolled up her sleeves and picked up an exquisite glass angel. Her hand wasn't quite steady—if only she was as confident as she had tried to appear.

Dominic was due back in to Sydney early this evening. *What if he hated the tree?* Surely he wouldn't. He seemed so happy with everything else she'd done for the party; surely he would fall in love with the tree.

But it would take a Christmas miracle for him to fall in love with *her.*

She longed for that miracle. Because she couldn't deny it to herself any longer—she had developed feelings for him.

Dominic had managed to get an earlier flight out of Minneapolis to connect with a non-stop flight to Sydney from Los Angeles. Nonetheless, it was a total flight of more than twenty hours. Despite the comfort of first class, he was tired and anxious to get away from the snow and ice of Minnesota and home to sunny Sydney. A bitterly cold Christmas wasn't quite as he'd remembered it to be.

Overriding everything else, he wanted to get home to Andie. He had thought about her non-stop the whole trip, wished she'd been with him. Next time, he'd promised Walter, he'd bring Andie with him.

As the car he'd taken from the airport pulled up in front of his house, his spirits lifted at the thought of seeing her. He hadn't been able to get through to her phone, so he'd called Party Queens. Eliza had told him she was actually at his house in Vaucluse, working on the decorations for the party.

On the spur of the moment, he'd decided not to let her know he'd got in early. It might be better to surprise her. He reckoned if she didn't know he was coming, she wouldn't have time to put on her fake fiancée front. Her first reaction to him would give him more of a clue of her real feelings towards him.

Because while he was away he had missed her so intensely, he'd been forced to face *his* real feelings towards *her*. He was falling in love with her. Not only was he falling in love with her; he realised he had never had feelings of such intensity about a woman.

Melody had been his first love—and sweet, damaged Melody had loved him back to the extent she was capable of love. But it hadn't been enough. That assault charge had happened because he had been protecting her. Protecting her from a guy assaulting her in an alley not far from the takeaway food shop where he'd worked in the kitchen in return for food and a few dollars cash in hand.

But the guy had been her dealer—and possibly her pimp. Melody had squealed at Dominic to leave the guy alone. She'd shrieked at him that she knew what she was doing; she didn't need protecting. Dominic had ignored her, had pulled the creep off her, smashed his fist into the guy's face. Then the dealer's mates had shown up and Dominic had copped a beating too. But, although younger than the low-lifes, he'd been bigger, stronger and inflicted more damage. The cops had taken him in, while the others had disappeared into the dark corners that were their natural habitat. And Melody had gone with them without a backward glance, leaving him with a shattered heart as well as a broken nose. He'd never seen her again.

Of course Melody hadn't been her real name. He'd been too naïve to realise that at the time. Later, when he'd set up the Underground Help Centre, he'd tried to find her but without any luck. He liked to think she was living a safe happy life somewhere but the reality was likely to be less cosy than that.

Then there'd been Tara—the next woman to have betrayed him. The least thought he gave to his ex-wife the better.

But Andie. Andie was different. He felt his heart, frosted over for so long, warm when he thought about her. *What you saw was what you got.* Not only smart and beautiful, but loyal and loving. He'd told her more about his past than he'd ever told anyone. He could be himself with her, not have to pretend, be Nick as well as Dominic. Be not the billionaire but the man. Their relationship could be real. *He could spend his life with Andie.*

And he wanted to tell her just that.

The scent of pine needles assaulted his senses even before he put his key in his front door. The sharp resin smell instantly revived memories of that Christmas Eve when he'd been eleven years old and the happy part of his childhood had come to its terrible end. Christmas trees were the thing he most hated about Christmas.

The smell made him nauseous, started a headache throbbing in his temples. Andie must be using pine in some of the decorations. It would have to go. He couldn't have it in the house.

He pushed the door silently open—only to recoil at what he saw.

There was a Christmas tree in his house. A whopping great Christmas tree, taking up half his entrance hallway and rising high above the banisters of the staircase.

What the hell? He had told Andie in no uncertain terms there was to be no Christmas tree—anywhere. He gritted his teeth and fisted his hands by his sides. *How could she be so insensitive?*

There was a team of people working on the tree and its myriad glitzy ornaments. Including Andie. He'd never thought she could be complicit in this defiance of his wishes. He felt let down. *Betrayed.*

She turned. Froze. Her eyes widened with shock and alarm when she saw him. A glass ornament slid from her hands and smashed on the floor but she scarcely seemed to notice.

'What part of "no Christmas tree" did you not get, Andie?'

She got up from her kneeling position and took a step towards him, put up her hands as if to ward off his anger. The people she was with scuttled out of the room, leaving them alone. But he bet they were eavesdropping somewhere nearby. The thought made him even more livid.

'Dominic, I'm sorry. I know you said no tree.'

'You're damn right I did.'

'It was a mistake. The tree was never meant to be here. There were some…some crossed lines. I wasn't expecting it either. But then I saw it and it's so beautiful and looks so right here. I thought you might…appreciate it, might see how right it is and want to keep it.'

He could feel the veins standing out on his neck, his hands clenched so tight they hurt. 'I don't see it as beautiful.'

Her face flushed. She would read that as an insult to her skills. He was beyond caring. 'Why? Why do you hate Christmas trees?' she said. 'Why this…this irrational dislike of Christmas?'

Irrational? He gritted his teeth. 'That's none of your concern.'

'But I want it to be. I thought I could help you. I—'

'You thought wrong.'

Now her hands were clenched and she was glaring at him. 'Why won't you share it with me—what makes you hurt so much at this time of year? Why do I have to guess? Why do I have to tiptoe around you?' Her voice rose with each question as it seemed her every frustration and doubt rushed to the surface.

Dominic was furious. How dared she put him through this…this humiliation?

'Don't forget your place,' he said coldly. 'I employ you.' With each word he made a stabbing motion with his finger to emphasise the words. 'Get rid of the tree. Now.'

He hated the stricken look on Andie's face, knowing he had put it there. But if she cared about him at all she never would have allowed that tree to enter his house. He could barely stand to look at her.

For a long moment she didn't say anything. 'Yes,' she said finally, her voice a dull echo of its usual husky charm. 'Yes, sir,' she added.

In a way he appreciated the defiance of the hissed 'sir'. But he was tired and jet-lagged and grumpy and burning with all the pain and loss he associated with Christmas—and Christmas trees in particular. Above all, he was disappointed in her that she thought so little of his wishes that she would defy him.

His house was festooned with festive paraphernalia. Everywhere he looked, it glittered and shone, mocking him. He'd been talked into this damn party against his wishes. *He hated Christmas.* He uttered a long string of curses worthy of Scrooge.

'I'm going upstairs. Make sure this tree is gone when I come back down. And all your people as well.' He glared in the general direction of the door through which her team had fled.

She met his glare, chin tilted upwards. 'It will take some time to dismantle the tree,' she said. 'But I assure you I will get rid of every last stray needle so you will never know it was there.' She sounded as though she spoke through gritted teeth. 'However, I will need all my crew to help me. We have to be here for at least a few more hours. We still have to finish filling the goody bags and setting the tables.' She glared at him. 'This is *your* party. And you know as well as I do that it must go on. To prove you're not the Scrooge people think you are.'

Some part of him wanted to cross the expanse of floor between them and hug her close. To tell her that of course he understood. That he found it almost impossible to talk about the damage of his childhood. To knuckle down and help her adorn his house for the party tomorrow. But the habits of Christmases past were hard to break.

So was the habit of closing himself off from love. Letting himself love Andie would only end in disappointment and pain, like it had with every other relationship. For her as well as himself. *It seemed he was incapable of love.*

'Text me when you're done,' he said.

He stomped up the stairs to his study. And the bottle of bourbon that waited there.

Andie felt humiliated, angry and upset. How dared Dominic speak to her like that? *'Don't forget your place.'* His harsh words had stabbed into her heart.

Jeremy poked his head around the door that connected through to the living room. She beckoned him to come in. She forced her voice to sound businesslike, refused to let even a hint of a tear burr her tone. 'I told you he wouldn't be happy with the tree.' Her effort at a joke fell very flat.

'Don't worry about it,' Jeremy said, putting a comforting hand on her shoulder. 'We'll get rid of this tree quick-smart. No matter your man is in a mood. The show has to go on. You've got two hundred people here for lunch tomorrow.'

'Thanks, Jeremy,' she said. 'Dominic has just got off a long flight. He's not himself.' But her excuses for him sounded lame even to her own ears.

Was that angry man glaring at her with his fists clenched at his sides the true Dominic? She'd known the anger was there bubbling below the surface, was beginning to understand the reasons for it. But she'd thought that anger that had driven him to violence was in his past. How could she possibly have thought she'd fallen in love with him? She didn't even know the man.

'What do you suggest we do with the tree?' Jeremy asked. 'There are no returns on cut trees.'

Andie's thoughts raced. 'We've got a Christmas Eve party happening elsewhere tonight. The clients have put up a scrappy old artificial tree that looks dreadful. We'll get this delivered to them with the compliments of Party Queens. Keep whatever ornaments you can use here; the rest we'll send with the tree. Let's call a courier truck now.'

Seething, she set to work dismantling the beautiful tree. As she did so, she felt as if she were dismantling all her hopes and dreams for love with Dominic. The diamond ring felt like a heavy burden on her finger, weighted by its duplicity and hypocrisy. While he'd stood there insulting her, she'd felt like taking the ring off and hurling it at him. If it had hit him and drawn blood she would have been glad. His words had been so harsh they felt like they'd drawn blood from her heart.

But of course she couldn't have thrown her ring at him while there were other people in the house. She would be professional right to the end. After all, wasn't she known for her skill at dealing with difficult people?

In spite of that, she'd had her fill of this particular difficult man. He'd got what he wanted from her in terms of his American deal. She'd got what her family needed for Timothy. Both sides of the bargain fulfilled. He'd been her employer, her fake fiancé—she'd liked to think they'd become friends of a sort. She'd wanted more—but that was obviously not to be. She'd stick it out for the Christmas lunch. Then she'd be out of here and out of his life.

The crew worked efficiently and well. When they were done and the tree was gone she waved them goodbye and wished them a Merry Christmas. But not before asking them to please not repeat what they might have heard today. Talk of Dominic's outburst could do serious damage to the rehabilitation of his Scrooge image.

By the time they had all gone it was early evening. She stood and massaged the small of her back where it ached. She would let Dominic know she was done and going home. But she had no intention of texting him as he'd asked. Not asked. *Demanded.* She had things to say that had to be said in person.

CHAPTER FOURTEEN

WITH A HEAVY HEART—wounded hearts *hurt*—Andie made her way up the stylishly decorated staircase, its tiny lights discreetly winking. She hadn't been up here before, as this part of the house was off-limits for the party. When she thought of it, she actually had no idea where Dominic could be.

The first two doors opened to two fashionably furnished empty bedrooms. The third bedroom was obviously his—a vast bed with immaculate stone-coloured linens, arched windows that opened to a sweeping view of the harbour. But he wasn't there.

Then she noticed a door ajar to what seemed like a study.

There was no response to her knock, so she pushed it open. The blinds were drawn. Dominic lay sprawled asleep on a large chesterfield sofa. The dull light of a tall, arching floor lamp pooled on him and seemed to put him in the spotlight.

His black lace-up business shoes lay haphazardly at the end of the sofa. He had taken off his jacket and removed his tie. The top buttons of his shirt were undone to reveal an expanse of bare, well-muscled chest her traitorous libido could not help but appreciate as it rose and fell in his sleep.

His right arm fell to the floor near a bottle of bourbon. Andie picked it up. The bottle was nearly full, with probably no more than a glassful gone. Not enough for him to be drunk—more likely collapsed into the sleep of utter exhaustion. She put the bottle on the desk.

There was a swivel-footed captain's chair near the sofa with a padded leather seat. She sat on the edge of it and watched Dominic as he slept. Darn it, but that wounded heart of hers beat faster as she feasted her eyes on his face, which had become so familiar. So…so—she nearly let herself think *so beloved.* But that couldn't be.

She swallowed hard at the lump that rose in her throat. Why on earth had she let herself fall for a man who was so difficult, so damaged, so completely opposite to the man who had made her so happy in the past?

Dominic's hair stood up in spikes. He obviously hadn't shaved since he'd left Minneapolis and his beard was in that stubble stage she found so incredibly sexy. She hadn't realised how long and thick his eyelashes were. His mouth was slightly parted. She longed to lean over and kiss it. She sighed. There would be no more kissing of this man.

He moaned in his sleep and she could see rapid eye movement behind his lids as if he were being tortured by bad dreams. She could not help but reach out to stroke his furrowed forehead. He returned to more restful sleep. Then his eyes flickered open. Suddenly he sat up, startling her. He looked around, disorientated, eyes glazed with sleep. He focused on her.

'Andie,' he breathed. 'You're here.' He gave a huge sigh, took her hand and kissed it. 'I didn't think I'd ever see you again.'

He didn't deserve to, she thought. But her resolve was weakening.

'Are you okay?' she said, trying to ignore the shivers of pleasure that ran up her arm from his kiss. He had been rude and hurtful to her.

'I've just had a horrible dream,' he said.

'What kind of dream?'

'A nightmare. I was in a cemetery and saw my own headstone.'

She shook her head. 'No, Dominic—I don't want to hear this.' The day of Anthony's funeral had been the worst day of her life. When she'd had to accept she'd never see him again. She couldn't bear to think of Dominic buried under a headstone.

But he continued in a dramatic tone she didn't think was appropriate for such a gruesome topic. 'It said: 'Here lies Dominic—they called him Scrooge'. And I think it was Christmas Day.'

Not so gruesome after all. She couldn't help a smile.

'You think my nightmare was funny?' he said, affronted.

'I'm sure it was scary at the time. But you'll never be called Scrooge again. Not after tomorrow. I…I'm sorry about what I said earlier. About your…your Scroogeness, I mean.'

He slammed the hand that wasn't holding hers against his forehead. 'The Christmas tree. I'm sorry, Andie. That was unforgivable. Pay your crew a bonus to make up for it, will you, and bill it to me.'

Did he think everything could be solved by throwing money at it?

'I'm also sorry about the tree, Dominic. It was an honest mistake. It's all gone now.'

Maybe she'd been in the wrong too, to imagine he might like the tree when he'd been so vehement about not having one in the house. But she hadn't been wrong about expecting better behaviour from him.

He shuddered. 'It was a shock. The smell of it. The sight of it. Brought back bad memories.'

She shifted in her seat but did not let go of his hand. 'Do you think it might be time to tell me why Christmas trees upset you so much? Because I didn't like seeing that anger. Especially not directed at me. How can I understand you when I don't know what I'm dealing with?'

He grimaced as if stabbed by an unpleasant memory. 'I suppose I have to tell you if I want you to ever talk to me again.'

'I'm talking to you now.'

She remembered what she'd said about recalling unpleasant memories being like reliving them. But this had to come out—one way or another. Better it was with words than fists.

'Christmas Eve is the anniversary of my parents' deaths.'

She squeezed his hand. 'Dominic, I'm so sorry.' That explained a lot. 'Why didn't you say so before?'

'I…I didn't want people feeling sorry for me,' he said gruffly.

'People wouldn't have… Yes, they would have felt sorry for you. But in a good way.' Could all this Scrooge business have been solved by him simply explaining that? 'Can you tell me about it now?'

'There…there's more. It was cold and frosty. My parents went out to pick up the Christmas tree. A deer crossed the road and they braked to avoid it. The road was icy and the car swerved out of control and crashed into a barrier. That's how they died. Getting the damn Christmas tree.'

She couldn't find the words to say anything other than she was sorry again.

'It was…it was my fault they died.'

Andie frowned. 'How could it be your fault? You were eleven years old.'

'My aunt told me repeatedly for the next six years it was my fault.'

'I think you'd better tell me some more about this aunt.'

'The thing is, it really *was* my fault. I'd begged my parents for a real tree. We had a plastic one. My best friend had a real one; I wanted a real one. If they hadn't gone out to get the tree I wanted they wouldn't have died.'

'You've been blaming yourself all these years? It was an accident. How any competent adult could let you blame yourself, I can't imagine.'

'Competent adult and my aunt aren't compatible terms,' he said, the bitterness underlying his words shocking her.

'I keep asking you about her; it's time you gave me some answers.' Though she was beginning to dread what she might hear.

'She used alcohol and prescription meds to mask her serious psychological problems. I know that now as an adult. As a kid, I lived with a bitter woman who swung between abuse and smothering affection.'

'And, as a kid, you put up with a lot in the hope of love,' Andie said softly, not sure if Dominic actually heard her. She could see the vulnerability in that strong-jawed handsome face, wondered how many people he had ever let be aware of it. She thought again of that little boy with the dark hair. Her vision of Dominic's son merged with that of the young, grieving, abused Dominic. And her heart went out to him.

The words spilled out of him now, words that expressed emotions dammed for years. 'She was particularly bad at Christmas because that's when she'd lost her sister—which was, in her eyes, my fault. When she got fed up with me, she locked me in a cupboard. The physical abuse stopped when I got bigger than her. The mental abuse went on until the day I ran away. Yet all that time she held down a job and presented a reasonable face to the world. I talked to a teacher at school and he didn't believe me. Told me to man up.'

'I honestly don't know what to say…' But she hated his aunt, even though she was aware she'd been a deeply troubled person. No child should be treated like that.

'Say nothing. I don't want to talk about it any more. I'm thirty-two years old. That was all a long time ago.'

'But, deep down, you're still hurting,' she whispered. 'Dominic, I'm so sorry you had to go through all that. And I admire you so much for what you became after such a difficult start.'

Words could only communicate so much. Again, she felt that urge to comfort him. This time, she acted on it. She leaned over to him and kissed him, tasted bourbon on his lips, welcomed the scrape of his stubble on her skin. Immediately, he took the kiss deeper.

The kiss went on and on, passion building, thrilling her. But it was more than sensual pleasure; it was a new sense of connection, of shared emotion as well as sensation.

He broke the kiss to pull her shirt up and over her head. His shirt was already half unbuttoned. It didn't take much to have it completely undone and to slide it off his broad shoulders and muscular arms. She caught her breath in awe at the male perfection of his body.

She wanted him. Dominic had got what he wanted from Walter. Timothy was booked for the treatment he needed. She had promised herself to go after what she wanted—him—and now was her time. It might never be more than this. She knew it and was prepared to take that risk. But she hoped for so much more.

She hadn't known him for long but she had the same kind of certainty—that it could be for ever—as she'd felt for Anthony. A certainty she'd thought she'd never feel again. *For ever love.* Had she been given a chance for that special connection again? She thought *yes*, but could she convince Dominic she could bring him the kind of happiness that had seemed to evade him—that he deserved?

He threw his head back and moaned his pleasure as she planted urgent kisses down the firm column of his throat, then back up to claim his mouth again. He tasted so good, felt so good.

He caught her hands. 'Andie, is this what you want? Because we have to stop it now if you don't,' he said, his voice husky with need.

'Don't you dare stop,' she murmured.

He smiled a slow, seductive smile that sent her heart rate rocketing. 'In that case…' He unfastened the catch on her jeans. 'Let's see if we can get these jeans to misbehave…'

Satisfied, replete, her body aching in the most pleasurable of ways, Andie drowsed in his arms as Dominic slept. But she couldn't let herself sleep.

If she'd been a different kind of person she would have stayed there. Perhaps convinced Dominic to shower with her when they woke. She would enjoy soaping down that powerful body. Heaven knew what kind of fun they could have with the powerful jets of water in his spacious double shower. Then they could retire to spend the rest of the evening in that enormous bed of his.

But Andie was not that person. There was the Christmas Eve party she had committed to this evening. As the party planner, she was obliged to call in to see all was well. She also had to check the big tree had made its way there safely—though the eighteen-year-old daughter had texted Andie to thank her, thrilled with the 'real tree'.

There was nothing like the smell of pine resin and the beauty of a natural tree. As eleven-year-old Dominic had known. Her heart went out to that little boy who lived in the damaged soul of the big male, sleeping naked next to her, his arm thrown possessively over her. She was also naked, except for her engagement ring, shining with false promise under the lamplight.

She had agreed to see her family tonight. Tomorrow, Christmas Day, would be the first Christmas lunch she had not spent with them. She was surprised her father had taken it so lightly. 'You have to stand by Dominic, love. That party is not just a job for you now. You're his future wife.'

If only.

Reluctantly, she slid away from Dominic, then quietly got dressed. She would see him in the morning. Tomorrow was Christmas Day, a holiday she loved and he hated. Now she could see why. She ached to turn things around for him—if he would let her.

She looked at his face, more relaxed than she had seen it, and smiled a smile that was bittersweet. They had made love and it had been magnificent. But nothing had changed between them. Tomorrow she was facing the biggest party of her career so far. She would be by the side of the man she had fallen in love with, not knowing for how much longer he would be a part of her life.

When the truth was, she wanted Dominic for Christmas. Not just his body—his heart as well.

Somehow, tomorrow she would have to confess to Dominic the truth of how she felt about him. That she wanted to try a relationship for real. She hoped he felt the same. If so, this would be the best Christmas she had ever had. If not... Well, she couldn't bear to think about *if not.*

CHAPTER FIFTEEN

DOMINIC AWOKE ON Christmas morning as he was accustomed to waking on December the twenty-fifth—alone. It was very early, pale sunlight filtering through the blinds. He reached out his hand to the sofa beside him in the vain hope that Andie might still be there, only to find the leather on that side disappointingly cool to the touch. He closed his eyes again and breathed in the scent of her that lingered in the room, on his skin. Then was overtaken by an anguished rush of longing for her that made him double over with gut-wrenching pain.

He remembered her leaving his side, her quiet footsteps around the room, the rustling as she slid on her clothes. Then her leaning towards him, murmuring that she had to go. She had duties, obligations. He'd pulled her back close to him, tried to convince her with his hands, with his mouth why she should stay. But she'd murmured her regret, kissed him with a quick fierce passion, told him he had jet lag to get over. Then she'd gone.

All he'd wanted to say to her still remained unsaid.

Of course she'd gone to the other people in her life who needed her and loved her. The only commitment she'd made to him was based on the falsehoods he'd engendered and coerced her into. She'd played her role to perfection. So well he was uncertain what might be fact and what might be fiction. But surely making love to him with such passion and tenderness had not been play-acting?

He noticed the bourbon bottle on the desk, lid on, barely touched. This would be the first Christmas he could remember that he hadn't tried to obliterate. The first Christmas that he woke to the knowledge that while Andie might not be here now, she soon would be. And that his perfect, empty house would be filled with people. People who had known hardship like he had and whom he was in the position to help by making their Christmas Day memorable.

Not for the first time, he thought of the possibility of opening a branch of the Underground Help Centre here in Sydney, where it was so obviously needed. Profits from the joint venture with Walter could help fund it. He had much to learn from Walter—he could see it was going to end up a friendship as well as a business partnership.

For the first Christmas in a long time he had something to look forward to—and it was all thanks to Andie.

He hauled himself off the sofa and stretched out the cricks in his back. The sofa was not the best place to sleep—though it had proved perfectly fine for energetic lovemaking. He paused, overwhelmed by memories of the night before. *Andie.* Hunger for her threatened to overwhelm him again—and not just for her beautiful, generous body. He prayed to whatever power that had brought her to him to let him keep her in his life. He hoped she would forgive the way he'd behaved—understand why. And know that it would never happen again.

He headed down the stairs and stood in the entrance hall. Not a trace of the tree remained, thank heaven. He breathed in. And none of that awful smell. Andie had been well meaning but misguided about the tree—now she understood.

The ballroom was all set up, with tables and chairs adorned in various combinations of red and white. A large buffet table area stretched along the wall closest to the kitchen. He'd approved the menu with Gemma and knew within hours it would be groaning with a lavish festive feast. The dishes had been chosen with the diverse backgrounds of the guests in mind—some were refugees experiencing their first Christmas in Australia.

He still couldn't have tolerated a tree in the house but he had to admit to a stirring of interest in the celebrations—more interest than he'd had in Christmas since he'd been a child. Andie was clever—children would love all this and adults should also respond to the nostalgia and hope it evoked. Hadn't she said Christmas was about evoking emotion?

Thanks to the tragedy on Christmas Eve all those years ago, thanks to the way his aunt had treated him in the years that followed, the emotions the season had evoked for him had been unhappy in the extreme. Was there a chance now for him to forge new, happy memories with a kind, loving woman who seemed to understand his struggles?

Andie had said he could trust her, but after his display of anger over the Christmas tree last night would she let herself trust *him*?

There was a large Santa Claus figurine in the corner with rows of canvas, sunshine-themed goody bags stacked around it. Of course it should have been a tree—but the Santa worked okay too as a compromise. The sturdy bags could double as beach bags, the ever-practical Andie had pointed out to him. She had thought of everything. There were gifts there for the volunteers too.

The house seemed to hum with a quiet anticipation and he could feel his spirits rise. Christmas Day with Andie in his house must surely be a step up on the ones he'd been forced to endure up until now.

He swung open the doors and headed to his gym for a workout.

* * *

An hour later Andie arrived with the chef and his crew. Dominic had long given her a pass code to get in and out of fortress Vaucluse.

She was wearing working gear of shorts, T-shirt and sneakers. Later she would change into her beautiful new red lace dress and gorgeous shoes—strappy and red with tassels—in time to greet their guests. She took her dress on its hanger and her bag into the downstairs bathroom. As she did, she noticed the doors to the garden were open and someone was in the pool. She went out to investigate.

Of course it was Dominic, his powerful body spearing through the water. No wonder he had such well-developed muscles with vigorous swimming like this. She watched, mesmerised at his rhythmic strokes, the force of his arms and powerful kick propelling him with athletic grace.

She didn't say anything but maybe her shadow cast on the water alerted him to her presence. Maybe he caught sight of her when he turned his head to breathe. He swam to the edge of the pool and effortlessly pulled himself out of the water, muscles rippling. He wasn't even out of breath.

She almost swooned at the sight of him—could a man be more handsome? Memories of the ecstasy they had given each other the night before flashed through her, tightening her nipples and flooding her body with desire.

His wet hair was slick to his head, the morning sunlight refracted off droplets of water that clung to his powerfully developed shoulders and cut chest, his veins stood out on his biceps, pumped from exertion. And then there were the classic six-pack, the long, strong legs. He didn't have a lot of body hair for such a dark man, but what there was seemed to flag his outrageous masculinity.

She wanted him more than ever. Not just for a night. For many nights. Maybe every night for the rest of her life. There was so much she wanted to say to him but, for all the connection and closeness and *certainty* she had felt last night, she didn't know how to say it.

Her engagement ring glinted on her left hand. The deal with Walter was done. Dominic's Scrooge reputation was likely to be squashed after the party today. How much longer would this ring stay on her finger? What, if anything, would be her role in Dominic's life? She wanted to say something about last night, bring up the subject of the future, but she just couldn't. 'Happy Christmas,' she said instead, forcing every bit of enthusiasm she could muster into her voice.

He grabbed a towel from the back of the chair and slung it around his shoulders, towelling off the excess water. 'H… Happy Christmas to you too,' he said, his voice rusty in the way of someone unused to uttering those particular words. She wondered how long since he had actually wished anyone the Season's greetings.

He looked down into her face and she realised by the expression in his eyes that he might be as uncertain as she was.

Hope flared in her heart. 'Dominic, I—'

'Andie, I—'

They both spoke at the same time. They laughed. Tried again.

'About last night,' he said.

'Yes?' she said.

'I wanted to—'

But she didn't hear what he had to say, didn't get a chance to answer because at that moment the chef called from the doors that opened from the ballroom that Gemma and Eliza were there and needed to be buzzed in.

Dominic groaned his frustration at the terminated conversation. Andie echoed his groan.

'Later,' she said as she turned away, knowing that it

would be highly unlikely for them to get another private moment together for the next few hours.

Dominic found the amount of noise two hundred people could generate—especially when so many of them were children—quite astounding. He stood on the edge of the party, still at the meet-and-greet stage, with appetisers and drinks being passed around by waiters dressed as Christmas elves.

Santa Claus, otherwise known as Rob Cratchit, his Director of Marketing, sidled up next to him. 'It's going even better than I expected,' he said through his fake white beard. 'See that woman over there wiping tomato sauce off the little boy's shirt? She's a journalist, volunteering for the day, and one of your most strident Scrooge critics. She actually called you a multi-million-dollar miser. But I think she's already convinced that today is not some kind of cynical publicity stunt.'

'Good,' said Dominic. Strange that the original aim of this party—to curry favour with Walter Burton—seemed to have become lost. Now it was all about giving people who had it tough a heart-warming experience and a good meal. And enjoying it with Andie by his side.

'Good on you for dressing up as Santa Claus,' he said to Rob. Andie had been right—Rob made the perfect Santa and he had the outgoing personality to carry it off.

'Actually, *you're* the Santa Claus. I talked to one nice lady, a single mum, who said her kids would not have got Christmas lunch or a Christmas present this year, unless a charity had helped out. She said this was so much better than charity. You should mingle—a lot of people want to thank you.'

'I'm not the mingling type,' Dominic said. 'I don't need to be thanked. I just signed the cheques. It should be Andie they're thanking; this was all her idea.'

'She's brilliant,' said Rob. 'Smart of you to snap her up so quickly. You're a lucky man.'

'Yes,' said Dominic, not encouraging further conversation. He'd never been happy discussing his personal life with anyone. The thought that—unless he said something to her—this might be the last day he had with Andie in his life was enough to sink him into a decidedly unfestive gloom.

He hadn't been able to keep his eyes off Andie as she flitted around the room, looking her most beautiful in a very stylish dress of form-fitting lace in a dusky shade of Christmas red. It was modest but hugged every curve and showed off her long, gorgeous legs. He tried not to think of how it had felt to have those legs wrapped around him last night…

'Well, mustn't linger,' said Rob. 'I have to be off and do the *ho-ho-ho* thing.'

As Rob made his way back into the throng, Andie rang a bell for attention and asked everyone to move towards the entrance hall. 'Some of the children and their parents are singing carols for us today.' She'd told Dominic a few of the adults were involved in street choirs and had been happy to run through the carols with the kids.

There was a collective gasp from the 'audience' as they saw the children lined up on the stairs, starting from the tiniest to the teenagers with the adults behind. Again Andie had been right—the stairs made the most amazing showcase for a choir. Each of the choir members wore a plain red T-shirt with the word *'choir'* printed in white lowercase letters. It was perfect, gave them an identity without being ostentatious.

Andie met his gaze from across the room and she smiled. He gave her a discreet thumbs-up. Professional pride? Or something more personal?

The choir started off with the Australian Christmas

carol 'Six White Boomers' where Santa's reindeer were replaced by big white kangaroos for the Australian toy delivery. It was a good icebreaker, and had everyone laughing and clapping and singing along with the chorus.

As Dominic watched, he was surprised to see Andie playing guitar up on the balcony with two other guitarists. She was singing too, in a lovely warm soprano. He remembered that photo of her playing guitar in the hallway of her parents' home and realised how much there was he still didn't know about her—and how much he wanted to know.

When the choir switched to classics like 'Silent Night' and 'Away in a Manger', Dominic found himself transported back to the happy last Christmas when his parents were alive and they'd gone carol singing in their village. *How could he have forgotten?*

The music and the pure young voices resonated and seemed to unlock a well of feeling he'd suppressed—unable perhaps to deal with the pain of it during those years of abuse by his aunt. He'd thought himself incapable of love—because he had been without love. But he *had* been loved back then, by his parents and his grandparents—loved deeply and unconditionally.

He'd yearned for that love again but had never found it. His aunt had done her best to destroy him emotionally but the love that had nurtured him as a young child must have protected him. The realisation struck him—he had loved women incapable of loving him back, and all this time had thought the fault was his when those relationships had failed.

Andie's voice soared above the rest of the choir. Andie, who he sensed had a vast reserve of love locked away since she'd lost her boyfriend. He wanted that love for himself and he wanted to give her the love she needed. How could he tell her that?

He tried to join in with the words of the carol but his throat closed over. He pretended to cough. Before he made an idiot of himself by breaking down, he pushed his way politely through the crowd and made his way out to the cabana, the only place where he could be alone and gather his thoughts.

But he wasn't alone for long. Andie, her eyes warm with concern, was soon with him. 'Dominic, are you okay?' she said, her hand on his arm. 'I know how you feel about Christmas and I was worried—'

'I'm absolutely fine—better than I've been for a long time,' he said.

He picked up her left hand. 'Take off your ring and give it to me, please.'

Andie froze. She stared at him for a long moment, trying to conceal the pain from the shaft of hurt that had stabbed her heart. So it had come to this so soon. Her use was over. Fake fiancée no longer required. Party planner no longer required. Friend, lover, confidante and whatever else she'd been to him no longer required. *She was surplus to requirements.*

Dominic had proved himself to be generous and thoughtful way beyond her initial expectations of Scrooge. But she must not forget the cold, hard fact—people who got to be billionaires in their twenties must have a ruthless streak. And he'd reneged on his offer that she could keep the ring—not that she'd had any intention of doing so. To say she was disappointed would be the world's biggest understatement.

She felt as though all the energy and joy was flowing out of her to leave just a husk. The colour drained from her face—she must look like a ghost.

With trembling fingers, she slid off the magnificent ring and gave it back to him, pressing it firmly into the palm of his hand. Her finger felt immediately empty, her hand unbalanced.

'It's yours,' she said and turned on her heel, trying not to stagger. She would not cry. She would not say anything snarky to him. She would just walk out of here with dignity. *This was her worst Christmas Day ever.*

'Wait! Andie! Where are you going?'

She turned back to see Dominic with a look of bewilderment on his handsome, tough face. 'You're not going to leave me here with your ring?'

Now it was her turn to feel bewildered. '*My* ring? Then why—?' she managed to choke out.

He took her hand again and held it in a tight grip. 'I'm not doing a good job of this, am I?'

He drew her closer, cleared his throat. 'Andie, I… I love you, and I'm attempting to ask you to marry me. I'm hoping you'll say "yes", so I can put your ring back on your wedding finger where it belongs, as your *real* fiancé, as a *real* engagement ring. Just like you told me you wanted.'

She was stunned speechless. The colour rushed back into her face.

'Well?' he prompted. 'Andrea Jane Newman, will you do me the honour of becoming my wife?'

Finally she found her words. Although she only needed the one. 'Yes,' she said. 'I say "yes".'

With no further ado, he slid the beautiful ring back into its rightful place. To her happy eyes it seemed to flash even more brilliantly.

'Dominic, I love you too. I think maybe it *was* love at first sight the day I met you. I never really had to lie about that.'

She wound her arms around his neck and kissed him. They kissed for a long time. Until they were interrupted by a loud knock on the door of the pool house. Gemma.

'Hey, you two, I don't know what's going on in there

and I don't particularly want to know, but we're about to serve lunch and your presence is required.'

'Oh, yes, of course—we're coming straight away,' Andie called, flustered.

Dominic held her by the arm. 'Not so fast. There's something else I want to ask you. What would you like for Christmas?'

His question threw her. She had to think very hard. But then it came to her. 'All I want for Christmas is for us to get married as soon as possible. I… I don't want to wait. You…you know why.'

Anthony would have wanted this for her—to grab her second chance of happiness. She knew that as certainly as if he'd been there to give her his blessing.

'That suits me fine,' Dominic said. 'The sooner you're my wife the better.'

'Of course it takes a while to organise a wedding. Next month. The month after. I don't want anything too fussy anyway, just simple and private.'

'We'll have to talk to the Party Queens,' he said.

She laughed. 'Great idea. I have a feeling we'll be the best people for the job.'

She could hardly believe this was true, but the look in his eyes told her she could believe it. She wound her arms around his neck again. 'Dominic Hugo Hunt, you've just made this the very best Christmas of my life.'

He heaved a great sigh and she could see it was as if the weight of all those miserable Christmases he'd endured in the past had been thrown off. 'Me too,' he said. 'And all because of you, my wonderful wife-to-be.'

CHAPTER SIXTEEN

ANDIE FOUND HERSELF singing 'Rudolph the Red-Nosed Reindeer' as she drove to Dominic's house five days later. She couldn't remember when she'd last sung in the car—and certainly not such a cheesy carol as 'Rudolph'. No, wait. 'Six White Boomers' was even cheesier. But the choir had been so wonderful at Dominic's Christmas party she'd felt it had become the heart of the very successful party. The carols had stayed in her head.

It had only been significant to her, but it was the first time she'd played her guitar and sung in public since Anthony had died. She'd healed in every way from the trauma of his loss, although she would never forget him. Her future was with Dominic. How could she ever have thought he was not her type?

She didn't think Dominic would be burdened with the Scrooge label for too much longer. One of his most relentless critics had served as a volunteer at the party—and had completely changed her tune. Andie had committed to heart the journalist's article in one of the major newspapers.

Dominic Hunt appears more Santa Claus than Scrooge, having hosted a lavish Christmas party, not for celebrities and wealthy silvertails but for ordinary folk down on their luck. A publicity stunt? No way.

She suspected Dominic's other private philanthropic work would eventually be discovered—probably by the digging of this same journalist. But, with the support of her love and the encouragement of Walter Burton, she thought he was in a better place to handle the revelations of his past if and when they came to light.

Dominic had invited her for a special dinner at his house this evening, though they'd had dinner together every evening since Christmas—and breakfast. She hadn't been here for the last few days; rather, he'd stayed at her place. She didn't want to move in with him until they were married.

But he'd said they had to do something special this evening as they wouldn't be able to spend New Year's Eve together—December the thirty-first would be the Party Queens' busiest night yet.

She was looking forward to dinner together, just the two of them. It was a warm evening and she wore a simple aqua dress that was both cool and elegant. Even though they were now engaged for real, they were still getting to know each other—there was a new discovery each time they got the chance to truly talk.

As she climbed the stairs to his house, she heard the sounds of a classical string quartet playing through the sound system he had piped through the house. Dominic had good taste in music, thank heaven. But when she pushed open the door, she was astounded to see a live quartet playing in the same space where the ill-fated Christmas tree had stood. She smiled her delight. It took some getting used to the extravagant gestures of a billionaire.

Dominic was there to greet her, looking darkly handsome in a tuxedo. She looked down at her simple dress in dismay. 'I didn't realise it was such an occasion or I would have worn something dressier,' she said.

Dominic smiled. 'You look absolutely beautiful. Anyway, if all goes well, you'll be changing into something quite different.'

She tilted her head to the side. 'This is all very intriguing,' she said. 'I'm not quite sure where you're going with it.'

'First of all, I want to say that everything can be cancelled if you don't want to go ahead with it. No pressure.'

For the first time she saw Dominic look like he must have looked as a little boy. He seethed with suppressed excitement and the agony of holding on to a secret he was desperate to share.

'Do tell,' she said, tucking her arm through the crook of his elbow, loving him more in that moment than she had ever loved him.

A big grin split his face. 'I'm going to put my hands over your eyes and lead you into the ballroom.'

'Okay,' she said, bemused. Then she guessed it. The family had been determined to give her an engagement party. Now that she and Dominic actually were genuinely engaged she would happily go along with it. She would act suitably surprised. And be very happy. Getting engaged to this wonderful man was worth celebrating.

She could tell she was at the entrance to the ballroom. 'You can open your eyes now,' said Dominic, removing his hands.

There was a huge cry of 'Surprise!' Andie was astounded to see the happy, smiling faces of all her family and friends as well as a bunch of people she didn't recognise but who were also smiling.

What was more, the ballroom had been transformed. It was exquisitely decorated in shades of white with hints of pale blue. Round tables were set up, dressed with white ruffled cloths and the backs of the chairs looped with antique lace and white roses. It was as if she'd walked into a dream. She blinked. But it was all still there when she opened her eyes.

Dominic held her close. 'We—your family, your friends, me—have organised a surprise wedding for you.'

Andie had to put her hand to her heart to stop it from pounding out of her chest. 'A wedding!'

She looked further through the open glass doors to see a bridal arch draped with filmy white fabric and white flowers set up among the rows of blue agapanthus blooming in the garden. Again she blinked. Again it was still there when she opened her eyes.

'Your wedding,' said Dominic. '*Our* wedding. You asked to be married as soon as possible. I organised it. With some help from the Party Queens. Actually, a *lot* of help from the Party Queens. Jake Marlow and some other friends of mine are also here.'

'It…it's unbelievable.'

'Only if it's what you want, Andie,' Dominic said, turning to her so just she could hear. 'If it's too much, if you'd rather organise your own wedding in your own time, this can just turn into a celebration of our engagement.'

'No! I want it. It's perfect.' She turned to the expectant people who seemed to have all held their breath in anticipation of her response and gone silent. 'Thank you. I say I do—well, I'm *soon* going to say I do!'

There was an eruption of cheers and happy relieved laughter. 'Here comes the bride,' called out one of her brothers.

Andie felt a swell of joy and happy disbelief. It was usually her organising all the surprise parties. To have Dominic do this for her—well, she felt as if she was falling in love with him all over again.

But the party planner in her couldn't resist checking on the details. 'The rings?' she asked Dominic. He patted his breast pocket. 'Both ready-to-wear couture pieces,' he said.

'And this is all legal?'

'Strictly speaking, you need a month's notice of intent to be married—and we filled out our form less than a month ago. But I got a magistrate to approve a shorter notice period. It's legal all right.'

Her eyes smarted with tears of joy. This was really happening. She was getting married today to the man she adored and in front of the people she loved most in the world.

Her fashion editor friend, Karen, dashed out from the guests and took her by the arm. 'Hey! No tears. I've got my favourite hair and make-up artist on hand and we don't want red eyes and blotchy cheeks. Let's get your make-up done. She's already done your bridesmaids.'

'My bridesmaids?'

'Your sisters, Hannah and Bea, Gemma, Eliza and your little niece, Caitlin. The little nephews are ring-bearers.'

'You guys have thought of everything.'

Turning around to survey the room again, she noticed a fabulous four-tiered wedding cake, covered in creamy frosting and blue sugar forget-me-nots. It was exactly the cake she'd talked about with Gemma. She'd bet it was chocolate cake on the bottom layers and vanilla on the top—Gemma knew she disliked the heavy fruitcake of traditional wedding cakes.

'Wait until you see your wedding dresses,' said Karen.

'Dresses?'

'I've got you a choice of three. You'll love them all but there's one I think you'll choose. It's heavy ivory lace over silk, vintage inspired, covered at the front but swooping to the back.'

'And a veil? I always wanted to wear a veil on my wedding day.' This all felt surreal.

'I've got the most beautiful wisp of silk tulle edged with antique lace. You attach it at the back of a simple halo band twisted with lace and trimmed with pearls. A touch vintage, a touch boho—very Andie. Oh, and your mother's pearl necklace for your "something borrowed".'

'It sounds divine.' She hugged Karen and thanked her. 'I think you know my taste better than I do myself.'

It *was* divine. The dress, the veil, the silk-covered shoes that tied with ribbons around her ankles, the posy of white old-fashioned roses tied with mingled white and blue ribbon. The bridesmaids in their pale blue vintage style dresses with white rosebuds twisted through their hair. The little boys in adorable mini white tuxedos.

As she walked down the magnificent staircase on her father's arm, Andie didn't need the guests' *oohs* and *aahs* to know she looked her best and the bridal party was breathtaking. She felt surrounded by the people she cared for most—and who cared for her. She wouldn't wish anything to be different.

Dominic was waiting for her at the wedding arch, flanked by his best man, Jake Marlow—tall, broad-shouldered, blond and not at all the geek she'd imagined him to be—with her brothers and Rob Cratchit as groomsmen.

She knew she had to walk a stately, graceful bride's walk towards her husband-to-be. But she had to resist the temptation to pick up her skirts and run to him and the start of their new life as husband and wife.

Dominic knew the bridesmaids looked lovely and the little attendants adorable. But he only had eyes for Andie as she walked towards him, her love for him shining from her eyes.

As she neared where he waited for her with the celebrant, a stray breeze picked up the fine layers of her gown's skirts and whirled them up and over her knees. She laughed and made no attempt to pin them down.

As her skirts settled back into place, their glances met

and her lips curved in an intimate exchange of a private joke that had meaning only for two. It was just one of many private connections he knew they would share, bonding and strengthening their life as partners in the years of happy marriage that stretched out ahead of them.

Finally she reached him and looked up to him with her dazzling smile. He enfolded her hand in his as he waited with her by his side to give his wholehearted assent to the celebrant's question. 'Do you, Dominic Hugo Hunt, take this woman, Andrea Jane Newman, to be your lawful wedded wife?'

CHAPTER SEVENTEEN

Christmas Day the following year.

ANDIE STOOD WITHIN the protective curve of her husband's arm as she admired the fabulous Christmas tree that stood in the entrance of their Vaucluse home. It soared almost to the ceiling and was covered in exquisite ornaments that were set to be the start of their family collection, to be brought out year after year. Brightly wrapped gifts were piled around its base.

Christmas lunch was again being held here today, but this time it was a party for just Andie's family and a few other waifs and strays who appreciated being invited to share their family's celebration.

The big Scrooge-busting party had been such a success that Dominic had committed to holding it every year. But not here this time. This year he'd hired a bigger house with a bigger pool and invited more people. He'd be calling in to greet his guests later in the day.

Andie hadn't had to do a thing for either party. She'd had her input—how could a Party Queen not? But for this private party the decorating, table settings and gift-wrapping had all been done by Dominic and her family.

After much cajoling, Andie had convinced her father to transfer his centre of cooking operations to Dominic's gourmet kitchen—just for this year. Although Dad had grumbled and complained about being away from familiar territory, Andie knew he was secretly delighted at the top-of-the-range equipment in the kitchen. The aromas that were wafting to her from the kitchen certainly smelled like the familiar traditional family favourites her father cooked each year. She couldn't imagine they would taste any less delicious than they would cooked in her parents' kitchen.

It was people who made the joy of Christmas and all the people she cherished the most were here to celebrate with her.

And one more.

The reason for all the disruption lay cradled in her arms. Hugo Andrew Hunt had been born in the early hours of Christmas Eve.

The birth had been straightforward and he was a healthy, strong baby. Andie had insisted on leaving the hospital today to be home for Christmas. Dominic had driven her and Hugo home so slowly and carefully they'd had a line of impatient cars honking their horns behind them by the time they'd got back to Vaucluse. He was over the moon about becoming a father. This was going to be one very loved little boy.

'Weren't you clever, to have our son born on Christmas Eve?' he said.

'I'm good at planning, but not *that* good,' she said. 'He came when he was ready. Maybe…maybe your parents sent him.' She turned her head so she could look up into Dominic's eyes. 'Now Christmas Eve will be a cause for celebration, not mourning, for you.'

'Yes,' he said. 'It will—because of you.'

Andie looked down at the perfect little face of her slumbering son and felt again the rush of fierce love for this precious being she'd felt when the midwife had first laid him on her tummy. He had his father's black hair but it was too soon to tell what colour his eyes would be.

Her husband, he-who-would-never-be-called-Scrooge-again, gently traced the line of little Hugo's cheek with his finger. 'Do you remember how I said last year was the very best Christmas of my life? Scratch that. This one is even better.'

'And they will get better and better,' she promised, turning her head for his kiss.

As they kissed, she heard footsteps on the marble floor and then an excited cry from her sister Bea. 'They're home! Andie, Dominic and baby Hugo are home!'

* * * * *

THE BABY WHO SAVED CHRISTMAS

ALISON ROBERTS

For Liz
With fond memories of our visit to
St-Jean-Cap-Ferrat
With love

CHAPTER ONE

SOMETHING WAS GOING very wrong for Alice McMillan.

She was not supposed to be enjoying herself right now.

'I'm sorry…'

Silent, one-sided communication had become a habit even though the feeling of connection had faded over the months of this year. Now it only served to increase the prickle of guilt.

'But it *is* gorgeous… You must have loved it, too.'

All those years ago. Twenty-nine, to be exact. A period of time that had included Alice's conception.

Having stepped off the bus from Nice in the heart of the small town of Villefranche-sur-Mer, Alice crossed the road to start walking downhill, skirting around a man on a ladder who was part of the team installing a huge pattern of tinsel that would hang over the centre of the main street like a giant tiara. She'd printed off a map before leaving Edinburgh and the route looked easy enough. All she had to do was find the beach and follow it. At the other end was the start of the peninsula that was St Jean Cap Ferrat and the address she was heading for looked like it was within easy walking distance.

There was a small market happening on a grassed

area opposite the bus stop. Stalls were selling things like cheese and preserves, hand-made soaps and Christmas decorations. There was music coming from somewhere and the smell of hot food made her mouth water. When had she last eaten? That bag of cheese and onion crisps and a bottle of water on the last leg of her long train journey didn't really count.

She had to edge her way through a group of people who seemed to be there to socialise rather than shop but they made way for her politely and the smile of the man at the stall was welcoming.

'*Bonjour, mademoiselle. Qu'est-ce qu'il vous fait aujourd'hui*?'

This might be her first day ever in France but Alice had been surrounded by the sound of this language since her arrival in Paris early this morning. She'd already learned that the best response was a smile and an apology that she didn't speak French.

The apology was genuine. Most people learned at the very least to say 'please' or 'thank you' in the language of a country they chose to visit and Alice could do that in Spanish or Italian. Even Greek. But not French.

Never French…

'One of those, please.' Alice pointed to a baguette that had been split and filled with a thick slice of ham and some cheese.

'Of course.' The man switched languages effortlessly. 'You are English?'

'Scottish.'

'Ah… Welcome to Villefranche.' The sandwich was being wrapped in paper. 'You are here on holiday?'

A holiday? A place you chose to go to relax and enjoy yourself? No. This journey was definitely no holiday.

But Alice smiled and nodded as she handed over some money because the truth was far too personal to tell a stranger and too complex to explain anyway. She wasn't even sure she understood herself why she had made the impetuous decision to come here and now that she *was* here she felt like she was on an emotional roller-coaster.

It was a relief to get away from all the people. The buzz of conversation and laughter faded and the group of people she passed near the tourist attraction of the old citadel were clearly English tourists.

There was a marina below the citadel and Alice found a bench where she could sit and eat her sandwich in the afternoon sunshine. There was a man working on a boat nearby. Joggers went past and people walking their dogs or pushing prams but nobody seemed to notice Alice and she gave herself a few minutes to bask in the sunshine, enjoy the delicious fresh bread with its perfect filling and get her bearings.

She could see the curve of the beach not far away—past a line of restaurants and cafés and she could see the tongue of land that had to be St Jean Cap Ferrat. She knew the main village was out of sight, on the other side of the peninsula, but there were lots of houses on this side and one of them was the address she was heading for. Right on the coastline, in fact. If she knew where to look, she would probably be able to see it from here.

But what, exactly, did she think was going to happen when she knocked on the door? That she would only have to come face to face with this famous racing-car driver called André Laurent and he would somehow recognise her as his daughter? Or that she would show him the faded photograph she'd found hidden in her mother's most private belongings to remind him of their relationship and then disbelief would morph into amazement and finally joy?

That she would, again, have at least one person that she could think of as family?

Nerves kicked in. This had been a stupid idea. She wouldn't be welcome. It was quite likely she would have to turn around immediately and retrace her footsteps and then what would she do? With the knowledge that the big city of Nice was so close and there was bound to be plenty of hotels, she hadn't even tried to book a room for the night or find out what time the buses stopped running.

Maybe she should just turn around now.

Alice closed her eyes and waited and, yes...there it was. That feeling that this was the right thing to do. That flicker of hope that it might even be the best thing she had ever decided to do. Okay, it was a huge gamble and it was quite possible that it would turn out to be her worst decision ever but there was only one way to find out.

And there was *something* important here.

She could feel it. A sense of...belonging?

Well, that wasn't so crazy, was it? She was half-French. She might have been brought up to dismiss this heritage as something to be ashamed of but there could be no denying that the lilt of the language around her and the feel of these streets and houses was touching a part of her she didn't recognise. A part that held whispers of contentment. Of being *home*...

Hence the silent apology to her mother.

Jeanette McMillan would have been so horrified by her making this journey it was no wonder that the very idea would have been unthinkable while she was alive. Even now, Alice could hear an echo of the words that had stopped any queries about her genetic history.

'Your father was *French…*' The biggest insult ever. 'And he tried to get rid of you…'

Curiosity about even the country had to be firmly squashed because she'd loved her mother and any intermittent yearning to find out who her father might be had been something that had needed to be kept even more private, especially in recent years when her mother had already been coping with more than anyone should have to bear.

How sad was it that she would never know if her mother had loved this place as much as Alice knew she might be capable of loving it herself?

She opened her eyes again and scanned the buildings she could see more closely. Maybe the bar where her mother had been working when she'd only been eighteen was nearby. Had it had a view of this sparkling blue bay of the Mediterranean dotted with yachts or had it been tucked away amongst the ancient stone buildings on the steep, cobbled streets of the old town?

That flicker of hope ignited into tendrils of excitement. Had her mother felt this sense of freedom as she'd embarked on her first adult adventure? Alice had left it far too long to stretch her wings but how could things have been any different with first her grandmother and then her mother having to suffer through such unbearably slow and debilitating terminal illnesses?

But she was here now and everything felt new and wonderful. This hadn't been a stupid idea at all. This was magic—as if she was taking the first steps into a real-life fairy-tale. It was a shame she didn't have time to explore this historic part of the small town right now but time was marching on and it was winter. Daylight wouldn't last past about five p.m., and she didn't want to be trying to find her destination in the dark.

Her breath came out in an incredulous huff at the reminder of the season. This bright warmth was another wave of the magic wand—like the feeling of the scenery and the sound of the language was proving to be. Had it only been two days ago that Alice had been wrapped up against the bone-chilling temperatures of a Scottish winter? She'd shed her coat hours ago but still felt overdressed in her long-sleeved jumper and skinny jeans that were tucked into short boots.

The coat felt heavy over her arm as she followed the signposted walkway to the beach. It was a good thing that the few items she'd deemed necessary for a trip that might only last a day or two had fitted into a small backpack so she didn't have anything else to carry in her hands.

The beach was almost deserted, wavelets lapping at the golden sand. Even now, the sea looked inviting and Alice knew that the water temperature would probably be warmer than any beach in Scotland in midsummer. No doubt it got horribly crowded here in the high season, though, given that it was such a popular playground for the rich and famous. Didn't people like Madonna come here for holidays?

And Monaco was only a short drive down the coast. The place where her father had apparently become so famous and another Mecca for the kind of people that had always seemed like an alien race to Alice McMillan. She wasn't just visiting another country right now—it felt like she was heading for a different planet.

The path seemed to end in a car park, which was momentarily confusing, but then Alice spotted the stairs tucked against the steep bank. There was a path that followed a railway line at the top of the stairs and moments later she saw a street with a sign that gave her a name she recognised. Pulling a now crumpled map from her back pocket, Alice kept walking and it was less than ten minutes later that she came to another road that clearly led down towards the coastline again. The view back over the bay to Villefranche was spectacular but there seemed to be a downside to living on this street. There was certainly no room for anyone to park. There were vans and trucks parked nose to tail, and further down the hill she could see a large group of people milling about.

As she got closer, she could see that a lot of them were holding cameras.

Paparazzi? Was Madonna taking a winter break, perhaps? In the same street her father lived in? It wouldn't surprise her. When she'd found the street on the internet, it had looked like every house could be an exclusive resort—the dwellings massive, with huge gardens and swimming pools of Olympic size. The gates advertised just how prestigious this real estate was. Ornate black iron with gold gilding that were at least twice Alice's height, decorated with security features like cameras and intercoms. There were even security guards standing in front of the most ornate she'd seen so far. This property was also the one attracting the attention of the media. There was more than one television crew set up amongst a bank of cameras.

Disconcertingly, as Alice skirted the back of the small crowd she discovered that this was the end of the road. There were no more houses. With her heart thumping, she checked the map again. Okay, she'd known her father was famous. But *this* famous...?

The voice so close to her ear made her jump. She crumpled the map in her hand but it was too late. The man had seen the red circle and her notes and he was asking her something in a tone that was unmistakeably extremely interested.

Alice didn't bother to apologise this time. She shook her head and stepped back.

'I don't understand. I don't speak any French. Not even a single word of it.'

The man only spoke louder. And faster. He even took hold of Alice's arm and started pushing her towards the crowd.

Alice tried to pull her arm free. She had no idea what was going on but she knew she'd made a mistake now and the sooner she got away from here the better. The fairy-tale was taking an ominous twist and she needed to think about this. About taking a different approach to reach her goal, maybe.

This was frightening. Her unwelcome companion was now talking to someone else. About *her*. Her hand tightened around the ball of the map. This was nobody else's business.

How awful would it be if the media discovered that André Laurent had an illegitimate child before he did?

'It's okay,' the second man said. 'You're not in trouble. My friend is just wanting to know why you look for the house of Monsieur Laurent?'

'I... I need to talk to him, that's all. About something...important.'

'*Talk* to him?' The reporter, if that's what he was,

couldn't have looked more astonished. '*Mon Dieu*… Don't you *know*?'

'Know what?'

But the two men were talking to each other again. In low voices, as if they didn't want to be overheard. They were still attracting attention, though.

'Come with me.'

'No… I think it might be better if I come back another time…'

But Alice was being firmly ushered forward. Towards the gate and the uniformed guard. Another rapid conversation followed, with the second reporter providing translation.

'He wants to know who you are.'

'My name is Alice McMillan. I'm…' Suddenly, this was terrifying. She was in a strange country and couldn't understand a word of what was being said around her. Something was going on and there was a grim note in the atmosphere. How was it that she hadn't noticed the presence of the police on the outskirts of this group? What if she found herself in trouble simply by having arrived in the wrong place at precisely the wrong time?

She seemed to have unwittingly walked into a nightmare situation and maybe the only way through it was to be honest.

She swallowed hard. And then she stood on tiptoe and spoke quietly enough that only the security guard could hear what she said.

'André Laurent is my father.'

The phone would not stop ringing.

You would have thought that after this morning

things would have settled, but there had been no sign of things calming down the last time he'd checked.

Without altering the stride of his pacing, Julien Dubois flicked a sideways glance at the floor-to-ceiling windows of the grand salon. Not that he could see more than a glimpse of the driveway between the trees edging such a private garden but he knew it led to the massive gates that locked the property away from the rest of the world. And he knew what was waiting on the other side of those gates.

What were the vultures outside the gate waiting for, exactly? A clip of a celebrity looking grief-stricken? Or better yet, *not* looking grief-stricken, which would give them permission to go digging into a background that was dripping with juicy topics.

How old was he when the mother died?

How long is it now since the tragic death of his sister?

What had caused such a family rift?

What reason could he have to hate a national icon like André Laurent so much?

Who are the people in the house with him?

What's going on?

On the other side of a room big enough to easily host a ball was a corner of the house that had a view of not only the main garden and the pool complex but a glimpse of the private beach with the background of the bay and Villefranche beyond.

Of course the owner of this house would have chosen this jewel as his man cave. The rich red of the Persian carpets was as sombre as the dark glow of the enormous mahogany desk. An entire wall was a gallery of trophies and photographs with a gilt-framed monstrosity of the man himself behind a dense spray of champagne as he celebrated one of his early wins in the Monaco race.

Julien's jaw tightened as he deliberately ignored the real reason he loathed the image but really…it was a shameful waste of a magnum of Mumm Champagne.

The muscles of the rest of his body were as tense as his jaw by the time he'd taken two steps into the room. He didn't want to be in here at all but he'd discovered it was a place that contained some particularly useful technology. Not the huge screen that had an endless loop of overpriced cars racing through the streets of Monaco. No…it was the smaller screen that provided a live feed to every security camera the property boasted. He knew which corners of the screen came from the cameras on the gateposts because checking them was becoming a half-hourly ritual.

He only needed the crowd to thin out enough and he would be able to escape a property he'd never intended setting foot inside in the first place. It wasn't as if he was getting anywhere on the mission that had brought him through the gates. It was clearly a stalemate.

The media interest didn't seem to have died down at all yet, unfortunately. And what on earth was going on right in front of the gate?

A girl looked, for all the world, as if she was *kissing* one of the security guards. No wonder he looked so shocked, stepping back and staring at her as if she was completely crazy.

Julien found himself leaning closer to the screen, as if that would help him see the image more clearly. The woman was nothing like any journalist he'd ever seen. Was it because she wasn't holding a camera or microphone? Maybe it was the odd accessory of what looked like a child's schoolbag on her back. Then she turned enough for him to see her face and he realised that his impression probably had more to do with body language than anything else. The confidence was missing. The pushiness…

Yes. She looked like a fish out of water. Bewildered even, as the guard moved further away from her, reaching for his phone.

Frightened?

The urge to offer protection was instinctive. Well honed. And quite enough to trigger a wave of a grief that he'd believed he'd come to terms with by now.

He'd tried, so hard, to keep Colette safe…

And he was failing her again, even now…

If only the tears of grief would come, they might wash away some of the anger building today but it wasn't going to happen here in this room of all places.

And it wasn't going to happen now. Not with a phone ringing yet again. And this was his personal mobile, not a house landline, which meant that it was a caller he needed to take notice of. His solicitor, probably. He'd walked out on the argument still going on in the small drawing room on the other side of the foyer but decisions had to be made about which legal documents had precedence. Was he going to win the battle he'd come here today to fight?

But this call was not a summons back to the tense meeting. It was coming from outside the gates, from a member of his own entourage.

A glance at the screen gave him the odd feeling of a breath of wind that targeted only the hairs on the back of his neck. As he answered the call, his gaze went straight back to the security images. He could see his caller. The bodyguard his solicitor had deemed necessary for this potentially volatile visit.

'Sorry to disturb you, Monsieur Dubois.'

'What is it?'

'There's a girl here…an English girl…'

His gaze shifted fractionally. Yes, he could still see her. Just standing there, looking lost. He wasn't the only one looking her way either. In the boring hours of waiting for something newsworthy, any distraction for the reporters was probably welcome.

'And?'

'And…' The security guard muttered something incomprehensible.

'Pardon? You'll have to speak up.'

'I'm not sure that's a good idea.' On the screen, Julien could see the guard turn his back on his audience and step even further away. He spoke in a hoarse whisper that hissed over the line.

'She's saying that Monsieur Laurent is her father.'

Julien's breath came out in a derisive snort. 'Of course she is. She won't be the first to turn up with a convenient claim like that now. Send her packing.'

'But…she wants to talk to him…'

'What?'

'I know. It's bizarre but she really doesn't seem to have any idea what's going on. I thought it might be better to deal with it away from prying eyes and ears.'

Julien closed his eyes and cradled his forehead in one hand, applying pressure to both temples.

Could this day get any more complicated?

After a long silence he forced his eyes open again and let his breath out in a defeated sigh.

'Fine. Send her up to the house.'

* * *

Alice McMillan wasn't used to being the centre of attention.

It was unnerving the way she could actually feel the intense interest of the crowd of people behind her as the massive gates were opened just far enough to let her squeeze through in the company of the security guard she had whispered her secret to. She could imagine the crowd pressing closer as they shouted questions at her.

She should feel safer shut away from the pack but, if anything, Alice felt like she was falling further into a rabbit hole, like the Alice she'd been named for. Tumbling into an alien world that she was not at all sure she wanted to visit. She lifted her chin. No…this was a fairy-tale, she reminded herself. She was Cinderella and she was being escorted to the palace where the ball was about to begin.

The guard escorting her to the house was completely silent and it was a long walk. Plenty of time to look around. At a perfectly manicured garden with enough palm trees to make it look like a tropical island and citrus trees with lemons bright jewels against a glossy green background. The blue of the infinity pool was an almost perfect match for the sea it blended into, and the house…

The house looked like the kind of mansion people paid good money for the privilege of being allowed to enter. Not quite a palace but an ancient, stately villa with pillared terraces and enormous windows that probably did have a ballroom tucked away, along with a whole wing for staff quarters. It loomed ever larger as Alice walked towards it and by the time they reached the stone paving leading to the biggest front door she had ever seen, she could feel the shadow of the house settling onto her like a dark cloud that was menacing enough to suggest an imminent storm. The heavy chopping beat of a hovering helicopter overhead added to the unreality and made her feel as if she'd stepped into a movie. A modern twist on an old fairy-tale. Some kind of psychological thriller perhaps.

The guard stopped and jerked his head towards the door.

'Allez. Il vous attend.'

The message was crystal clear. Somebody was expecting her arrival.

Her *father*?

Oh, Lord…this was all far more dramatic than she'd ever imagined it could be. Maybe she should have paid more heed to the advice her gran had given her so many years ago.

'Don't ever go looking for your father. You're better off not knowing…'

Too late now. She was here and…and the door was opening, possibly by the very man she had come here to meet. Despite the hammering of her heart, Alice took a deep, steadying breath and walked on. She even summoned a smile as if that would somehow make her more welcome.

Disappointment that the wrong person had opened the door was remarkably crushing and her smile died instantly. Who was this young man who'd been sent to greet her? An employee? Yes, that seemed most likely. A personal assistant maybe. Or a press secretary.

Someone who'd been given clear instructions to get rid of her as quickly as possible judging by the look on his face. The glare from those dark eyes, along with the fact that he was dressed from head to toe in black, made it all more sinister. A glance upwards and he then seemed to melt into the shadow of the house as he stepped back.

'Come inside, please,' he said. 'There will be photographers in that helicopter and they have very sophisticated lenses.'

His English was perfect but his accent more than strong enough to reveal his nationality. He looked French, too. Following him across an ornate foyer and through a room with a parquet floor that was easily big enough to entertain a couple of hundred people in, Alice had plenty of time to notice those superbly tailored clothes and that smoothly combed hair that was long enough to have been drawn back into a small ponytail.

She could almost hear her grandmother clicking her tongue and muttering darkly about foreigners and their incomprehensible habits but a wayward thought sneaked in that if there was any casting going on for this real-life fairy-tale, this man might have blown any competition out of the water as far as the role of the handsome prince went.

A room like a conservatory could be seen leading from the end of this ridiculously large room. Behind glass doors was a forest of indoor plants and cane furniture and beyond that Alice could see the mirror-like surface of a swimming pool. She was led towards the other side of the house, however. Into a room that was overwhelming full of...stuff. Pictures and trophies and even a wide-screen television that had a movie playing silently.

And then she saw the enormous portrait in its elaborately gilded frame and her mouth went completely dry.

This was her father's office. These were his trophies. He was probably the driver in that speeding car in the movie.

Wow... He was larger than life in every sense in here. Supremely successful, charismatic...incredibly wealthy. Would it matter to him that she wasn't any of those things? Would he accept her for simply being his child? *Love* her even...?

The hope was so much stronger now. A happy ending was beckoning. She couldn't wait to meet him. Okay, she was nervous and knew she might be shy to start with but this meant *so* much to her. Surely he would sense that and give them a chance to explore their connection?

Her guide shut the door behind them. He walked past Alice and then turned. For a long, long moment he simply stared at her. Then he gestured towards an overstuffed chair that was probably a priceless antique.

'Take a seat.'

It was more like a command than an invitation and it ignited that rebellious streak that Alice thought she'd left behind with her schooldays. She stayed exactly where she was.

'As you wish.' The shrug was subtle. The way he shifted a large paperweight and perched one hip on the corner of the desk was less so. This was his space, the action suggested. Alice was the intruder.

Another piercing stare and then a blunt question. 'Who are you?'

'My name is Alice McMillan.' It was the first time she had spoken in his presence and her voice came out more softly than she would have liked. A little hoarsely even. She cleared her throat. 'And you are...?'

The faint quirk of an eyebrow revealed that his bad manners had only just occurred to him.

'My name is Julien Dubois. Who I am doesn't matter.'

Except it did, didn't it? He was a gatekeeper of some kind and he might have the power to decide whether her quest had any chance of success.

'Where are you from, Miss McMillan?'

'Call me Alice, please. Nobody calls me Miss—even the children in my class.'

'You are a teacher?'

'Yes. Pre-school. A nursery.'

'In England?'

'Scotland. Edinburgh at the moment but I was brought up in a small village you won't have heard of. Where it is doesn't matter.'

Good grief...where was this urge to rebel coming from? The feeling that she'd done something wrong and had been summoned to the headmaster's office perhaps? It was no excuse to be rude enough to fling his own dismissive words back at him in exactly the tone he'd used.

That eyebrow flickered again and he held her gaze as another silence fell. Despite feeling vaguely ashamed of herself, Alice didn't want to admit defeat by looking away first. His eyes weren't as dark as they'd appeared in the shadows of the entranceway, she realised. Much lighter than her own dark brown, they were more hazel. A sort of toffee colour. He had a striking face that would stand out in any crowd, with a strong nose and lips that looked capable of being as expressive as that eyebrow, but right now they were set in a grim line, surrounded by a jaw that looked like it could do with a shave.

'And you claim that André Laurent is your father?'

The disparaging snap of his voice brought her drifting gaze sharply back to his eyes.

'He is.'

'And you have proof of this?'

'Yes.'

'Show me.'

Alice slipped the straps of her backpack from her shoulders. She sat on the edge of the uncomfortable chair to make it easier to open the side pocket and remove an envelope. From that, she extracted a photograph. It was faded now but the colour was still good enough to remind her of the bright flame shade of Jeannette McMillan's hair and that smile that could light up a room. A wave of grief threatened to bring tears and she blinked hard, focusing instead on the man in the picture. She raised her gaze to stare at the oversized portrait again.

With a nod, she handed the photograph to Julien.

'My mother,' she said quietly. 'I wouldn't have known who she was with except that she kept these magazine clippings about him.' She glanced down at the folded glossy pages still in the envelope. 'Well hidden. I only found them recently after she...she died.'

If she was expecting any sympathy for her loss it was not forthcoming. Julien merely handed the photograph back.

'This proves nothing other than that your mother was one of André's groupies. It's ancient history.'

'I'm twenty-eight,' Alice snapped. 'Hardly ancient,

thanks. And my mother was not a "groupie". I imagine she was completely in love…'

'Pfff…' The sound was dismissive. And then Julien shook his head. 'Why now?' he demanded. 'Why *today*?'

'I… I don't understand.'

'Where have you been for the last week?'

'Ah… I went home to my village for a few days. And then I've been travelling.'

'You don't watch television? Or read newspapers?' He raised his hands in a sweeping gesture that her grandmother would have labelled foreign and therefore ridiculously dramatic. 'How could you not *know*?'

'Know what?'

'That André Laurent crashed his car three days ago and killed himself. That his funeral was *today*.'

'Oh, my God…' Alice's head jerked as her gaze involuntarily flicked back to the huge portrait. 'Oh… *no*…'

From the corner of her eye, she could see that Julien was following her gaze. For a long second he joined her in staring at the image of a man that was so filled with life it seemed impossible to believe that he was gone.

But then, with the speed of a big cat launching itself at its prey, Julien snatched up the paperweight from the desk and hurled it towards the portrait, creating an explosion of shattering glass, leaving behind a horrified silence that only served to magnify his chilling words.

'I wish he'd done it years ago… If he had, my sister wouldn't have married him. She would still be *alive*…'

CHAPTER TWO

THE SHOCK WAS mind-numbing.

The pain this stranger was feeling was so powerful that Alice could feel it seeping into her own body to mix with the fear of knowing that she was alone with an angry man who was capable of violence. Compassion was winning over fear, however. His sister had been married to André Laurent. Presumably she'd been in the car with him in that fatal crash. She wanted to reach out and offer comfort in some way to Julien. To touch him…?

No. That would be the last thing he would accept. She could see the agonised way he was standing with every muscle clenched so that male pride could quell the need to express emotion. With a hand shading his eyes to hide from the world.

And self-pity edged its way into the overwhelming mix.

Alice had lost something here, too.

Hope.

She'd tried to keep it under control. Ever since she'd finally found the courage to return to the cottage that had been the only real home she'd ever known because it had been time she faced the memories. Time to accept that she'd lost her only family and that she had to find a way to move forward properly from her grief. To embrace life and every wonderful thing it had to offer and to dream of a happy future.

It had been time to sort through her mother's things and keep only those that would be precious mementos.

She'd grown up in that tiny house with two women. Her mother and her grandmother. Strong women who'd protected her from the disapproval of an entire village. Women who had loved her enough to make her believe that the shameful circumstances of her birth didn't matter. That she was a gift to the world simply because she existed.

Maybe it had been a bad choice to make the visit so close to Christmastime, when the huge tree was lit up in the village square and the shops had long since decorated their windows with fairy-lights and sparkling tinsel. The sadness that this would be her first Christmas with no family to share it with had been the undercurrent threatening to wash away the new direction she was searching for, and finding that envelope that had provided the information about who her father was had given that undercurrent the strength of an ocean rip.

Had given her that hope that had exploded into something huge the moment she'd walked into this room and seen that portrait. She had been ready to love this man—her unknown father.

She'd still had a family member. Someone who'd been denied any connection with the women who had raised her but with a connection to herself that had to mean something. She was a part of this stranger.

His daughter.

It felt quite possible she had loved him already. And

now she had lost him before she'd even had the chance to meet him. She would never know if there were parts of her personality she might have inherited from that side of her gene pool. Like that rebellious streak maybe. Or the unusual gurgle of her laughter that always turned heads. Her brown eyes?

Yes. Even behind the shards of broken glass clinging to the frame of that portrait and the mist of the champagne spray, Alice could see that her father's eyes were as dark as her own.

He looked so happy. Confident and victorious. And there was no denying how good looking André Laurent had been. Despite the disparaging reaction of the silent man beside her, Alice just knew that her mother had been in love and had had her heart broken. Why else had she never tried to find another relationship?

She would never even discover whether André remembered her mother. If she had, at least, been conceived in love on both sides.

Yes. That hope of finding something that could grow into a new but precious version of family was gone. It was dead and had to be buried. Like her father had been only this morning.

Her breath hitched and—to her horror—Alice felt the trickle of tears escaping.

And then she heard a heavy sigh.

'*Je suis désolé*. I'm sorry.' Julien's voice had a very different timbre than she had heard so far. Softer. Genuine? Whatever it was, it made his accent even more appealing. 'I should not have done that.'

Alice swallowed the lump in her throat. The fear had gone. This man wasn't violent by nature. He had just been pushed beyond the limits of what anyone could bear. She knew what moments of despair like that could feel like.

'It's okay,' she said, in barely more than a whisper. 'I understand. I'm very sorry for your loss.'

The response was a grunt that signalled it was not a subject that he intended to discuss any further.

Alice was still holding the photograph of her parents. It was time to put it back in the envelope, along with the clippings that had supplied the name missing from her birth certificate. She slipped the envelope into the side pocket of her backpack and zipped it up. Then she picked up the straps to put it back on.

'Where are you going?'

Alice shrugged. 'I'll find somewhere. It doesn't matter.'

Julien moved so that he was between her and the door. 'You can't go out there. You can't talk to those reporters. They would have a—what do you call it? A... paddock day with a story like this.'

There was a faint quirk of amusement to be found in the near miss of translation. 'A field day.' She shook her head. 'I won't talk to anyone.'

'They'll find out.' Julien's headshake was far sharper than her own had been. 'They'll discover who you are and start asking questions. Who else knows about this... claim of yours?'

Alice was silent. What did it matter if he didn't believe her? Nobody else knew anything more than what had been impossible to hide. That her mother had gone to work for a summer in the south of France. That she had come home alone and pregnant.

'Do you have any idea what the Laurent estate is worth?' Julien's gaze flicked over her from head to foot, taking in her simple, forest-green jumper, her high-street jeans and the well-worn ankle boots. The back-pack that dangled from her hands. 'No… I don't suppose you do.'

He was rubbing his forehead with his hand. Pressing his temples with long, artistic fingers that made Alice wonder what he did for a living, which was preferable to feeling put down by her appearance. Was he a surgeon, perhaps, or a musician? The black clothes and the long hair fitted more with a career in music. She could almost see him holding an electric guitar—rocking it out in front of a crowd of adoring fans…

'I need to get advice.' Julien sounded decisive now. 'Luckily, I have my solicitor here in the house with me. And I expect a DNA test will soon sort this out.'

'There's no point now.'

'Pardon?'

'I came here to meet my father. If he'd needed that kind of proof I wouldn't hesitate but it's…too late now. It doesn't matter because I'm never going to meet him, am I?'

'But don't you want to know?'

Did she? Maybe it would be better to find out that André Laurent *wasn't* her father, however remote that possibility was, because then she could walk away knowing that she hadn't lost something that had been real and so close to being within her grasp.

And if he was, she wouldn't be haunted by knowing that her father was still out there in the world somewhere but impossible to find. She knew in her heart that she was right but there was something to be said for having written confirmation of some things, wasn't there?

So Alice shrugged. 'I guess so.'

'Come with me.' Julien opened the door. 'I do not want to be in this room a second longer.'

With what was probably going to be her last glance at her father's portrait, Alice followed him out of the office. She expected to traverse the length of the enormous room again but, instead, Julien stayed at this end of the house and threw open the glass doors to the conservatory. He waited for her to enter, his face expressionless. Perhaps the effort of keeping that anger under control left no room for anything else.

Even a hint of a smile would do.

The memory of that soft tone in his voice when he'd apologised was fading. Oddly, Alice wanted to hear it again. Or to see something that would suggest it had been genuine. That she was correct in thinking that she'd caught a glimpse of the real person buried under this grim exterior. A person she had, for an instant of time, felt a connection with.

But his tone was just as empty as his face. All that was left was the accent that still tickled her ears and made her feel as if there was a secret smile hovering just over her lips, like a butterfly waiting to alight.

'Have a seat,' he said. 'Are you hungry? I can ask the housekeeper to provide something for you.'

'No. Thank you. I had lunch not long ago.'

'As you wish. I shouldn't be too long. Please, wait here.'

She didn't really have a choice, did she? She could walk out of the house but those security guards wouldn't open the gates without getting permission and even if it was given, she would then face the media pack and... and she'd always been hopeless at lying.

Probably thanks to her father's genes, Alice had failed to receive more than the blue eyes that every member of the McMillan clad had had. She had been quietly thankful that she had escaped the flaming red hair that ran through generations of her mother's family. It hadn't been banished entirely, but her version was a rich auburn instead of orange. It was a shame she'd missed the olive skin that had been evident in that portrait of her father, though. She had pale, Scottish skin—inclined to freckle with any sunshine and turn a bright red when she blushed.

Which was what she always did if she tried to tell a lie.

Walking between the cool green fronds of huge, exotic ferns in tall terracotta urns, Alice headed for a cane couch with soft-looking, cream upholstery. Unbidden, a memory surfaced that provoked a poignant smile.

She had been about four years old and she'd done something bad. What had it been? Oh, yes... She'd been rebellious even then and she had gone to play somewhere she hadn't been allowed to go alone—behind the hen house and down by the creek. Knowing that the mud on her shoes would reveal her sin, she had taken them off and hidden them under a bush. When the query had come about their whereabouts, tiny Alice had given innocence her best shot and she'd said she didn't know where her shoes were. The fairies must have taken them.

Her mother and her grandmother had simply looked at each other.

'She's blushing, Jeannie. She's no' telling the truth.'

'Aye...'

And then the two women who'd ruled her universe had turned their gazes on Alice. She'd never forgotten what that silence felt like as they'd waited for her to confess. The guilt and the shame of it. They'd never had to wait that long again.

Not that she had any intention of confessing to any reporters but Julien was probably right. They already knew her name because they'd been right there when she'd introduced herself to the security guard. It wouldn't take long for them to chase down a story and if she was confronted by leading questions, her skin would betray her.

She could feel a prickle of heat in her neck, just *thinking* about having to lie.

At least she was safe here. The world outside those gates could be as far away as her home as she sat here in this quiet space amongst the greenery, looking out over the reflection of palm trees on the swimming pool. Her gaze was automatically drawn further—to where the water fell over the end and made it look as if the cruise ship in the distance was sharing the same patch of ocean.

And then Alice felt a shiver dance down her spine. The atmosphere had changed as noticeably as if a cool breeze had blown through the room. She didn't have to turn her head to know that Julien had returned.

Maybe she didn't feel so safe in here after all.

She was sitting on one of the couches, looking out at the view.

Julien could only see her profile but it made him realise he hadn't really looked at her until now. Or rather he'd looked at her as simply another issue that had to be dealt with on one of the darkest days of his life.

Now he could see her as media fodder and wouldn't

they have a feast? This Alice McMillan was tiny. A few inches over five feet perhaps and slim enough to wear children's clothing. That bag she was carrying looked like an accessory to a school uniform.

And there was no denying how pretty she was. That tumble of richly coloured, wavy hair… Given how unpretentious the rest of her clothing was and the fact that her nails weren't even painted, it was highly likely the colour was natural and it all added up to a brand of woman that Julien had no idea how to handle due to an almost complete lack of experience. Even his own sister had morphed into one of the polished beauties that every man wanted to be seen with. Did other men always have that nagging doubt about how genuine they really were?

The memory of tears slipping from chocolate-brown eyes that had reminded him of a fawn made him groan inwardly. Imagine how that would go down in a television interview. She would have the whole world on her side.

André Laurent and—by association—his sister and then he himself would be branded as heartless rich people who were uncaring of an impoverished relative. If, of course, her claim was true. And why wouldn't it be? Given the endless stream of women in that man's life, the probability of a legacy like this was certainly believable and, according to the legal expert he'd just been speaking to, the implications were enormous. He kept his tone light enough not to reveal the can of worms that was potentially about to be opened, however.

'The news is good,' he said. 'We have made some enquiries and apparently there have been great advances in DNA testing and a result can be found within a matter of a few days. All we need is a simple mouth swab from you. Someone is coming to the house soon, to do what is needed.'

She nodded slowly and then bent her head, a thick curl of her hair falling across her cheek. She pushed it back as she looked up again.

'But they would have to match it, wouldn't they? It's too late to get a sample from my…from André. Monsieur Laurent,' she added quickly, as though she didn't have the right to be so familiar.

'M'sieur.' Without thinking, Julien corrected her pronunciation to make the 'n' silent. She really didn't know a word of French, did she? Then he shrugged. 'It seems that there are many items that may suffice. Like his toothbrush. Someone is coming who is an expert. He works with the police.'

'The *police*?' A look of fear made her eyes look huge against that pale skin.

It was like that moment after he'd hurled the paperweight at the image of the man he'd despised so much and he realised he'd scared her enough to make her cry. A shameful thing. He didn't treat women like that. He didn't treat *anyone* like that. This whole disaster was turning him into a person he really didn't like and this woman was making it that bit harder to sort out the issue that was so personally—and urgently—important. This made her someone he needed to remove from his company at the earliest opportunity so it shouldn't matter at all how she was feeling.

But it did.

It made him want to reassure her. Comfort her even.

He turned away so he didn't get trapped in those eyes. He shrugged off the unwelcome sensation that something very private was being accessed. Like his heart? How long had it been since he'd felt the urge to protect a woman? Maybe he'd given up on trying to care after Colette had made it so clear he'd been wasting his time. That he didn't understand. All those years and, in the end, they had counted for nothing.

'A coincidence,' he said, the words coming out more sharply than he might have chosen. 'This man also runs a private paternity testing company.' A sigh escaped that had a whisper of defeat about it. The need to reassure was too powerful. 'You are not being accused of anything.'

Yet, he added silently. But then he made the mistake of looking at her again. No. She wasn't here to chase five minutes of fame or a share in a vast fortune. There was no mistaking her sincerity. Or her vulnerability. She not only believed that André was her father, it held a huge significance for her. It had to be simply another coincidence that she had arrived with such unfortunate timing.

It could be an hour or more before the DNA expert arrived from Nice with his testing kit and it would be extremely impolite to leave her waiting here alone and it would be imprudent to antagonise her. For everybody's sake, this matter had to be kept as private as possible.

'So...' Julien lowered himself onto a couch facing Alice. 'You are a teacher?'

'Yes.'

'You like children, then?'

'Of course.'

'Do you have any of your own?'

That startled her.

'No… I'm not…um…married.'

'Neither was your mother.'

Maybe she wasn't quite as vulnerable as he'd thought. A flash of something like anger crossed her face and her chin lifted.

'She suffered for that. There are communities where it's still considered shameful to produce an illegitimate child.'

Julien blinked. If the mother had suffered, it was logical to assume that the child had as well.

'Why did she go back, then?'

The stare he was receiving made him feel like he'd asked a very stupid question. There was something even more disturbing in that look, however. Pity? Was he missing something fundamental?

'Brannockburn was her home. She was very young and her heart was broken. She needed her mother.'

A broken heart? Well, she probably hadn't been the only woman who'd believed that she might be the one to tame André Laurent. He could hardly brand her as a complete fool when his own sister had fallen under the same spell decades later.

'I'm sorry…' Her apology was unexpected.

'What for?'

Alice was twisting a lock of hair in her fingers as she shifted her gaze to the doors that led back into the house. 'You've lost your sister. You must have family here. Your mother perhaps? I'm intruding on a very personal time. I'm sorry. Obviously, I wouldn't have come if I'd had any idea of what had happened.'

'My only family was my sister,' Julien said quietly. 'And I lost her three months ago. She died in childbirth.'

* * *

A heavy silence fell but Alice didn't dare look back at him.

Had the baby died as well? Had they both recently lost their only living relatives? Not that there was any real comparison. He'd known his sister and she'd only lost the potential of knowing her father. But she knew what it was like to lose the person who was the emotional touchstone in one's life. Her mother had seemed far too young to be taken but how old had Julien's sister been? Probably only in her thirties, as he looked to be himself.

This was a tragedy in anybody's terms and Julien clearly blamed her father and hated him for it. She had come here claiming a close relationship to André so it was no wonder she wasn't welcome. Had André been as reckless on public roads as he'd been on a racing circuit? That would give credence to the idea that the crash had been his fault but Julien had said his sister had died in childbirth months ago. How could André be blamed for that?

A cold chill ran down Alice's spine. Had it been an abortion that had gone horribly wrong? That was part of her own history, in a way. The only reason she existed had been because her mother had refused to go along with what had been deemed compulsory.

The silence grew heavier. And more awkward.

And then it was broken by something totally unexpected.

The wail of a baby.

CHAPTER THREE

ALICE FOUND HERSELF staring at the doors as the sound grew louder. Julien had gone pale. He got to his feet and walked past her without a word. Without thinking, Alice stood up and followed him.

There seemed to be two groups of people at the other end of the huge room. Two men wearing dark suits, facing each other and talking loudly. Behind the second man were two women. One was older and wore an apron. A younger woman was carrying the baby, who couldn't be more than about three months old. The age of the youngest of the children who attended the preschool educational centre she worked for.

The age Julien's nephew or niece would have been by now?

Julien was walking swiftly, as though he intended to stop them coming any further. Alice was a few steps behind by the time they all stopped.

They spoke French, of course, so she couldn't understand a word but she could pick up a sense of what was going on. There was a problem of some kind and Julien wanted nothing to do with it. She couldn't be sure that he'd even looked at the baby, having positioned himself alongside one of the men so that he was only facing the other man and the older woman. Their voices rose over the sound of the baby crying and the younger girl was looking ready to cry herself.

Alice might teach the older pupils at the Kindercare Nursery School but she had had enough experience with the youngest children to know that this baby wasn't well. The crying was punctuated by coughing. He had a runny nose and kept rubbing at his eyes with a small fist. His mother, if that's who she was, jiggled the bundle she held with what looked like a desperate attempt to comfort him. When she looked away from the heated discussion happening between the others, she met Alice's gaze and there was a plea in that look that Alice could not ignore.

She moved closer, her arms outstretched in an invitation to give the mother a break from a stressful situation. Astonishment gave way to relief as Alice took the baby, unnoticed by anyone else. She walked away, back towards the conservatory, with the thought that she could at least give them a chance to talk without having to shout over the wailing, which was probably becoming a vicious cycle as the loud voices distressed the baby further.

'It's okay, sweetheart,' she told the baby. 'You're just miserable, aren't you? Look, it's cooler in here. Let's get that blanket off you and let you cool down, shall we?'

The tone was one she used with any unhappy child and her movements were calm and confident as she unwrapped the covering that would be far too hot for a baby who was probably running a temperature.

'You've got a cold, haven't you?' Spikes of damp, dark hair covered the baby's forehead and Alice smoothed them back. 'They're rotten things, colds, but you know what?'

The exaggeration of her question seemed to have finally caught the baby's attention. He hiccupped loudly and opened his eyes to look up at Alice.

Dark eyes that had that baby milkiness that made it hard to decide whether they were blue or brown.

'Colds go away.' Alice smiled. 'In a day or two you're going to feel ever so much better.'

She unsnapped the top fastenings of the sleep suit to allow a bit more fresh air to cool the baby's skin. Miraculously, he'd stopped crying now, so Alice rocked him gently and started singing softly. It was amazing how comforting it was to hold this tiny person. For the first time Alice felt as if she was welcome in this house.

Needed even.

The baby's eyes drifted shut and only moments later there she was sitting in the conservatory again but this time holding a sleeping infant.

A quiet one.

For a few seconds Alice watched the baby's face as it twitched and settled deeper into sleep. Who was he? Julien's child perhaps? Was that young woman his wife? Or his girlfriend perhaps, given the speed with which he'd suggested it wasn't necessary to be married to have a child. If either scenario was correct, her opinion of him was dropping rapidly. He should have been trying to help, not making things worse.

Not that she could hear the sound of any arguments any more.

In fact, it was so quiet she glanced up with the worrying thought that they might have all gone somewhere else and left her with the baby.

To her horror, she found that there were five people watching her from the doorway.

Julien looked angry again. His words were cold.

'What, exactly,' he bit out, 'do you think you are *doing*?'

Wasn't it obvious? Alice said nothing. The younger woman was standing with her head down as if she knew she had done something wrong. Julien said something and she started to move towards Alice but then the older woman halted her with a touch on her arm and spoke. Another discussion started amongst the group with rapid, urgent-sounding words.

At the end of their conversation the two women and the men turned and walked away. Alice knew her face would be a question mark as Julien turned back but he didn't meet her gaze.

'It seems that this is the first time the baby has slept in many hours. It would be to his benefit not to disturb him for a little while.'

'He's not well. I think he's running a temperature.'

'A doctor has been summoned.'

Julien stopped his pacing amongst the greenery with his back towards Alice.

Alice broke the silence. 'What's his name?'

'Jacques.'

'Is he your son?'

Julien turned very slowly and his expression was… shocked. Appalled even—as if the very idea of having a child was the worst fate he could imagine.

'Of course not.'

Alice frowned. 'Then why is he here? Whose baby is he?'

Julien closed his eyes. 'My sister's.'

It was Alice's turn to be shocked. That made him Julien's nephew. An orphan who had only just lost his father and was in desperate need of any remaining family. But Julien didn't seem to want anything to do with little Jacques. Because he was also André's son?

Oh… Another shock wave rocked Alice. If André *was* her father, then that made this baby her half-brother.

Part of her own family…

She loved children anyway and would do anything to help one who was in distress but her compassion towards this infant had just morphed into something much bigger. Something totally unexpected and potentially hugely significant.

She stared at the sleeping infant's face, the dark fan of eyelashes over cheeks that were too red. A patchy kind of red, like a rash of tiny spots. Even asleep, his tiny hands were in fists and he still felt too hot. The patch of skin she had exposed by unbuttoning the sleep suit was also red. Spotty, even.

The mind-blowing implications of a genetic relationship were pushed aside. Alice pulled open the suit a little further. Yes…the rash was everywhere. Faint but unmistakeable.

'Oh, no…'

'What?'

She looked up to find Julien had stepped closer. It was the first time she'd seen him look directly at the baby and it was a fleeting glance, almost as if he was afraid of what he might see. Perhaps he had good cause to feel afraid…

'I thought he only had a cold,' Alice said. 'But…but this looks like it might be measles.'

'How do you know?'

'I've seen a lot of pictures. There was an outbreak in Edinburgh last year and we had a lot of our children absent because of the quarantine necessary. One of them had an older sister at school who got very sick.'

'Quarantine?'

'Measles is a notifiable disease in most countries. It's highly contagious and it can be dangerous. The girl I was talking about got one of the worst complications—encephalitis—and she…she died.' Alice paused to draw in a breath. 'Even one case and anybody who's been within possible contact has to be quarantined for about two weeks. Unless they've been immunised or have had measles themselves.'

'Have you had measles?'

'Yes. When I was a child. Have you?'

'How am I supposed to know something like that?'

'From health records perhaps. An immunisation card that your mother would have kept.'

He shook his head. 'I don't know of anything like that.' He had taken a step back, as if that was enough to protect himself, and that bothered Alice. She cuddled Jacques a little closer.

'You've been in the same house,' she said, rubbing in the unwelcome information. 'The same room. Contacts can spread measles before they start feeling sick themselves. There was a case in the States last year where everybody was placed in isolation because they'd been sitting in a doctor's waiting room where there'd been a case of measles earlier that day.'

Julien shook his head again, more slowly this time. 'That is not going to happen here. It cannot. The situation is difficult enough as it is.' He took another step back. 'It's not as if I've touched the child.'

Alice felt a stirring of real anger. Why *not*? This baby had never known his mother and his father had died days ago. Had there only been hired help to offer comfort? He wasn't even looking at Jacques again now. As if he could make the problem disappear by ignoring it. And then he spoke again, on the end of a sigh.

'I have been forbidden to see Jacques,' he said. 'Ever since my sister died. But she made me his guardian and that is why I'm here today. To collect him.'

It still made no sense. 'But you still haven't *touched* him? Seen him even?'

'The Laurent family have another court order. His grandmother is arriving later today also with the intention of taking guardianship of Jacques. That is why the solicitors are here. It is a very delicate situation. My solicitor advised me not to make things worse and… for me…'

He *was* looking at Jacques now. With an expression that broke Alice's heart.

'For me, I knew it would only make things so much harder if I saw him and then…he was taken away.'

So he really *did* care.

Any anger Alice was feeling towards Julien evaporated. She had no idea why he'd been refused contact with his nephew after his sister had died but, whatever the reason, it had to be unfair. Cruel, in fact. If there were sides to be taken in this dispute, she had just put herself firmly on Julien's side.

The impression lasted only for a heartbeat. Julien's almost desperate expression vanished as his attention was caught by something he heard. He turned his head towards the windows.

'Someone is arriving,' he announced. 'Let's hope

it is the doctor, who can sort this out. Let's hope that you are wrong.'

Or was it the DNA expert who had been summoned to sort out the other problem that was pending? Was he hoping she was also wrong about who she thought her father was?

To Alice's relief, the doctor looked like a kindly man. Grey-haired and a little overweight, with deep smile lines around his eyes—a quintessential family GP. He came into the conservatory accompanied by the two women.

The older woman went to take the baby from her arms and he whimpered the moment as she touched him. Alice rocked him again. She didn't want to let him go.

'Shh,' she whispered. 'It's okay, little one. We all want to help you.'

He cried out more loudly when the woman touched him for the second time and the doctor cleared his throat and then spoke in excellent English.

'Perhaps it's better if the baby stays with you while I examine him, *mademoiselle*. He seems to like you.'

Alice nodded. Was it too far-fetched to imagine that the baby was aware of a connection between them? Or maybe it was because she knew how unwelcome *she* was in this house as far as Julien and probably any other members of the household were concerned. This baby had no idea of the trouble she was causing and now he was causing trouble himself, poor little thing, so there *was* a connection to be found quite apart from any yet-to-be discovered genetic one. They were both problems. He needed protection, this little one, and she was just the person to provide it.

She held the baby while the doctor took his temperature and listened to his heart and lungs. She helped him undress the baby down to his nappy so that he could see his skin. Jacques whimpered miserably at the disturbance.

'He needs paracetamol, doesn't he?' Alice asked the doctor. 'And sponging with lukewarm water?'

'Indeed. You are familiar with nursing children?'

'I'm a pre-school teacher. We often have to deal with sick children and I've done some training. I've never dealt with a case of measles, though. Is that what it is?'

'It would seem very likely. He has all the symptoms, including Koplik's spots inside his cheeks. Are you immune?'

'Yes. I had measles as a child.'

'Do you have documentation to prove your immunity?'

'No...' Alice closed her eyes on a sigh. The need for such documentation would never have occurred to her as she'd embarked on this impulsive journey.

'Are you aware of how serious this is?'

She nodded. 'I've kept up with news of outbreaks since we had a scare in Edinburgh.'

'Then you'll know that a case has to be reported and that there are very strict isolation and quarantine procedures that must be followed. I need to offer immunisation and prophylactic treatment to everybody who cannot prove their immunity.'

Julien had been standing within earshot. 'Quarantine is completely out of the question for me. I am due in Paris for filming in the next day or two. It's a Christmas show that's been planned for many months and cannot be postponed.'

The doctor sighed. 'I know who you are, Monsieur Dubois—of course I do. My wife is one of your biggest admirers but…' he raised his hands in a helpless gesture '…rules cannot be broken, I'm afraid. Not when it could put the health of so many others at risk.'

Alice blinked. The doctor looked to be in his sixties and his wife was one of Julien's biggest fans? If he wasn't in an edgy rock band, what sort of music did he produce? Romantic French ballads perhaps, with the accompaniment of an acoustic guitar? Was he doing a collection of Christmas carols for a seasonal show? No. Somehow it didn't fit—especially right now, with that angry body language.

With a sound of pure frustration Julien pulled a mobile phone from his pocket and walked away as he held it to his ear. The doctor turned to the two women and began speaking in French again.

Concerned expressions became horrified as he kept talking. The younger woman burst into tears. Voices rose as panicked questions were asked. Behind her, Alice could hear Julien also raising his voice on his telephone call. Everybody was sounding upset and all Alice could do was to sit there and hold the baby. It was the doctor who finally noticed that Alice was being completely left out of the conversation.

'Marthe—the housekeeper here—has grandchildren at home and she's worried,' he explained. 'Nicole—Jacques's nanny—has much younger siblings that she visited only yesterday. They are both very scared and want to take their quarantine periods in their own homes. This is possible, as their contacts will also have to be isolated. I will be visiting their households as soon as I leave here.'

Alice looked down at the baby she was still holding. And then she looked up at the doctor and nodded her head. 'I can look after Jacques.'

'I can see if there is a nurse available who is prepared to come into the house for the quarantine period but I doubt that any arrangements could be made until tomorrow. It would be very good if you could care for him until then.'

Julien snapped his phone shut. 'No,' he said. 'Mademoiselle McMillan cannot stay in this house. She will have to find a hotel.'

'That would be the very worst thing she could do. This is a very serious matter, Monsieur Dubois. I can take a blood sample from her but it may take a few days to prove immunity and even then she may be discouraged from leaving the house.'

'You don't understand. There's another matter that is pressing.'

'Oh?'

Julien turned his gaze to Marthe and Nicole, who were whispering together near the doorway, looking desperate to escape and get back to their own families. A few words from Julien and they both disappeared.

Julien continued speaking in French to the doctor, who blinked in astonishment as his gaze settled on Alice. She could feel the prickle of a blush starting. Any moment now and the colour of her cheeks would rival that of Jacques's.

There was sympathy in the doctor's smile when Julien had stopped speaking.

'You are having quite a day, my dear, are you not?'

'Mmm...' The kind tone almost undid her but Alice was not going to cry in front of Julien again.

'The reason you came here is not important right now. What matters is that you *are* here and we are lucky that you have experience with young children. Or maybe it's more than lucky.' There was compassion in this kindly doctor's eyes. This was a man who'd spent a lifetime caring for people who were sick and vulnerable. Who had a wealth of understanding of the intricacies of human relationships. 'It could be that you are this little one's big sister, yes?'

Alice nodded slowly, her throat suddenly too tight to swallow. The tears were harder to hold back now. She would have stepped up to care for this baby no matter who he was, but the idea that she had a member of her own family who desperately needed her help was overwhelming.

She had come to this place to try and find the only living relative she might have.

This might be a bizarre twist to her fairy-tale but it seemed like she might have actually achieved her goal. And it came with an entirely new world of hope.

And, for one night at least, she could hang onto that hope.

The doctor patted her shoulder. 'Tomorrow will be a new day. In the meantime, I will leave you all the medications you might need. Here, let's give him his first dose of paracetamol and then I will take the blood samples I need from you and Monsieur Dubois.'

It was Julien's turn first. And then it was Alice's turn and she couldn't free an arm while she was still holding Jacques.

She looked at Julien.

The doctor looked at Julien.

It was crystal clear what the logical solution was

but Julien seemed frozen. Alice could sense his fear. He'd never touched this baby. Was he afraid that he would drop him or was his reluctance due to something deeper? An even harder barrier to overcome?

She could hear the echo of those heart-breaking words.

'...it would only make things so much harder if I saw him and then...he was taken away.'

Touch was a far more powerful sense than sight, wasn't it?

But he cared. And, like herself, Jacques was his relative. Was he feeling the same kind of overwhelming connection that she was?

He had more right than she did to feel like that. More right than she did to know the joy of cuddling this small person.

Slowly, she walked towards Julien. She held his gaze, trying to offer both reassurance and encouragement. When she was so close that the baby was touching them both, his arms came up. So slowly. And then she felt the weight being transferred and Julien's gaze dragged itself away from hers and dropped to the face of his tiny nephew. He turned away then, as though he wanted to keep this moment private.

Mon Dieu...

How shocking was this?

The first time he had touched his sister's child.

He'd had no choice but to back away from any desire to see his nephew while André had still been alive. Even today, in the hours he'd known he was in the same house, it had been easier to comply with the legal advice to keep his distance. Maybe he'd known what he would feel in this moment. This emotional connection. The vulnerability of a tiny being that would suck him into offering not only his protection but his love. A breeding ground for feelings of guilt and worry and love that might eventually be thrown back at him as not having been good enough, but nothing could prevent him from providing any of it. He already loved this nephew despite trying to hide from that knowledge. He'd never intended being in this position again. He didn't know if he was strong enough.

But, once again, it seemed that he had no choice and he'd come here to do what his sister had asked him to do—to take guardianship of his child if anything happened to her. And now that he was holding him, how could he ever let him go? If he lost the legal battle with Madame Laurent, it was going to haunt him for the rest of his life.

The baby's eyes were wide open. Perhaps he was as shocked as Julien was at this unexpected physical contact. Could babies sense what people were thinking? Did he know he presented a threat out of all proportion to his size?

Maybe he did. Maybe he wanted to be back in the embrace of Alice's arms. How strange was it that she had been the only person able to comfort him in his misery? Did he sense the likely connection between them? A half-sister was a closer relation than an uncle.

Dark eyes stared up at him, making Julien wonder again how much was being understood. Too much, it seemed. The tiny face began to crumple. The small body squirmed like a fish that had been landed and needed to get back to the water to survive. And then that dreadful, unhappy wailing began again.

He paced back and forth as he waited for Alice to swap the ball of cotton wool she was pressing to her elbow for a plaster. He watched the doctor pack his things back into his bag and heard him say that he would deal with all the precautions needed for everybody who would be leaving the house to enter quarantine in their own homes—including the solicitors. He saw him leave and knew that in a very short space of time he would be alone in this house with Alice McMillan.

And still the baby was crying. More quietly, though. An exhausted sound of misery.

And there was a terrible smell. It was the odour that was really the final straw. Julien's sense of smell and taste were finely honed. They had to be to be as good at his work as he was and this…this was making him feel decidedly ill.

He needed help.

The doctor had been right. It really was very lucky that Alice was not to be allowed to leave the house.

Julien did his best to summon a smile as he moved closer. Preferably one that was apologetic. She hadn't bargained on any of this when she'd come to this house, had she? He'd not only been rude to her, he'd been violent in front of her and now she was as much of a prisoner here as he was, at least until the results of those blood tests came back. She had every right to be angry with him. To refuse to help even.

The smile came out a bit broken and he knew he was frowning fiercely so he had to say something.

'Alice…' The tone of her name came out as a plea

that made him wince inwardly but this was a moment when he simply had to swallow his pride. ‘I think that I…need your help. *Please…*’

CHAPTER FOUR

IT WAS SOMEWHAT startling to discover that she really liked this man.

Maybe it was the way he said her name, with an inflection and accent that made it sound so much more exotic. More like *Elise* than Alice.

Maybe it was the desperate edge to the word 'please'.

Or maybe it was the expression in his eyes. This was not someone who was used to feeling out of control of any situation and he was hating every second of this but he was too emotionally exhausted to fight any longer. Of course he was. He'd been dealing with who knew how much grief and hatred and mistrust, maybe even fear, all in the space of the short time Alice had been there?

It wasn't that she felt obliged to help. She would have gladly cared for Jacques without anybody even asking. He was her brother, for heaven's sake.

But now her heart went out to Julien in spite of everything. She wanted to help *him* just as much.

Silently she held out her arms and took the baby. She couldn't help screwing up her nose.

'Phew… He needs a clean nappy.'

Julien nodded. He was taking a step back, the

way he had when he'd heard about the possibility of measles.

'Where's the nursery?'

'I have no idea.'

Alice kicked herself inwardly as she remembered that he'd never been allowed to see his nephew so, of course, he hadn't visited this house. There was a lot more going on here than she had any knowledge of. Undercurrents that were powerful and dark.

Through the glass walls of the conservatory she could see cars leaving. The doctor's car with the housekeeper and the nanny. Then two other cars that presumably held the men in suits. The idea that the three of them were now alone in this vast house should have been alarming but this was simply another twist in the strangest day of her life and Alice felt curiously calm.

Thankfully, Jacques was settling in her arms, with just an occasional hiccup to let them know he still wasn't happy. She took a slow, inward breath as she shifted his weight to hold him more comfortably.

'Let's go and find it, then, shall we?' She offered a tentative smile with the suggestion. She might be the one who knew what to do but she didn't want to be left to do it entirely by herself. It felt as if she was doing something wrong, taking over the house of complete strangers, let alone taking over the care of their child. 'I expect it will be upstairs somewhere?'

Alice could sense Julien's hesitation so she held eye contact. Her message was silent but firm.

There's only the possibility that this baby is my brother. He's definitely your nephew. I know you think it might make things harder for you but you know what the right thing to do is...

His nod was so subtle she wouldn't have picked up on it if she hadn't been deliberately attempting a bit of telepathy.

And maybe there was a silent message coming back in her direction.

I know. I'll try...

Nothing was said aloud and, with Jacques now drowsy, it was in complete silence that they both left the huge room. The foyer was much bigger than Alice had noticed when she'd first come in. Had she not even looked up to see the gallery of the second floor that ran around three sides of this incredibly high, square space? No. She'd been focused on the fact that the man who'd greeted her was far too young to be her father. On his dark clothing and the ponytail that would have made her grandmother shake her head disapprovingly.

It didn't bother Alice. In fact, she quite liked it. There was no doubt that Julien was a very good-looking man and the smoothness with which his hair was combed back made it look as elegant as his clothing, but the short tail had a curl to it. Did he wear it loose when he was performing? Did it frame and soften his face and brush his shoulders in soft waves?

She'd quite like to see that…

The brief distraction of her train of thought vanished as she let her gaze roam the towering space. It was too much like a museum to feel like a home. The floor was marble and there were pillars supporting scalloped archways that were echoed on a smaller scale all around the second floor. A life-sized sculpture was in one of the archway recesses, illuminated by small floodlights. It wouldn't have surprised her to see a tour group appear in the wake of a guide, except that she could feel the emptiness of the vast house almost echoing around them.

Julien didn't say anything until they reached the top of the stairs. Behind them they now had a birds'-eye view of the impressive foyer. Directly in front of them was a massive painting in an ornate gilt frame that looked as if it was by some famous artist. A scene of overdressed people with heavy-looking wigs and miserable expressions and cherubic children with cheeks as pink as Jacques's. On either side they were faced with the wide balcony and its choice of countless doors.

'Incroyable...'

'Pardon?'

He swept his hand in a gesture that took in everything around them. 'I don't understand,' he said. 'This is not a home. It's a...a...'

'Museum?'

'*Exactement*. A gallery to display wealth. How could anyone want to *live* here?'

His sister had wanted to. Was that what he couldn't understand?

'I expect Jacques's grandmother is just as wealthy?'

'It's not the money,' Julien said. 'It's the way of thinking. The...first thoughts?'

'Priorities?'

'Oui.'

Walking briskly, Julien was throwing open doors. Alice caught glimpses of over-furnished bedrooms with four-poster beds and heavy velvet drapes. An overly masculine one and then a very feminine one beside it. Had his sister not shared a room with her husband?

Interior doors stood open to give a glimpse of bathrooms with marble floors and golden tapware. There was a huge sitting room with luxurious cream leather seating and a television screen big enough to make it a private movie theatre.

'I just thought of something.'

'What?'

'The grandmother. She won't be allowed to come to the house, will she?'

'No…' Julien turned his head as they walked further down the gallery that ran parallel with the front of the house.

'Or to take Jack away. Not for…for ages. A couple of weeks perhaps. Will that give you enough time?'

'I don't know if time will be enough.'

'It couldn't hurt, though, could it? Showing that you can care for him?'

Julien was silent. He had opened another door and here it was. A room that looked like an interior designer had used to fill a brief for the perfect nursery.

The ceiling was a pale blue with fluffy white clouds and a golden sun with a smiley face. The blue blended into the top of the walls but then gave way to green canopies of trees that sheltered every farm animal you could think of. The grass they stood on was sprinkled with a rainbow of flowers. Piles of toys that Jacques was far too young to appreciate—like model racing cars that were miniature Ferraris and Maseratis—filled the corners of the room but the important things were there as well. A comfortable chair for someone who needed to feed a baby. A cot with a colourful mobile hanging above it and a row of teddy bears at the foot end. On the wall behind the cot huge wooden letters in primary colours spelled out the name 'JACQUES'.

Each letter was intricately adorned with tiny pictures of animals and toys.

Alice went straight towards a change table that had shelves stuffed with disposable nappies and wipes and creams and gently put Jacques down on the soft, washable surface. She stroked his hair back and smiled as he opened his eyes.

'You were loved, little one, weren't you? What a beautiful room they made for you.'

Julien said nothing. He was still opening doors.

'There's a small kitchen,' he reported. 'And a bathroom. And a bedroom that must be for the nanny.'

'Are there bottles and things in the kitchen? Tins of milk formula?'

'There's a lot of things.' Julien's voice faded as he moved back. 'Yes…bottles and cleaning things. A microwave oven.' She could hear a cupboard door closing. 'Many tins. It looks like the baby section of a supermarket.'

A rubbish bin with a tightly fitting lid was available for the soiled nappy and wipes, and by the time Julien had finished exploring and arranging items that might be useful on the bench Alice had given Jacques a quick sponge bath and fastened a clean nappy in place. Now he was sucking on his fist and grizzling.

'I think he's hungry. I'll make up some formula.'

'Do you know how?'

'I've seen it done. I don't work with the very young children at our nursery school very often but our staff kitchen is shared by everyone. There'll be instructions on the tin if I forget.'

'In French,' Julien reminded her.

'Oh...of course. Could you translate for me?'

'Of course.'

'Could you hold him? I'll need two hands.'

'Why don't you hold him and tell me what to do? I'm used to being in kitchens. I can follow a recipe.' He took off his black jacket and rolled up the sleeves of his black shirt.

He was avoiding contact again but Alice let it go. Something had changed since they'd entered the nursery. The cold, empty feeling of this vast house had been left behind in favour of these bright colours and attention to detail—the evidence that this little person had been wanted and loved. Some of the weirdness and tension had gone.

Julien actually looked a lot happier in this small kitchen as he found the measuring spoons and distilled water and made up the bottle of formula. Clearly, he could have easily done it by himself by following the instructions but Alice found herself enjoying watching. He had clever hands and his movements were deft and confident. He only frowned when he took the bottle from the microwave.

'I haven't found a thermometer. How can we check the temperature?'

'Sprinkle a few drops on the inside of your wrist. It shouldn't feel hot.'

Jacques's whimpers became a demanding cry as he spotted the bottle and Alice hurried towards the chair near the cot. She could see Julien wiping down the bench in the kitchenette as she settled back to feed the baby and it struck her as odd that a rock god could be so domesticated.

Nice odd, though.

* * *

The bench was as spotless as possible and all the kitchen items were back in place. There was no reason for him to stay here any longer.

Except…he didn't want to leave.

As he turned away from the bench he could see Alice sitting in the chair, feeding the baby. The light in the room was fading rapidly and she'd turned on the nearby lamp.

His sister had never had the chance to sit like that—her head bent and one hand supporting the end of the bottle. Had she dreamed of what it might be like to have a baby staring back at you like that, with a tiny hand that also seemed to be holding the bottle?

Memories raced even further back as he leaned a shoulder against the kitchen door. Had Colette felt the kind of love for this infant before he was born that their mother had given the two of them once, so long ago? The kind of love that had made him protect his little sister against so many odds? Had those dreams and that love stirred these poignant feelings of loss and regret but also shone a light of hope into a dark space?

The hope that came from a fresh beginning. A chance to start again and make things right this time.

He could feel that hope himself and it was like nothing he'd ever felt. But, then, he'd never been so emotionally exhausted. So beset with problems that were coming at him from so many directions. This was a brief moment when he could actually avoid thinking about any of those problems.

Or maybe not. The buzz of the phone in his pocket came a split second before the ringtone.

He moved to the windows as he answered the call.

It was dark outside now but he could see the glow of light from the street beyond the gates. A car that was waiting for permission to enter.

He raised a hand in an apologetic gesture towards Alice as he headed for the door and she smiled her understanding as she nodded.

A dreamy kind of smile, he noticed only after he'd left the room. Did holding babies automatically have that kind of effect on women? Maybe it had something to do with the soft glow of light bathing the chair and making Alice's hair glow like the last embers of a fire. Or how dark her eyes were in that pale face. Or simply how tender that smile had been.

Whatever it was, it had changed Julien's perspective. She didn't need to enhance or bleach her hair colour or have some stylish cut. She had no need of the layers of make-up he thought any attractive woman relied on. Alice McMillan wasn't simply pretty, as he'd first thought.

She was stunning.

The realisation came on top of that strange feeling he'd got watching her with the baby. It was still sucking him back in time as he hurried downstairs. Sending him over ground so old it felt new again.

How much of all this was his own fault?

If he only spent more time with Colette, she wouldn't have been able to hang out with her friends so much, using movies and trashy magazines to sculpt her view of a perfect life where only money was needed to put the world right and give her everything she could possibly want. He'd fed that belief himself, in fact, by working so hard and being so careful of every euro he earned.

If he'd been more of a father figure, perhaps she

wouldn't have fallen for a man who'd been thirty years older than her.

The regret was so intense it was painful but somehow, in the back of his mind, he could still sense that smile Alice had given him. Could still feel the softness of that moment of hope.

Crazy, considering everything that had happened today. Was it any wonder his thoughts were so scrambled? He was heading out to the gates to meet the DNA expert—a bizarre twist to this dreadful day that he could never have imagined. The quarantine on top of that was like a bad joke.

But Julien wasn't laughing.

What was that saying? You had to laugh or you would cry?

He couldn't do that either.

He seemed to have forgotten how.

Minutes ticked by in the quiet nursery.

Jacques had finished his bottle of milk and Alice lifted him to her shoulder and began to rub his back. He nestled against her and she could feel his breath on her neck. The misery of his day had caught up with him and now that he was clean and fed, she could feel the heaviness of an infant slipping into deep slumber.

His body didn't feel unnaturally hot now but that was probably because of the paracetamol the doctor had administered. He would need some more during the night. His warmth was comforting and Alice loved the tiny snuffling sounds he was making. She had probably been sitting here cuddling him for too long, though. He needed his own bed and a good sleep to help him on his journey to recovery.

He made no protest as Alice laid him gently into his cot. She pulled the blanket back and tucked him in with only a sheet for cover. She would check again soon to make sure he was neither too warm nor cold. There was a lump down the side of the cot and when she pulled it out, Alice found it was an old toy. A faded rabbit that looked as if it had been knitted out of brown fabric.

A very different toy from all the bright new offerings in the room so it had to be special in some way. She tucked it in beside Jacques, with just the head and ears above the sheet.

She needed to find somewhere to sleep herself before too long—in the nanny's room perhaps. Not that sleep would come easily if she didn't get something to eat. Lunch seemed a very long time ago now and her stomach was rumbling.

And where was Julien? It had to be more than half an hour ago that he'd received that phone call and vanished but she couldn't go looking for him. The house was far too big to hear a baby crying. She certainly couldn't hear any sounds coming from downstairs. It was too quiet, in fact. Reaching up, Alice wound the handle on the mobile above the cot. The carousel of bright toys began turning slowly to the soft notes of 'Brahms's Lullaby'.

It was then that she noticed the baby monitor handset on the shelf beside the cot, tucked in between a soft toy unicorn and a dragon. She turned it on and suddenly an image of Jacques appeared on the screen above a speaker grill. Startled, Alice looked around and finally spotted the camera mounted on the wall at the end of the cot.

She'd heard parents discussing baby cams but had

never seen one in action. This was perfect. She could go in search of something to eat and not only hear if Jacques woke up, she'd be able to see him. A quick visit to the nursery bathroom to freshen up and Alice was ready. Eager even.

It was only because she was alone in a strange house, she told herself. Any adult company would do. It wasn't that she wanted to see Julien again.

So why did her heart do a funny double beat thing when she tiptoed out onto the gallery and saw the tall, dark figure coming towards *her*?

Julien was carrying something.

'I have the testing kit,' he told her. 'We couldn't allow the DNA expert to come into the house but he's given me very detailed instructions on how to take the test. He's waiting outside the gate to collect it when we finish. I've already found the items that might be sufficient from… André.'

The hesitation was tiny but spoke volumes. How much did you have to hate a person to make it difficult to even say his name?

And the reminder of why she had come here in the first place had wiped out that warm glow that cuddling a sleepy baby had given Alice. It had certainly eliminated any inexplicable excitement that seeing Julien had provoked. This was business. A necessary step that might give him permission to send her packing. How could she have forgotten how unwelcome her arrival had been? That she might only have a single night to clasp that hope of family to her heart?

'Fine.' Her voice was tight. 'Tell me what to do.'

'No. I have to do it. I'm the one who has been briefed.'

Julien's tone was brisk. 'Come with me. We need a place with good light.'

He took her to one of the bedrooms that they had opened a door on during their first exploration of this second floor. The feminine one. They went through the bedroom into the en suite bathroom, which was clinically bright once all the lights had been snapped on.

Alice put the monitor handset on the marble top of the vanity unit.

'What's that?'

'A monitor. So I can hear when Jack wakes up. See?' Alice touched the screen and the image of Jacques's face appeared. Like all babies, he looked like an angel with that cupid's bow of a mouth relaxed in sleep. The sweet sound of the lullaby still playing made the picture all the more adorable.

'Jacques.' Julien corrected her pronunciation, emphasising the soft 'J' as he busied himself pulling items from the bag he was carrying.

'We do two tests. One is a back-up in case there isn't enough DNA in the first sample.' He placed two small, plastic vials on the vanity top. Then he took a long packet and peeled open the end to reveal a stick that he took hold of carefully.

'I must not touch the swab or I might contaminate it.' He stepped closer to Alice. 'Open your mouth, please.'

Suddenly, this was excruciatingly embarrassing. She had a strange, *extremely* good-looking man standing close enough to kiss her and he'd asked her to open her mouth. Alice had to close her eyes as she complied. She could feel the prickle of heat rising rapidly from in front of her neck to her face. Please, let this be over quickly, she begged silently.

'I have to scrape the inside of your cheek for forty-five to sixty seconds,' Julien told her. 'The pressure will be firm. I have to collect cheek cells, not your saliva.'

Oh… God… How long could sixty seconds feel like?

For ever, that was how long. The swab on the end of the stick was like a toothbrush made of firm cotton balls. She could feel it moving up and down on the inside of her cheek. She could feel Julien's hand so close to her face she was sure that her lips were registering the warmth of his skin.

It was doing something very odd to parts of her body that had nothing to do with this test. Quite apart from the blush, her heart was hammering and there were butterflies dancing deep down in her belly.

'Bien…' The swab was finally removed from her mouth and then Julien concentrated on opening the plastic vial and inserting the swab into the liquid it contained. Then he pressed a spike on the end of the stick that released the swab and allowed him to screw back the lid of the vial. She watched his face in the mirror as he focused on his task. His hair wasn't as smooth as it had been. A thin tress had escaped the ponytail and flopped forward.

The butterflies, which had almost stopped dancing when the procedure had finished, started beating a new tattoo as Alice failed to head off a totally ridiculous desire to reach out and smooth that wayward tress back into place.

It was unfortunate that Julien chose that moment to raise his gaze and caught her looking at him in the mirror. For a heartbeat, time stopped as they stared at each other in the mirror. The bright lighting made it so easy to see the way his eyes darkened. Had he guessed that

Alice was thinking about touching him? Had the urge suddenly become contagious?

Hurriedly, she dropped her gaze and Julien cleared his throat at exactly the same moment.

'One more,' he said. 'And then we're done.'

This time, Alice stood like a statue while her other cheek was scraped and she didn't risk any glance towards the mirror as he dealt with the swab and then sealed both vials into a plastic specimen bag.

There was a moment's silence when he'd finished and Alice almost wished to hear a baby's cry from the monitor, which would give her an excuse to flee. Was Julien looking into the mirror again? Looking at *her* as she avoided looking at *him*?

It was still heavy in the air—that moment when they hadn't been able to look away from each other's reflections. Something had happened. Some nameless, unexpected, *unwanted*...thing.

'You need to sign this consent form. Here—I have a pen.'

He handed her the pen and as he did so his hand brushed hers.

No more than a whisper of a touch but it felt like her skin had been burned.

Alice's signature had never been quite this shaky before. She folded the paper and handed it back and this time she looked up at Julien.

There was no getting away from it. Now that it had happened, this thing couldn't be taken back. Even if she didn't look, she had been sure it was still there.

And looking had just confirmed it.

CHAPTER FIVE

WHAT, IN GOD'S NAME, had just happened there?

The last few days—ever since he'd heard about André's accident—had made Julien feel as if his world was tipping on its axis, and the events of today had already made the angle a lot steeper. At the precise moment he'd met Alice's gaze in the mirror for the second time, it had felt like he'd just fallen off the edge of it.

Those *eyes*...

Who was this woman? This flame-haired Scottish pixie who'd not only crossed his path so unexpectedly, she was now an integral part of his life being brought to a crashing halt.

And...it felt...*good*?

Who knew where that moment could have gone if her stomach hadn't suddenly rumbled too loudly to be ignored—a sound that made Alice blush scarlet.

'Oh...pardon *me*.'

The way the colour flooded her face was fascinating but Julien wasn't going to make things any more weird by staring. And how was it that he'd only just noticed how intimate a space a bathroom was?

'You're hungry.' He turned on his heel as he made the redundant announcement. 'Come... I will get these delivered to the gate and then we'll find out what the kitchen has to offer.'

He kept a step or two ahead of Alice as he led the way downstairs but he was acutely aware that she was following. Was she still blushing? He'd never met a woman who blushed. Or whose stomach rumbled like a train, for that matter. Julien's lips twitched at the thought of either of those occurrences happening with any of the sophisticated, perfectly groomed women who'd always been available and more than willing to share his companionship and his bed.

This foreign pixie was certainly very different.

Nice different. It made him think of times with Colette before she'd learned to be sophisticated.

Not that it was unusual to remember things from the past—especially in the last few months when the grief had had to be endured, but this was the first time it could bring even an inward smile. When something poignant but sweet was stronger than any associated pain.

He sent the samples out with the security guard and remembered to issue instructions that no one else was to come through the gates, no matter how certain they were about their rights. Madame Laurent could be referred to his solicitor for more information. Or her own, for that matter. Both those men were now probably confined to their own homes and less than happy about it but what could they do?

What could any of them do about it?

At least he could do the thing that was guaranteed to relieve stress.

He could cook.

'Oh, my goodness…' Alice stopped in the doorway to the kitchen. 'This looks like a commercial kitchen.

You could cook enough to feed an army in here. Or run a restaurant.'

And it was clean, Julien noted with satisfaction, eyeing the expanse of stainless-steel benches.

'There's no fridge!' Alice exclaimed. 'How strange…'

'There'll be a cold room, I expect. And a pantry. You're right…this has been set up as a commercial kitchen. Look…' Julien walked past the hobs and ovens and through an arched doorway into a scullery. Sure enough, there was a pantry and if he'd thought the cupboard in the nursery had looked like a section of a supermarket, it was nothing on what was stocked in here. The cold room was just as well stocked.

'Oh…' Alice's eyes were round with surprise. 'Look at all that *cheese*…' She grinned at Julien. 'I *love* cheese…'

It was the first time he'd seen her really smile and he got that strange falling sensation all over again. He found himself smiling back because he couldn't help it.

'Take some out,' he told her. 'See if you can find some bread and olives. There'll be a wine cellar somewhere but we'll make do with what's cold. Here…take this one. I'll see what I can find to cook with.'

'But it's champagne… *French* champagne.'

Julien's lips twitched again. 'I wasn't aware there was any other kind.'

'But…'

'Mmm?' Julien was gathering some ingredients. Minced beef and garlic and chilli. Greens and parmesan cheese. He needed something quick and easy. Pasta and salad should be perfect. Reaching for a bottle of balsamic vinegar, he became aware of the silence behind him. He turned to find Alice looking bewildered. He raised his eyebrows.

'Champagne is for celebrating something,' she said quietly.

Julien stopped thinking about food. 'Maybe we can find something to celebrate, then.'

Her eyes widened. 'Like what?'

Oh, no… How insensitive was it to suggest that she should be celebrating something when she'd just found out that her probable father was deceased? He had to think fast as he moved past her to drop his armload on a bench.

'You may have discovered a brother,' he suggested. 'And…and have you ever been to France before?'

'No…never…'

'*Donc*… There you go. That is definitely worth celebrating.'

'And what about you? What have you got to celebrate?'

'Ah…' Julien stared down at his ingredients without seeing them. Nothing. He was revisiting the grief from losing his sister. He had a major problem in what to do about the show that filming was due to start on within days. He probably had to face a court case over custody of his nephew that was highly likely to get very nasty.

No. Nothing to celebrate there.

He looked up, ready to admit defeat and agree that champagne might not be the most appropriate thing to drink.

And then he got caught by those eyes again.

What was it that he could see?

Hope?

Optimism?

A belief in fairy-tales, even?

Something shifted in his chest and he found himself saying something he hadn't thought of until now.

'I got to hold my sister's baby for the first time today.' The words came out as little more than a whisper and he was embarrassed that he was showing so much emotion in front of a stranger. He cleared his throat. 'And I have a reprieve from having to deal with Madame Laurent.' He offered a crooked smile. 'That is absolutely worth celebrating, *n'est-ce pas*?'

She'd made him smile.

Sort of. One of those oddly endearing lopsided ones like he'd given her when he had asked for her help with Jacques, but it felt like a victory because there was something very sombre about Julien's face—especially his eyes—and she got the impression that he didn't smile, let alone laugh, very often.

She sat at the big central table in this enormous kitchen, with the baby monitor in one hand and a glass of champagne in the other, and watched Julien cook.

The champagne was astonishingly delicious and Julien...well, he was just as astonishing. The way he chopped vegetables with a speed that made her blink and then scooped them up to drop them into a food processor as if it was the easiest thing in the world to do without making a mess. He got two frying pans going on gas flames on the hobs and in one of them he was adding things to minced beef like mustard and balsamic vinegar and a huge handful of herbs that had also been chopped with lightning efficiency. The smell was starting to make Alice feel very, very hungry and the champagne on her empty stomach was making her head spin a little. She watched as Julien tossed the contents of the pan, which mixed the contents more efficiently than a wooden spoon, which would have been her choice of implement.

'You really know your way around a kitchen, don't you?'

A snort that could have been laughter came from Julien. 'I should hope so. I've been working in them for twenty years now.'

'Twenty years? You don't look old enough to have been working that long.'

'I'm thirty-five.'

'You started working when you were fifteen? After school?'

'No.' Julien carelessly sprinkled a handful of sea salt flakes into a pot of boiling water and then tipped a packet of pasta in. 'I had to drop out of school.'

'Why?' Alice wouldn't normally ask such personal questions of someone she had only just met but the champagne was making her reckless.

'My mother died. I had to get my sister away from our stepfather and I had to support her. The only job I could get was washing dishes in a restaurant. Sometimes I was given other jobs to help the chefs and...and I was good at it.' He lifted his glass in a toast. 'And so I learned to cook.'

He'd taken off his tie and unbuttoned the top of his shirt before he'd started work in the kitchen and his sleeves were pushed up as far as they could go. The escaping tress of his hair had been joined by a couple more and his cheeks were pink from the heat of the stove. He looked dishevelled. And...as delicious as the smell of whatever he was cooking. Alice could only begin to imagine how many fans he must have.

'And you're a musician as well…'

'*Pardon? Je ne comprends pas…*'

The puzzlement on his face made the meaning of his words clear.

'The show you were talking about? The film crews? I thought…you must be a singer. In a band.'

He was looking at her as if she'd lost her mind. 'It's a show for television. Food television.'

Alice's jaw dropped. 'Food television? You're a… *chef*?' Images of a rock star were being blown apart. No wonder the doctor's wife was such a fan. Maybe the media waiting outside the gates had nothing to do with how famous her father had been.

'*Exactement*. The Christmas show I was talking about? It is for a morning television show on Christmas Eve. I am demonstrating a traditional English Christmas dinner to compare with another chef who is doing the French one.' Julien drained his glass of champagne and came over to the table to refill both their glasses. 'The actual cooking will be pre-recorded but I will be a guest on the live show to talk about it on the day. If my test doesn't confirm my immunity so that I can leave this house, it will be a mess that will be very difficult to deal with. A lot of people will be extremely annoyed.'

As if in sympathy with the statement, a whimper came through the monitor. It was a startling reminder of the responsibility they both had to Jacques and for a long moment they both stared at the screen of the handset but, with another tired-sounding cry, the baby settled back into sleep.

Julien sank into the chair opposite Alice, his gaze

still focused on the screen, his brow furrowed. 'What is that?'

'What?'

'In the bed with him? That…'

'Oh…it's a toy. A rabbit. I thought it must be special because it looks very old.'

The way Julien's throat moved suggested that he was having trouble swallowing.

'It's *le lapin brun…* It was Colette's special toy when she was tiny. I…didn't know she had kept it.' His voice cracked. 'She must have put it in the nursery before he was born because… I don't think she ever saw him after he was born…'

Tears sprang to Alice's eyes. 'That's so sad…' Then she shook her head slowly, in disbelief. 'Such a tragedy… Was…was she very sick?'

'*Non*. She had come to see me only the week before. The first time I had seen her in over a year and she had never looked so well. She was so excited about the baby. It made her want to reconnect with her own family, she said. It made her remember…'

He had closed his eyes and that gave Alice permission to let her gaze linger on his face as he seemingly became lost in his own thoughts.

Dear Lord, even when you couldn't see those astonishing eyes, he was a beautiful man with those strong features and such a sensitive-looking mouth. Eyelashes that caught your attention because they were a little longer than you'd expect on a man—like his hair.

This was no time to ask what had caused such a rift between these siblings. Whatever it had been, it sounded like they'd been ready to forgive and forget. 'What did she remember?' Alice asked softly to break the silence.

'That her first memories were of how I'd looked after her. How important I'd been in her life for ever. That she didn't want to lose that and that, maybe, this baby could help bring us back together. And I thought she was right. She texted me when she went into the hospital and so I went to visit and...and I saw her die...'

'Oh, my God... *No*...' It was instinctive to reach out to touch him. To cover his hand with her own.

His eyes were open again and the shock of his words cut even deeper as she saw unshed tears making them glisten.

'They said it was an *embolie*. I don't know the word for it in English...'

'An embolism?'

'*Probablement*.' Julien shook off the translation as unimportant. 'Something to do with the water around the baby and it gave her an attack of the heart and... *Il ne pouvait rien faire*... They tried. I *saw* how hard they try...'

That his English was fractured only made this more heart-breaking. Alice could feel Julien's distress so deeply that, unlike him, she couldn't stop tears escaping, but he didn't need her reaction to make the memories worse. He needed something very different.

Comfort.

With a huge effort Alice banished her tears and steadied her voice. She squeezed Julien's hand as she spoke.

'I love it that Jacques has the rabbit,' she said softly, paying careful attention to pronouncing the name correctly. 'One day you'll be able to tell him how special it is. And how much his mother must have loved him to give it to him.'

The glance she received was almost bewildered. And then Julien gave his head a tiny shake as if he was sending those memories back where they belonged. In the past. He stood up, sliding his hand from beneath Alice's with no acknowledgment that she had touched him, and her fingers curled as she pulled her hand back.

She could only see his back now.

'Let's eat. My penne ragout will be ready.'

He was too tired to feel particularly hungry.

Or perhaps his brain was too occupied with other things to notice he was only picking at his food.

The words Alice had spoken were turning slowly, a new ingredient that was going to simmer in his head, along with everything else that had happened today, like a kind of emotional ragout.

Memories associated with the brown rabbit were strong enough to throw the mix off balance. The sight of it shocking enough to make him talk to someone about that terrible day for the first time.

Maybe it was easier to be open with a stranger?

Except that it hadn't felt like he'd been with a stranger. Alice was different. She was real. And she cared. That human touch of comfort had almost left a brand on his skin that he could still feel.

He hadn't seen that toy for so many years he had forgotten how important *le lapin brun* had been. Colette would not go to sleep without it. And if he'd taken her to hide—under a bed perhaps—to escape one of their stepfather's drunken rages, then brown bunny made it so much more bearable. Little Colette would cuddle the toy. And he would cuddle Colette.

And now Jacques was sleeping with it and Alice

had found something good about that. Something to celebrate…

But that was confusing the flavour he'd been so sure was the right one for whatever recipe his head and heart were inventing—the cocktail of grief and resentment and even hatred. He could imagine Colette putting the toy into the bed she had prepared for her baby and gifting him the thing that had brought her such comfort, but for him to have it suggested that André had known of the toy's significance and he'd wanted his son to have something precious that had belonged to his mother…

Because he'd cared?

Because he'd loved Colette that much?

If that was true, then he himself had been wrong in trying to stop the marriage by persuading Colette what a terrible mistake she was making. It would make those strained months of him not being welcome in his sister's home—after the wedding he'd refused to attend—a stupid, wasted opportunity. And the sworn hatred between the two men wouldn't have overridden almost everything else at Colette's funeral.

He knew he had failed her but maybe it was in a different way than he'd thought.

'This is amazing…' Alice's words broke the increasingly negative spiral of his thoughts. 'It's the best pasta I have ever eaten. It's…it's *magnifique…*'

Her passable attempt at a French word made Julien tilt his head in acknowledgement of both her effort and the compliment. It made him look up and catch her gaze and it seemed like every time that happened it became more familiar and the hit of whatever it was that the eye contact gave him became more powerful.

He couldn't identify what it was but there was no

getting away from the knowledge that it warmed something deep inside his chest. It was something as real as the comforting touch she had given him. Maybe he hadn't known how precious little of anything that real there was in his life.

'*Merci beaucoup.* I am delighted that you like it.'

Suddenly Julien felt hungry himself. Really hungry. He loaded up forkful of the pasta coated in the spicy sauce and could taste it properly now. Yes, that balsamic vinegar had added a perfect, balancing note to the sweetness of the tomatoes and the bite of chilli.

A small thing in the grand scheme of things but it was often the small things that could be unexpectedly important, wasn't it?

Like an old, battered toy…

By the time Alice had finished eating her delicious meal it was obvious that she could barely keep her eyes open.

'Dessert?' Julien offered. 'Some coffee, perhaps?'

'No, thank you. I… I should go and check on Jacques and then I think I need some sleep myself. I thought I would use the nanny's bed, if that's all right? That way I'll be close when he wakes. He may need a night feed and I'm sure he'll need some more paracetamol before morning.'

Morning. The start of a new day and who knew what new problems might present themselves? Julien rubbed his temples. He had more than enough to deal with now. Too much. Top of that list would be to call a teleconference and try to organise a way to manage the fallout if he couldn't film the Christmas show. He had tried to contact the head of his production team as soon as the doctor had dropped the quarantine bombshell but he hadn't got through. And then he'd been completely distracted, hadn't he—at first by the appalling thought of Alice having to stay in the house and then by the emotional roller-coaster that had started the moment he'd held his sister's child in his arms for the first time ever.

It was all too much. He needed some time out and maybe it wasn't too late to try and make the first of those calls tonight. He pulled his phone from his pocket and was already scrolling his contacts list as he spoke.

'I'll use one of the rooms near the nursery,' he told Alice. 'You can call if you need help with anything.'

'Don't worry… I'm sure I can cope.' There was a moment's silence and he knew Alice was looking at him, waiting for him to look up, but he resisted the urge. Enough was enough. If that peculiar sensation he got when he met her eyes kept happening, he might have to try and identify it so that he would know how to deal with it. And he had the funny feeling that giving it a name might only open a whole new can of worms.

He knew she had gone by more than the sound of her boots on the flagged floor of the kitchen.

Her departure also left the room feeling disturbingly empty.

CHAPTER SIX

THE MESSAGE HAD been crystal clear.

It felt like they'd been so close in those moments when Alice had been holding Julien's hand as he'd told her about the tragedy of his sister's death but he hadn't even looked at her when she'd excused herself to check on Jacques, and whatever barrier he'd put up around himself, having pushed her away, was still firmly in place the next morning.

He barely came near the nursery for the whole morning, other than to bring her a tray of coffee and some amazingly melt-in-the-mouth croissants, still warm from the oven, at seven a.m. At nine a.m., with a phone in his hand, he came briefly to the door to ask if Jacques was any worse and if she needed the doctor to visit today. He vanished as soon as she shook her head.

Being abandoned upstairs with an unwell baby should have felt lonely. Scary even, but the time was passing quickly and, for such a huge house with only one other adult in it, it felt surprisingly busy.

Phones were ringing at frequent intervals and delivery vans began arriving from mid-morning. From the nursery windows Alice could see them coming up the driveway, and if she was near the door to this suite of rooms she could hear Julien talking downstairs or faint clattering sounds from the direction of the kitchens.

Would he deliver another tray for her lunch? And then dinner after a whole afternoon alone with Jacques? By one p.m. Alice felt like she'd been sent to Coventry—as punishment perhaps for engaging in a conversation that had become too personal. She didn't even try and ignore her rebellious streak this time. As soon as Jacques was down for a sleep after a lunchtime feed, she took the baby cam monitor and marched downstairs.

Her determined stride faltered at the bottom of the stairs. There were boxes littering the foyer. A suitcase. And…

'Good *grief…*'

Julien appeared from the kitchen, wiping his hands on a dish towel.

'*C'est horrible, n'est pas*?'

'Horrible.' Alice tried to repeat the word. 'It's a…a *monster.*'

A monster bright blue teddy bear that was in the corner beside the door.

'It is a gift from Madame Laurent. It has a tag that says, "For my beloved grandson".'

Alice let out an incredulous huff. 'It's five times the size of her grandson. It would probably terrify him.'

'That is why I have left it down here.'

'And the suitcase?'

'Some clothing and other things I needed. I can arrange for some to be brought for you?'

'I'll manage. I have a spare shirt and…' a blush threatened as she stopped herself mentioning underwear '…things. I'm fine. I just came down for…' *Some company.* 'For something to eat.'

'Come.' Julien's hand wave encompassed the boxes. 'I have had many things delivered, including some work that needed extra food.'

Alice followed him into the kitchen. There were pots simmering on the stove and the table was covered with sheets of paper, most of which had glossy photographs along with the text.

'Is that a recipe book?'

'They are the—how do you say it—proofing pages?' Julien began scooping them into a heap. 'There is a deadline and I want to check some of the recipes by cooking them again. What would you like for your lunch? A mushroom risotto perhaps? Or chicken Dijon?'

Alice chose the risotto. He presented it to her on a tray but Alice didn't want to leave the room, even if he was busy working. She sat at the table and watched him. She hadn't intended interrupting him any further but she only took a few mouthfuls before her good intentions evaporated.

'How do I say "I love it" in French?'

The smile was the kind of lopsided one he'd given her more than once now. Maybe that was the only way Julien smiled. It meant something, though, because he stopped what he was doing and came to sit opposite her.

'Je l'aime.'

Alice repeated the phrase. 'And if I want to say "I *don't* like it"?'

'Je ne l'aime pas.' Julien frowned. 'You *don't* like the risotto?'

She grinned. 'No. *Je l'aime*. A lot.'

'Beaucoup.' He listened to her repetition. 'You have a good accent,' he told her.

The praise was unexpected and Alice felt suddenly

shy. 'I think I'd like to learn French,' she admitted. 'I was never allowed to take it at school and I haven't really listened to it properly before but…it's beautiful. Like music.'

'It is a beautiful language.' Julien gave her a curious look. 'Why were you not allowed to learn at school?'

Alice had to look away. 'Because of who my father was, I imagine. My mother never talked about it but my grandmother hated anything French.'

Julien let her eat in silence for a minute. 'Perhaps your mother hated André Laurent, too, after the way he treated her.'

'I don't think so. If she had, she might have found someone else she could fall in love with and she never did. I don't think she even tried.'

'Perhaps your village was too small.'

'It was small but Mum trained to be a nurse after I was born and she met a lot of people through her work.'

'And shc had you to carc for.'

'Yes.' Alice glanced at the monitor as she ate another mouthful of the delicious risotto. 'I can imagine loving my child so much that I would be wary of anything that might change my life.' Then she laid down her fork and sighed 'Or maybe her heart had just been broken too badly. I know a lot of people think it's nonsense but—for some—I think there really is only "the one".'

Julien was giving her another one of those odd, unreadable looks. 'And you? Are you one of the "some"?'

Again, Alice had to look away. How silly was it that her heart had started thumping so loudly she was afraid he might hear it? But she nodded slowly.

'Yes. I think I'm one of those people.'

Julien's chair scraped as he pushed it back abruptly. 'I hope you find this "one", then, Alice.'

She took her plate over to the sink beside which he was working again. 'Sometimes that's not enough,' she told him. 'He will have to find me, too.'

It was the sound of the baby crying early the next morning that woke Julien.

It was still crying as he pulled on his jeans. A sharp cry that was suddenly alarming.

Still too sleepy to think clearly, he threw open his door and ran to the nursery. Jacques was in his cot. Alice was nowhere to be seen.

'Alice?'

There was no answer. The kitchenette was deserted and there was no sound of running water from the bathroom.

The noise level was still increasing. Julien walked to the cot and stood looking down at his nephew. He had no idea what he should do. Surely Alice would come through the door and rescue him?

Jacques was sobbing. His little fists were waving in the air and his face was bright red.

'Shh…' Julien said. *'Alice vient bientôt. Tout est okay...'*

Except it wasn't okay. Jacques let out a piercing shriek and he couldn't stand there and do nothing. Reaching into the cot, he picked up the baby and then held it against his chest. A still-bare chest, he realised belatedly that now had a warm little head resting on it as he rocked the baby and tried to make soothing noises into the miniature ear.

Miraculously, it seemed to be working. The shrieking lessened to a wail and then to a series of hiccupping sobs. And then Jacques started rubbing his nose on Julien's chest and the movement got slower and slower and then stopped. Julien noticed two things. That Jacques seemed to have gone back to sleep and that one tiny fist was locked around his thumb.

No. Make that three things. He had picked up this distressed baby and had been able to comfort him. He felt proud of himself. And then he felt…something much deeper. This tiny person was trusting him enough to fall asleep in his arms. To protect him from any evil that might be present in the unknown world around them. Such absolute trust from a being so completely vulnerable was doing something peculiar to his heart because it felt so full it could burst.

He should go and find Alice and hand over the care of the baby because this was precisely what he had been afraid of. Feeling the kind of bond that would inevitably lead to heartache, no matter how this situation got resolved.

He had known it would only make it harder to hold his sister's baby and Alice couldn't be far away so he could escape.

He just didn't want to move quite yet.

Alice had been running up the stairs as she'd heard that alarming shriek over the monitor.

She'd gone down to the kitchen to find something for her breakfast because Julien wasn't awake yet and she'd stupidly left the monitor there to go and find a downstairs bathroom. How long had he been crying like that?

She wasn't even halfway up the stairs when the increased force of the baby's cries made her check the screen of her monitor and that was when she saw that Jacques wasn't alone.

Julien was standing beside the cot. Half-dressed. Good grief, he hadn't even fastened the button of his jeans and she could see the white fabric of his underwear exposed. As for the rest of him…oh, my… A torso and arms with sculpted muscle that begged to be traced with gentle hands. A face that was so twisted with indecision that a sympathetic smile tugged at Alice's lips and she wanted to hug even more than stroke this man.

She should keep going and rescue him because he clearly had no idea what to do about Jacques but Alice's steps involuntarily came to a halt. She was holding her breath when she saw Julien reach into the cot and then she had to swallow past a huge lump in her throat as she saw him cradle the baby against his bare chest and start rocking him.

It was an image that would have melted any woman's heart but it was bigger than that for Alice because it got added to her memory of whatever had happened between them that had been reflected in the bathroom mirror and had since been banished.

He was an extraordinary man, wasn't he?

Completely out of her league, of course. A television star, for heaven's sake. Probably extremely wealthy and able to take his pick of a vast array of eager women.

What would she have to offer that could possibly interest someone like Julien Dubois?

Obviously nothing, which was why he had backed off so quickly. Alice started walking again. She took a deep breath and tried to shove her thoughts somewhere that wouldn't show on her face by the time she got to the nursery. If there had been a 'thing' and it hadn't been simply her imagination, then Julien had banished it and she needed to follow suit unless she wanted to totally humiliate herself.

The 'thing'—along with that heart-stealing sight of him holding Jacques—had to be jammed into a mental jar like the ones that Julien brought out from the pantry when he was cooking. Big, square glass jars with metal lids that held things like caster sugar or salt. The thing needed to be trapped and the lid tightly screwed into place. The jar couldn't be opened and the thing couldn't be allowed to grow because that might shatter the glass and possibly be as catastrophic as the way the glass on her father's portrait had shattered when Julien had hurled the paperweight at it.

So Alice wasn't even going to *think* about the muscles on that bare chest and arms. Or those unfastened jeans…

She would keep her gaze firmly on the baby when she entered the room. She would keep out of Julien's way as much as possible and when they were together she would stick to something completely safe—like the basic French lessons he had started giving her over dinner last night.

It should work.

It *had* to work.

CHAPTER SEVEN

THE PHONE RANG at exactly nine o'clock in the morning.

The way it had for three mornings now.

'Tell him that the rash is fading on his face,' Alice called in response to Julien's query. 'It certainly hasn't spread any further down his body and his temperature is normal quite a lot of the time.'

'Do you want the doctor to visit today?'

Alice shook her head, adjusting the weight of the freshly changed and fed baby in her arms from her position on the gallery, looking down to the foyer that Julien was crossing as he headed for one of the landlines in the house. 'We might need some more paracetamol syrup, that's all.'

There would be no problem having it delivered, along with any other supplies Julien deemed necessary. Vans were still being admitted through the gates every day. More gifts had arrived from Madame Laurent. Nothing as awful as the giant teddy bear but none of them had got as far as the nursery—they were piling up around the blue monstrosity in the foyer, which Alice could see from the corner of her eye as she walked with Jacques around the gallery instead of going straight back to the nursery.

Maybe she wanted to hear the sound of Julien's voice as he carried on his conversation with the doctor. No sooner had it stopped than the phone rang again. A shorter conversation this time and then a much longer silence. So long that Alice decided it was time to return to the nursery, so the sound of her name being called again startled her.

'Alice?'

Elise. It still gave her a tiny flutter of butterflies in her stomach, the way Julien pronounced her name. She turned to peer down into the foyer again.

'I'm here.'

'Could you come downstairs, please?'

Alice's heart skipped a beat. Something had changed. She was used to the level of tension in this house and how serious and almost aloof Julien was but there was a note in his voice that she had never heard before and it made her feel as if she was being summoned to the headmaster's office because she had done something wrong and she was in trouble. Her heart was in her mouth by the time she got to the bottom of the stairs.

Had the blood-test results come back to prove her immunity to measles? Was she about to be sent away and the care of Jacques assigned to someone else? Or was Julien also safe and he could escape to meet the deadline of filming his Christmas show in Paris? Alice wasn't sure which scenario would be worse. She didn't want anything to change, she realised. Not just yet.

'What is it?'

'Come…' Julien led her across the foyer, not towards the grand salon, as she might have expected for a formal discussion, but into the kitchen. This was the only room that she'd spent much time in other than the nursery.

It felt like home. Despite the size and how professional this area of the house was, it didn't have the kind of museum feel the rest of the house did, with the opulent architecture and priceless antiques so carefully positioned. Julien probably felt more at home here as well, which was why he'd chosen to use it as an office as well as a test kitchen.

Not that there were any papers strewn over the table yet this morning.

'Sit down.' The invitation was terse enough to make it sound like a command but, for once, any rebellious streak on Alice's part was dormant. She sank into a chair beside the table and shifted Jacques so that he was sitting on her lap, cradled in one arm. She rested her other hand on the tabletop, ready to provide extra support quickly if it was needed. Jacques looked up at Alice and then reached out a chubby hand to grab a fistful of her hair. He was only holding it, not tugging, so Alice let it be and shifted her gaze to Julien, who had sat down at the end of the table right beside her.

This was different, too. If they ate together, he sat opposite her. This felt more intimate. More serious. Alice swallowed hard. Something bad must have happened and the news was going to be broken gently. But she was an orphan already and had no other family so what did she have to lose?

'Oh…' Alice whispered. 'The DNA results have come back, haven't they?'

'*Oui*. The call came just after I spoke with the doctor.'

The sinking feeling was so horrible that Alice had to close her eyes. 'I was wrong, wasn't I? I'm not André's daughter. Jacques is not…not my brother…'

'Au contraire...' The touch of Julien's hand covering hers as it rested on the table made Alice's eyes snap open. 'That is exactly the truth. You are, without doubt, the child of André Laurent. And you are Jacquot's sister.'

Alice gasped. The flood of emotion revealed how much she had had resting on this news. There was grief there. For the father she would never know. For her mother who had lost the man she loved and then lost her life far too soon. But there was joy, too. Immeasurable joy and hope for a future she had never imagined.

She tried to smile but imminent tears made it impossible. She tried to fight them. Tried not to be so acutely aware of how her skin felt where Julien's hand was covering hers. It felt like support. Protection. And something much more visceral. Attraction mixed with both grief and hope felt remarkably like being in love, didn't it?

She couldn't go there... Couldn't even let the thought rest long enough to take a recognisable shape.

'Jacquot?' she queried, her voice choked.

Julien shrugged. 'It is a... How do say it? A pet name? Like Jamie instead of James.' He smiled at the baby, reaching out to touch his cheek gently. 'It seems you have a big sister, little Jacquot.'

Alice lost the battle with the tears. The skin on her hand was still tingling where he'd been touching it and she knew exactly what the stroke of that finger on the baby's cheek would feel like. Tender. Caring...

The tears rolled down her cheeks in big, fat droplets.

Julien glanced up and then stared at her, his brow furrowed. 'This news has made you unhappy?'

Alice shook her head. What had Julien said? *'Au*

contraire,' she managed on a stifled sob. 'I… I couldn't be happier.'

A sudden tug on her hair made her look down and, as if he knew how momentous this news had been, Jacquot stared back up at the two adults.

And then it happened. His little face crinkled and then split into a grin—the first real smile Alice had seen him make.

The alchemy of her emotional turbulence found a new direction. The one it should have had all along. This was the moment that she fell completely in love with this baby.

Her *brother…*

It was a crooked little grin. Rather like the only way she'd seen his uncle smile. Alice lifted her gaze and that might have been a mistake because it hit her again. It was so huge, this love that she had for Jacquot. Her heart could burst with the enormity but it wouldn't because some of that love was spilling out and Julien was somehow caught up in the fallout. Words formed and came out in a whisper.

'He looks like you.'

Julien met her gaze. His eyes looked bright—with unshed tears perhaps? 'I was just thinking how much he looks like Colette.'

The poignant undertone of his words made Alice want to gather him close and cuddle him the way she was cuddling Jacquot. The corners of her own mouth were still curling, as they had done in an instant response to the baby's smile, but now she could feel them wobble. She could see exactly the same struggle between happiness and sorrow hovering over the edges of Julien's lips and when she was brave enough to catch his gaze again, there it was.

The thing…

And this time it was powerful enough to feel like a punch in her gut, maybe because she recognised it for what it was. How could she not, when she'd just fallen utterly in love with her little brother?

Julien Dubois wasn't just caught up in the fallout of what she was feeling for her little brother. He was a part of what was causing this tsunami of emotion. She had somehow slipped past the warning signs that she might be in danger of falling in love with him.

For some reason she couldn't identify, there was a sense of connection in that particular look they had shared more than once now that was sucking her in and making her imagine things that couldn't possibly be true. How ridiculous was it to get a flash of thought that this man could be the person she had been searching for ever since she'd been a naïve teenager and had begun dreaming of a fairy-tale happy ending in her search for love?

They didn't even speak the same language, for heaven's sake.

They had absolutely nothing in common, other than a genetic connection to a small, orphaned child.

No wonder she hadn't been able to dismiss the memory of how that eye contact had made her feel. Or how it had been magnified by the sight of Julien standing half-naked with Jacquot in his arms. With the skin of her hand still buzzing with the memory of his touch even though it had been removed now, the air around her felt volatile. As if something could very well explode.

That imaginary glass jar perhaps?

Alice dragged her gaze free of Julien's so fast he didn't have a chance of being the first to break that contact.

They both seemed to feel the need to change the subject and they both spoke at exactly the same time.

'The doctor said…'

'I think I'd better…' Alice stopped and blinked. 'What did the doctor say?'

'That the nanny, Nicole, is showing signs of having caught measles. She has the spots inside her cheeks. I've forgotten what he called them.'

'Koplik's spots. Oh, no… That makes this a more serious outbreak, doesn't it?'

'It would appear so. But he said that Jacques will not be contagious within another day or two and he's found a children's nurse who can come into the house and care for him. Marthe—the housekeeper—could also return as her tests have shown her to be immune.'

'*No…*' Alice surprised herself with the vehemence of her response so it was no wonder that Julien's eyebrows shot up. 'I want to look after him,' she added. 'He's…' A smile curved around her soft words. 'He's my brother.'

Julien frowned. 'It may take some time before your relationship to Jacques can be legally acknowledged. The French system of law is complicated and offices will close down for some time over the Christmas period.' His frown deepened. 'There have been repeated calls from Madame Laurent—his grandmother. She is impatient to have the child collected and taken to her home in Geneva at the earliest opportunity.'

'Have him *collected*?' Alice was shocked. 'This is her *grand*son. How could she be prepared to let total strangers come and take him away from his home? How frightening would that be? It's hard enough that he has people he doesn't know looking after him when he's sick but at least he's in a familiar place.'

'She buried her only son a few days ago. I imagine it's a taxing time for an elderly woman.'

'How old is she?'

'Given that her son was in his early sixties, I expect she's well over eighty.'

Far too old to be taking on the task of raising a baby, then. But then another thought struck Alice and it made her catch her breath.

'Good grief…do you realise that Madame Laurent is also *my* grandmother?'

Julien's chair scraped as he pushed it back. 'Of course. I hadn't thought of that.'

And it was clearly an unpleasant thought. Alice was closely related to a man he loathed. He was disappearing behind the barriers again and Alice didn't want him to go. It wasn't fair to dismiss her because of who her father or grandmother was.

'Did the doctor say anything about the blood tests? Do we know if we're cleared for immunity for measles now?'

Julien shook his head as he got to his feet. 'No. Those results are not back and although he expects it won't be any later than tomorrow, they will be too late to help. A decision about my travelling has to be made today. This morning. So the show will have to be cancelled. There is no way around it and it is a disaster.'

'You would have been allowed to travel if you had proof of immunity?'

'Yes. And I expected it would have come well before

this or I would have taken the offer of being immunised again but it is too late now.'

'But other people who are immune are allowed to come into the house, aren't they? Like the nurse that we don't need?'

'It would seem so.' But Julien wasn't really listening. He had his mobile phone in his hand and was staring at the screen as he moved towards the door.

He was moving further away with every heartbeat and Alice could feel the distance growing. She should just let him go. If she couldn't see him, maybe she could clear her head—and her heart—of the nonsense that had taken root.

But her mouth opened before she could stop it.

'Why can't you film the show here?'

'Quoi?' Julien stopped in his tracks and turned to face Alice. 'What did you say?'

'It's just an idea…' And probably a stupid one judging by the look on Julien's face. 'This is a huge kitchen. It could be in a restaurant somewhere. How many people do you need to film a show?'

Julien shrugged. 'A skeleton crew might be only a cameraman and a sound person and someone to do the set-up and lighting. My producer perhaps.'

'What if you could find people that had proof they were immune to measles? Or if they had no chance of catching it? The kitchen has a back door, doesn't it? They wouldn't need to go into the house and I could keep Jacquot out of the way…'

The look of concentration on Julien's face was as fierce as he'd looked when he'd been cooking in the last couple of days.

'I don't know… There would be a lot of questions

that need to be asked. An impossible amount of organisation to do if it was possible…but…'

But there it was.

A glimmer of hope in what had been an insurmountable problem that Julien had been putting off making a decision about because the repercussions were so huge.

Nobody in his management team would have thought of this possibility because they had no idea what the kitchens were like in the Laurent mansion but why hadn't it occurred to him?

Yet again, the little Scottish pixie had waved a magic wand.

Perhaps.

There were a dozen or more phone calls that needed to be made and Julien didn't want to waste a single minute.

An hour of calls being made and received stretched into two hours and then three. Strings were pulled. Concessions made. Permission granted. Plans put into action.

Julien took the stairs two at a time. He burst into the nursery and Alice whirled around from where she had been bent over the cot, tucking the baby in for a sleep.

The curtains had been pulled to dim the room but a shaft of sunlight had found the gap between them and Alice turned into it, her hair glowing like a halo around her head.

Julien took a stride towards her. And then another. He caught her shoulders in her hands and bent his head to kiss her on one cheek and then the other. A perfectly ordinary greeting between French friends.

'You are an angel,' he told Alice. 'You have solved

the problem of the show. *Merci, chérie. Merci beau-coup.*'

Maybe it was the way his heart had been captured by a baby smile that had made him remember his little sister with such a burst of love. Maybe it was the way Alice's eyes were shining with such joy at his exuberant appreciation of having the wheels of a solution already turning. Or maybe this had just been something that had become inevitable ever since that first moment of being caught by those extraordinary eyes.

Instead of leaving the kissing within those polite parameters, Julien bestowed a third kiss. Directly on Alice's lips.

A brief kiss—but not nearly brief enough because now he knew what it was he'd been trying to avoid defining. That peculiar sensation he got when he looked into her eyes was nothing compared to the electric shock that came from touching her skin. Touching her hand had been manageable. Kissing her cheeks even. But the touch of his own lips on hers?

It was so powerful. This sense of…recognition.

Of finding something you hadn't had any idea you were even looking for.

It couldn't be real. It had started when he'd been in an emotionally exhausted state and right now he was high on the relief of a massive problem being on the way to resolution.

Julien needed to remember that this woman was the daughter of the man who'd been his enemy. Who had put the knife in and twisted it in those first awful moments of trying to come to terms with his sister's death.

'You'll never see her son. My son—unless it's over my dead body...'

And she was the granddaughter of Madame Laurent—the matriarch of the family he despised who was just as determined to take his nephew out of his reach.

He was already on his way out of the room as the shock waves of his impulsive action faded into ever smaller ripples.

Julien needed to make sure he didn't touch Alice McMillan again, that was all. And that should be easy with the chaos that was about to descend on this house.

The kitchen was out of bounds for Alice as soon as the first of the convoy of trucks and vans began arriving later that day. The sound of voices and furniture scraping and even loud hammering could be heard coming from the kitchens as she wandered around upstairs with Jacquot in her arms, keeping him amused while he was awake.

Julien brought her a mug of coffee and a fresh baguette filled with ham and cheese as a late lunch.

'Filming will start very soon. There will be more than enough food for dinner later but it may be quite late. Will you be okay to wait?'

'I'll be fine. Good luck—I hope it goes well.'

Alice filled in the time easily to begin with. Jacquot was clearly feeling much better today and the smiles came more often. He even giggled when she squeaked one of his toys in his bath and Alice ignored how wet she was getting from the splashing as she leaned over to kiss him.

'You are adorable, Jacquot. I love you so much…'

It was a joy to feed him after his bath and to sing softly to him as he fell asleep and it was in the quiet moment before she put him into his cot for the night that the idea first occurred to Alice.

She could raise her little brother. She could give him a home and love him to bits, and if Julien could be persuaded that it was a good idea they could both be all the family this little boy could need. Surely the grandmother would agree that it was best? She was an old woman and it wasn't as if it was someone outside the family taking on Jacquot's care. She was his sister but she could be a mother as well.

The idea grew wings as she tucked Jacquot into his cot. Maybe Madame Laurent—and possibly Julien—would insist that Jacquot be brought up in France but Alice could manage that. She would learn this beautiful language. Julien could keep teaching her.

She could keep seeing her tiny brother's uncle. Become part of his life and maybe he would kiss her again…

Alice found she was touching her lips with her fingers as she stood there looking down at the sleeping baby. It took very little imagination to pretend that this feather-light touch was how it had felt when Julien's lips had touched her own.

Suddenly the time that needed to be filled became interminable. There was nothing Alice needed to do unless Jacquot woke again and, with the baby cam handset, she was free to wander anywhere in the house.

Downstairs…where Julien was…

She fought the desire for a while but it got the better of her and eventually Alice crept downstairs with the intention of maybe peeping through the kitchen door. As she got closer, the alluring aroma of roasting meat made her stomach growl so loudly she had to stop and press her hand against her belly, willing it to be silent.

Another few steps and she could hear Julien's voice. He was speaking in French and the tone was confident. Light. As if he was smiling as he spoke?

She had to see. The kitchen door wasn't completely shut and the space inside was brightly lit. Surely nobody would notice if she pushed it open a fraction more and watched for a few minutes?

No heads turned as she pushed the door open further and then Alice forgot to worry about interrupting what was going on. She barely recognised the space. It wasn't so much the professional lights and microphones on the end of long poles that looked as much out of place as the man with a huge camera balanced on his shoulder. It was more that the kitchen had been turned into a Christmas wonderland.

Long ropes of greenery threaded with fairy-lights hung in loops on the walls a little below ceiling height. A tall tree stood in the corner, with tiny lights sparkling amongst red and silver themed decorations, and a wreath of mistletoe hung from a central light fitting. The huge kitchen table had been pushed to one side of the room and decorated as if a family was about to sit down for Christmas dinner.

Fine white china, gleaming silverware and crystal glasses marked each place setting. Christmas crackers with red and silver paper lay beside each plate. There were places for platters of food to rest on wrought-iron trivets and any remaining space on the table was covered with candles in glass holders with wreaths of greenery studded with red berries. The flickering flames of the candles glinted on the silver cutlery and champagne flutes.

There was Christmas music playing softly in the background. Carols that were instantly familiar and beloved to Alice because they were being sung in English. Memories of Christmas dinners shared with her mother and grandmother brought a lump to her throat and Alice had to look away from the table.

To where Julien was standing behind the island bench, smiling into a camera as he spoke. His hair was neatly tied back in the usual ponytail but his face looked different. Had make-up emphasised those thick, dark eyebrows and lashes, the shadowing of his jaw and the beautiful olive tone of his skin or was it the white chef's tunic he was wearing, underneath a striped apron, with the neck unbuttoned and the sleeves rolled up? Maybe the difference was simply that he was smiling in a way Alice hadn't seen. A non-crooked way.

He looked happy. More than that—this was a man who was sharing something he was totally passionate about. The superb knife skills as he diced an onion and celery sticks and the way he could toss a frying pan full of tiny pieces without spilling a thing might be showmanship but they were as natural as breathing to Julien.

Such a contrast to how she'd seen him standing—bewildered—staring down at his howling nephew when he'd had no idea of what to do.

The sight of him now made her catch her breath but the memory of him holding Jacquot had caught her heart completely.

She might think she'd stayed in control but, in retrospect, that had probably been the moment she'd gone past the point of no return when it came to falling in love with Julien Dubois.

Or had that moment been when she'd caught his gaze when they'd both been under the spell of Jacquot's first smile?

Or maybe when he'd brushed that kiss on her lips this morning?

Trying to identify when it had happened was pointless. It was probably the combination that had filled that jar past bursting point. Alice could almost feel the pieces shattering and the emotions the jar had contained rushing out to fill every cell of her body.

It was creating a heat like nothing she had ever experienced.

Desire that was so much more than purely physical.

She'd never wanted the touch of any man the way she wanted Julien Dubois.

As if he felt the force of that desire, Julien suddenly glanced up from what he was doing and his words stopped in mid-sentence. His hands froze in mid-air just as he was about to add another handful of ingredients to the frying pan and for an insanely long moment it felt as if the world had stopped turning.

He knew exactly what she was thinking and…for that moment Alice could swear he had caught that desire like a match to a fuse and it was about to explode.

The moment was shattered by a bark of incredulous sound that came from a man holding a clipboard and the cameraman sounded like he'd uttered a succinct oath as he lowered his camera to turn and stare at Alice. Filming had clearly been interrupted and it was only then that Alice realised she wasn't peering around the edge of the door any more. When had she stepped right into the kitchen without noticing herself moving? In that delicious stretch of time when her bones had been melting and she'd been unable to think of anything but her longing to be with Julien?

What on earth had she done? Was it possible to pick up filming at the place they had stopped or would they have to film that whole demonstration of preparing whatever it was in the frying pan again? A peek in Julien's direction revealed that he was as angry as everybody else in this space. A girl holding the microphone and somebody else beneath a light stand had moved so they could join in the incredulous staring.

She didn't need to understand a word of French to know that more than one person was telling her to go away and not come back but it was Julien who made sure she understood by translating.

'Go away, Alice. Do not come near here again.'

It sounded more like *Do not come near me again*.

Mortified, Alice could feel the worst blush ever flood up from her neck into her face. Even her ears felt like they were burning.

'I'm sorry,' she said. 'I'm terribly sorry...'

She closed the kitchen door behind her as she fled.

CHAPTER EIGHT

HEADLONG FLIGHT DIDN'T leave any room for rational thought.

Instead of running upstairs to the safety of the nursery suite, Alice found she had gone in the direction of the first place she'd felt safe in this house.

The conservatory.

The room was dark but there were muted floodlights in the garden that illuminated the swimming pool and filtered in through glass walls to provide a hint of green on the dark shapes of the indoor trees and made the white furniture easy to find. It was the same couch she'd sat on when she had held Jacquot for the first time that Alice chose to curl up on to wait out the shame of the trouble she'd caused.

And the pain of the way Julien had dismissed her.

She'd been remembering her family the last time she'd come in here alone. The way her mother and grandmother had always been able to know if she wasn't telling the truth. Would they be able to see what felt stupidly like a broken heart right now?

He's French, her grandmother might have sniffed. *What did you expect?*

But her mother? Might she have given her comfort

because she would understand? Had André sent her away looking like he'd never wanted to see her again when she had already gifted her heart to him? When she had been carrying his baby in her belly?

She had no idea how long she sat there, failing to win a battle with tears of self-pity, but Alice finally pulled herself together.

It was ridiculous to feel like she had a broken heart. This wasn't a fairy-tale, this house was not a palace and Julien wasn't any kind of fantasy prince. He'd been forced to live in the same house as her with the rest of the world shut away and, yes, there had been moments where she could convince herself that something amazing was happening between them but he was back in his real life now and she had absolutely no part in it. It had been the promise of being able to do that that had led to him kissing her in the first place.

The worst part of it all was that he'd seen the desire that must have been glowing from her face like a neon sign. He'd been so shocked he hadn't been able to look away. It wasn't that he felt the same way at all. He'd been...appalled.

There was no point wallowing in it. It might be as soon as tomorrow that the results of those blood tests came through and that Jacquot would be deemed to be no danger to others. This quarantine would end. Jacquot would be taken into the care of his grandmother and she herself would have to go home and she would never set foot in this house again. The opportunity to find out anything about her father that she couldn't find printed in a magazine or revealed in a television interview would be lost for ever.

Her heart thumping, Alice got to her feet and went

to the room that Julien had taken her to when she had first arrived. Flickering screens from the security system showed her where she could turn on a desk lamp rather than the main lights of the room. Even in the soft light the shards of glass still clinging to the oversized portrait of her father was a shocking reminder of that violent action of Julien's and the pent-up grief and hatred it had revealed, but Alice pushed any thoughts of him away. She was here in the hope of finding something that might let her believe her father hadn't been a man worthy of that kind of hatred. Maybe something she could keep to give Jacquot in years to come.

There were stacks of magazines with pictures of André Laurent on their covers. Silver trophies and framed photographs of André with people that Alice could recognise as being famous. Film stars and someone she thought had been a French president. Moving behind the desk, she found a smaller photograph in a heart-shaped silver frame. A much older-looking André with his arms around the waist of a very beautiful, young, dark-haired woman who had to be Julien's sister.

Alice picked up the image and studied it. They were looking at each other rather than the camera and it was impossible not to catch the impression that they were very much in love. It was a picture of a private moment and it made Alice catch her breath, wishing that the photo of *her* parents had been this revealing.

It was a double frame that could be closed and in the other side was a photo of a baby with tufts of dark hair. Jacquot. Had it been taken on the day he'd been born? When André had lost the mother of the only child he'd known he had? It didn't matter. What did matter was that it showed how important his brand-new family had been to André and it was something that Jacquot would treasure when he was old enough to understand. Alice set the frame carefully to one side of the desk.

She would come and get it when she was leaving the house and then somehow, some time she would find a way to give it to her little brother.

She sat there for a long moment and then idly began opening desk drawers. Maybe she was hoping she might find cards that had been kept with messages of love in them but there seemed to be only stationery items like embossed paper and pens. A lower drawer had a business diary and appointment cards. Plane tickets to Geneva had been booked for Christmas Eve and there were passports with the tickets…two of them. One had a shiny, unmarked cover and had been issued only last week—a baby's first official document.

Alice closed the drawer slowly. Had André been planning a family Christmas to help him get through the grief of this first celebration without his wife? Would Madame Laurent be struggling with her own sadness and that was why she was so eager to collect Jacquot? It could be that she might welcome her as well.

Movement from the screens caught her eye and she watched as the headlights of cars and vans lit up the driveway and went out the gates. The road outside looked empty. Had the media finally given up on getting a story or pictures? It was another clue that normal life would be resumed in the near future but it felt curiously as if something important was slipping through her fingers.

The baby cam monitor showed Jacquot to be sleeping peacefully and maybe it was time for Alice to follow his example. The delicious smell of the Christmas feast that had been prepared in the kitchens should have been just as enticing when Alice reached the foyer but, despite her earlier hunger, her appetite was nothing like it had been when she had come downstairs earlier.

And when she saw who was emerging from the interior kitchen door, it vanished completely.

Julien had shed the striped apron. He'd unbuttoned the white tunic completely so that it hung open and most of his chest was bare. He was wearing faded denim jeans that had been hidden by the apron and maybe he'd kicked his shoes off because his feet were also bare.

And he'd taken the fastening off his ponytail. This was the first time Alice had seen him with his hair loose and she'd been right about how it framed and softened his face and brushed his shoulders in soft waves. It took away that professionally polished look and gave him an almost disreputable edge. A muted but irresistible hint of 'bad boy'.

And then she noticed how tired he looked.

And how his face changed when he saw her.

Her mouth went very dry. 'I'm so sorry, Julien,' she said quietly. 'I hope I didn't disrupt the filming too much.'

He flicked his hand. 'It was of no matter. We redid that part when I could concentrate again. It is finished now and only needs editing.' He was giving her an intense look that Alice couldn't interpret.

'I have never lost my focus like that,' he said, walking slowly towards her. 'What is it about you that can do that to me, Alice McMillan?'

'I… I…' *Have absolutely no idea*, she wanted to say. *Maybe it's the same thing that you do to me…*

Her words had evaporated and she didn't need them anyway because Julien hadn't stopped moving and now he was standing right in front of her. As close as he'd been standing that first night when he'd taken the sample from the inside of her cheek.

Once again, she was aware that she had an impossibly gorgeous man standing close enough to kiss her but this time it wasn't embarrassing. This time it was the most amazing moment of her life because she knew that that was exactly what *was* going to happen.

And it wasn't going to be an afterthought to a friendly kiss on both cheeks. Oh, no… The way Julien's hand slid behind her neck and cradled the back of her head meant that this was going to be a *real* kiss…

Except it wasn't. It was so far away from anything Alice had ever experienced that it was a fairy-tale kiss from a handsome prince. A prince who sensed that her bones were melting and scooped her into his arms and held her against his bare chest as he carried her upstairs and into a room well away from the nursery. It must have been the one he'd chosen on the first night here because it had the black clothes he'd been wearing carelessly thrown over the back of a chair.

The huge four-poster bed fitted right into this fantasy and, if Alice had had any qualms about whether she should let this go any further with a man she'd only met days ago, they vanished the moment Julien laid her on that bed and his lips covered hers again. Had he sensed a heartbeat of indecision? The gentle touch of lips suggested exactly that and the moment Alice knew she was completely lost to this overwhelming desire was the moment that gentleness got edged out by an increasingly fierce passion.

The buttons on her shirt popped open and then his lips were on the swell of her breasts and Julien was telling her how beautiful she was. How irresistible. That he was saying it in French didn't matter. In fact, there could be no other language that could make words like this so compelling. So believable…

How on earth had he been able to focus enough to finish filming that show when all he'd wanted to do had been this from the moment he'd seen her standing in the doorway, looking at him the way she had?

And he wasn't disappointed. *Au contraire*, he might have had a great deal of experience in lovemaking but it had never been this good. Because he'd never touched or been touched by a Scottish pixie with magic in her eyes. And in her hands. And in the soft sounds she made as she responded to every move he made. The cry she couldn't stifle when he took them both over the edge and into paradise…

She stayed in his arms as he waited for his heart rate and breathing to get back to within normal parameters, her head snuggled in the dip between his shoulder and his heart as if the space had been created for just that purpose.

The silence could have been awkward—as these moments usually were—but it was far from that. It was good. Too good because he felt like he'd like to stay like this for ever, and that meant the moment had to be broken before he had time to think about it any longer.

'*C'etait bien*?' he asked softly. 'It was good?'

'Oh…*oui*…' He could feel the curve of her lips against his chest. '*Je l'aime.*'

It felt like the chuckle came from a place he'd forgotten existed. Amusement that was a mix of pride and a deep fondness and possibly a twinge of sadness as well. The only person in his life who had ever made him feel something like that had been Colette—when she'd been young and trying to do something grown up but could only manage cute. Another silence fell, which made him wonder if Alice was trying to think of something else she could say in his language. Instead, the silence was broken by the loud growl of her stomach, which made him smile again.

'You are hungry, *chérie.* I happen to know where there is a Christmas dinner that will still be warm. *Est-ce que tu voudrais diner avec moi*?'

Some of the food had been left in one of the massive ovens to stay warm.

Apparently more than one version of things had been cooked because the filming had needed different stages of the cooking process within a short time period. Most of it was stored in the cold room now and Julien warned Alice that she might be eating Christmas dinner more than once.

Alice sat at the end of the table with a flute of champagne in her hand and watched as Julien placed platter after platter of amazing-looking food in the spaces between the dozens of flickering candles.

A turkey and a jug of aromatic gravy with a curl of steam above it. Wedges of roasted pumpkin and crispy, browned potatoes. Sweet glazed carrots and Brussels sprouts. Bread sauce.

'Oh...you did pigs in blankets. My absolute favourite.' Alice picked up one of the tiny sausages wrapped in bacon and baked until crisp. 'Oh, yum. How do you say "yum" in French?'

Julien had a carving knife in one hand and a sharpening steel in the other. '*Miam-miam*,' he told her.

He'd just put his faded jeans and his black shirt on before they'd left his bedroom and the shirt was only buttoned halfway up but it didn't matter that he wasn't wearing his white tunic or even that he hadn't tied back his hair again once he began sharpening that knife. He was every inch the professional chef and this had to be the sexiest thing Alice had ever seen a man doing.

Her pig in its blanket remained barely tasted and her champagne was forgotten. The pleasure Alice was getting from simply watching Julien was as much as she could cope with because it took far more than just her eyes. Her whole body was watching and remembering every touch he had given her. Every stroke and every kiss and—if she never experienced it again—she would never forget this blissful afterglow if she lived to be a hundred and two.

With the succulent meat carved and served, Julien piled their plates with a sample of everything else he had cooked for his traditional British Christmas dinner.

Alice wondered what the other chef had done for his French version but she didn't want the conversation to turn professional. She wanted to bask in this delicious glow for a little longer. To talk about things that mattered only to themselves.

But she didn't want to say too much either. Whatever was happening here was new and fragile and there was a danger of breaking it with the pressure of words that were too heavy or smothering it with a layer of too much emotion. Maybe talking about food was safer.

'This is the best Christmas dinner I've ever tasted,' she told him. 'As much as I adored my mum and my gran, they could never cook like this. The turkey was always dry.'

'Putting butter under the skin makes a difference. This is how I do it in my restaurant.'

'Are you open on Christmas Day?'

'No. But we serve Christmas meals for two or even three weeks of December. By the time Christmas Day comes, the last thing I want to eat is a goose. Or a turkey.'

'So what do you cook to celebrate Christmas Day?'

Julien shrugged. 'It's not something I celebrate. It means nothing to me other than a day to be alone and rest.'

Alice stopped eating. So there was no significant other in his life who he would spend a special day with? It should be a relief to know that but, instead, it was almost frightening. Was Julien a lone wolf? Was he alone by a choice that was unlikely to change? She stared at her half-eaten meal but, however delicious it was, she had no inclination to eat anything more.

'What about when you were a child?'

Julien followed her example and put down his fork, picking up his glass instead. 'Celebrations were something to be feared when I was a child.'

There was nothing Alice could find to say in response. She could only look at Julien's face in the soft light of the candles and hold her breath until the ache in her chest eased a little.

Julien drained his glass of champagne and reached for one of the bottles of wine on the table. The ruby-red liquid filled the crystal glass and he offered it to Alice but she shook her head, remaining silent as he closed his eyes and took a long sip of his wine. And then another. And then he opened his eyes again but kept his gaze on the glass in his hand as he began talking quietly.

'My father walked out on us when I was five years old. He'd married my mother because she was pregnant but he told us many times that he'd never wanted a child. When it became apparent that another child was on the way, it was too much and he left.'

'Oh, *Julien*...'

Alice's heart ached for that little boy who'd known he hadn't been wanted. Who had probably believed that it was his fault that his father had abandoned them.

'My mother couldn't cope alone so she married again as soon as she could. She chose an angry man who could use words as well as his fists as weapons and the worst times were always when he drank too much. Celebrations like birthdays and especially Christmas were the days he always drank too much.'

As if the reminder disgusted him, Julien put his glass down and pushed it away. 'It's too easy to hurt a child,' he murmured. 'That's why I will never have one of my own.'

The ache around Alice's heart took on a hollow edge as if it was surrounded by a bottomless pit. 'But you have Jacquot now. You are his guardian...'

'Which means I have to ensure that he is safe and cared for. I can't bring up a child. I work long hours in my restaurant. I have to travel a lot for my television work and my recipe books. Other time is taken up with production and editing. It would be impossible to live with a baby.'

'But he has to be *loved*,' Alice whispered. 'That's just

as important as being safe and cared for. Maybe *more* important.' She'd seen how much it had meant to him that Colette's precious rabbit toy had been bequeathed to her baby. And the way Julien had looked when Jacquot had smiled at them both. 'You said he looks like Colette and…and I know you loved your sister…'

He must have loved her very much to have dropped out of school to protect her from their stepfather.

'How old were you when your mother died?' Alice asked, when Julien said nothing.

'Fifteen.'

'And Colette was…?'

'Ten. A child.'

He hadn't been much more than a child himself. 'And you were allowed to be Colette's guardian when you were so young?'

'I would have lied about my age if anyone had asked but it turned out there was nobody who cared enough to find out.'

'That must have been *so* hard…'

Julien picked up one of the pigs in blankets from his plate with his fingers and bit into it, tilting his head to shrug off her comment.

'I worked,' he said a moment later. 'First one job and then two. Even three at one time. I had found a cheap apartment for us. Colette went to school and she looked after herself after school. She knew it was the only way we could stay together. We were the only family we each had. We had to help one another.' He looked at the food in his hand and then put it down, as though his appetite had vanished.

'It only worked because she was old enough to do

that,' he added. 'I couldn't have cared for a baby then. I couldn't now.'

'You *could*...' Alice whispered. 'If you wanted to.' *If I helped you...*

But her offer remained unspoken because Julien had raised his hand as if warning her off.

'I *don't* want to. I've been down that path before. Tried to protect someone and keep them safe and...and I did not do it well enough... *C'est tout.*'

Alice could hear the pain in his words. He had loved his sister so much. She didn't understand why he was taking so much blame for her death but maybe it was because it was still so recent. Grief was not helpful to rational thinking, was it?

She spoke quietly into the silence.

'She knew how amazing it was—what you did for her. That's why she made you the guardian of her child.'

Julien gave that half-shrug. This wasn't something he really wanted to analyse. 'So she said. I think I told you that she came to see me just before her baby was due to be born. She wanted to give me the legal document about the guardianship. It was the first time I'd seen her in more than a year. Since she'd married André. A marriage that I'd tried to stop.'

'Why?'

'Because he was far too old for her. And he was well known for his excesses. Fast cars. Beautiful women. Too much alcohol...'

So this was why he blamed himself? Because he hadn't protected her from a relationship that had led to a baby's birth that had proved fatal? It wasn't logical. It wasn't even acceptable. 'But they loved each other.'

'Pfff...' The sound was as dismissive as when Julien had made it in response to her suggesting that her mother had been in love with André.

Julien had been both a brother and a parent to his sister and he knew about that kind of protective love, but had anyone ever protected *him*? Did he even realise it could be safe, given that his parents had failed him and even his beloved sister had walked away from his life when he'd thought he was still protecting her? Had he ever allowed himself to be *in* love? Or *felt* truly loved by someone?

It would seem not.

What on earth made her think she had any chance of breaking through a barrier like that?

It would need a miracle.

But miracles did happen sometimes, didn't they? And what better time of year to find one than at Christmas?

There was a clock ticking, though, and it wasn't just counting down the hours until Christmas Day.

And miracles needed to be planted to have any hope of growing.

Alice took a deep breath.

'If you're Jacquot's guardian, you will get to choose who can raise him, won't you?'

'That's my hope. And if it's away from the Laurent family I will still be able to visit him. To watch over him as he grows up and help when or if I'm needed.'

'He needs to be with someone who loves him,' Alice said again. 'I love him. He's my brother. Choose me, Julien.'

He met her gaze and Alice's heart skipped a beat.

But then, after a long moment, he looked away.

'*Non. C'est impossible.*'

CHAPTER NINE

THOSE EYES…

He would never forget how they looked in this moment. He had crushed something beautiful. Naïve perhaps but something so genuine that it felt like he was hurting a child by not protecting it from the harshness of reality.

'*Je suis vraiment désolé, chérie…* I am truly sorry…'

He touched her face as he spoke and the way she tilted her head to press her cheek against his fingers was heart-breaking.

He had to take his hand away before he gave in to the urge to hold her in his arms and start kissing her. Promising her things that it would be foolish to even consider. He used his hand to massage his own temples as he let his breath out in a sigh.

'You are single, yes? You don't have a boyfriend or fiancé?'

The blush was a display of intense emotion he was getting used to from Alice. That flash of pain that could also be anger made him realise how stupid the question was. She had just given him more in bed than any woman ever had. And this was Alice. She did not have a deceitful bone in her body. She would never cheat on any man.

'You work as a teacher. You love your work?'

'Yes, but—'

'But you would sacrifice your lifestyle in order to care for a child?'

'Isn't that what you did for your sister?'

Julien shook off what sounded like admiration. He had only done what he'd had to do. And he hadn't done it well enough, anyway.

'You would not be viewed as a suitable guardian to raise a baby,' he said. 'And you would want to take him out of the country.'

'Not necessarily.'

'You have a house in Scotland, yes?'

'Yes…'

'Jacquot is French. The last member of what has been a very powerful family in France. His father has always been adored as a national icon.'

'But didn't you say that Madame Laurent lives in Geneva?'

'The border between France and Geneva is merely a formality for many French people. Besides, it is only one of her houses. I understand she has a luxury apartment in Cannes and she may choose to live here in *this* house, which I believe was the family home when André was a child himself.'

A house they both knew was a mausoleum totally unsuited to raising a child.

'I could live in France.' There was determination in those liquid brown eyes now. Passion even. 'I'm half-French.'

'That would be difficult. You don't speak our language.'

Her chin lifted. 'I'm learning.'

She was. The shy echo of her words when he'd asked whether their lovemaking had been good—*Je l'aime*—gave him an odd tightness in his chest that made it hard to draw in a new breath.

'Yvonne Laurent is a powerful woman who is used to getting her own way. I don't even know if I can win what I want to get from her. It may be up to the courts to decide whether the relationship of an uncle is more important than that of a grandmother.'

'I'm his sister...'

'A half-sister. And that would probably have to be endorsed by a court as well. The French legal system can be very slow. Especially if someone has the money to delay proceedings. Cases can drag on for months. Years even, and that would not be a good thing for a child. Small children can understand more than you might think...'

Like he had when he'd started protecting Colette from the moment she'd been born? So she would never know that it was also her fault that their father had gone?

He could see the empathy in her eyes now. He shouldn't have told her so much about his childhood. She could read between lines, couldn't she? She knew how bad it had been and she wanted to make it better somehow.

To make him feel loved?

The pull was so powerful it was painful but he couldn't give in to it. There was no room in his life for someone to be that close. No room in a heart that was too scarred to love and lose again.

'But you are going to fight,' Alice said softly. 'To get what you want. Custody of Jacquot?'

'No.' Julien shook his head. That would mean he would become a parent again. He would have the kind of responsibility he had already proved with his sister that he could not honour well enough. 'I simply want regular access. For the boy to know I am his mother's brother and that I will help him in whatever way he needs as he grows up.'

'Maybe I could have access, too?'

He had to admire her optimism. The hope she could find in every dark corner. Like the way she had seen something good in an ancient toy that was waiting patiently to be of importance one day.

'Maybe fighting isn't the way to win,' Alice said slowly. 'This woman doesn't know that she is my grandmother. If Jacquot is so important to her, it could be that she might listen to her other grandchild. If I don't threaten her, maybe I can persuade her.'

'*Peut-être*.' Alice McMillan could probably persuade anybody if she looked at them like that. He was in danger of being persuaded that he could gift his heart to someone again and he knew that wasn't true. He had found the safe place to be years ago. Away from someone who would see him as a husband and father.

He needed to break the spell that was being woven around him here, in the light of all these romantic candles. In a kitchen that was a room that would always feel like home, no matter where he was. In a Christmas setting that was always redolent with the idea of family…

'Have you had enough to eat? There is a plum pudding with brandy sauce. And custard. Would you like to taste it?'

'*Peut-être*,' Alice enunciated again, carefully. And then she smiled at him. 'Actually, yes, please. I would love to.'

It was good to move. To take the plates of their unfinished first course away and make a clear space to start again. To move on.

A little showmanship with the pudding came as naturally as breathing these days and it was comforting, too, because it was a demonstration of who he was. What his life was about.

He put the pudding on its platter in front of Alice and moved a candle closer. He held a silver ladle full of brandy over the flame of the candle to warm it and then tipped it just enough to catch the flame and ignite. He never got tired of the magic of that blue flame and the way it flowed so dramatically over the curve of the pudding as he slowly poured it.

'*Oh...*' Alice's gasp of appreciation was another echo of their time in his bed and Julien couldn't dampen a hunger that had nothing to do with food.

He stayed quiet as he served their dessert but Alice had something to say.

'It won't be long, will it? Until...until our quarantine is over.'

'No. I'm hoping the test results will come through tomorrow. I hope also that they are good because I have to go to Paris the next day. It's Christmas Eve and I need to be present on the live broadcast of the show if possible. To appear by a remote connection would not be good enough.'

'Hmm...' Alice paused, a spoonful of pudding halfway to her lips. 'We only have a short time together, then…'

'This is true.' He couldn't tell her that her words gave him a sinking feeling, as if a huge stone had lodged in his gut. To imagine there could be any time together after this was as impossible as the notion of her becoming the guardian for her little brother.

Alice's head was bent, her gaze on her spoon. And then she peeped up through a thick tangle of dark lashes with a look that would have rendered any red-blooded male completely helpless. 'We should make the most of it, then…'

Julien took the spoon gently from her fingers. He cupped her chin and raised it so that he could kiss her with equal gentleness.

'Je suis d'accord. Absolument.'

It couldn't do any real harm, could it? To enjoy the company of such an intriguing woman? At least, this time, he wouldn't have to make the decision to walk away—the way he always did when a woman was getting too close. It was going to happen naturally so why not make the most of every moment they had left? It might only be a matter of hours.

Starting with what was left of this already remarkable night. With luck, Jacquot was well enough to sleep in his own bed right through until morning as long as he was fed and clean and, thanks to the baby monitor, there was no need for Alice to return to *her* own bed.

He was more than happy to share his.

It was the first time little Jacquot Laurent had slept through the night.

It was also the first time he had woken and not immediately cried for attention. Instead, the sounds that came through the monitor handset were soft chirrups and coos, as if the baby was experimenting with talking to himself.

Alice awoke to the sounds with a smile already curving her lips. And then she realised she was still snuggled against Julien's bare chest with his arm around her and his fingers carelessly draped across her breast and the smile seemed to turn inwards.

She had never felt contentment like this. A weariness that felt blissful because of what had been experienced instead of sleep. Alice tilted her head so that she could see Julien's face. Relaxed in slumber, he had lost the solemn air and intensity she had grown accustomed to. A tress of that surprisingly soft hair had caught on his lashes and lay across his cheek and lips. Alice reached up and gently brushed it back into place. Maybe her grandmother would have disapproved of Julien's hairstyle but Alice was never going to forget the thrilling tickle of that hair on her skin when Julien had been kissing and tasting her body. Her neck…her breasts…her belly…and, *oh*…

A pair of gorgeous hazel eyes were on her face and Alice knew she was going to blush so she ducked her head.

'Jacquot is awake. Listen…'

Julien also smiled. 'He sounds happy.'

'He must be hungry. I need to go to him.'

'Of course. And I should go and do something with that disaster of a kitchen. Shall I bring you some coffee before breakfast?'

'Please…' Alice rolled away but Julien's arm tightened around her and pulled her back.

'You have forgotten something, *chérie*.'

'Oh? What?'

'This…' Julien kissed her. A brief caress and then a more thorough one. 'It is a French custom, the morning kiss…'

'Mmm…' If it hadn't been for a more demanding cry coming from the monitor, the morning kiss would no doubt have become much more than that.

Was it too much to hope that they could have one more night together? Alice wondered as she hastily pulled on her clothes and made her way to the nursery. This felt like the start of something new. Something wonderful. Something that was too good to be true?

She heard the phone ringing as she had Jacquot in his bath, squeaking the rubber duck to make him smile and kick his feet. Was it nine a.m. already? The doctor was as reliable as an alarm clock. She had her little brother dressed and ready for his new day by the time Julien came to the nursery, carrying a steaming mug of delicious-smelling coffee. A wide grin appeared on the baby's face.

'He knows you,' Alice said. 'Here…he needs a cuddle from his uncle.' She took the mug of coffee from his hand and eased the bundle of baby into Julien's arms. Neither of them made any protest about the contact and Alice beamed at them both before taking her first sip of coffee.

This was progress. If Julien could bond with Jacquot as much as she had, they could join forces to make sure this baby had what he needed so badly—people to love him to bits.

'Was it the doctor who rang? Did you tell him how happy Jacquot sounded this morning?'

'It was and I did. He said that there doesn't need to be any further restriction to keeping him in the house if he's well enough to go out.'

'Oh…' That meant that he could be taken out, didn't it? Taken away…

'He also said that the results of our blood tests are finally back. We are both immune to measles. There are no further restrictions on either of us either. I have already booked an early flight to Paris tomorrow morning. And…'

Alice held her breath. Julien was looking down at the baby in his arms, who must have been enjoying the sound of his voice as much as she was because he smiled again, so energetically it made his whole little body wiggle. And Julien was smiling back but then he looked up at Alice and his smile faded.

'And Madame Laurent is driving down from Geneva this afternoon to make arrangements. She intends to take Jacquot back to her home tonight.'

The lump in Alice's throat was too big to swallow. 'What time is she due to arrive?'

'I'm not sure. Early this evening, I expect.' Julien's face was as sombre as the first time she'd met him but there was a depth of softness there that was very new. 'I'm sorry, *chérie*…there seems to be nothing I can do to stop this. Nothing I can do to help you.'

Alice looked away as she blinked back tears but all she could think about was the man standing there, holding the small baby. They were both the people she now cared about more than anyone else in her world.

And she had less than a day to be with them both. She pulled in a shaky breath.

'There is one thing you could do.'

'What is that? I have a few urgent matters I must attend to first, like discussing how to handle this with my solicitor, but I will have time this afternoon. If I can do this thing for you, I promise you I will.'

Alice turned back. 'I will have to leave France tomorrow and I feel like I haven't seen nearly enough. Could you take me somewhere that I will remember? Maybe somewhere…' her voice became quieter, hopeful '…that is special to you?'

She saw a flicker of doubt in his eyes. Was he reluctant to let her any further into his life?

'We would have to take the little one with us.'

Alice nodded. 'I know where things are. Like the nappy bag and a pram. Or there's a front pack. I can make up a bottle of formula that any café could warm for us.' She bit her lip. 'Have those journalists gone? You don't get harassed in public for being famous, do you?'

'I know how to deal with that.' His expression changed. A decision had been made and there was a hint of a smile on his lips. 'And I think I know where I can take you. Somewhere special enough for your last day in France. I will attend to what I must do and you get yourself and Jacquot ready.'

Alice took the baby from his arms and smiled up at him. 'Will I like it?'

'You will love it.' He turned to leave the nursery.

'You have forgotten something, Julien.'

'Oh…?'

Alice stood on tiptoe, leaning over the baby to kiss him. 'It's a Scottish custom,' she said softly. 'The goodbye kiss…'

It was even better than the kiss, she decided moments later—the way she'd made him smile.

* * *

Some time out to clear his head was the best thing he could do for this afternoon. After a string of telephone conversations between himself, his solicitor and Madame Laurent's solicitor, it had been agreed that a brief family meeting might be the best first step. Nothing official, such as taking Jacquot away from the house, would happen before tomorrow.

This was the opportunity Julien had requested for the key players to discuss the situation without outside input and legal arguments to inflame tempers. Alice's words had stayed in his mind—that perhaps persuasion might be more effective than threats. He had called for a temporary truce and, amazingly, Madame Laurent had agreed. The only thing she didn't know was that there were now three key players rather than two. And that the third one was a granddaughter she didn't know existed.

Alice could either be an ace up his sleeve or be seen as a threat that could close doors for ever. It was impossible to know which way the dice might roll but Julien was trying to channel some of Alice's optimism. It might help all of them.

Being recognised was not usually a problem and the media contingent outside the gates had given up and gone elsewhere days ago but Julien did need to be careful this time. He was breaching the court order that the Laurent family solicitors had arrived with on the day of the funeral to prevent him taking his nephew anywhere, and there was still the problem of Alice's connection to the family becoming public before Yvonne Laurent had time to accept the bombshell. It might have been easier to stay discreetly in the house for one more day but he'd made a promise and he was not about to dishonour that.

So he wore a black fisherman-style pullover under a coat with its collar turned up and hid his hair beneath a black woollen beanie that he wore low on his forehead because the day was too overcast to warrant sunglasses. Fortunately the chances of being recognised were low anyway, because the last thing anybody would expect would be to see him out with a woman who had a baby in a front pack, well bundled up for any winter chill with tiny arms and legs poking out of the contraption like a miniature snowman.

It hadn't been hard to think of an appropriate place to take Alice to give her a taste of France at Christmastime. He and Colette had been taken there once, as children, and it was probably the happiest memory of his entire childhood.

It was a bonus that the clouds were thick and dark enough to make it seem much later in the day than early afternoon because it made the Christmas lights of Nice's *marché de Noël* almost as bright as they would be at night. The enormous pine trees along the Promenade du Paillon were thickly dusted with artificial snow as they walked through the park to the Place Massena, and as they got closer they could see that the ice-skating rink was full of families out with their children and the giant Ferris wheel was turning. The massive Christmas trees were sparkling and there were crowds of shoppers at the stalls selling hand-crafted gifts and food and mulled wine.

And Alice looked as excited by it all as Colette had been when she'd still been a small child of about seven or eight. Those brown eyes that had captured him from the moment he'd seen them produce tears in André's office that first day were shining with joy now and Julien felt his chest expand with his own pleasure in having chosen this experience as his gift for her last day here.

That she was here with her baby brother in her arms made it even more special.

'Stand here, so that the Ferris wheel and the Christmas trees are behind you. I will take a photo for you.'

He would keep a copy of that photograph himself. If the sadness from the past tried to suck him back, he would be able to look at that smile and remember his Scottish pixie, who could always find something to celebrate.

He was missing Alice already. How stupid was that?

Would she miss him? Would she remember this time with him? Maybe a memento would help. A gift from one of the stalls perhaps?

Alice had turned to watch the Ferris wheel. Or was she watching the people on the skating rink? It was a colourful scene. There were coloured lights around the edges of the rink and overhead. Many people were dressed in Christmas shades of bright red and green and most of them were wearing Santa hats or reindeer horns. The people closest to them right now were a man and a woman who were holding the mittened hands of a small boy as he wobbled on his skates between them. A family, enjoying a Christmas outing. If she could have what she was wishing for, Julien thought, that could be Alice in a few years' time, with the father figure she chose to share her life with as she raised her baby brother.

The thought sat uneasily. He didn't want to imagine Alice with another man but it was inevitable, wasn't it? What man could resist those eyes? That spirit of optimism or that generosity as a lover? And it was no more than she deserved—to find that man and have babies of her own to cherish. He had no right to feel the way he did. Resentful almost?

Julien shook off the unwelcome train of his thoughts. He was here to give Alice a happy memory of France. He went to take her hand so that he could lead her towards the stalls and find a gift but her hands were busy, adjusting the straps of the front pack.

'Is it heavy? Would you like me to take him for a while?'

There was surprise in her eyes. And then something he couldn't identify but it looked curiously like satisfaction.

'Yes, please,' she said. '*Merci beaucoup*, Julien.'

It felt completely natural to take Julien's hand, once the front pack was securely in place and his hands were free. There was so much to look at as they wove their way slowly through the crowds, admiring the goods on offer at the stalls, but Alice kept looking sideways.

Was there anything more appealing than the sight of a tall, broad-shouldered man with a tiny baby on his chest?

And when you loved them both, was there anything that could make you feel more like your heart was so full it might simply break from joy?

She needed to find something else to look at before that joy escaped as tears.

'Oh, look...those hats have sparkles. Aren't they pretty?'

They were only woollen hats but they had large diamantes glued all over them and soft, furry pompoms on the top.

'Would you like one?' There was a furrow just visible under Julien's hat. 'I hadn't noticed that you didn't have a hat. Are your ears cold?'

'No, but I would love a hat anyway.' As much as she loved the concern in his voice and the idea that he cared if her ears were cold or not. 'The sparkle would always remind me of where it came from and when.'

'What colour would you like?'

'Black.' There was no hesitation on Alice's part. It would match Julien's hat but with a bonus. 'It makes the sparkles stand out more.'

Julien spoke to the woman running the stall and money changed hands. Instead of having the hat put into a bag, he put it on Alice's head, tucking her hair back from her face. Then he touched her nose with his finger.

'*Très mignon*,' he pronounced. 'Very cute. *Tout comme tu*.'

The stall owner said something then and Alice saw the warmth in his eyes vanish.

She nudged Julien. 'What did she say?'

He shook his head, turning away. Confused, Alice glanced back at the woman. Her confusion was being reflected back at her and the woman raised her hands in a puzzled gesture.

'I say only that he has a beautiful wife and the most beautiful baby in the world.'

Oh... That would have been a shock to a man who was a lone wolf and had decided long ago that he would never have a child of his own. No wonder the pleasure of this outing began to fade. When Jacquot finally woke a short time later and let them know he was hungry and needed changing, it was obvious that Julien was relieved to hand the baby back to Alice.

And the spell was broken. Even the lights and music

and the crowd of happy people couldn't fix what had been broken and it was Alice's turn to feel relieved when Julien suggested it was time to go back to the house.

They drove back in Julien's car in silence and he used a remote to open those extraordinarily ornate gates that had been Alice's first glimpse of this property.

It was only the second time she had passed through these gates into her father's estate. The first had been nearly a week ago but it felt like for ever because of how it had changed her life.

It felt like yesterday, too, because that time was etched into her memory for ever. She'd been so hopeful on her arrival but nervous as well. There'd been the media crowd to get through, helicopters hovering overhead and a grim man who'd met her at the door.

How different things were now. The media had given up and gone. There were no helicopters and she'd seen through the grimness that Julien had been wearing like a cloak to cover the vulnerability of a man who was capable of loving greatly but only felt safe to pour that passion into his work.

A man she had utterly fallen in love with.

But she felt far more nervous than she had that first time she'd been escorted up this driveway because there was a car parked on the curve of the driveway where it looped past the front doors to the mansion. A huge, gleaming black car. The kind that a very wealthy woman might be chauffeured to her desired destination in. The chauffeur was still sitting in the car but the back seat was empty.

Madame Laurent had clearly arrived and must have had a key to her son's house. She was waiting for them inside.

The nerves were there because Alice knew that this perfect day was almost over. That—very soon—she might have to say goodbye to both the man and baby she loved so much.

But the woman waiting for them was also the grandmother she had never met.

There was still a glimmer of hope.

CHAPTER TEN

YVONNE LAURENT WAS a perfect example of aristocratic elegance.

A tall, slim woman with beautifully coiffed silver hair and expertly applied make-up, she was wearing a twin set and pearls beneath the jacket and skirt of a tailored suit.

Alice was still wearing her forest-green jumper over one of the two shirts she'd been washing out every day and the jeans that were probably overdue for a wash were tucked into boots that had been getting a little more scuffed every day. And she had a silly hat with a pompom and sparkles on her head.

The visitor awaiting their arrival in the foyer barely gave her—or Jacquot—a second glance.

'*Bonjour*, Julien.' Her voice was as measured and controlled as her appearance but Alice understood nothing more than the greeting as a rapid conversation followed the polite kissing on each cheek. Julien ushered the older woman into the drawing room opposite the entrance to the grand salon and then turned back to Alice.

'She thinks you're a nanny,' he said in a low voice. 'I will explain why you are really here but it may be best if you take the little one up to the nursery in the meantime.'

Her nod of acquiescence was stiff. She could excuse the lack of interest in someone thought to be no more than hired help but she had this woman's grandchild cuddled against her chest and Madame Laurent had made no effort to try and see the baby's face. And this was supposed to be her precious grandchild that she was determined to care for?

The hope that she might welcome an adult granddaughter was evaporating. It was a relief to go upstairs. To change Jacquot and hold him in her arms while she fed him his bottle. To sing to him softly as she tucked him into his cot for what was possibly going to be the last time.

To wait. It felt like her future was lying in the hands of others but there was nothing she could do but wait.

And hope…

'Madame Laurent… I'm sorry that it has taken circumstances like this to meet you.'

She'd been at Colette's funeral, of course, but she'd been by André's side and Julien had kept his distance. He hadn't been welcome. At his own *sister's* funeral…

He couldn't afford to let any bitterness loose right now, however. And they were both dealing with the grief of losing a loved one. Surely that gave them a connection that would allow persuasion rather than threats—as Alice had suggested?

'I realise that this is a difficult time for you,' he said quietly. 'I am truly sorry for your loss, *madame*.'

The pale blue eyes he was looking into filled with tears. Yvonne Laurent lowered herself onto the overstuffed cushion of a small couch and opened her handbag to extract an embroidered handkerchief that she pressed to a corner of one eye and then the other. Finally, she spoke.

'My grandson is the only family I have left in the world.'

'Indeed.' Julien sat on the edge of another couch, facing her. This certainly wasn't the time to tell her that she was wrong. That she actually had another grandchild.

'It is the same for me, *madame*. Which is why I hope we can find agreement to keep him safe. Cared for. Loved…' The last word brought another echo of Alice's voice to the back of his mind. It felt like she was here in the room with him and it made it all the more important to make this work.

Even Madame Laurent's sniff was elegant. This time she pressed the handkerchief to her nose.

'That is exactly what I will do for Jacques. I am the one who can care for an infant. You…you have important work that must keep you extremely busy. You would not have the time for such a young child.'

Julien stiffened. He could *make* time, if he had to.

'You are a national icon, Julien.' Yvonne looked up to meet his gaze and her smile was poignant. 'My son was also. I understand the kind of pressure that goes with such a status.' When she blinked, her eyes glistened with tears again. 'I adored my son. I will give the same love and attention to my beloved grandson. I will provide the best nannies. Find the best schools.'

Julien dipped his head in acknowledgment. He could well believe that no money would be spared in providing for Jacquot but that wasn't the point.

'He's my nephew. My sister's child. I want to be part of his life.'

'Of course…' There was empathy in her tone now. 'I understand how important that is. I know there were… ah…difficulties in your relationship with my son but that is of little consequence now. This is about what is best for Jacques, is it not?'

'Yes.' Julien hadn't expected Madame Laurent to be so accommodating. He found himself smiling at her.

'I am not a young woman,' she said. 'While I can, of course I wish to provide a home for my grandson but I know there will come a time when he needs more than a safe nursery. A time when he needs a father figure. A time…' her indrawn breath was shaky '…when I will not be here to help him.'

'I want him to know who I am. I want to be part of his life.'

Madame Laurent tilted her head. 'You may visit whenever your schedule makes it possible. You will be made welcome at my estate.'

'And if anything happens to make it impossible for you to care for him?'

'I hope that will not be for a long time but, in that event, your guardianship will take priority.' Yvonne Laurent tucked her handkerchief back into her handbag. She got to her feet. 'If you're happy, I will have all of this documented by my solicitors and will bring the papers with me tomorrow when I come to collect my grandson.'

Happy? He should be. Madame Laurent had just agreed to everything he'd been trying to win when he'd come here in the first place. More, even. To be assigned indisputable guardianship of Jacquot if it became necessary in the future was an insurance policy that made this better than he could have hoped. But something was stopping any personal celebration and he knew what that something was.

Alice.

'Before you go, *madame*, there is something I should tell you about.'

'Oh…?'

'You have more than your grandson here in this house.' Julien took a deep breath. 'You also have a granddaughter.'

Madame Laurent stared at him. '*Non…c'est impossible…*'

Alice felt like she'd been waiting for ever.

Had Julien told Madame Laurent that she now had two grandchildren? Should she go downstairs? Brushing her hair, Alice wished she had packed some more clothes other than a spare shirt and clean underwear for this trip. Not that she owned anything like a power suit herself but why hadn't she thought to include a dress? Because she hadn't thought to present anything other than who she really was when she'd come in search of her father and that how the package was wrapped was of no importance?

Julien had seen through her lack of designer wear and sophistication. Or had he? If she had simply been a diversion from the boredom of being confined, it wouldn't have mattered what she looked like. Considering her an acceptable companion in the kind of world he normally inhabited might be a very different matter, especially if the people in that world were anything like

Madame Laurent. And if they were, a tiny voice whispered, would she even want to be there?

It needed every ounce of her courage to make the decision to go downstairs. Alice retrieved the photograph of her parents from her backpack, pushing aside the memory of how Julien had initially dismissed this evidence of her mother's relationship with André. The DNA test had been done and there could be no dismissal now. She hesitated a few moments more, however, checking—as she always did—that the baby cam was on and working before leaving the nursery.

But she didn't even get as far as the door because it was blocked by someone coming in.

Madame Laurent.

'Miss McMillan, it appears that you have a very unexpected connection with the Laurent family.'

Her English was so perfect it had virtually no accent and it made Alice realise how much she loved the way Julien spoke her language and could make it sound so much softer and almost as musical and inviting as his native tongue. How much she loved the way he said her name. It made the way this woman spoke seem so much harsher. Controlled and clipped. Cold…

She looked past Madame Laurent's shoulder in the hope that Julien had come upstairs as well but the doorway and the gallery beyond were empty.

She was alone. With her grandmother.

'I… I'm very happy to meet you,' she said quietly. 'I'm so very sorry for your loss. It's been devastating for me to have come here too late to be able to meet my father.'

Yvonne was staring at her but there was no more

warmth in either her expression or her body language than there had been in her voice. Then her gaze ran down the length of Alice's body, pausing as it reversed its journey.

'What is that?'

'Oh… It's a photograph. The only one I have of my parents together. It's what made me come here…' It was a wonder Alice's hand wasn't shaking as she held it out. 'Would you like to see?'

The focus of this woman's stare was unnerving.

'Her name was Jeannette McMillan. She came to work here in a gap year when she was eighteen. It was where she met your son, André.' Alice knew she was speaking too fast. Saying too much, but she needed desperately to break through what seemed an impenetrable barrier. 'Where she fell in love…'

Yvonne Laurent's breath was expelled in a dismissive snort. An echo of Julien's reaction. Was it a cultural thing to discount an extreme emotional connection? Surely not. Everybody knew that Paris was the city of love.

'I remember her.' The words dripped ice. The glance Alice received then sent a chill down her spine.

'I fail to understand what went wrong. The arrangements had been made. I had paid their exorbitant fees myself so that the unfortunate pregnancy could be dealt with discreetly.'

The mix of emotion that hit Alice was peculiar. There was anger that someone had been prepared to pay a lot of money to make sure she didn't exist. But there was a flash of something close to joy there as well. So it hadn't been her father who'd been the driving force in trying to get rid of her? It had been *this* woman. Her grandmother.

'*I* was that pregnancy,' she said slowly. 'And I was loved. By my mother. And by my *other* grandmother.'

Any rebuke her words held fell on deaf ears.

The huge diamonds in her rings flashed in the soft light of the nursery as Madame Laurent smoothed her perfectly groomed hair.

'I should sue that clinic,' she said. 'They told me the procedure had been completed. That the girl had been sent out of the country and would no longer be a problem.'

'Maybe they took pity on my mother when they saw how frightened she was. Or how much she wanted the baby of the man she loved.' Alice's voice was low. She was talking aloud to herself rather than trying to make conversation with someone she now knew she could never connect with.

Another derisive sound from Yvonne Laurent made her lift her chin and stare back at her, probably with the same kind of disgusted look she had been subjected to herself. This was unexpectedly devastating and a part of her needed to hit back.

'Perhaps it was André who made different arrangements,' she said. 'Perhaps he paid the clinic an even more exorbitant fee so that he could keep my mother safe. From *you*...'

'No. My son would not have done that. His racing career was everything to him. He was young. He could not have kept doing it if I hadn't provided the funding and he knew that was going to stop if he had anything more to do with a—a *waitress* who'd been stupid enough to try and catch him by producing an unwanted brat. She wasn't the only one. He was pursued by a great many like her. *Les salopes*... Trash...'

Alice stepped back as if she could get out of range of such venom. Her steps took her closer to the cot where Jacquot lay sleeping. It was then that fear stepped in. Not for herself—it didn't matter what this woman thought of her—but she was suddenly and dreadfully afraid for this innocent baby who was in danger of being brought up by a woman who was giving every impression that she was incapable of compassion, let alone love.

'And Jacquot?' she heard herself whisper. 'Is *he* an unwanted "brat" as well?'

'Of course not,' Yvonne Laurent snapped. 'He is a legitimate child and the heir to the Laurent name and fortune.' Her eyes narrowed. 'If you think you'll be getting any money from me, *mademoiselle*, think again. Maybe I wasn't careful enough the first time I tried to deal with you but I will not be making *that* mistake again.'

'Are you *threatening* me?'

'I am giving you some advice. Go back to the village you came from and do not ever come here again.'

Alice's inward breath was a gasp of horror. 'Jacquot is my *brother…*'

'No.' The word was final. 'Jacques Laurent is my grandchild. My *only* grandchild. You…' The rings on her hand flashed again in a gesture that could have been used to brush dust from a polished surface. 'You are *rien. Nothing.*'

'You don't care a jot about him,' Alice hissed. 'You haven't even *looked* at him since you came into this house.'

Madame Laurent's eyebrows rose just a little. Enough to suggest a refined astonishment.

'The child will have the best care that money can provide. And I will raise him to be as much of a credit to the Laurent name as his father was.'

Alice let out a long breath. 'I wish I'd met my father,' she said slowly. 'I wish I could have thanked him for making sure I didn't grow up here—with you as my grandmother. I was genuinely loved and that…that is of far more value than anything money can buy.'

The moment's silence was brief.

'Have my grandson ready to travel by tomorrow afternoon. And be ready to leave yourself. I do not wish to see you again.'

And with that, Madame Laurent turned and left the nursery, having not taken a step closer to Alice. Or any nearer the cot that contained her *only* grandchild.

Alice was shaking from head to toe as she did something that would probably be frowned on by any babycare guides. She lifted a soundly sleeping infant so that she could hold him in her arms and press her cheek gently against his downy head.

'I won't let it happen,' she whispered. 'I love you. Your uncle Julien loves you too, I know he does…and…and I love *him*…and I wouldn't have fallen in love with anyone who could let this happen so I know that you will be safe…'

Alice came downstairs as Madame Laurent's car was on its way to the front gates.

She looked pale. Shocked even.

Yvonne Laurent had looked a little pale herself when she'd come down a few minutes ago but that was understandable. To be presented with a relationship to an adult was a very different thing from meeting a vulnerable child and they would both need time.

And it wasn't really his business, was it? Nothing had changed. On leaving, Madame Laurent had only confirmed that she would be here tomorrow afternoon with their agreement legally documented.

So he smiled at Alice.

'All is well that ends well—is that how you say it?'

'Sorry?'

'A good result. I did not expect Yvonne Laurent to be so understanding. To agree to more than I had requested, in fact.'

'I… I don't understand…'

Alice had stopped moving. She sank down and sat very still, staring at him.

'There will be no need to go to court. She has agreed that I will be a part of Jaquot's life. That I will see him regularly and that, in the future, when she is no longer able to devote her life to her grandson, I will become his guardian.'

'Devote her life to him?' Alice looked horrified. 'Are you *kidding*? She doesn't care a jot for him, Julien. I don't think she even loved her own son. She wouldn't even *look* at Jacquot and she certainly isn't going to acknowledge me as his sister. She's an evil woman, can't you *see* that? She said the most horrible things about my mother. About *me*…'

The anguish in Alice's eyes was unbearable and it was too much like the kind of pain Julien had seen in other eyes, so long ago. It wasn't something he could fix and it might make things worse if he tried. To get too involved would only bring pain and hadn't he caused enough of that already? He was still too raw to cope with fresh wounds. He hadn't been able to protect Colette so what made him think he could help Alice?

At least he had protected Jacquot to the best of his ability.

And he could protect himself. He could feel himself turning inwards already, in search of that safe place.

'I expect that communication was difficult. Perhaps she wasn't able to express herself very well in your language.'

'Her English was perfect,' Alice said. 'Better than yours.'

If anything, her gaze was more intense now. 'You love Jacquot. You can't let this happen to him.'

She was looking at him the way she had when he'd told her so much about his childhood. As if she wanted to wave her magic wand and make him feel better.

Make him feel loved...

He couldn't go there. He didn't want to feel loved because that's how it all started. The need to give back. To love in return and to give everything you had. Then all you could do was wait for the inevitable pain when it got ripped away from you.

Just a few more steps and he could be in that safe place again. Couldn't Alice understand?

'You make everything about love,' he said. 'But that gets in the way of thinking with your head and not your heart and that's a dangerous path where too many people get hurt. Yes, my heart knows I love Jacquot but my head knows that what has been arranged is best. For everyone.'

Alice's eyes were huge in her pale face. 'You're afraid to take that path but you know that's what really matters. For everybody. *Especially* Jacquot...'

* * *

Her heart was breaking. She could feel it happening and the pain was unbearable.

The barriers were there again and more solid than ever.

The doubts she'd had during that awful time of waiting in the nursery surfaced again and this time they had vicious claws.

Julien had never said he loved her. He'd never even hinted that their time together would continue. He'd given her this special day because he'd known it was going to be their last and…and he'd been relieved when it was over. Look at the way the pleasure had been sucked out of the day when the woman at the hat stall had suggested they were a real family.

The spell had been broken then and now it was no more than a little sparkly dust. It would take no more than a heartfelt sigh to send that dust into oblivion.

He'd told her all along that it wasn't real. That it wasn't simply his work that stopped him from being able to raise a child. That he didn't *want* to…

Was there any point in trying to tell him that Jacquot's grandmother was an evil monster? What could she do? He'd been offered the perfect solution in which he could stay in that safe place he'd invented. The place where he didn't have to take the risk of truly loving.

Or being loved.

It was so obvious that Alice had reached the end of the road. That she was defeated.

'It makes no difference that I'm his sister, does it? That I can love him with all my heart and soul?'

That I could love you like that, too…

But she couldn't tell Julien that she loved him because he didn't *want* to be loved. Being rejected by Madame Laurent was one thing. To invite rejection from Julien was another thing entirely. Why make this even worse for herself?

And he wasn't going to tell her that he loved *her* because…because he didn't. It was that simple. He didn't know how to. She'd been right. She'd been no more than a distraction during a difficult time.

'I know you love Jacquot.' Julien's tone softened. 'And I…'

Something flashed in his eyes. It was a fleeting glimpse through the barriers. An echo of the 'thing'—that extraordinary connection they had found with each other. Oh, God…had she been wrong? Was he going to say that he loved *her*? That would change everything. They could fight this together. And *win*…

'And I must thank you for everything that you've done for him.'

The disappointment was crushing. Why did she keep buying into that fairy-tale when she should know better by now? Alice dropped her gaze so that Julien wouldn't see her pain.

'Maybe, one day, I can arrange for you to see him again but, for now, things must be as they are. *Je suis désolé.*'

Alice stared at her hands. It was really over.

'I'm sorry, too,' she whispered. 'More than you'll ever know.'

Julien was moving away. Towards the grand salon. Towards her father's office perhaps?

'I have to speak to my solicitor. Madame Laurent is returning tomorrow and it might be easier for you if you are not in the house. I will arrange for someone to come and care for Jacques until I get back from Paris. Marthe perhaps. And I will see if a flight can be arranged to take you home. Would you prefer to fly into Glasgow or Edinburgh?'

Alice pushed herself to her feet and turned her back as she prepared to head back upstairs. Her response felt strangled. Like her heart.

'Edinburgh.'

It was so late by the time he had all the arrangements in place there was no time for anything more than another strong cup of coffee, a shower and a change of clothes before his taxi would arrive to get him to his early flight to Paris.

Julien left the printout of the plane ticket to Edinburgh he had finally managed to secure on the kitchen table where Alice would find it when she came down for breakfast. He had also printed out the voucher for the taxi that would come and collect her. Marthe would be here by then and he would be getting on his return flight from Paris. By the time he was landing in Nice, her plane would have just taken off. They would both be in the sky at the same time, but flying in very different directions.

He would never see her again.

Along with the ticket and taxi voucher, Julien left the colour image he had used the technology in André's office to print. The photograph of Alice, with Jacquot in her arms, at the Christmas market in Nice.

He owed her at least a small memento.

No. He owed her much more than that but if he began to count then it would only make everything more difficult. More painful.

The picture said it all. That this time had been pretence. No more than a Christmas time fairy-tale and real life wasn't like that.

Could he leave without saying goodbye?

No. Of course he couldn't. The force that was still pulling him towards this extraordinary young woman was too overwhelming to even begin resisting and surely he could cope. He just needed to peep through the window of his safe place—he didn't have to step outside it.

There was no sound coming from the nursery but the door was ajar and there was the soft glow of a nightlight to be seen. Julien pushed the door open a little further but then he stopped, his planned speech of farewell and thanks evaporating.

He'd heard Jacquot crying when he'd been downstairs and again when he was getting out of his shower but now the baby was a silent bundle in the cot and Alice was curled up in the chair asleep with her head in the crook of her arm. Her hair was a tangle of curls and her face looked as if tears had dried to leave streaks.

If he woke her, would she cry again?

And, if she did, would he be able to stop himself taking her into his arms and holding her close to his heart?

Buying into that dream again for just a few moments longer? Making those promises he knew he had no hope of keeping? Making things worse for them both in the long run?

It was the hardest thing he'd ever done, turning to walk silently away from that room, but it was best that he did.

Best that he focused on what he had to do in a matter of only a few hours, which was to present to the world the face of a man whose absolute passion was his career. A career that might once have seemed as much of a fairy-tale as a happy family but was reality.

And he had to hang onto that for all it was worth.

Because, when all was said and done, it was all he really had to count on.

CHAPTER ELEVEN

JULIEN HAD GONE.

Alice knew that she and Jacquot were alone in the house from the moment she awoke.

Because it felt like a part of herself was missing.

The part she had given to Julien…

Jacquot was still asleep after a fretful night, probably due to the distress he must have sensed in her, so she moved slowly and quietly around the nursery, her feet feeling as heavy as her heart. After a brief shower she packed her few items into the backpack she had arrived with. The photo of her parents—now more precious than ever—was tucked carefully back into the side pocket. The action reminded her of the photograph she'd found in André's office of Jacquot's parents and her vow to find some way to give it to him one day. She needed to remember to go and fetch it.

It was still dark well after the baby stirred and Alice gave him his breakfast bottle and then bathed and dressed him. She gave him extra kisses and cuddles this morning and talked to him.

'I'll find you one day, sweetheart. I expect you'll learn to speak English and I'm going to take French lessons, so by the time I see you again we'll be able to talk to each other.'

She thought of all the baby milestones Jacquot would have in the next few years, like saying his first words and taking his first wobbly steps. The pain of knowing she wouldn't be able to witness or celebrate those milestones was astonishingly painful.

She'd found what she'd come to France in the hope of finding. Someone that was family to her. Jacquot had accepted her from the moment they'd met. Even now, the memory of how she'd been the only one able to comfort him when he'd been sick and miserable brought a smile to her lips. One that twisted in what felt like grief as she acknowledged that this gift of family was going to be wrenched from her in a matter of just a few hours.

And Julien hadn't even said goodbye.

The tears would come, nothing was surer, but Alice wasn't going to let it happen in the scant time she had left with her little brother. So she pasted a smile on her face.

'Shall we go downstairs, darling? So that Alice can have a cup of coffee?'

There would be no warm, buttery croissants ready for her this morning but it didn't matter. She couldn't have eaten anything anyway. Her stomach already felt like a stone and that stone became a painful boulder when she walked into the kitchen to find what had been left on the table for her.

The note was written in elegant handwriting. She could actually see Julien's hand holding the pen as she picked it up. Those long, clever fingers that were capable of magic in the kitchen. And in the bedroom…

Marthe would be arriving at ten-thirty a.m., the note

informed her. Half an hour before her taxi was due to arrive to take her to the airport.

'Merci, chérie,' the brief note ended. *'Au revoir.'*

Au revoir. One of the language lessons over a meal had been about saying goodbye. And this really meant goodbye. If you intended seeing someone again, you said something like '*à demain*'. Until tomorrow. Or '*à bientôt*'. Soon.

The endearment was probably automatic. Like a London cab driver calling you 'love'.

It meant nothing.

Except that wasn't true, was it? She'd seen a part of Julien Dubois that instinct told her very few other people saw.

That 'thing'. That connection they'd found when they'd looked at each other in the bathroom mirror that first night had been an attraction that went very much deeper than anything physical. She knew, beyond a shadow of a doubt, that Julien had felt it too. He was choosing to deny it. To run away.

And she understood. She might hate it but she had thought about nothing else in the sleepless hours before she'd finally succumbed to exhaustion last night.

She had told him that he was too afraid to take the path of love and it was true. He was protecting his heart but who could blame him when he'd lost everybody he'd given his heart to? His father had abandoned him at an impressionable age. He'd said himself that small children understood more than you would think and that was why he wanted to spare Jacquot the insecurity of having people fighting over his custody.

His mother had died at another impressionable age, when he'd been in that awkward transition period between child and adult, but he'd been mature enough to take responsibility for his young sister and devote his life to supporting and protecting her. Alice wasn't sure what had happened in recent years but the rift when he'd tried to protect Colette from marrying someone he hadn't trusted had to have been devastating. And just when it had looked like they were about to reconnect, he had lost his sister under tragic circumstances that were still raw.

No wonder he couldn't offer anyone else a part of his heart to keep for ever. There weren't that many parts left. And yet he'd tried, with Jacquot. He had been fighting to at least be a meaningful part of his nephew's life the day she had arrived here. There'd been an enforced disruption to the negotiations thanks to the quarantine but now he had exactly what he'd intended fighting for.

He had no idea what Madame Laurent was really like and, in trying to tell him, she had only made the distance between them greater. Maybe he hadn't been able to hear what she'd had to say because, if he believed her, it would destroy the victory he thought he'd won. Maybe that was why he hadn't risked waking her to say goodbye?

Had he felt the connection with her that he'd been unable to deny when he'd printed out this photograph of her at the Christmas markets?

Or had he remembered, instead, the shock of that stallholder assuming they were the parents of the small baby in their company? A happy little family. That he had a child of his own when he'd vowed that he would never let that happen.

As if he knew his part in the fantasy, Jacquot reached

up and caught the corner of the photograph in his small fist, crumpling it with surprising strength.

'Oops…' Alice gently extracted the glossy image. However painful it was in this moment, she was going to keep this. It didn't matter that it was now crumpled because she'd remember the tiny hand that had caused the damage and that made it even more precious.

She barely glanced at the plane ticket and taxi voucher because her intention of putting this photograph into her backpack beside the one of her parents had reminded her of the other photograph she was planning to take with her. The one in the heart-shaped, silver frame.

'Come on.' She smiled down at Jacquot, who now had a handful of her hair. 'Let's go to Daddy's office.'

She hadn't been in here since the night she'd interrupted the filming of the Christmas show that was probably being aired on television right now, with the hosts of the breakfast show chatting to Julien between clips. Was he wearing his white chef's tunic and that blue and white striped apron? Had it only been the night before last that he had emerged from the kitchen to kiss her senseless and give her the most memorable night of her life?

Such a contrast to the first memorable moment he'd given her, when he'd hurled that paperweight at her father's massive portrait. She stood in front of it for a long moment, ignoring the shards of glass and even the reason for the photograph. Instead, she looked into her father's eyes. Dark eyes, so like her own, that gleamed with such confidence and joy.

A man capable of great passion. Like Julien. But her father hadn't been afraid to love more than his career. He'd loved Colette, she was sure of that. Picking up the photograph in the silver frame only convinced her more. She clicked it shut. She was going to believe that André Laurent had loved *her* mother, too. He had been a victim of his upbringing perhaps. Overindulged and dependent financially on a woman who had no heart.

It was more of a stretch to believe that he'd helped Jeanette to escape the planned termination of her pregnancy but maybe her mother had severed contact so completely he'd known there was no point in trying to find her. The birth of his son at such a late age must have been a miracle. How sad that it had come at such a price, though. Had he been distraught? Had that contributed to his reckless driving that had taken his life?

He hadn't intended to die. Sinking into the desk chair, Alice used her free hand to open the drawer she'd opened the last time she had been in here. Yes. There were the tickets and passports ready to take Jacquot to his grandmother's house for his first Christmas.

Alice actually shuddered at the thought of being in that woman's company for anything, let alone a celebration like Christmas.

It was just as well she wasn't going to be here this afternoon to see Jacquot handed over to a woman who had no love in her soul. The family name was all Madame Laurent cared about, not the person who was carrying that name.

A flash of anger cut through weariness that went bone-deep.

How could Julien even think of allowing that to happen?

Maybe he wasn't the person she thought he was. Maybe she'd invented a prince for her fairy-tale and then she'd been stupid enough to fall in love with him.

No. In her heart of hearts she knew that wasn't true. Julien didn't know the truth or he would not let this happen. Nobody would.

Her arms tightened around Jacquot as she ducked her head to plant a kiss on his head. She'd promised this tiny person that she wouldn't let it happen. That his Uncle Julien wouldn't let it happen. But…but…

Alice blinked tears away as she raised her head, her glance grazing the drawer and its contents again as she did so.

Unbidden, her hand went out to pick up one of the items.

Jacquot's passport.

The idea was ludicrous. An act of rebellion that would get her into far more trouble than any of her childhood pranks.

But it wasn't impossible, was it?

Marthe wasn't coming here for another few hours. She had a voucher for the taxi company that included a phone number. If they spoke English—as most people seemed to here—she could change the time of her pick-up.

She had a plane ticket. A three-month-old baby didn't need a plane ticket because it got held in its mother's arms.

And who was going to check whether she actually was his mother? It was Christmas Eve and bound to be bedlam at any international airport.

She could keep Jacquot safe even if it was only for a short time before she was caught. She could keep him safe for his first-ever Christmas. Make him feel wanted and loved for no more than who he was. Her brother.

The idea was growing wings. The mix of nervousness and excitement felt rather like when she'd first arrived here. It would take courage to do it because she knew how wrong it was.

But then she looked down at a tiny face and Jacquot looked back and her and grinned his crooked little grin.

No. It wasn't wrong. It wasn't exactly the right thing to do either.

It was the *only* thing to do.

The airport was so chaotic Julien didn't remember to turn his phone back on until he'd finally managed to flag down a taxi and was stuck in the crazy Christmas traffic as he headed back to St Jean Cap Ferrat.

Ten missed calls from Marthe?

He knew his heart actually stopped for a moment because he felt the painful thump of it restarting.

Something had happened to Jacquot.

Or Alice.

His fingers shook as he tapped the screen to return the call. A moment later the housekeeper's voice was a distressed garble.

'I don't understand. Of course Alice has gone. Her plane will have taken off by now.'

He'd seen a British Airways plane taking off as he'd hurried through the crowds to escape the airport and he'd wondered if that was Alice disappearing from his life for ever. It had only made it more urgent to escape. To do what had to be done and then retreat into the only life he knew he could depend on. His own.

He was only half listening to Marthe's next words.

'How could she have taken Jacquot with her? You were there when the taxi came.'

He closed his eyes as he listened to the explanation. The taxi company had been and gone by the time Marthe had arrived at the house. Alice had left a note to say not to worry but the plan had been changed. That Julien would know why. So she'd been trying to ring him. Again and again.

But his phone had been turned off. Of course it had. He couldn't afford to have it ring when he was on a live television show and he hadn't bothered turning it back on when he had been about to fly.

If Alice had been on that plane he'd seen taking off, she hadn't been alone. She was taking her little brother back to Edinburgh and from there to whatever isolated little village she came from. What was its name? She had told him once. It would come to him.

Right now, the enormity of what had happened was sinking in as his taxi cleared the worst of the traffic and picked up speed. There was only an hour or two at most before Yvonne Laurent arrived to collect Jacquot and when she found out what had happened all hell would break loose. Would she think that he'd had a part in this himself? Would it send them all back to square one in a battle for Jacquot's custody?

How long did it take to fly to Edinburgh? No more than three hours, he suspected. Time enough for the full force of the law to be unleashed. Alice would be arrested the moment she arrived. Prosecution by the Laurent solicitors would be relentless and unforgiving. Jacquot would be taken away from her and brought back to France by strangers. He would be frightened and that was enough to make Julien angry. Very, very angry.

How could she do that?

What had she been *thinking*?

There was no reason for Marthe to stay in the house. Julien sent her home to her family. He screwed up the note Alice had left and hurled it to the floor of the kitchen. And then he began pacing, still unable to believe what she had done. He went in the direction of the nursery, as though he had to see for himself that it was uninhabited.

Which, of course, it was.

There was no sign that Alice had even been here but the absence of the baby whose name was proclaimed in those bright wooden letters on the wall was horrific.

The cot had been neatly made and propped against the soft bumper pad at the head end was a toy.

Le lapin brun.

Somehow that was even more shocking than Jacquot's absence. Alice had known how precious this toy was. She had said herself that she was happy it was there for him. That, one day, Julien would be able to tell him how special it was. How much he must have been loved.

He had to pick it up and, as he did so he remembered the last time he'd reached into this cot. When he'd been half-asleep and half-dressed and had gone into the nursery in response to that alarming cry from Jacquot.

And he remembered how he'd felt, holding that tiny baby against his bare chest. The pride in being able to comfort him. The absolute trust he was being endowed with to protect this baby from any evil in the world.

He could hear a whisper that sounded like Alice's voice.

She doesn't care a jot for him… I don't think she

even loved her own son... She's an evil woman, can't you see that?

Alice had felt that same level of trust from Jacquot, hadn't she? And she'd been brave enough to do something about it, however ill advised that had been. Anger was fading now, being replaced with something that felt more like respect. Admiration even.

But now Julien had the battered old bunny in his hand and he remembered the feel of it as if it was only yesterday that he had been handing it to his little sister to comfort her. How she would take it and clutch it to her chest and then wriggle into his arms to be held and comforted some more.

And finally...having not cried since his father had walked out when he'd been only five years old—even when his stepfather had beaten him or when his mother had died, leaving a scared youth to try and fight back against an unfair world—Julien was able to cry for his sister.

Racking sobs that felt like they were tearing his heart apart as he sank into the chair he'd seen Alice asleep in only this morning. Tears that soaked the toy he had pressed against his cheek. But curiously the pain didn't seem to be destroying what was left of his heart. When he was finally spent, there was an odd calmness to be found.

The beginning of peace perhaps?

It was only then that Julien became aware of something in the chair he'd been sitting in. Something with uncomfortably sharp edges. He reached underneath his legs and pulled out the handset to the baby monitor. Its red light was glowing but there was no point in keeping it on when there was no baby to watch over, was there?

Julien pushed a button but the light stayed on. He pushed another one and, unexpectedly, an image filled the screen. Did this state-of-the-art baby monitoring equipment actually make a video recording when it was switched on?

Apparently it did.

And the last time it had been switched on had been last evening. When Yvonne Laurent had gone up to the nursery after receiving the shocking news that there were *two* grandchildren of hers in the room.

He watched—and listened—in growing horror. Was this really the same woman whose words and tears had convinced him that they shared the same dream for Jacquot's future?

'The arrangements had been made. I had paid their exorbitant fees myself so that the unfortunate pregnancy could be dealt with discreetly.'

'...a waitress—who'd been stupid enough to try and catch him by producing an unwanted brat...'

'Jacques Laurent is my grandchild. My only grandchild... You... You are rien. *Nothing.'*

How hurtful must that have been? Words could hurt just as much as fists and he knew only too well what it was like to feel so unwanted. Rejected.

His little Scottish pixie had come here wanting nothing more than to find family in time for Christmas.

She'd found that her father had died only days before.

She'd found a tiny brother she could love and she'd been desperate to be allowed to raise him herself.

And she'd ended up being dismissed as *nothing.*

The anger was there again now but it wasn't directed at Alice. When the vicious old woman that his nephew was unfortunate enough to have as a grandmother arrived he was going to tell her exactly how wrong she was about Alice McMillan. Nothing? She was *everything* that Yvonne Laurent could clearly never be. Warm. Loving. Vibrant. Able to make life something to be celebrated, no matter what.

And…

Julien caught his breath as he focused on the small screen again. What was that? He studied the buttons on the handset properly this time so he could rewind and play that part again that he'd barely noticed during his outraged thoughts.

'I love you. Your uncle Julien loves you too, I know he does...and...and I love him...and I wouldn't have fallen in love with anyone who could let this happen...'

Mon Dieu…

The cascade of emotion was enough to bring tears to his eyes again but these were not tears of grief.

They felt more like joy.

And then Julien heard the doorbell ring. It was probably his solicitor, who was due to arrive before Madame Laurent in order to check that the legal paperwork was irrefutable. Paperwork that would now need to be ripped into shreds.

He got to his feet, the brown bunny in one hand and the handset of the monitor in the other.

Alice had left him one final gift, hadn't she?

The weapon he needed to win this battle, once and for all.

No. Make that two.

Unintentionally, she had also given him words of love.

Would they still hold true when he'd dismissed what she'd told him about that encounter with her grandmother? When he'd done what must have seemed so unforgiveable in her eyes? When he'd turned away from her so deliberately in order to protect himself?

There was only one way to find out.

But there were other matters to attend to first.

It was dark by the time the plane landed at Edinburgh airport even though it was only three p.m. Leaden skies held the weight of a snowstorm that everyone was hoping would hold off for at least twenty-four hours to give families time to gather for Christmas.

In rural Scotland, well to the north, it was already snowing. Tiny flakes sparkled in the headlights of her rented car as Alice finally parked in front of the cottage that had been her home since the day she was born.

The home she had celebrated every single Christmas in, with the decorations her mother had loved strung from every available anchoring point, a tree with flashing fairy-lights and gifts underneath, a fire burning brightly in the grate, Christmas carols coming from the CD player and the smell of a feast being prepared in the kitchen.

Home…

Jacquot was asleep in the car seat she had also rented. She carried him into the small stone house.

A very cold and dark stone house.

Aside from her brief visit back here last week, nobody had been living here for many months and there was no power on. No fire in the grate. Probably very little food in the pantry even. The shops would be shut and she didn't even have a close neighbour she could call on. There was no Christmas tree, no decorations and no music.

It was so quiet she could hear her own heart beating.

Until Jacquot woke and started to cry.

Alice undid the safety harness and scooped him into her arms. She wanted to cry herself.

What had she done?

What had she been *thinking*?

CHAPTER TWELVE

CHRISTMAS MORNING.

Somehow they'd survived the night.

Leaving Jacquot cocooned in blankets, tucked into the car seat that doubled as a carrier, Alice had used the light of her phone to find candles and then she'd built a fire in the ancient Aga stove in the kitchen that her grandmother had insisted on keeping because she'd been cooking on it ever since she'd come here as a young bride. At the same time she started a fire going in the open grate of the only living area in the house.

Feeding Jacquot was no problem now that she had a means of heating water because she had packed plenty of formula into the nappy bag, along with everything else she might need for a baby for a few days. She must have looked a sight at Nice airport yesterday, with her backpack on, a baby strapped to her chest and a well-stuffed carrier bag in each hand, but she'd been right in guessing that officials had been too busy to ask awkward questions. Instead, she'd found people eager to help a struggling young mother who'd had too many burdens to juggle. She'd got priority boarding and had been allowed to take all her bags onto the plane instead of checking any in, which had made for a much faster getaway when they'd arrived in Edinburgh.

That had been the worse time. The flight had been long enough for Alice to convince herself that Julien had arrived back in St Jean Cap Ferrat and would have been as furious as Madame Laurent to discover what she'd done. That the police would have been called. She had fully expected them to be waiting for her at Edinburgh airport.

But they hadn't been there.

And now she was several hours' drive away and, as if fate was lending her a helping hand, snow had fallen heavily all night. With any luck, it would take at least until tomorrow for roads to be clear enough to access Brannockburn easily.

She might not have the luxury of a few days' grace but it felt like she could count on having today.

Christmas Day.

And that was what mattered, wasn't it? This was Jacquot's first Christmas and she wanted it to be filled with all the love it was possible for a family to share. All the magic of Christmas.

Except there was nothing that said 'Christmas' about this house, except for the candles that she'd lit again once she was up for the day.

It was warm now, thank goodness. Rather than using the bedrooms upstairs, Alice had slept on the couch all night, getting up to look after Jacquot, who had slept in his nest of blankets, and stoking the fires each time.

But there was no tree. No decorations and no music. And certainly no smell of anything delicious being prepared in the kitchen—only the faint reminder of the can of baked beans Alice had heated for her breakfast.

They needed a tree.

'When I was little,' she told Jacquot, 'we all used to put our wellies on and go out to the big old pine tree beside the henhouse. I was allowed to choose the branch and Mum would saw it off. We had a red bucket full of sand that we kept on the back porch beside the firewood pile and we stood the branch up in that.'

The red bucket was still there. She'd seen it last night when she'd hurried in and out with armloads of small logs to fill the indoor basket.

She tickled Jacquot's tummy as he lay on the cushion of folded blankets, kicking his legs, and he grinned up at her.

With Julien's grin…

No…she couldn't go there… She wasn't going to cry today. Not on Christmas Day. She needed a distraction. Fast.

'What do you think, sweetheart? Shall we do it? If we were very quick, and chose a branch close to the ground, it wouldn't take long enough for us to get *too* cold because it's not snowing at the moment. And I know where the decorations are—in the boxes under Gran's bed. We won't be able to have the fairy-lights and I'm sorry I don't have any gifts for you but…but we could still make it *feel* right and I can take photos so that, one day, you'll know how special your sister wanted to make your first Christmas.'

There was another bonus to her plan. It would take most of the day to do everything she was suddenly desperate to do and it would stop her sitting around, thinking about Julien. The hardest moment came when she realised she needed a hat before she went tramping around in the snow and the only hat she had was the one Julien had bought for her at the markets in Nice. She pulled it over her head anyway.

'It's Christmas,' she told Jacquot, as she slipped her arms into the straps of the front pack. 'We need all the sparkles we can find.'

The daylight hours had come and gone in a flash. Here it was, four p.m., and it felt like night-time. Alice pulled the curtains over the windows to keep the warmth inside and she could see the starry shapes of fresh snowflakes sticking to the dark glass and piling up on the windowsills.

She was cutting them off from the outside world but it felt good. This was a private celebration and, as she turned and caught the full effect of the living room, it was perfect enough to make her catch her breath.

Okay, the hastily harvested tree branch was lopsided but it didn't matter because it was staying upright in the red bucket. And it didn't matter that it didn't have sparkling lights because it was plastered with every bauble Alice had found in the old boxes and with so many candles on the old sideboard and the mantelpiece, as well as the firelight, the glossy decorations were twinkling anyway.

Garlands of fake spruce and ivy, generously sprinkled with bunches of red berries, were looped above the doorways and from the heavy beams in the ceiling.

The beautiful stockings that her grandmother had lovingly embroidered were hanging above the fire and Alice had put tiny tea-light candles in glass tumblers on the hearth. The huge wickerwork reindeer her mother had loved stood guard on either side of the fireplace, proudly wearing their red collars and golden bells.

It didn't matter that there were no gifts under the tree either. Jacquot was too young to know the difference and Alice had the best gift she could possibly have already.

Family.

'We need a photo,' she told her tiny brother. 'I've never done a selfie before but here goes.'

She was wearing a Santa hat she'd found amongst the decorations and she'd dressed Jacquot in a little red sleep suit she'd packed with his things. Standing in front of the tree, with the baby tucked into the crook of one arm, Alice used her other hand to try and hold her phone far enough away to capture both their faces and some of the background.

It wasn't working. If she tilted the phone enough to put Jacquot's face in the picture, it cut off the top half of her own head and the tree was nowhere to be seen. 'I give up,' she sighed finally. 'I'll just take a picture of you and then we'll use my phone to have some Christmas music.'

The battery was not going to last much longer so Alice had to choose a favourite carol to listen to while she prepared Jacquot's Christmas dinner of a bottle of milk.

With the much-loved sound of 'The Little Drummer Boy' playing, she cuddled Jacquot for a minute longer, singing softly along with the song.

And then she froze.

No…it couldn't be…

But then she heard it again.

An insistent rapping on the front door of her house. Her time with Jacquot was about to end.

She'd been caught. It was time to face music that would have none of the joy of any Christmas carols.

She kept her head down as she opened her door, expecting to see the polished boots of more than one police officer.

She did see boots but they were old and soft looking, like a favourite pair a cowboy might wear. And they were beneath a pair of faded denim jeans. Alice's head jerked up.

'*Julien...*'

She had been hunted down by the person she was most ashamed to see and she could feel her face flood with burning colour as she thought of how much trouble she must have caused him.

But he was smiling. '*Bonjour, Alice. Joyeux Noël.* May I come inside?'

Speechless as she absorbed the sound of his voice again, Alice could only nod as she stood back. He was carrying a suitcase in one hand. No...it wasn't a case, she realised as he came into the light of the living room. It looked like...like a *picnic* hamper?

And he was holding something in his other hand as well.

Brown bunny.

Julien saw the direction of her gaze and held up the toy.

'I think you forgot something,' he said softly, holding it out to her. 'Something important.'

Her hand was trembling as she took the toy and she still couldn't think of a single word to say. This was the last thing she'd expected. Why wasn't he furious? Berating her for the crime she had committed in kidnapping Jacquot? Snatching him from her arms and disappearing back into the gloomy chill of the dark, snowy afternoon?

Finally, she found her voice, already sounding rusty. 'How did you find me? How did you *get* here?'

'I remembered the name of your village. Getting here was a little more problematic, especially when my car got stuck in the snow, but a very nice man with a tractor rescued me and, even better, he knew where your house was. I have walked the last mile or so. My feet are very cold.'

'Oh…come over near the fire.'

'Soon.' Julien put the hamper down and took off his coat. Then he pulled the hat off his head and the hair that had been tucked out of sight fell softly to touch his shoulders.

He stepped closer. 'You have forgotten something else. Or maybe you didn't know about it.' He bent to kiss Jacquot's head and then touched Alice's cheek with equal gentleness as he met her gaze.

She couldn't look away. The 'thing' was still there but it had changed. Grown. In fact, it was so huge it seemed to be sucking all the oxygen out of this room. Not that it mattered because she was too stunned to think about taking a breath anyway.

His hand traced her cheek, brushed her ear and then slid beneath her hair to cup the back of her head. Alice's lips were already slightly parted as she looked up, her heart so full of love it felt painfully stretched, and Julien matched his own lips with hers so perfectly it was like a dance as much as a kiss as they moved together.

'It is a French custom,' he whispered. 'The Christmas kiss.'

Vision blurred by tears made Alice blink. She couldn't believe any of this. It was a dream. A fairy-tale. Real life wasn't like this.

Except, right now, it appeared that it was.

Julien was stepping back. He picked up the hamper. 'There was so much food still in the cold room,' he said, 'I thought I would bring you Christmas dinner.'

Alice had thought that the traditional meal was the one thing she had needed to complete this Christmas celebration for Jacquot. But, in the wave of a magic wand, it had now appeared and she knew she'd been wrong.

What she had really needed to complete this perfect little Christmas was to be with both the people she now thought of as family.

Jacquot *and* Julien.

A single tear escaped and trickled down her cheek.

Miracles really did happen at Christmastime, didn't they?

'I have champagne, too,' Julien added. 'Because we have something to celebrate.'

'We do?'

'*Oui.* But first I must apologise. I had no idea about the terrible things Madame Laurent said to you. I had no idea what sort of person she really was because, I think, her acting skills are excellent. I should have listened. I will always listen in future, *mon amour. Je suis vraiment désolé.*'

That French was being spoken in this house, of all places, should have felt like a betrayal to her grandmother and mother but instead it felt like the two halves of who she was had finally been fitted together like a jigsaw puzzle. Or maybe she was feeling whole because Julien was here with her. Whatever the reason, the picture that the neatly fitting pieces were making was beautiful.

Jacquot's whimper reminded her that it was time for him to be fed but Alice hesitated. The shock of seeing Julien was wearing off and questions were filling her head. Serious questions.

'How do you know what she said? Did she *tell* you? Why? And where is she now? What's going to happen to me?'

Julien smiled. 'One question at a time, *mon amour.* Here, give Jacquot to me or would you like me to prepare his bottle?'

In answer, Alice transferred the bundle of baby from her arms to his and Jacquot, bless him, looked up at his uncle and forgot he was hungry. He practised his best smile instead. Julien followed Alice to the kitchen and watched as she reheated the pot of boiled water on the hotplate over the oven.

'Did you know that the baby cam could record things?'

'No.' Alice spooned formula into the bottle. If she had, she might have gone back to watch a particular scene more than once. The one where Julien had picked up his tiny nephew and held him against his bare chest. A scene that had captured her heart so decisively.

'It was lucky that you'd turned it on before Madame Laurent came into the nursery. It recorded everything she said.'

Alice's eyes widened. 'That's right… I'd turned it on because I'd been about to come downstairs and find you…'

'It gave me the evidence I needed to confront her.

My solicitor reminded her that what she had done had been ill advised and illegal if your mother had been more than twelve weeks pregnant. That, in any case, if this recording became public, her reputation would be ruined and if she contested the issue of guardianship any further, then that was exactly what would happen.'

Alice gasped. 'She must have been *so* angry.'

Julien nodded, a sombre expression on his face. 'So angry the doctors said later that it must have raised her blood pressure to a terrible level and that is why she had the… I don't know the word…*un accident vasculaire cerebral…*'

'A stroke?' Alice guessed, shocked. 'Oh, my God… Is she…is she still alive?'

Julien nodded again. 'But she is badly affected. I rang the hospital this morning before I left to check on her progress and it is thought she will need specialist care for a long time.'

Alice absorbed this information slowly as she shook the bottle and then tested the temperature of the formula on her wrist.

'So she can't take Jacquot even if she wanted to fight for custody?'

'No. My guardianship will be uncontested. Ironically, that was part of our agreement that she had already signed. That if anything happened to her, this is what would happen. From now on, he will be in my care.'

Alice nodded slowly, trying to take it all in. So that was why Julien had come instead of the police. He was here to take Jacquot back to France with him.

'Would…?' She had to clear her throat so her voice didn't wobble. 'Would you like to feed him?'

'You give Jacquot his dinner.' Julien gently transferred the baby back to her arms. 'I would like to give you *your* dinner and I need to make it hot.' He was smiling now. 'Do you remember the last Christmas dinner we ate together?'

How could she forget, when it had happened after he had taken her to his bed for the first time? By the look in his eyes right now he was remembering exactly the same thing.

'And do you remember I said you might be eating Christmas dinner more than once?'

Alice's knees felt a little weak. Was Julien referring to a repetition of more than eating a traditional meal? She needed to sit down while she fed Jacquot, who fell asleep before he had even finished his milk.

And then Julien brought her a glass of champagne and sat beside her on the old couch as they drank it. Silently, they sat together, soaking in the warmth and light of this Christmas scene Alice had created today.

'You really are a pixie,' Julien told her finally. 'You make the world a special place wherever you are.'

He took her empty glass and put it on the coffee table with his and then he put his arm around her and Alice snuggled against him, tilting her face up to receive one kiss and then another. They couldn't go upstairs to a bedroom and leave a baby in a room with a fire and a dozen candles but, unexpectedly, this felt better than sex. Deeper.

More like real life instead of a fairy-tale?

'Why did you leave *le lapin brun* behind?' Julien asked softly. 'Did you know I would find it?'

Alice nodded, loving the feel of Julien's chest beneath her cheek. She could hear his heart beating.

'I hoped so,' she said. 'I knew how much it meant to you. That it was the one thing Colette had given her baby that had been hers from her childhood. It was the link…the *love*…and I hoped that one day you would be able to give it to Jacquot so that the chain of that love wouldn't be broken.'

'Colette used to hold it when she was frightened.' Julien's voice cracked as he spoke. 'And I used to hold her. Like this…' His arm tightened around Alice and she snuggled closer.

'I'm not afraid to take the path of love,' he whispered, his lips very close to her ear. 'Not any more. I will love Jacquot for every day that I live and I will protect him in every way that I can.'

Alice pressed her lips together to stop them trembling. 'You will take him back to France?'

'I have to, *cherié*. You know that, yes?'

Alice nodded.

'But there is something I am also hoping…'

Alice tilted her head so that she could see his face.

'I am hoping that you will come back with us. That you will help me raise Jacquot and give him the love that only his sister or mother could provide.'

Alice stopped breathing. Was that all Julien was hoping? His eyes were telling her more than that but was he really not afraid to take an even bigger step into trusting that he could not only give love but *be* loved in return?

'*Je t'aime*,' he whispered. '*Tu as volé mon coeur. Tu as changé mon vie et...je pense que tu es la dernière pièce de mon casse-tête.*'

Oh… Alice's eyes filled with joyous tears. Could there ever be a more beautiful language for words of love? She didn't need a translation.

Or maybe she did.

'What does that mean? What is a *casse-tête*?'

'A puzzle. I said that I think *you* are the last piece of *my* puzzle.'

'Oh…that's exactly what I was thinking about you. I… No… *Je t'aime*, too, Julien. I always will. For ever.'

'*Pour toujours*,' Julien confirmed. And then he kissed her, so tenderly that the tears in Alice's eyes escaped to dampen both their faces. Or had Julien shed some of his own?

The smell of the heating turkey and gravy wafted into the room at that point. Alice's stomach growled loudly and Julien tipped back his head as he laughed.

'I am home,' he declared. 'And it is time to feed my woman.'

He stood up, lifting Alice to her feet, but instead of leading her to the kitchen he wrapped his arms around her again.

'This is only the first of many,' he whispered. 'And I will try to make each one happier than the last. *Joyeux Noël, mon amour*.'

'*Joyeux Noël*,' Alice echoed. And then she stood on tiptoe so that she could kiss Julien again. 'It's a Scottish custom, too,' she murmured. 'The Christmas kiss…'

* * * * *

A VERY SPECIAL HOLIDAY GIFT

BARBARA HANNAY

For Elliot, with huge, *huge* thanks for your unfailing faith in my writing... It would never have happened without you.

CHAPTER ONE

THE PHONE CALL that changed Chloe Meadows's life came when she was poised on tiptoe, on a chair that she had placed on top of a desk in a valiant attempt to tape a loop of Christmas lights to the office ceiling.

It was late on a Wednesday evening, edging towards nine p.m., and the sudden shrill bell in the silent, empty office was so unexpected Chloe almost fell from her precarious perch. Even so, she slipped as she scrambled down awkwardly in her straight grey business skirt and stocking feet.

She was slightly out of breath as she finally grabbed the phone just as it was due to ring out.

'Hello? ZedCee Management Consultants.' She wondered who would call the office at this late hour. On a Wednesday night.

There was a longish beat before she heard a man's distinctly English voice. 'Hello? I'm calling from London. Could I please speak to Mr Zachary Corrigan?' The voice was officious, like the command of a bossy teacher.

'I'm sorry. Mr Corrigan isn't in the office.' Chloe politely bit back the urge to remind the caller that it was well after office hours in Australia and that her employer was almost certainly at a social function.

On any given week night, Zac Corrigan was likely to be socialising, but that possibility had become a certainty *this* week, the week before Christmas, when almost everyone was at some kind of party. Everyone, that was, except Chloe, whose social calendar was *quiet* even at this busy time of the year.

Sadly, the red letter date in Chloe's festive season was the office Christmas party. This was the third year in a row that she'd put up her hand to be the party's organiser. She'd ordered the champagne, the wines and beer, as well as a selection of delicious canapés and finger food from François's. And she'd been happy to stay back late this evening to decorate the office with festive strings of lights, shiny balloons and bright garlands of tinsel and holly.

Secretly, she loved this task. When she'd first landed her job at ZedCee she'd also moved back home to care for her elderly parents, who weren't overly fond of 'gaudy' decorations, so this was her chance to have a little Christmas fun.

'To whom am I speaking?' the fellow from London barked into the phone.

'I'm Mr Corrigan's PA.' Chloe was used to dealing with bossy types, matching their overbearing manner with her own quiet calm. 'My name's Chloe Meadows.'

'Ms Meadows, this is Sergeant Davies from The Metropolitan Police and I'm ringing from The Royal London Hospital. I'm afraid the matter is urgent. I need to speak to Mr Corrigan.'

'Of course.' Instantly alarmed, Chloe forgave the policeman his bossiness and reached for a pen and paper.

She was appalled to think that this urgent matter was in any way connected to her boss. 'I'll call Mr Corrigan immediately and tell him to ring you.'

Sergeant Davies dictated his number, Chloe thanked him and her stomach clenched nervously as she connected straight to Zac Corrigan's mobile.

The zip in the young woman's black silk dress slid smoothly downwards and the fabric parted to reveal her delightfully pale back. Zac Corrigan smiled. She was lovely. Tipsy after too many champagne cocktails and without very much to eat, but at least they'd escaped the party early, and she was quite irresistibly lovely.

With a practised touch, he caressed the creamy curve of her shoulder and she giggled. Damn. Why did champagne make girls giggle?

Still. Her skin was soft and warm and her figure was exquisite and, for a repeat of the night they'd shared last weekend, Zac could forgive her giggling.

With a firm hand cradling her bared shoulders, he leaned closer to press a kiss to the back of her neck. His lips brushed her skin. She giggled again, but she smelled delicious and Zac's anticipation was acute as he trailed a seductive line of kisses over her shoulder.

The sweet moment was spoiled by the sudden buzz of his mobile phone and Zac swore beneath his breath as he sent a frustrated glare in the direction of the armchair where he'd dumped the phone along with his jacket and tie.

'I'll get it!' the girl squealed.

'No, don't bother. Leave it.'

Too late. She'd already wriggled free and was diving for the chair, laughing excitedly, as if answering his phone was the greatest game.

Chloe suppressed a groan when she heard the slightly slurred female's voice on the line.

'Hi, there!' a girl chirped. 'Kung Fu's Chinese Takeaway. How can I help you?'

'Hi, Jasmine.' Chloe was unfortunately familiar with most of her boss's female 'friends'. They were usually blessed with beauty rather than brains, which meant they were always ringing him at work, and Chloe spent far too much time holding them at bay, taking their messages, placating them with promises that Mr Corrigan would return their calls as soon as he was free, and generally acting as a go-between. 'Hold the jokes,' she said now. 'And just put Zac on.'

'Jasmine?' The voice on the end of the line was slightly sloshed and distinctly peeved. 'Who's Jasmine?' Her voice rose several decibels. 'Zac, who's Jasmine?'

Oops. Under other circumstances, Chloe might have apologised or tried to reassure the silly girl, but tonight she simply spoke loudly and very clearly. 'This is Mr Corrigan's PA and the matter is urgent. I need to speak to him straight away.'

'All right, all right.' The girl was sulky now. 'Keep your hair on.' There was a shuffling, possibly stumbling sound. 'Mr Corr-i-gan,' she said next, sounding out the syllables in a mocking sing-song. 'Your PA wants you and she says you'd better hurry up.' This was followed by a burst of ridiculous giggling.

'Give that here!' Zac sounded impatient and a moment later he was on the line. 'Chloe, what's up? What the hell's the matter?'

'An urgent phone call has come through for you from London,' she said. 'From the police. At a hospital.'

'In *London*?' There was no missing the shock in his voice.

'Yes. I'm afraid it's urgent, Zac. The policeman wants you to call him immediately.'

There was a shuddering gasp, then another sound that might have been—

No. It couldn't have been a sob. Chloe knew her ears were deceiving her. During three years in this job she'd never detected a single crack in Zac Corrigan's habitual toughness.

'Right.' His voice was still *different*, almost broken and very un-Zac-like. 'Can you give me the number?'

Chloe told him and listened as he repeated it. He still sounded shaken and she felt a bit sick. Normally, she refused to allow herself any sympathy for her boss's personal life, which was as messy as a dog's breakfast, as far as she was concerned. But this situation was different. Frightening. She couldn't recall any connection between her boss and London and she thought she knew almost everything about him.

'I'll let you know if I need you,' he said.

Zac was as tense as a man facing a firing squad as he dialled the London number. This emergency *had* to involve Liv. He was sure of it. He'd been trying to convince himself that his little sister was an adult now and quite capable of running her own life, especially after she'd ignored his protests and left for England with her no-hoper boyfriend… But…

Liv.

His baby sister…

All that was left of his family…

His responsibility…

'Hello,' said a businesslike English voice. 'Sergeant Davies speaking.'

'This is Zac Corrigan.' His voice cracked and he swallowed. 'I believe you're trying to contact me.'

'Ah, yes, Mr Corrigan.' The policeman's tone was instantly gentler, a fact that did nothing to allay Zac's fears. 'Can I please confirm that you are Zachary James Corrigan?'

'Yes.' What had Liv done? Not another drug overdose, surely? When he'd rung her two weeks ago, she'd promised him she was still off the drugs, *all* drugs. She'd been clean for over a year.

'And you're the brother of Olivia Rose Corrigan?'

'Yes, I am. I was told you're calling from a hospital. What's this about?'

'I'm sorry, Mr Corrigan,' the policeman said. 'Your sister died a short while ago as the result of a road accident.'

Oh, God.

It wasn't possible.

Shock exploded through Zac, flashing agonising heat, threatening to topple him. Liv couldn't be dead. It simply was *not* possible.

'I'm sorry,' Sergeant Davies said again.

'I—I see,' Zac managed. A stupid thing to say, but his mind was numb. With terror. With pain.

'Do you have any relatives living in the UK?' the policeman asked.

'No.' Sweat was pouring off Zac now. Vaguely, he was aware of the girl, Daisy, with the black dress dangling off her shoulders. She was hovering close, frowning at him, her heavily made-up eyes brimming with vacuous curiosity. He turned his back on her.

'Then I take it you'll be prepared to be our contact for any arrangements?'

'Yes,' Zac said stiffly. 'But tell me what happened.'

'I'll pass you onto someone from the hospital, sir. The doctor will be able to answer all your questions.'

Dizzy and sick, Zac waited desperately as the phone went through several clicks and then a female voice spoke.

'Mr Corrigan?'

'Yes,' he said dully.

'This is Dr Jameson from the maternity ward.'

Maternity? She was joking, surely?

'I'm very sorry, Mr Corrigan. Your sister was brought to our hospital after a vehicle accident. There were extensive head and chest injuries.'

Zac winced. Head and chest. The worst.

'Olivia was rushed to theatre and we did our very best, but the injuries were too extensive.' A slight pause. 'I'm afraid we couldn't save her.'

Zac went cold all over. So there it was. Two people had confirmed the impossible. His greatest fear was a reality. After all these years when he'd tried and failed with Liv, he'd now failed her abysmally…

And it was too late to try again.

He couldn't breathe, couldn't think. Horror lashed at him as he fought off images of Liv's accident. Instead he clung to a memory of his beautiful, rebellious young sister from years ago when she was no more than sixteen… He saw her on the beach, during a holiday on Stradbroke Island, her slim tanned arms outstretched, her dark gypsy hair flying in the sea wind, her teeth flashing white as she laughed and twirled with child-like joy.

He remembered it all so clearly. With her brightly coloured sarong over a skimpy yellow bikini, she'd looked so tanned and beautiful. Innocent, too—or so Zac had thought—and, always, *always*, so full of fun.

That was how he'd thought of Liv back then—full of fun and life.

Now...he couldn't believe that her life had been extinguished.

'But we were able to save the baby,' the English doctor said.

Baby? Now Zac sank in weak-kneed horror onto the edge of the bed. What baby? How could there be a baby?

'Are you there, Mr Corrigan?'

He swallowed. 'Yes.'

'You're listed as your sister's next of kin, so I'm assuming you knew that Olivia was pregnant?'

'Yes,' he lied when in truth he'd had no idea. When he'd phoned Liv only two weeks ago, she hadn't said a thing about being pregnant. Right now, he felt as if the world had gone quite mad.

'Your sister was already in labour,' the woman said. 'We believe she was on her way to hospital when the accident occurred.'

'Right.' Zac sagged forward, elbows on knees. 'So—' he began and then he had to stop and take a shuddering breath, which wasn't much help. He forced himself to try again. 'So—this baby. Is it OK?'

'Yes, a beautiful baby girl, perfectly unharmed and born by Caesarean section only a couple of weeks before her due date.'

Zac pressed a shaking hand to his throbbing forehead. His stomach churned. He was sweating again. This woman was trying to tell him that some crazy twist of fate had snatched his beautiful sister's life and left a baby in her place. How bizarre was that?

He wanted to drop the phone, to be finished with this absurd conversation. No way did he want to deal with the gut-wrenching news that had just been so calmly delivered.

But, of course, he knew he had no choice.

With a supreme effort, he shut off the hurt and pain and, like the cool-headed businessman he usually was, he forced his mind to confront practicalities.

'I presume you've contacted the baby's father?' he said tightly, recalling the man who'd convinced Liv to run away with him. A guy from a band—a band no one had heard of—an older man with dreadlocks streaked with grey and restless eyes that could never quite meet Zac's gaze.

'Your sister wasn't able to tell us the name of the baby's father. There was a man in the car with her, but he assured us he was only a neighbour and not the father, and our blood tests have confirmed this.'

'But he could tell you—'

'I'm afraid he doesn't know anything about the father's identity.'

'Right.' Zac drew a deep, shuddering breath and squared his jaw. 'So this baby is, for all intents and purposes, my responsibility?' Even as he said this, he knew it hadn't come out right. He'd sounded uncaring and hard. But it was too late to try to retract his words. He could only press on. 'I'll…er…make arrangements to come over to London straight away.'

* * *

Chloe had just finished pinning the last decoration in place when her boss rang back.

'Chloe, I know it's late, but I need you to book me a flight to London.' His voice was crisp and business-like, but tight, too, the way people spoke when they were fighting to keep their emotions in check. 'You'd better make it the soonest flight possible. First thing tomorrow morning, if you can.'

'Of course, and would you like a hotel reservation as well?' Chloe hoped she didn't sound too surprised, or worried… If there was a crisis, the last thing Zac needed was an anxious, fussing PA.

'Yes, book a hotel room, please. Somewhere central.'

'No problem.' Already she was firing up her computer.

'And I'll need you to sort out those accounts with Garlands.'

Chloe smiled to herself. 'All done.'

'Already?' He sounded surprised. 'That's great. Well done.'

'Anything else?'

'Could you ring Foster's and tell them that Jim Keogh will represent me at tomorrow's meeting.'

'No problem.' Chloe paused, in case there were any more instructions. 'That's all then?'

'Actually, Chloe…'

'Yes?'

'You'd better book two flights to London. Just two one-way seats at this stage. I'm not sure how long I'll need to be over there.'

Ridiculously, Chloe's heart sank. An annoying reaction. Why should she care if her boss wanted to take the giggling girl who'd answered the phone with him on an all-expenses-paid trip to London? Of course,she couldn't help wondering how much use the girl be would if Zac had been called away to something urgent.

'What name for the second ticket?' she asked smoothly as the company's preferred airline's website came up on her computer screen.

'Ah…good question. Actually…'

Another pause. Chloe began to fill the boxes on the flights search. Point of departure… *Brisbane, Australia.* Destination… *London, UK*. Date of flight…

'How busy are you, Chloe?'

'Excuse me?'

'Could you spare a few days?'

'To fly to London?'

'Yes. This is an emergency. I need someone…capable.'

Chloe was so surprised she almost dropped the phone. Was Zac really asking her to go to—to London? *At Christmas?*

'I know it's short notice and it's almost Christmas and everything.'

Her head spun, first with shock and a fizz of excitement, and then with dismay as she thought about her elderly parents at home, waiting for her, depending on her to look after the shopping and to cook Christmas dinner and to drive them to church. They would never cope without her.

'I'm sorry, Zac. I don't really think I could get away at such short notice.'

As she said this, there was the sound of a door opening behind her and she jumped. Turning, she saw her boss striding into the office. Of course, he'd had his phone in the hands-free cradle while he was driving.

As always, Chloe's heart gave a pitiful little skip when she saw him, but at least she was used to that nuisance reaction now. She knew it wasn't significant—pretty much the automatic reaction shared by most women who encountered Zac Corrigan's special brand of tall, dark and handsome.

This evening he looked paler than usual and his grey eyes betrayed a shock he hadn't been able to shake off.

'If you can come with me, I'll pay you a hefty Christmas bonus,' he said as he strode across the office to Chloe's desk.

But he'd already paid her a generous Christmas bonus. 'Can you explain what this is about?' she asked. 'What's happened?'

What's happened?

Zac lifted his hand and rubbed at his brow, where a headache had been hovering ever since he took the call from the hospital and now throbbed with renewed and vicious vengeance.

'Are you all right, Zac? You look…'

Abruptly, Chloe pulled a swivel chair from the nearest desk and pushed it towards him. 'Here, sit down.'

He held up a hand. 'It's OK, thanks. I'm fine.'

'I'm sorry, but I don't think you are.'

To Zac's surprise, his PA took a firm grasp of his elbow, gripping him through his coat sleeve. 'I think you should sit down now before you fall down.'

Zac sat.

'Can I get you a cup of tea?'

If he wasn't feeling so strung out, he might have

smiled at this old-fashioned response from his conservative and over-conscientious PA. She was dressed in one of her customary businesslike suits. Her white blouse was neatly buttoned and tucked in, and there wasn't a strand of her light brown hair out of place. Good old, reliable Chloe.

He was so relieved to see her tonight. He'd been desperate to get away from the giggling Daisy and, by contrast, cool, collected Chloe was a reassuring and comforting sight.

'I don't need tea,' he said. 'I'd just like to get these flights sorted, and I could really do with your assistance in London.'

'I assume this is all because of the phone call…from the hospital.'

'Yes.' Zac swallowed, trying to clear the sharp, persistent pain that seemed to have lodged in his throat. 'I'm afraid it wasn't good news,' he said with quiet resignation. 'It was bad. Really bad. The worst.'

'Oh, no… I'm so sorry.'

Sorry… Zac was sorrier than he'd ever thought possible. He looked away from the sympathy in Chloe's soft brown eyes. Then, staring bleakly at a spot on the grey office carpet, he told her the rest of his news…

When he finished, Chloe took ages to respond. 'I…I don't know what to say,' she said at last. 'That's so terrible. I…I never realised you had a sister.'

'Yeah…well…' He couldn't bring himself to admit his estrangement from Liv, or that he hadn't known about the baby, that Liv had never even told him she was pregnant, that she almost hadn't told him about going to England.

How could he admit to this prim and conscientious

cliché of a secretary that his reckless sister's pregnancy was just another of the many secrets she'd hidden from him?

'I guess you'll need help…with the baby girl…if they can't find her father,' Chloe suggested awkwardly.

'Yes. I'll be it's…I mean…*her* guardian.' He knew this, because the one thing he'd insisted on after Liv's overdose was that she made a will. He'd hoped that a measure of reality would shake some sense into her. 'I couldn't possibly manage on my own.'

Babies had never registered on Zac's radar. He'd always supposed they were a dim possibility in his far distant future…when he eventually settled down and chose a wife and all that went with a wife… But, even though he was a godfather twice over, he'd never actually held a baby. There had always been plenty of women with willing arms and he'd been more than happy to buy expensive gifts and the best champagne to wet the baby's head and then stay well in the background…

'I'm sure we can find someone.' Chloe was busy at her computer screen, scrolling through some kind of spreadsheet.

'Find someone?' Zac asked, frowning. 'How do you mean? What kind of someone?' He didn't need to *find* someone. He had Chloe.

She turned back to him with a smile that was almost sympathetic. 'This is a list of your personal female contacts.'

'You have them on a spreadsheet?'

'Well, yes. How else do you think I manage to—?'

'All right, all right.' He gave an impatient wave of his hand. He knew Chloe was a marvel at managing his female friends—sending them the appropriate invitations or flowers, birthday or Christmas presents, get well cards, even, at times, offering excuses on his behalf…but he'd never given any thought to how she kept track of them.

'What about Marissa Johnson?' Chloe said now. 'She always struck me as sensible.'

'No,' Zac said curtly, remembering the awkward way he and Marissa Johnson had broken up. He jumped to his feet, seized by a fit of restless impatience. 'Look, there's no point in looking at that list. I don't want any of *them*. I want you, Chloe. We've worked together for three years now and I know you'd be perfect.'

To his surprise her cheeks went a deep shade of pink—a becoming shade of pink that unsettled him.

'I don't know very much about babies,' she said.

'Really?' Zac frowned at her. She was female, after all. 'But you know enough, don't you? You know how to put on a nappy. And when it comes to bottles and that sort of thing, you can follow instructions. It's just for a few days, Chloe. There's a remote possibility that I might have to bring this child home. I'll need help, just till I have everything sorted.'

Not that he had any idea how this problem could be sorted. At the moment he was still too shocked. Too sad. He didn't want to think about a little new life when Liv was—

'I'm sorry,' Chloe said quickly. 'I'd like to help, but I'm not really free to rush overseas at the drop of a hat. Not at this time of year. I have my parents to consider…'

'Your parents?' Zac frowned again. Why would a woman approaching thirty be so concerned about her parents? Then again, he knew he was out of touch with the whole family thing. His own parents had died when he was eighteen and he'd been managing without them for almost seventeen years.

But now there was a baby…a niece…another little girl who was his responsibility. A slug of pain caught him mid-chest. History was repeating itself in the most macabre way.

'It's Christmas,' Chloe said next, as if that explained everything. She looked up at the surprisingly attractive decorations she'd arranged about the office. 'Would you like me to look into hiring a nanny?'

Zac let out a weary sigh. 'The last thing I need now is to start interviewing nannies.'

'I don't mind doing the interviews.'

'No,' he snapped. 'We don't have time.'

Besides, for this delicate operation, he needed someone he already knew, a woman who was loyal and trustworthy, and sensible and efficient—and a woman who wouldn't distract him with sex.

Chloe Meadows ticked every box.

CHAPTER TWO

CHLOE COULDN'T QUITE believe it was actually happening. Here she was in the executive lounge of Brisbane International Airport, enjoying coffee and croissants with her boss, with a boarding pass for a flight to London in her handbag, a grey winter jacket and rosy pink scarf folded on the seat beside her, and a neatly packed carry-on bag at her feet.

She still wasn't quite sure how Zac had convinced her to do this, but from the moment he'd learned she had an up-to-date passport the pressure had begun. He'd argued that the company was winding down for the Christmas break anyway and, thanks to her superb organisational skills, the office Christmas party could run brilliantly without her.

He'd brushed aside her concerns that she knew very little about babies. After all, the child's father might yet be found.

To Chloe's amazement, even her very valid concerns about her parents had been duly considered by her boss and then swiftly and satisfactorily smoothed away.

She'd been stunned when he'd asked last night if he could visit her parents. She'd tried to protest. 'Sorry, no. Mum and Dad will be in bed already.'

'Why don't you ring them to check?' he'd said confidently.

To Chloe's surprise, her mother and father were still up, watching *Carols in the Cathedral* on TV, and, even more surprisingly, they said they'd be happy for her boss to call in, if he didn't mind finding them in their dressing gowns and slippers.

Zac said he didn't mind in the least.

'Chloe, there's sherry in the pantry and we can break open that box of shortbread you bought last week,' her mother suggested, sounding almost excited.

Zac had poured on the charm, of course, and, when it came to being charming, her boss was a genius. Even so, when he offered to put her parents up in the Riverslea Hotel, all expenses paid, with all their meals, most especially Christmas lunch, included, Chloe was sure they would refuse. It would be all too flash! They didn't like flashiness.

But, before her parents could object, Zac had thrown in a car with a driver to take them to church on Christmas Day, or to the doctor, or anywhere else they needed to go, and he'd offered to hire a nurse to check daily that they were keeping well and taking their correct medication.

Chloe's mother had looked a bit doubtful about this, until she'd received an elbow in the ribs from her dad.

'It would be like a holiday, love,' he'd said.

Still, Chloe had expected her parents to have second thoughts and say no. But then Zac also told them with commendable sincerity how extremely important, no, *invaluable,* their daughter was to him and how much he needed her for this very important mission in the UK.

Somehow he'd struck just the right note, which was

clever. If he'd praised Chloe to the skies, her parents would have been suspicious and he would have blown it.

Instead, by the time he'd finished, they were practically squirming with delight, like puppies getting their tummies rubbed just the way they liked it.

And now…this morning, her parents, with their out of date, simple clothes and humble, shabby luggage, including her dad's walking frame, had looked a trifle out of place in the luxurious hotel suite with thick white carpet, floor-length cream linen curtains, golden taps in the bathroom, not to mention panoramic views up and down the Brisbane River…but the grins on their faces had said it all.

'Chloe, you go and look after your nice Mr Corrigan,' they'd said, practically pushing her out of the door. 'Don't you worry about us.'

Chloe had closed her gaping mouth.

Remembering her parents' delight, she could almost imagine them exploring their hotel room like excited children, checking the little bottles of shampoo and bubble bath, flushing the loo and bouncing on the king-sized mattress. Zac Corrigan had achieved a minor miracle.

And Chloe was going to London!

Right. Deep breath. She only hoped she wasn't making a very serious mistake. After all, she knew why her boss had been so keen to avoid asking any of his female 'friends' to accompany him on this very personal journey. He liked to keep his relationships casual and this sojourn to London would be anything but casual.

Chloe also knew why her boss regarded her as a suitable choice. She was capable, conscientious and uncomplicated, and he trusted her to remain that way. Which suited her just fine. It did. Really.

Yes, there was a danger that those annoying longings she sometimes felt for Zac would surface, but she'd had plenty of practice at keeping them in check and she was sure she could survive his close proximity for a few short days.

So perhaps it was OK now to admit to herself that she was a tiny bit excited, or at least she would be if she wasn't concerned for Zac and the sad ordeal that still awaited him when they landed.

Eventually, they boarded and took off, making the long flight across Australia, and now they were, according to the map on the screen, flying high above the Indian Ocean…

The cabin lights were dimmed, Zac and Chloe had eaten an exquisite meal and had drunk some truly delicious wine, and their business class seats had been turned into beds.

Beside Chloe, her boss appeared to be asleep already, stretched out in jeans and a black T-shirt, with his shoes off and his belt removed and his feet encased in black and purple diamond-patterned socks. He had also plugged in earphones and was listening to music and he had slipped on the navy silk eyeshade the airline provided.

He was used to flying and she supposed he would sleep now, possibly for hours. He'd probably had very little rest during the previous night and she was sure he needed to sleep. Actually, Chloe's night had been sleepless as well, so she knew it would be sensible to try to follow his example. Otherwise, she'd end up in London, useless with jet lag, with a boss who was ready and raring to go.

Unfortunately, however, Chloe was too *wired* to sleep. The past twenty-four hours had been such a whirlwind and the thought of London was simply too exciting. She'd acquired her passport in happier times, when she'd thought she knew exactly where her life was heading…

But she'd never used it. So she'd never been on an international flight before, had never flown business class, and had certainly never been to England. It was hard to believe she would soon be seeing the famous Tower Bridge and Big Ben and Buckingham Palace.

Needing to calm down, she fished in her bag for the magazines she'd bought from the airport newsagent while Zac was busy with a phone call. The mags were all about mothers and babies and parenting and Chloe hoped to find an article or two about caring for newborns. Just in case…

Luckily, there were plenty of stories and columns covering all kinds of newborn issues. Chloe soon discovered what to do if a baby had colic, jaundice, an umbilical hernia…and masses of information about bath time, skin care, crying, feeding, burping…

She read the information conscientiously, trying to take it all in, wondering if she would actually be called on to apply any of this in practice and hoping she'd remember the important details. Her real-life experience of babies was limited to admiring her friends' offspring, and she'd found them cute to cuddle or play with and then she'd been happy enough to hand them back to their mothers.

After her life turned upside down several years ago, she'd given up her own dreams of motherhood, so she'd never given much thought to the finer details of green nappies or colic or projectile vomiting.

Even now, she blocked those images. Not every baby had those problems, surely?

Instead, Chloe allowed herself to picture a tiny, warm, sweet-smelling bundle in her arms, a dear little baby girl, with soft pink skin and perhaps dark hair like Zac's. A darling rosebud mouth.

'Aren't you sleepy?' murmured a deep voice beside her.

Startled, she turned to see that Zac had lifted his eye-shade and removed an earplug, and was watching her with marked curiosity.

Chloe's insides began to buzz—an annoying reaction to having him so close. 'I…er…thought it might help if I read for a bit first,' she said.

Zac leaned closer, frowning. 'What on earth are you reading?'

The magazine in her lap was unfortunately open at a full-page picture of a tiny baby attached to an enormous breast.

Chloe felt her cheeks heat. 'I…um…just thought…in case…you know, the baby…it would be handy to have a few clues.'

'It would indeed.' Zac spoke smoothly enough, but his eyes once again held the bleak shadows that had arrived with the terrible news about his sister. 'Good thinking, Ms Meadows.'

Chloe swallowed. It was more than a little unnerving to find herself lying so close to her boss's disconcerting, sad grey eyes. She could see his individual thick, dark eyelashes and the grainy texture of the skin on his jaw. She hadn't been this close to a man since—

'I'm sure I'll be sleepy soon,' she said quickly, before her thoughts could be hijacked by haunting memories.

'Tell me something you've learned,' Zac said, keeping his voice low so he didn't disturb the other passengers, many of whom were sleeping. 'I'm intrigued.'

'Something about babies?' Chloe whispered back.

He cast another glance at the photo in her lap. 'Or breasts, if you prefer.' He gave her a teasing smile.

Despite the rising heat in her cheeks, Chloe sent him a drop-dead look and closed the magazine.

'Babies then,' Zac amended, his lips still twitching in a smile. 'Tell me what you've learned about babies.'

In truth, she'd learned an awful lot that she hadn't really wanted to know—about a newly delivered mother's hormonal fluctuations, the stitches she might have in awkward places, her leaking or sore and swollen breasts.

'OK,' she said as she remembered a snippet of practical information that was safe to share with him. 'Did you know that you should wash the baby's bodysuits and nightgowns in hypoallergenic dye- and scent-free detergent?'

'Fascinating.' Zac yawned, clearly already bored.

Good, he might leave her in peace.

Chloe waited for him to replace his eye mask. Instead, he pointed to one of the magazines in her lap. 'Do you mind?'

This time, she didn't try to hide her surprise. 'You want to read one of these? A mother and baby magazine?'

Her corporate executive playboy boss could not be serious. The Zac Corrigan she knew wouldn't be caught dead with such an incriminating piece of reading material in his hands, not even in the relative anonymity of an international flight.

'Yes, please,' he said, holding out his hand and smiling blandly. 'I'd like to be educated.'

Lips compressed to stop herself from making a smart retort, Chloe handed him a magazine that focused on a baby's first six months. She supposed he was probably teasing her, but he might be trying to distract himself from thinking too much about his sister.

It was even possible that he genuinely wanted to learn. After all, if a father for Liv's baby couldn't be traced, Zac might soon find himself in complete charge of a newborn.

For a while they both read in peaceful silence, the small glow of their reading lights making golden cones in the otherwise darkened cabin. But Chloe couldn't relax. For one thing, she was too curious about how Zac might be reacting to the contents of his magazine.

But it wasn't long before he leaned close, speaking softly. 'Did you know that babies can stare at you while they sleep?'

'Excuse me?'

He smiled. 'It says here that they can sleep with their eyes half open. It looks pretty spooky, apparently.'

Although his smile, up close, was dangerous for Chloe's heart health, she couldn't help smiling back at him. 'Well, the article I'm reading warns that babies sometimes don't sleep at all.'

'No.' Zac feigned complete shock. 'That can't be right.'

'Well, I guess they sleep eventually, but some stay awake for much longer than they're supposed to.'

'A bit like us,' he said, looking around the business class cabin at all the other passengers, who appeared to be contentedly sleeping.

Chloe sighed. 'I guess we really should turn our lights out and try to sleep.'

'Yes, we should.' He closed the magazine and handed it back to her. 'Thanks for that. Most enlightening.'

By the time she'd stowed the magazines away, Zac had turned off his reading light, pulled down his eye-shade and folded his arms over his wide chest. 'Goodnight, Ms Meadows.'

He usually only addressed her this way when he was in a playful mood, which wasn't very often, mostly when he'd pulled off some extraordinarily tricky business coup. Chloe wondered if the playboy was coming out in him now, simply because he was lying beside a young woman who was close enough to touch and kiss.

That thought had no sooner arrived than her body reacted, growing warm and tingly and tight.

Oh, for heaven's sake.

Where had such a ridiculous reaction sprung from? Chloe gave herself a mental slap and glared at Zac.

'Goodnight, sir,' she said icily.

'And try to sleep.' He spoke without lifting his shade and he sounded now like a weary parent. 'We've a long way to go.'

Chloe didn't answer and she was relieved that she would not have to speak to her boss again until morning. She pulled on her own eye mask and tried to settle comfortably, hoping that the steady vibration of the plane and the hum of its engines would soothe her.

Her hopes were not realised.

She couldn't relax. She was too upset by her mental slip about kissing and touching her boss. Too busy delivering a good, stern lecture to herself. After all, she knew very well that Zac had asked her to accompany him on this trip precisely because he needed a female companion to whom he was *not* sexually attracted.

Her momentary lapse had no doubt been brought on by her over-tiredness. She knew nothing like *that* would happen. Zac had spent a good section of almost every working day in the past three years in her company without once trying to flirt.

Besides, she didn't want it to happen. She was far too sensible to ever fall for her boss's superficial good looks and charming wiles. Apart from the fact that she'd had her heart broken once and never wanted to experience that pain again, there was no way on this earth that she would allow her name to end up on the spreadsheet of his *Foolish Females*.

Unfortunately, her attempt to sleep only lasted about ten or fifteen minutes before she had to wriggle and fidget and try for a more comfortable position. Beside her, she heard a weary sigh. 'Sorry,' she whispered.

Zac lifted the eye mask again and pinched the bridge of his nose.

'Sorry,' Chloe said again. 'I disturbed you, didn't I?'

He shook his head. 'Not really.' He yawned. 'I'm dog-tired, but I have a feeling I'm not going to sleep tonight.'

'Do you normally sleep on long haul flights?'

'Eventually.'

She wondered if he couldn't stop thinking about his sister. Was he simply too upset to sleep? She wished she could help.

'I don't have any brothers or sisters,' she said tentatively.

Zac frowned.

'Sorry,' she said quickly, wincing at her third apology

in as many minutes. 'I just thought you might want to talk, but I shouldn't have—'

'No, no, it's OK.' He sighed again, and lay staring into space, apparently thinking…

Chloe waited, not sure what else to say.

'Liv was eight years younger than me,' he said quietly. 'When our parents died, she was only ten, so I felt more like her father at times.' His mouth was a grim downward curve. 'She was my responsibility.'

Chloe stared at him now as she tried to take this in. Was the poor man blaming himself for his sister's accident? Did he feel completely responsible? 'But you must have been very young, too,' she said.

'I was eighteen. An adult.'

Only just, by the skin of your teeth. 'How awful for you to lose both your parents so young.'

'Yeah,' he agreed with another sigh.

Chloe didn't like to ask, but her imagination was running wild. 'How did it happen, Zac? Was there an accident?'

He shrugged. 'We'll never know for sure. My parents were sailing somewhere in Indonesia when their boat just disappeared. My father was a geologist, you see, and my mother was a marine biologist and they were mad keen on science and exploration, always on the lookout for a new discovery. I suppose you'd call them nutty professors. Eccentrics.'

So they'd just disappeared…? Poor Zac. How terrible to have his parents simply vanish, to never know if they'd been taken by pirates, or capsized in a tropical storm, or drowned when their boat struck a coral reef…

'They—they couldn't be still alive, living on some jungle-clad island, could they?'

Zac's mouth tilted in a wryly crooked smile. 'I've played with that fantasy, too. But it's been seventeen years...'

Chloe couldn't imagine how awful it must have been for him—a mere eighteen years old and forced to carry on living without answers, just with terrible possibilities.

'Right from the start I was worried about Liv,' he said next. 'I couldn't bear to see her disappear into a foster home, so I applied to be her guardian. I dropped out of uni and got myself a job, so we could live together and I could look after her.'

'Goodness,' Chloe said softly, hoping she didn't sound as surprised as she felt.

Zac's lips curled unhappily. 'It was possibly the stupidest decision I ever made.'

'Don't say that. I think it was incredibly brave of you.'

She was stunned to realise that Zac had sacrificed his own goals to try to keep what was left of his family intact. All she'd ever known about his private life was the revolving door of lookalike leggy blonde girlfriends. He'd never seemed to really care about any of them beyond their sex appeal and she'd assumed the 'care factor' gene was missing from his DNA.

But it was clear to her now that he'd cared very deeply about Liv.

'I couldn't keep her on track,' Zac said, so softly Chloe almost missed it. 'Liv never really looked on me as a parent. She wouldn't accept me in a fathering role, so I had very little influence, I'm afraid. I think she was mad at our parents for disappearing the way they did and she saw me as an inadequate substitute. Before she was out of her teens she was into drinking and trying drugs. And then she was like a nomad, never wanting to settle. She didn't want to study and she would never stay in one job for long enough to get any real skills. She was like a butterfly, always searching for a brighter flower.'

'Might she have inherited that urge from your parents?'

'Quite possibly, I guess.'

He stared unhappily up at the cabin's ceiling and Chloe wished she could offer him wise words of consolation.

She did her best. 'Honestly, I don't think you should blame yourself for this accident, Zac.'

But he simply shook his head and closed his eyes.

It was ages before Chloe drifted off to sleep and when she woke a soft grey light filled the cabin and flight attendants were bringing around hot towels to freshen their hands and faces, as well as glasses of orange juice.

'Morning, sleepyhead.'

Zac's seat was already back in the upright position and he looked as if he'd been to the bathroom and washed and shaved.

Chloe yawned and hoped her hair wasn't too messy. In a minute she would follow his example and freshen up. 'What time is it?'

'Seven forty-five. That's Greenwich Mean Time, of course. If we were still at home it would be five forty-five in the evening.'

So...her parents had almost completed their first day in the hotel. Chloe hoped they were still enjoying themselves.

If she'd been in Brisbane, she would be putting the final touches to the office's decorations and making last minute checks about the drinks and ice.

'I hope you're not worrying about your parents.'

'No, I'm not.' She knew they were in good hands and she'd left the hotel desk, the hired nurse and the chauffeur with all the phone numbers and information they could possibly need. 'I was thinking about the office Christmas party tonight, actually.'

'Really, Chloe?' Zac was frowning at her now, although his eyes glinted with puzzled amusement.

'I was looking forward to the party,' she admitted, no longer caring if this revealed her inadequate social life.

'You were looking forward to watching half the office staff get plastered and then staying behind to clean up their mess?'

She opened her mouth to protest.

Zac's smile was gently teasing. 'You're going to see London at Christmas. I promise you that's a thousand times better than the office do.'

'I suppose it would be. When should we get our first glimpse of England?'

'Oh, in about an hour.'

CHAPTER THREE

It was raining when they touched down at Heathrow, but somehow that couldn't dim Chloe's excitement. As business class passengers with only carry-on baggage, she and Zac didn't have to hang around in long queues and soon they were outside, suddenly very grateful for their warm overcoats and scarves.

While they waited for a taxi she made a quick phone call to her parents.

'We're about to go down to the dining room,' her mum told her excitedly. 'We've already checked out the menu and we're having lamb cutlets and then rhubarb crumble. Give our love to Zac.'

They were having the time of their lives and, within moments, Chloe was climbing into a proper shiny black London taxi and her excitement mounted as they whizzed along busy rain-slick streets filled with other taxis and cars and bright red double-decker London buses. Ahead, on a pedestrian crossing, people huddled beneath umbrellas glistening with rain.

Zac asked the taxi driver to stop at their hotel to leave their luggage and Chloe caught a brief impression of huge glass doors, massive urns filled with greenery and enormous gold-framed mirrors in a white marbled foyer.

'Now, we'd better head straight to the Metropolitan Police,' Zac said when he returned.

'Yes.' Chloe dug out her phone and checked the arrangements she'd made for Zac to meet with Sergeant Davies. She gave their driver the address and then they were off again.

Three blocks later, they had stopped at traffic lights when she saw the trio of soldiers. The tall, broad-shouldered men were simply standing and chatting as they waited to cross a road, but all it took was the sight of their camouflage uniforms and berets to bring back memories of Sam.

It could still happen like that, even though she'd had three and a half years to recover. The smallest trigger could bring the threat of desperate black grief.

Not now...I can't think about him now...

But now, on the far side of the world with her handsome boss, this painful memory was a timely reminder of the heartache that came with falling in love. Chloe knew she had to be super-careful…and she was grateful she'd trained herself to think of Zac as nothing but her boss…glad that she'd become an expert at keeping a tight lid on any deeper feelings…

At the police station, Sergeant Davies was very solicitous as he ushered them into his office. He told them that Liv's death had been clearly accidental and there was no reason to refer it to the coroner.

'The young man who was driving your sister to the hospital is definitely in the clear,' he added. 'He's a Good Samaritan neighbour. He was injured, but he's going to be OK. A badly broken leg, I believe.'

Zac sat stiffly, his face as grim as granite, as he received this news.

'We'll be laying serious charges against the driver of the other car,' the sergeant then told them.

'Driving under the influence?' Zac asked.

This was answered by a circumspect nod of assent.

Zac sighed and closed his eyes.

Outside, Chloe wanted to suggest that they found somewhere for a coffee. She was sure Zac could do with caffeine fortification, but perhaps she shouldn't have been surprised that he was determined to push on with his unhappy mission. At work he always preferred to confront the unpleasant tasks first. It was one of the things she'd always admired about him.

Within moments of hitting the pavement, he hailed another taxi and they were heading for the cold reality of the Royal London Hospital.

Once there, Zac insisted on seeing his sister, but as Chloe watched him disappear down a corridor, accompanied by a dour-looking doctor in a lab coat, she was worried that it might be a mistake. Her fears were more or less confirmed when Zac returned, white-faced and gaunt, looking about ten years older.

She had no idea what to say. There was no coffee machine in sight, so she got him a drink of water in a paper cup, which he took without thanking her and drank in sips, staring at the floor, his eyes betraying his shock.

Eventually, Chloe couldn't bear it. She put an arm around his shoulders and gave him a hug.

He sent her a sideways glance so full of emotion she felt her sympathetic heart swell to bursting. He offered her a nod, as if to say thanks, but he didn't speak. She was quite sure he *couldn't* speak.

For some time they sat together, with their overcoats

bundled on the bench beside them, before one of the hospital staff approached them, a youngish woman with bright red hair. 'Mr Corrigan?'

Zac lifted his gaze slowly. 'Yes?'

The woman's eyes lit up with the predictable enthusiasm of just about any female who met Zac. 'I'm Ruby Jones,' she said, holding onto her bright smile despite his grimness. 'I'm the social worker looking after your case.'

'Right. I see.' Zac was on his feet now. 'I guess you want to speak to me about the…the child?'

'Yes, certainly.' Ruby Jones offered him another sparkling smile, which Chloe thought was totally inappropriate. 'Am I right in imagining that you'd like to meet your niece?'

'Meet her?' Zac looked startled.

'Yes, she's just on the next floor in the maternity ward.'

'Oh, yes, of course.' He turned to Chloe. 'You'll come, too, won't you?'

'Yes, if you like.'

Ruby, the social worker, looked apologetic. 'I'm afraid—in these situations, we usually only allow close family members into—'

'Chloe is family,' Zac intervened, sounding more like his usual authoritarian self.

Chloe stared at the floor, praying that she didn't blush, but it was a shock to hear Zac describe her as family. She knew it was an expedient lie, but for a crazy moment her imagination went a little wild.

'I'm sorry.' Ruby sounded as flustered as Chloe felt. 'I thought you mentioned a PA.'

Zac gave an impatient flick of his head. 'Anyway, you couldn't count this child's close family on two fingers.' He placed a commanding hand at Chloe's elbow. 'Come on.'

Chloe avoided making eye contact with Zac as the social worker led them to the lift, which they rode in silence to the next floor.

'This way,' Ruby said as they stepped out and she led them down a hallway smelling of antiseptic, past doorways that revealed glimpses of young women and bassinets. From all around were sounds of new babies crying and, somewhere in the distance, a floor polisher whined.

Zac looked gloomy, as if he was hating every minute.

'Have you ever been in a maternity ward before?' Chloe asked him out of the side of her mouth.

'No, of course not. Have you?'

'Once. Just to visit a friend,' she added when she saw his startled glance.

Ahead of them, the social worker had stopped at a glass door and was talking to a nurse. She turned to them. 'If you wait here at this door, we'll wheel the baby over.'

Zac nodded unhappily.

Chloe said, 'Thank you.'

As the two women disappeared, Zac let out a heavy sigh. His jaw jutted with dismal determination as he sank his hands deep into his trouser pockets. Chloe was tempted to reach out, to touch him again, to give his elbow an encouraging squeeze, but almost immediately the door opened and a little trolley was wheeled through.

She could see the bump of a tiny baby beneath a pink blanket, and a hint of dark hair. Beside her, she heard her boss gasp.

'Oh, my God,' he whispered.

The trolley was wheeled closer.

'So here she is.' The nurse was middle-aged and hearty and she gave Zac an encouraging smile. 'She's a proper little cutie, this one.'

Chloe couldn't help taking a step closer. The nurse was right. The baby was incredibly cute. She was sound asleep and lying on her back, giving them a good view of her perfectly round little face and soft skin and her tiny nose—and, yes, her perfectly darling rosebud mouth—just as Chloe had imagined.

The baby gave a little stretch and one tiny hand came out from beneath the blanket, almost waving at them. There was a hospital bracelet around her wrinkled wrist. Chloe saw the name Corrigan written on it and a painful lump filled her throat.

Zac was staring at the baby with a kind of awestruck terror.

'So what do you think of your niece, Mr Corrigan?' asked Ruby, the social worker.

He gave a dazed shake of his head. 'She's tiny.'

'Her birth weight was fine,' the nurse said, sounding defensive, as if Zac had directly criticised her hospital. 'At least seven pounds.'

The social worker chimed in again. 'Would you like to hold her?'

Now Zac looked truly horrified. 'But she's asleep,' he protested, keeping his hands rammed in his pockets and rocking back on his heels as if he wished he could escape. For Chloe, by contrast, the urge to pick the baby up and cuddle her was almost overwhelming, as the maternal yearnings that she'd learned to suppress came suddenly rushing back.

She saw a frowning look exchanged between the nurse and the social worker and she worried that this was some kind of test that Zac had to pass before they could consider handing the baby into his care.

'Go on,' Chloe urged him softly. 'You should hold her for a moment. You won't upset her. She probably won't even wake up.'

Zac felt as if the air had been sucked from his lungs. He couldn't remember when he'd ever felt so out of his depth. The nurse was peeling back the pink blanket to reveal a tiny baby wrapped tightly in another thinner blanket. This was going to happen. They were going to hand her to him and he couldn't back out of it.

'Our little newborns feel safer when they're swaddled firmly like this. It also makes them easier to hold,' the nurse said as she lifted the sleeping bundle.

Reluctantly, Zac drew his hands from his pockets and hoped they weren't shaking.

'Just relax,' the nurse said as she placed the baby in his arms.

Relax? She had to be joking. It was all right for her. She did this every day. He was still getting over the agony of seeing Liv. And now he was so scared he might drop her baby…

She was in his arms.

He could feel the warmth of Liv's baby reaching him through the thin wrap. Could feel her limbs wriggling. Oh, dear God, she was so real. Alive and breathing. He forced himself to look down into her little pink face, so different from the deathly white one he'd so recently witnessed…

And yet…the similarity was there…

He found it so easily in the baby's soft dark hair, in

the delicate curve of her fine dark eyebrows, and in the tiniest suggestion of a cleft in her dainty chin.

'Oh, Liv.'

His sister's name broke from him on a desolate sob. His vision blurred as his throat was choked by tears.

Chloe's heart almost broke when she saw the silver glitter in Zac's eyes.

Even now, under these most difficult circumstances, it was a shock to see her boss cry. Zac was always so in control. In the day-to-day running of his business, it didn't matter how worried or upset or even angry he was, he never lost his cool. Never.

He usually viewed any kind of trouble as a challenge. In fact, there were days when he seemed to thrive on trouble and conflict. Twice, to her knowledge, he'd taken his company to the very brink of economic peril, but he'd never lost his nerve and had emerged triumphant.

Of course, there was a huge gulf between the challenges of the business world and a personal heartbreaking tragedy.

Now Zac Corrigan, her fearless boss, was caught in the worst kind of heartbreak and he was shaking helplessly as tears streamed down his face.

'Here,' he said, thrusting the baby towards Chloe. 'Please, take her.'

Her own emotions were unravelling as she hastily dumped their coats to accept the warm bundle he pressed into her arms. The poor man had been through so much—*too* much—in such a short time and, on top of everything else, he was dealing with jet lag. But, even though he had every reason to weep, Chloe knew he would be mortified to break down like this in public.

She wasn't at all surprised when Zac turned from them and strode back down the corridor, his head high and his shoulders squared as he drew deep breaths and fought for composure.

Watching him, she held the baby close, inhaling the clean and milky smell of her. She thought how perfectly she fitted in her arms.

Beside her, Ruby, the social worker, said, 'It's such a very sad situation.'

Indeed, Chloe agreed silently.

The baby squirmed now and beneath the blanket she gave a little kick against Chloe's ribs. Chloe wondered if this was how it had felt for Liv when she'd been pregnant. *Such a short time ago.*

Oh, help. If she allowed herself to think about that, she'd start weeping, too.

Perhaps it was just as well that she was distracted by Zac's return. He seemed sufficiently composed—although still unnaturally pale.

'I'm so sorry for your loss,' the nurse said.

Zac held up a hand and gave a brief nod of acknowledgement. 'Thank you.' His manner was curt but not impolite. Then he said, in his most businesslike tone, 'I guess you need to bring me up to speed.' He shifted his now steady gaze to the social worker. 'What's the current situation? Has anyone been able to locate the father?'

Ruby shook her head. 'I'm afraid we've had no luck at all.'

'You've definitely ruled out the fellow who was in the car with Liv?'

'Yes.'

At this news, Zac looked bleaker than ever.

'We've also interviewed the people who lived in the

share house with your sister,' Ruby said next. 'But they haven't been able to help us. They said Olivia wouldn't tell anyone the father's name. She simply told them that he wouldn't be interested in a child and she didn't want anything more to do with him.'

Zac stared at her for a long moment, his grey eyes reflecting a stormy mix of emotions. Eventually he nodded. 'That sounds like my sister, I'm afraid. But there was a boyfriend. I'm pretty sure Liv was still with him last Christmas. An Australian. A singer in a band.'

'Bo Stanley?'

Zac nodded grimly. 'Yes, I'm pretty sure that's his name.'

Again, she shook her head. 'A housemate did mention him and he's still in the UK, so we made contact and had him tested. It was easy to disqualify him. He's completely the wrong blood type.'

This time, Zac stared at her as if he was sure she had to be mistaken, but eventually he gave an unhappy shake of his head and shrugged. 'I guess he's off the hook, then.'

In Chloe's arms, the baby gave a little snuffling snort. When Chloe looked down she saw that her eyes had opened. The baby blinked and stared up at Chloe, straight into her eyes.

How much could those newborn dark grey eyes see? The baby's expression was definitely curious. Trusting, too. Her intense, seemingly focused gaze pierced Chloe's heart and she was enveloped by a rush of warmth, a fierce longing to protect this tiny, sweet girl. *It would be so easy to love her.*

She realised that Zac was watching her.

His gaze lingered on her as she stood there with the

baby in her arms. Surprise flared in his eyes and then a softer emotion. Chloe held her breath and for a winded moment her mind played again with hopelessly ridiculous possibilities…

Fortunately, Zac quickly recovered. 'OK,' he said, looking quickly away and becoming businesslike again. 'I guess my next question is about the baby.'

'What would you like to know?' the nurse asked guardedly.

'Is she healthy?'

'Perfectly.' She sniffed as if his question had offended her. 'You would have been informed before now if there was a problem.' Then, more gently, she asked, 'Do you have a particular concern?'

Zac grimaced uncomfortably. 'My sister had a drug habit, or at least she used to.' He shot a quick glance to Chloe and then looked away, as if he was embarrassed to have his employee hear this admission. 'It was some time back,' he added quickly. 'And Liv assured me she's been clean ever since, but I assume you've run the necessary tests?'

'Yes, Mr Corrigan. I can reassure you there were no signs that the baby has been adversely affected by alcohol or drugs.'

'Well, that's good news at least.' He swallowed. 'So…' Looking from the nurse to the social worker, he summoned a small smile, a glimmer of his customary effortless charm. 'What's next?'

Ruby, the social worker, was clearly surprised. 'Well…as you're next of kin and you've been named as guardian—'

'Yes, I've brought a copy of my sister's will if you need to see it.'

'And you've come all the way from Australia,' Ruby continued. 'I—I mean *we* were assuming that you planned to care for the baby.'

Zac nodded and his throat worked as he swallowed again.

Chloe knew he felt overwhelmed. He'd fielded successive shocks in the past twenty-four hours and she felt compelled to speak up. 'We've only just arrived from Heathrow and Mr Corrigan hasn't had any time to adjust, or to buy any of the things the baby will need.'

The nurse nodded. 'Of course. I understand.'

Shooting Chloe a grateful look, Zac added, 'If the baby could remain in your care for a little longer, I'd be happy to pay for any additional costs.'

This could be arranged, they were told, and Zac was also given a list of funeral parlours, as well as the name and address of Liv's share house, so that he could collect Liv's belongings. On that sobering note, they departed.

Outside the hospital a brisk December wind whipped at them, lifting their hair and catching at the ends of their scarves. Standing on the footpath on Whitechapel Road, Zac almost welcomed the wind's buffeting force and the sting to his cheeks. He dragged in an extra deep lungful of chilled air, as if it might somehow clear the raw pain and misery that roiled inside him. But there was no way he could avoid the two images that kept swimming before his vision. The pale, bruised, lifeless face of his beautiful sister and the small, red, but very much alive face of her tiny newborn daughter.

His niece.

His new responsibility.

The frigid air seemed to seep into Zac's very blood

along with this chilling reality. This baby, this brand new human being had no other family. He was *it*. She would be completely dependent on him.

He shot a glance to Chloe, whose cheeks had already turned quite pink from the cold. The high colour made her look unexpectedly pretty and he thought how fabulous she'd been this morning. In fact, his decision to bring his PA with him to London had been a stroke of pure genius. On the long flight, at the police station and again at the hospital, Chloe's no-fuss efficiency and quiet sympathy had been exactly the kind of support he'd needed.

'I vote we go back to the hotel now,' he said. 'We can check in and get a few things sorted.'

Chloe nodded. 'I'll check out those funeral parlours, if you like. It might be hard to find a—a place—with Christmas and everything.'

Zac was about to agree, but then he remembered the heartbreaking decisions he might be required to make. 'I'd better talk to them, Chloe. Anyway, you're probably exhausted.'

'I feel fine, actually.' She smiled. 'Being outside and grabbing a breath of fresh air makes all the difference.'

You're a breath of fresh air, he almost told her, and then thought better of it. Even minor breaches of their boss-PA boundaries seemed to make Chloe uncomfortable and now that she'd given up her Christmas and had come all this way, he didn't want to upset her. Instead he said, 'And I'll also make contact with the share house people.'

'Yes, it might be worth finding out what Liv's already bought before you start shopping.'

Zac frowned. Suddenly, his mega-sensible PA wasn't making any sense at all. 'Shopping?'

'For the baby.'

'Oh.' He gulped nervously. 'Yes, of course.'

A vision of a mountain of nappies and prams and tins of formula mushroomed in Zac's imagination. He felt overwhelmed again as he raised a hand to hail their taxi.

In a matter of moments, they were heading back into the city centre. Chloe leaned back in the seat and closed her eyes. She was probably worn out, even though she'd denied it. Zac had never seen her like this—with her eyes closed, her dark lashes lying softly against her flushed cheeks, her lips relaxed and slightly open.

She looked vulnerable and he found his attention riveted…

This wasn't the first time he'd entertained the idea of kissing Chloe, of making love to her, but, just as he had on the other occasions, he quickly cut off the thought.

From the start, when he'd first employed Chloe, he'd quickly recognised her value as his PA and he'd set himself clear rules. No office affairs. Ever.

Of course, there'd been times when he'd wished to hell that he wasn't so principled where Chloe was concerned. More than once they'd been deep in a business discussion when he'd been completely distracted by her quiet beauty, but it was almost certainly for the best that his common sense had always prevailed.

And now, once again, Zac dismissed ideas of tasting her softly parted lips and he wrenched his thoughts back to his new responsibilities.

A tiny baby…such an alarming prospect for a commitment-shy bachelor. If he took Liv's little daughter into his care, she would rely on him for everything—for food, for shelter, clothes…love. As she grew older she would look up to him for wise guidance, for entertainment, for security. She would require vast amounts of his time and patience.

No doubt she would view him as her father.

Her daddy…

The thought brought shivers fingering down Zac's spine. He couldn't deny he'd been hoping that the baby's biological father would emerge and make a claim, but he'd also been worried by the prospect. Knowing Liv, the guy was bound to be a no-hoper. Now, the possibility of a father galloping up on a white charger to save the day was fast disappearing and this left Zac with a different, but equally worrying set of problems…centring on his own, very real inadequacies…

He was very aware that his personal life was at best…haphazard…but there was a good reason for that—in more recent years he'd been making up for lost time.

Liv had been so young when their parents died, and for many years Zac had made her his first priority. He'd juggled several part-time jobs so that he could be at home for as much of Liv's out-of-school time as possible.

It was only *after* Liv had turned eighteen and struck out on her own, that he'd decided he might as well have some fun, so when it came to dating women he'd been a late starter. By then he'd also discovered he had a head for business as well as a talent for attracting gorgeous girls. He'd enjoyed the combination of work and play so much that he hadn't felt a need to settle down.

Now…as he stared out at the busy London traffic, at the towering modern buildings and the occasional ancient stone church hunkering within the skyscraper forest, he wondered if adoption might be the best option for Liv's baby.

It wasn't the first time Zac had toyed with the idea. Ever since the first shocking phone call from London , the possibility of adoption had been there, nagging at the back of his thoughts.

A huge part of him was actually quite willing to hand the baby over, and not because he was keen to shirk his responsibility, but because he was so totally scared of failure. With Liv, he'd tried his damnedest and he'd failed spectacularly, so how could he hope to be any more successful with her baby?

And yet…

Zac dragged an agonised hand over his face as guilt squirmed unpleasantly inside him. Could he really bring himself to hand that tiny bundle, that little 'mini-Liv', over to strangers?

After all, his sister had named him as guardian of her children in her will, and surely she wouldn't have made that weighty decision if she'd wanted her baby to be adopted.

Problem was…if the child was *not* adopted, there were very few alternatives. He certainly couldn't care for a baby on his own and he shuddered at the idea of a procession of housekeepers and babysitters and nannies.

He had to find a better solution. Fate had handed him a second chance to care for a member of his family and he simply *had* to get it right this time.

Liv's child needed security and continuity and she needed someone else besides him, someone who would balance his strengths and weaknesses. But a baby also needed someone who would really care about her and love her and, most importantly, stay with her…

What the poor kid needed was a mother…

With a heavy sigh, Zac closed his eyes, recalling a long ago image of Liv as a baby. He could picture their house in Ashgrove in a street lined with Bunya pines. Their mother was bathing Liv in a special little baby bath on the kitchen table, holding her carefully in the crook of her arm as she squeezed water from a facecloth over her fat little tummy.

Their mum had made a game of it and every time the water touched Liv's tummy, the baby would laugh and splash. Zac remembered the happiness of that squealing baby laughter, remembered the shining joy and impossible-to-miss love in his mother's face.

At the time he'd been a bit jealous and oh, so aware of the vital importance of a mother's love.

Oh, Liv, Liv...you should have been a mother, too.

Watching from the seat in the taxi beside Zac, Chloe saw his face twist with pain. He was looking away, out of the window, and he had no idea he was being observed. His mouth was trembling and then he grimaced and bit down hard on his lip as if to hold back a sob, and she could see tears again, could see the raw, agonising pain in his face. She longed to reach out, but she knew he would hate to be caught on the brink of breaking down yet again.

Still staring bleakly through the window, Zac's weary mind threw up a picture of Chloe at the hospital this morning. He remembered how perfectly the baby had fitted into the cradle of her arms, remembered the warm glow in Chloe's chocolate eyes as she looked down at her. He remembered the equally warm, melting sensation that he'd felt as he'd watched the two of them.

So natural and right…

Yes, there could be no question. What the baby needed most definitely, *absolutely*, was a mother.

And suddenly, arriving with the lightning jolt swiftness of every great idea, Zac discovered the perfect solution.

'You know what this means, don't you?' he announced in sudden triumph.

Beside him Chloe jumped and blinked as if she'd been woken from sleep. 'What?' She was frowning. 'Excuse me?'

'This baby,' Zac said impatiently. 'Liv's baby. There's only one way to take proper care of her.'

Despite Chloe's puzzled frown, her eyes widened with curiosity. 'What is it?'

'I'll have to take the plunge.'

'What plunge?'

'Into wedded bliss.' He tried to sound more excited. 'I'll have to get married.'

CHAPTER FOUR

MARRIED?

Zac Corrigan married?

Chloe stared at her boss, too stunned to speak. There was every chance she wasn't breathing and she had huge doubts about her hearing.

Surely she must have dreamt that Zac, the serial dater, truly wanted to get married?

He was watching her with a smile that didn't quite reach his worried eyes. 'Don't look so shocked,' he said.

She gave a dazed shake of her head, as if to clear it, and sat up straighter. 'Sorry. I think I must have nodded off and didn't hear you properly. What did you just say?'

'I've found the perfect solution to the baby problem.'

'Which is…?' she prompted cautiously.

Zac lifted his hands in a gesture of triumph, as if he was announcing the latest boost in company profits to a group of delighted shareholders. 'It's obvious that I need to get married.'

Good grief. She had heard him correctly.

For no more than a millisecond the word 'marriage' uttered by Zac Corrigan sent a strange thrill zinging through Chloe, skittering across her skin and lifting fine hairs. But, almost immediately, she came to her senses.

He was pulling her leg, of course. If she hadn't been so tired she would have seen the joke immediately.

'Marriage?' She laughed. 'Yeah, right.'

'I'm serious, Chloe.'

'Yes, of course you are.'

'I mean it.' He said this forcefully, as if he was growing impatient with her. 'It's the perfect solution.'

For some men, possibly, but not for you, Zac.

Clearly, jet lag had caught up with her devilishly handsome playboy boss. Jet lag plus too many personal shocks in a short space of time.

Unless...

Chloe supposed it was possible that Zac had fallen deeply in love very recently, without her knowing. 'I should have asked,' she said quickly. 'Do you already have a lucky lady in mind?'

Please, don't let it be that giggling girl who answered his phone the other evening.

Perhaps it was just as well that their taxi pulled up outside their hotel at that precise moment. Zac didn't answer Chloe's questions and the crazy conversation was dropped. Instead, he turned his attention to signing for the fare, making sure it included a generous tip.

Then a young man, resplendent in a uniform with tassels, opened the taxi door for Chloe. She had an almost film star moment as she went up the short flight of stone stairs with Zac to enormous glass doors, opened for them by another man in livery.

Once inside the glamorous high-ceilinged foyer with an exquisitely decorated soaring Christmas tree, they were greeted by more smiling staff who attended to the business of collecting their luggage and checking in.

It all went super-smoothly, with a level of service

that exceeded Chloe's experiences on previous business trips. She'd certainly never stayed anywhere this glamorous before.

Zac had interrupted her last Wednesday evening, when she'd been about to make the hotel booking.

'Hang on,' he'd said, as he hunted in his desk and produced a business card. 'Try this place. I stayed there once. It's central and rather good.'

It was much pricier than his usual budget, but Chloe hadn't liked to argue and now, here they were, in a lift with an intricately tiled floor and mirrored walls, taking them silently swishing upwards…

Seconds later, they were standing in the carpeted hallway outside their adjoining rooms. 'Take your time settling in,' Zac said. 'Perhaps you'd like to rest up for a bit?'

Chloe was tempted, but she knew it wouldn't be wise. 'If I fall asleep now, I'll probably find myself wide awake and prowling around at midnight.'

To her surprise, he responded with a sparkling-eyed, slightly crooked smile.

She frowned. 'Did I say something funny?'

'No, as always you were eminently sensible, Chloe, but I have a very curious imagination. I couldn't help playing with the idea of my Ms Meadows on a midnight prowl.'

To her dismay, her mind flashed an image of the two of them meeting out here in the corridor when she was wearing nothing but a nightie and heat flared as if Zac had struck a match inside her. 'Don't be ridiculous,' she snapped.

He wiped the smile, but irritating amusement still lurked in his grey eyes. 'Seriously, it's probably best if you can manage to stay awake until this evening. How about we meet in half an hour for lunch?'

'Sounds fine. Would you like me to make you a cup of tea, sir?' She added this in her most deferential manner, to remind them both of the very clear lines drawn between his status and hers.

Zac's response was another unsettling smile and, for a moment, he looked as if he was going to make yet another inappropriately playful remark, but then he gave a slight shake of his head and the amused light in his eyes died. 'No, thanks. I'll manage.'

Chloe was annoyed that she still felt unsettled as she slid the key in her lock and went into her room.

But she was soon distracted by the room's jaw-dropping gorgeousness. It had an enormous bed, a thick, pale carpet and comfortably padded armchairs, as well as vases of roses. Everything was in tasteful shades of pink and cream, and the view was beautiful, too, through elaborately draped windows to green English parkland with enormous ancient trees spreading winter-bare branches above smooth velvet lawns.

She set her bag down and took off her coat and scarf and laid them carefully on the end of the bed. She slipped off her shoes, and when her stockinged feet sank into the deep pile carpet she gave a blissful little twirl and then a skip.

She thought of her parents back in Brisbane, enjoying their lovely hotel stay, which was also courtesy of Zac. It seemed wrong somehow that both she and her parents were enjoying a luxurious and other-worldly experience for such a very sad reason.

Sobered by this thought, she located the tea-making facilities hidden discreetly behind white-painted doors.

Soon she had the jug boiled and a bag of Lady Grey tea brewing in a delicate china cup and, with milk and a half-teaspoon of sugar added, she took the cup to an armchair. For the first time in days, she had a little time to herself, to relax and unwind. But she couldn't stop thinking about her boss and the difficult phone calls he was making right next door.

As an only child, she didn't know what it was like to lose a sibling, but she knew all too well what it was like to lose someone she loved...and, without warning, she was swamped by memories.

Once again she was feeling the crushing weight of the raw grief caused by Sam's death. It had sent her retreating home to her elderly parents and, once there, their increasing age and health issues had become her excuse to withdraw from the pain of her old life...

Now, curled in the armchair, clutching the lovely cup to her chest, Chloe wept for Sam, her fiancé...and for her lost dreams...and also, in a more complicated way, she found herself weeping, as well, for her boss.

'Are you sure you're OK, Chloe? You're looking a little peaky,' Zac commented when they met again thirty minutes later.

She looked surprised. 'I'm perfectly fine, thanks.'

He might have quizzed her further, but he knew he probably looked rather pale and drawn, too. He'd certainly felt flattened after his discussions with the funeral director.

'Liv's share house is in Islington,' he said, referring to one of the other phone calls he'd made. 'It's probably just as easy to take the Tube and we can go out there first thing in the morning.'

Chloe nodded.

'I was hoping you'd come, too.'

'Yes, of course.'

The enormity of his relief was out of all proportion but, with that small issue settled, they headed for Oxford Street, hunting for a place to eat. Or at least that was Zac's plan until Chloe was completely captivated by the extravagant Christmas displays in the shops' windows.

He was patient enough while she admired them—blinding white snow scenes complete with pine trees and clever mechanical toys, glittering tables laden with sumptuous feasts, fantastic fashions displayed against a stunning snowy backdrop.

He knew the shop windows were incredibly inventive and artistic, but he found it difficult to enjoy them. He was finding it impossible to shake off the burden of his new and weighty responsibilities.

He'd been slightly miffed that Chloe had laughingly dismissed his brilliant solution of marriage without giving it so much as a moment's thought. He was also surprised she'd been so forthright. Usually, if his PA disagreed with him, she kept her opinions to herself, unless he specifically asked for her input.

Of course, he'd never discussed his private life with Chloe until now, but everything had changed last Wednesday evening. And it had changed again this morning when he saw his sister's tiny baby. He was overwhelmed anew by the huge pressure of his *duty*, and now, as Chloe turned from a clever display of robots made from children's building blocks, he was gripped by a new kind of urgency.

'You know, I'm at a loss about this child,' he said. 'I can't possibly care for her on my own.'

Perhaps he spoke a little too loudly. A woman rushing past them, laden with shopping parcels, sent Chloe a distinctly disapproving glance.

Fortunately, Chloe ignored her and simply stepped closer to Zac, lowering her voice. 'You can have all kinds of help with a child, you know. There are nannies and—'

Zac cut her off in a burst of impatience. 'Nannies come and go. I want—' He sent another glare to the steady stream of Christmas shoppers flowing around them and gave an impatient shake of his head. They couldn't talk about this here, and the cafés in Selfridges were bound to be packed at this time of the year.

'Come on.' He tugged at her coat sleeve. 'I've remembered a pretty good pub just around the corner.'

As Zac charged off, Chloe almost had to run to keep up with him.

She soon forgave him, though, when he located the pub. It had a very appealing wonderfully 'old English' atmosphere created by small paned windows with white trims, a green door and a window box spilling red, white and purple petunias.

Inside, the dark, timber-panelled space was as warm and cosy as the outside had promised. Appetising aromas drifted from the kitchen, and there was a friendly buzz in the room as diners, who were taking a break from their Christmas shopping, chatted quietly at tables covered in white linen.

Chloe and Zac took off their coats and scarves and hung them near the door, which was quite a novel experience for Chloe after subtropical Brisbane, and a friendly young waiter showed them to a table in a corner.

Several of the female diners turned and unashamedly

followed Zac with their eyes. Chloe was used to this, of course, but Zac hardly seemed to notice them.

As they made themselves comfortable, Chloe was tempted to relax completely and soak up the centuries-old atmosphere, but she was too conscious of the tension coming off Zac in waves. She wondered if he was still stewing over his crazy marriage idea. Surely he would soon wake up to himself?

At least he didn't try to raise the delicate subject until after they'd ordered. Chloe chose a Stilton and potato soup with a glass of white wine, while Zac ordered a beef and Guinness pie and half a pint of beer.

With that settled, Chloe decided that she should at least humour her boss. 'So are we still discussing this marriage plan, Zac?'

His grey eyes narrowed. 'On the assumption that you're prepared to be reasonable.'

'Of course I'll be reasonable, but you never did tell me if you had a future wife in mind.'

'Well...no.' He smiled a little ruefully. 'I'll admit that's a problem.'

Chloe stomped on the ridiculous flush of relief that swept through her.

'But I'm still quite sure marriage is the perfect solution.'

'Because...?'

'The baby will need a mother,' Zac said simply.

Ah, yes...

In a heartbeat, Chloe was remembering the sweet little bundle in her arms, the warm weight of Liv's baby, and she was reliving that amazing moment when she'd looked deep into the baby's bright little eyes and had felt her heart turn over.

The memory made her throat ache and she had to swallow before she could answer. 'Finding a mother would be the ideal solution,' she said, hoping the emotion didn't show in her face. 'But plenty of babies have been brought up by nannies.'

Ridiculous tears threatened and she looked away quickly to the end of the dining room. What on earth was the matter with her? She had to be very careful that she didn't become too emotionally caught up in Zac's problems. There was no point in becoming maudlin just because she'd given up her own dreams of a family when she'd gone home to her parents.

She turned her attention to the far wall, where a huge mantelpiece lent the restaurant a gracious Victorian air. With her gaze centred on it, she said lightly, 'Wasn't the British Empire practically raised by nannies in its heyday?'

Zac's jaw stiffened, a clear sign that he was annoyed. 'Let's stick to the twenty-first century.'

She tried again, in placating tones. 'I believe the modern nannies are very well trained.'

'But no nanny these days is going to stick with a child until she's an adult.'

'That might be a stretch.' Across the table, Chloe eyed her boss boldly. 'Then again, modern marriages don't always last very long either.'

A stubborn light gleamed in Zac's eyes as he stared unblinkingly back at her. 'I still think marriage is the most sensible option. I want this child to have stability, parents who'll stick around, perhaps a little brother or sister—a life as close to normal as possible.'

Such an alluring picture…

Chloe took a deep breath. Zac wanted to give the

baby everything Liv had lost.He wanted this quite badly, and desperate times required desperate measures. 'You have to do what you think is right, Zac. It's none of my business, anyway.'

'Actually…that's not quite true…'

Her heart began a frantic hammering. What did he mean?

'I thought you might be able to help me,' Zac said.

'Really? How?'

'You have that spreadsheet. We could go through it together—take another look at the possibilities.'

The spreadsheet… It was so ridiculous to feel disappointed in him. Why on earth might she have thought…?

'Please tell me you're joking,' she said quickly.

'I'm not. I'm deadly serious.'

'But trawling for a wife through a database is so—' *So wrong on so many levels.* 'So unromantic.' Chloe had to look away again.

She was remembering the day Sam proposed. They'd been walking in the rain along a cliff top, with the sea crashing and foaming on the rocks below. Sam had produced a ring and he'd actually gone down on one knee. It was *so-o-o-o* romantic. He'd told her how madly he loved her and their kiss in the rain had been the most exciting moment imaginable…

'I mean,' Zac was saying. 'For all we know, these modern marriages might fail for the very reason that they're based on romantic notions instead of common sense and logic.'

'So what are you saying now, Zac? That you don't believe in romance?'

Before he could respond, the waiter approached with their drinks.

'Meals won't be long,' the young man said cheerfully.

Zac thanked him and, as the waiter left, he raised his glass and smiled. 'Anyway...here's to you, Chloe Meadows, best PA ever.'

It was such a sudden turnabout, she knew she looked flustered and was possibly blushing. Again.

'I'm extremely grateful to you for agreeing to come here at such short notice,' Zac went on. 'And at such a difficult time of the year.'

As they clinked glasses, his smile was so sincere that Chloe gave a little laugh to cover her reaction.

'How could I turn down an all-expenses-paid trip to London?' she said, but she was actually wondering how Zac could be so exasperating one moment and then so charming the next.

After a sip of wine, which was exceptionally fine, she veered back to their previous discussion. Now that Zac had raised the thorny subject of marrying someone with the aid of a computer spreadsheet, it was like a prickle buried in her skin that she had to dig out. 'So I take it you don't believe in romance?' she challenged him again.

He shrugged. 'I think romance is problematical. I don't see how people can make a decision that lasts a lifetime based purely on their feelings. It's highly possible that there would be more successful marriages if everyone took a more practical approach.'

'Like arranged marriages?'

'Why not? They seem to work quite well in many cultures.'

Chloe took a deeper sip of her wine as she considered this. She had to admit it was true that arranged marriages often worked. Her parents' neighbours from Afghanistan were prime examples. The Hashimis' marriage had been arranged by their parents when they were still in their teens and they'd been happily together for forty years. In fact, Mr Hashimi seemed more devoted to his wife than ever.

'You know, you're *almost* making sense,' she said. 'Except—'

'Yes?' Zac prompted eagerly, but then the waiter appeared again with their meals.

Chloe was grateful for the interruption. She'd been about to say that she couldn't imagine many Australian women falling for Zac's scheme, but then she'd remembered the names in the list of his *Foolish Females* and she knew that quite a few of those girls would probably leap at the chance to marry her boss. After all, Zac Corrigan was exceptionally eligible.

'So it sounds as if you'd like to approach this marriage like a business strategy?' she said instead as she sprinkled croutons over her soup.

Zac nodded as he cut into his crusty pie to reveal rich dark meat and gravy. 'As a starting point, at least.'

'And how would you make your choice? Draw up a list of the attributes you want in this wife? Then try to find the perfect match from the *Fool*—from the list of girls you've already dated?'

'Exactly,' he said with a grin. 'I knew you'd come on board.'

An hour later, they were still in the pub.

Having finished their meals and drinks, they were onto their second cups of coffee, hoping to keep jet lag at bay for a little longer, and Chloe, to her own amazement, was helping to draw up Zac's list of wifely qualities.

'OK, let's see what you have so far.' She read from the

notes she'd typed into her phone. 'We—I mean *you*—want someone who's sensible—' She'd been majorly surprised that this had headed his list. 'Smart, sympathetic, reliable, has a sense of humour, likes kids, is not too loud…'

Zac nodded. 'That sounds about right.'

What about size eight and blonde? This described most of the girls he liked to date, but somehow Chloe restrained herself from asking this and took a kinder approach. 'I don't think you really need a database, Zac. You must already know which of your girlfriends has these qualities.'

A deep frown furrowed his brow as he stared at his coffee cup. 'It's hard to find them all in one person, though, isn't it?'

When he looked up, he seemed genuinely perplexed. 'Angie Davis has a great sense of humour and she's probably good with kids, but I'm not sure she's all that reliable. And Sasha Franks would run a terrific household, but she's a bit…cold.'

'What about Marissa Johnson?' Of all Zac's girlfriends, Chloe had liked Marissa the best. She was a very friendly young woman who worked in a sports store on the Gold Coast, and she had short dark hair and a natural, make-up-free glow of the outdoors about her, which made her a little different from his usual choices.

Zac, however, was shaking his head. 'Why does Marissa's name keep cropping up? You told me to invite her here to London and I said no then.'

Chloe shrugged. 'I just think she's really nice, the sort of girl I could be good friends with.' She smiled sheepishly.' But I don't suppose that's helpful to you.'

'Actually, you're probably right about Marissa.' He

sighed heavily. 'But of all the girls I know, she's probably the least likely to be interested in marrying me.'

'Are you sure?'

He nodded. 'I'm afraid I stuffed things up with her. I…er…kind of forgot to mention that I was still seeing someone else.'

Chloe groaned. 'For heaven's sake, Zac.'

He shrugged. 'The other girl was in Melbourne and it was only ever occasional, but Marissa still gave me the boot.'

Good for her, Chloe thought, but she kept the thought to herself. Instead, she found herself saying, 'You never know, she might forgive you if you asked very nicely. Putting a ring on her finger could make a world of difference.'

She wished she felt happier about offering that last piece of unasked-for advice. It didn't help that Zac's response was a gorgeously brooding smile that made her wonder what he was thinking.

Was he actually in love with Marissa?

Why should I care? It's not as if I want him for myself. Chloe knew she was far too sensible to make such a foolish mistake.

'I've never actually asked about *your* credentials,' Zac said suddenly.

'Mine?' A zap, like an electric spark, shot through Chloe. 'Wh-what d-do you mean?'

'Well, here I am seeking your advice and I don't even know if you're qualified. I know nothing about your social life. You're such a private girl, Chloe. I've never heard you mention going on a date.' He was looking at her now as if she was a very amusing riddle. 'For example…is there a boyfriend I should have apologised to when I dragged you away at Christmas?'

Chloe gulped. 'No—there's…er…no one at the moment.'

'You're a lovely girl…so there must be an explanation.'

Stifling her delight at his use of the word 'lovely', she decided that she wouldn't tell him about Sam. How could a man who didn't believe in romance possibly understand her pain, or why she'd retreated so completely from the dating scene?

Zac was still smiling, but the expression in his grey eyes was piercing now. It seemed to skewer her. 'You're not going to share that explanation, are you?' he said.

'No, I'd rather not.'

He frowned and, for the longest time, he regarded her with a look that was unexpectedly sympathetic, but, to Chloe's intense relief, he dropped the subject.

They walked back to their hotel through the gathering gloom of a wintry London afternoon. Street lights had already come on and the window displays made eye-catching splashes of colour.

Zac was beginning to feel a little better after a warming meal and a reasonably profitable chat with Chloe, as if he'd been trapped in a nightmare but was gradually finding his way out. He would certainly give the Marissa option more careful thought.

'I suppose you might have to think of a name for the baby,' Chloe said suddenly when they were about a block from their hotel.

'A name?' With a soft groan, Zac threw back his head

and stared helplessly up at the dark lowering clouds. 'I wouldn't have a clue where to begin.'

'Oh, I'm sure you'll have fun once you get started, Zac. There are so many pretty girls' names.'

'I guess.' But when he tried to think, he could only think of past girlfriends' names and he didn't want any of them. Beyond these, however, his mind drew a blank. 'Do you have any suggestions?'

Chloe laughed. 'Where do I start? Mind you, I'm no expert, but I think all the old classic names are still very popular—names like Emma and Sophie or Rose. Or, let me see, there's Isabella or simply Bella.'

'Bella's cute,' Zac admitted, thinking of the tiny pink-cheeked baby he'd been handed at the hospital.

'I guess you'd also want to choose something that went well with Corrigan.'

'Would I? Yes, I guess…'

'For example, Chloe Corrigan would sound a bit off.'

Inexplicably, Zac's chest tightened. 'Would it?'

'Definitely,' Chloe said gruffly. 'Too many Cs and Os. Although Kate or Katy might work. Katy Corrigan sounds catchy. Or maybe something pretty starting with M like Megan or Molly or Mia—or, if you wanted to be modern, you could go for something like Mackenzie.' His PA was obviously warming to this task.

'Molly,' Zac said quickly. 'I don't mind that. I don't know why, but the baby sort of looks like a Molly, doesn't she?'

Chloe turned to him. She was smiling, but her brown eyes were so soft and warm with emotion that the band around his chest pulled tighter.

'Molly's very cute,' she said. 'Or if you wanted to tie in a Christmas link, you could always go for Holly.'

'No, I'm warming to Molly,' Zac said. He liked to arrive at firm decisions. 'Molly Corrigan sounds all right, doesn't it? Or are there too many Os?'

'Molly's great.'

'Or Lucy. What about Lucy Corrigan? That sounds better, doesn't it?'

'Yes, Lucy's lovely,' Chloe said softly.

'Lucy Francesca Corrigan,' Zac refined, proud of his sudden inspiration.

'Oh, Francesca's gorgeous. What made you think of it?'

'It was my mother's name, although most people just called her Fran or Frannie.'

'It would be very fitting to name the baby after her grandmother. Lucy Francesca's so pretty. I love it!'

'Excellent. We can sleep on it and see if we still like it in the morning.'

For a moment, Zac thought he saw a glistening dampness in his PA's eyes, but she turned quickly to study another shop window, so he couldn't be sure.

He wondered if he'd said something wrong.

CHAPTER FIVE

ZAC WASTED NO time in getting to the share house the next morning. Having finally succumbed to jet lag on the previous evening, he and Chloe had opted to skip dinner in favour of much needed sleep and, consequently, they'd both woken early. A hearty hotel breakfast and a Tube ride later, they stood outside the house Liv had shared for the past twelve months.

Zac had no idea what to expect, but he wasn't totally surprised when his knock was answered by a girl with purple hair and a silver ring through her nose.

'Good morning,' he said rather formally. 'I spoke to someone called Skye on the phone.'

'Yeah,' the girl said. 'That's me.'

Zac lifted the empty suitcase he'd brought to collect Liv's belongings. 'I'm Zac Corrigan.'

Skye's face broke into an unexpectedly warm smile. 'Lovely to meet you, Zac.' She offered her hand, complete with black nail polish. 'Liv told us so much about you.'

'Really?' He couldn't hold back his surprise.

'Yeah, of course she did. She was dead proud of you, you know.'

But as she said this, her eyes filled with tears and—dammit—Zac felt his own eyes begin to sting.

'Come on in,' Skye said in a choked voice, blinking hard as she opened the door wider and stepped back to make room for them. 'Pete and Shaz have both left already for work.'

'We're not holding you up, are we?'

She shook her head. 'I don't work Saturdays.'

In the narrow hallway a faint smell of incense lingered. Zac introduced Chloe.

'Pleased to meet you.' Skye smiled now and regarded Chloe with interest. 'Are you Zac's girlfriend?'

'PA,' Zac and Chloe said together.

The girl gave a slightly puzzled frown, then shrugged and headed down the hall, nodding for them to follow.

'We miss Liv so much,' she said over her shoulder. 'But you must know that, Zac. You know what she was like. Such a live wire and always so lovely and kind.'

'Yes,' Zac said faintly as they entered the lounge room, which wasn't nearly as dilapidated as he'd expected.

The furniture was almost certainly second-hand and the sofa was draped in a hand-knitted shawl of red and purple wool, while the walls were hung with huge amateurish paintings in equally bright and gaudy oils. But everything was clean and tidy and the overall effect was surprisingly appealing. Artistic and cosy.

'Before I show you Liv's room,' Skye said, 'I thought I should mention that Father Tom dropped by last night.' Her eyes widened with the importance of this news. 'He said he could squeeze in a funeral on Monday morning, even though it's Christmas Eve...' The girl looked from Zac to Chloe. 'That is, if you'd like a church funeral.'

Zac hoped he didn't look as surprised as he felt. Avoiding Chloe's gaze, he asked, 'Did—did Liv attend church?'

'Oh, yeah.' The look Skye gave him was almost pitying. 'Every Sunday morning and on Wednesday evenings as well. We all go together. It's lovely.'

'Um…what kind of church?' he dared to ask.

'Oh, you can check it out for yourself, Zac. It's the little chapel around the corner. Father Tom's marvellous. You should see the work he does in the streets around here.'

'I see.' Zac swallowed. 'I'm afraid I had no idea about this. I've…er…made arrangements with a funeral director for a cremation.'

'But wouldn't you want a church service with Liv's friends as well?'

He realised he'd given no thought to the friends Liv might have made. She'd only been in England a year and he'd somehow pictured her wandering around with the guy from the band, pretty much alone and drifting…

Somewhat dazed, he looked Chloe's way and she immediately smiled and sent him an encouraging nod.

'A church service would be…perfect,' he said.

'Wonderful. I'll give Father Tom a ring, shall I?'

'Thank you.'

'Right. It's this way to Liv's room.' Skye was pointing. 'Feel free to take any or all of her things. Anything left, we can sort out.' Her voice wobbled and suddenly there were tears in her eyes again and her nose was distinctly pink. 'And stay as long as you like.'

'Thank you. You're very kind.' Still feeling dazed, Zac went to the doorway and then came to an abrupt halt when he saw his sister's room.

As a teenager, Liv's bedroom had always been a dive, with the bed unmade and clothes left lying on the floor where she'd climbed out of them, the waste basket overflowing with scrunched balls of paper and drink cans. For Zac, the messy room had been a constant battleground, but in the end he'd hated carrying on like an Army sergeant major and he'd given up trying to get her to tidy it.

In this room, the bed was covered by a smooth, spotless white spread and there was an arrangement of bright flowers in a vase on the bedside table. On top of a chest of drawers sat a small yellow teddy bear and neatly folded piles of baby clothing. Beside that a collection of toiletries…talcum powder and baby lotion and a glass jar filled with snowy cotton wool balls.

Taking pride of place in the corner stood a white bassinet of woven cane made up with clean sheets and with a soft pink blanket folded over one side, ready and waiting for a tiny occupant.

Stunned, Zac sagged against the doorpost.

The room said it all. His little sister had grown up and changed beyond recognition. Liv had found a true home here in London and she'd obviously been looking forward to motherhood. All evidence pointed to the fact that she'd planned to be a perfect mother, until fate cruelly robbed her of that chance, that *right*.

Without warning, he was swamped by a fresh deluge of sorrow and his chest swelled to bursting point as he felt his heart break all over again. He had no hope of holding back his tears.

It was a while later when he heard Chloe whisper softly behind him, 'Zac.'

He felt her hand on his arm, rubbing him through

his coat sleeve, and he found her touch unexpectedly comforting.

Straightening, he scrubbed a hand over his face. 'Sorry. I'm afraid I lost it again.'

'Oh, don't worry,' she said, swiping at her eyes. 'I've been blubbing, too.'

'It was such a shock.' He waved a hand at the room. 'I wasn't expecting this. Everything's so damn...*neat*.' He managed a broken laugh.

'It's charming,' Chloe said. 'Picture perfect.'

'The little monkey. Liv would never tidy a thing for me.'

They both laughed shakily, and stood looking about them. Then, drawing a deep breath, Zac set down the empty suitcase on a mat at the end of the bed. 'If only I had a clue where to start.'

Chloe crossed the room to the chest of drawers. 'I guess you'll definitely need these baby things.' She picked up the top item of clothing and held it out to him.

It was the tiniest singlet he'd ever seen. 'Wow, it's so little.'

'It's minuscule,' Chloe whispered, sharing his awe.

'I can't imagine trying to dress a wriggling baby in that,' Zac added with mild alarm.

Chloe smiled, but made no comment and he thought how lovely she looked. Actually...what man wouldn't be entranced by those shapely legs, that shiny, touchable hair? And how could he ignore the lovely warmth of her dark brown eyes? Bizarrely, in the midst of these saddest of circumstances, Zac found himself wondering why he'd always been so black and white about the boundaries he maintained with his PA.

'I'll get started, shall I?' she said, turning to open

the top drawer. 'I'm assuming you'll only take the baby clothes?'

'I think so.'

'There are plenty here. It looks like Liv was well prepared.'

Zac nodded and pledged to concentrate on the task at hand. 'If we set Liv's clothes to one side, Skye will know what to do with them.'

'But you'll want to keep things like this, Zac.'

'Like what?'

Chloe was holding out a small blue album. 'Take a look,' she said, sending him a significant glance.

It was a photo album, he quickly realised as he turned to the first page. It showed a professional photograph of his family taken in a studio when he was around ten.

His mother had used this photo to make a personalised Christmas card, he remembered. And there his mother was...looking youthful and beautiful with short dark hair and lively grey-green eyes, and wearing her favourite dress of tailored green linen.

Beside her, his father was wearing a white business shirt and dark trousers with a maroon tie. His father's hair had already started to grey at the temples, but his face was tanned from all the time he spent outdoors in the bush, tracking down the plants and animals that were endangered by extensive mining.

His mum had dressed them all in Christmas colours, so Zac was wearing a dark red polo shirt with pale chinos, while Liv, aged two, was in a white dress with a green and red tartan sash. Zac smiled, remembering how hard it had been to get Liv to sit still for the photo.

Now...they were all gone.

He was the only one left...and, suddenly, looking

at the photo was unbearable. He shut the album with a snap. He'd had more than enough heartbreak for one day.

Without speaking, he walked over to the suitcase and dropped the album into it. Chloe glanced at it and then up at him, but she didn't say a word. Her eloquent dark eyes told him that she understood. For that, he almost hugged her.

It was as they were leaving and thanking Skye yet again that Zac remembered to ask, 'Do you know if Liv had any names chosen for the baby?'

Skye laughed. 'She had hundreds. You should have seen the lists. Liv knew she was having a girl, of course.'

'Did she have a favourite name?'

'Not as far as I could tell. The name seemed to change almost every day. The only thing Liv was certain about was that she wanted her mother's name, Francesca, for the middle name.'

'Ah...' Zac caught Chloe's eye and they shared a smile and he felt an unexpected glow inside. It was incredibly reassuring to know that his first important decision about the baby had been on the right track.

'Are you going to check out the church?' Chloe asked when they were once again outside.

'Yes, good idea. I wouldn't mind meeting this Father Ted, too, if he's around.'

'Tom,' Chloe corrected. 'Father Tom.'

Zac grinned. 'Thanks, Ms Meadows. I suppose the chances of finding him on a Saturday morning are slim.'

They saw the tiny stone church as soon as they rounded the corner. Surrounded by a narrow fringe of green lawn, it was like a relic from the past, smack bang next to a row of brightly painted modern shops.

The front door of the church was open, offering an enticing glimpse of a nativity scene, complete with a stable and straw and a plaster donkey. When Zac and Chloe detoured around it, they found two women in the church's darkened interior, arranging white gladioli and bunches of holly in tall copper urns.

'I was hoping to find Father Tom,' Zac told the nearest woman.

She nodded towards a small wooden arch-shaped door in the far wall. 'Over there in the vestry.'

'Thank you.'

'He's very busy with Christmas and everything, and there'll be a wedding here in an hour or so.'

'I won't take up much of his time.'

As he turned to head off, Chloe held out her hand for the suitcase. 'I'll look after that.'

'OK, thanks.' Leaving Chloe sitting in a pew, Zac realised how quickly he'd become used to having her right beside him. *Almost as if…*

He cut off that thought before it distracted him from the task at hand.

At the vestry he gave two short knocks and the door was opened by a young sandy-haired fellow in jeans and a black knitted sweater.

'Hi there,' he said. 'How can I help you?'

'I was hoping to speak to Father Tom.'

The young man grinned. 'And so you are.'

This was Father Tom? Zac swallowed his shock. He'd expected a grey-haired old fellow, possibly stooped and wearing spectacles. This Father Tom, with his designer stubble and flashing blue eyes and no hint of a dog collar, looked more like a rock star than a priest.

'How can I help you?' Father Tom asked.

'I'm Zac Corrigan. I—'

'Zac, of course, of course… Wonderful to meet you. Come on in.' The young priest opened the door wider and stepped back. 'Take a seat,' he added as he scooped a pile of hymn books from a chair.

Once the books were deposited on a crammed shelf, he held out his hand. 'Please accept my condolences.' His hand gripped Zac's firmly. 'Liv was an amazing girl, just wonderful. We're all devastated.'

'I'm very grateful that you've offered to fit in a funeral for her at such short notice.'

'Only too happy to help.' Father Tom sat behind his desk, pushed some paperwork aside and leaned forward, hands clasped. 'Is there anything else I can do for you while you're here?'

Zac deliberately tried to relax, with an ankle propped on a knee. 'I know you can't break confidence,' he said carefully. 'But I wondered if Liv ever spoke to you about the baby's father.'

'About his identity?'

'Yes.'

Father Tom shook his head. 'I had no luck there, I'm afraid. Of course, I did raise the question with Liv. I asked her if the father was going to be able to help her or at least support her. She was straight upfront and said that this was *her* baby and she would be the one to care for it. The father was completely out of the scene.'

Zac realised he'd been holding his breath and now he let it out slowly, surprised by an unexpected sense of relief. He wasn't sure how or when it had happened but, some time in the past twenty-four hours, he'd arrived at a point of acceptance and his feelings about the baby had changed. He would be disappointed now if a strange man stepped up to claim her.

'Of course I did talk to Liv about the challenges of being a single mother so far from home,' the priest said. 'I was concerned about her secrecy and I probed to make quite sure that she didn't want the father's help. She assured me that the baby's father hadn't abused her in any way. In fact, she impressed on me that he wasn't a bad guy, but she said she'd put a lot of thought into her future and she knew exactly what she was doing.'

He fixed Zac with a steady gaze. 'She liked to talk about her family and she told me all about you.'

'Her annoying big brother.'

Father Tom gave a smiling shrug.

'She never told me about her pregnancy.'

'Ah, yes, Liv admitted that. She seemed to think she'd given you enough worry over the years. She knew you would have felt compelled to rush over here and to—'

'Interfere,' supplied Zac, tight-lipped.

This brought another sympathetic smile. 'Micro-manage, perhaps.'

Zac nodded. He knew Liv was right. He would have been over here like a shot, bossing her around, trying to order her to come home.

'Liv certainly planned to tell you once the baby was born. She said—I want to show Zac that I can be a brilliant mum and I want him to be finally proud of me.'

Finally? Zac cringed and the back of his neck burned. 'I was already proud of her,' he said gruffly. 'I might have been bossy, but I—I loved her.'

Damn it, he was *not* going to break down again, and certainly not in front of this man.

'I know you loved her,' Father Tom said gently. 'And

I'm sure Liv knew it, too. She was looking forward to showing you her baby. She told me that she couldn't wait to meet you at Heathrow and she fantasised about the moment she handed you your little niece.'

Oh, God. Zac groaned with the effort of holding himself together. Somehow he managed to lurch to his feet and thank Father Tom for his time. They spoke briefly about the service on Monday.

'Thanks for calling in, Zac. I'll see you then.'

They said farewell and Zac was still shaking inside as he strode back through the church to Chloe.

'No leads on the baby's father,' he said tersely and he was infinitely grateful that Chloe didn't press him with further questions as they went outside, where the clouds had parted at last to reveal a glimmer of pale English sunshine.

Chloe knew Zac was tense after his discussion with the clergyman. As the Tube train rushed back into the city, she tried to talk about practical things.

'I don't think we need to buy many more clothes for the baby, unless we see something *really* cute. I've done a little research on the Net and, for now, I think we probably only need formula and bottles and a steriliser, although we should check with the airline to see what they provide for babies on long haul flights.'

'Yeah, and I suppose we'd better ring the hospital and arrange a time to collect Lucy.' Zac looked a little self-conscious as he said the baby's name and Chloe gave him an encouraging smile.

Unfortunately, the look in his eyes when he returned her smile made her stomach drop as if she'd plunged from a great height.

Which was a definite problem. She'd had a few too many of these moments recently. Spending so much time with Zac was taking its toll.

She told herself that it was only natural, that sharing his personal tragedy was bound to have an impact on her own emotions. But now she was beginning to worry about the future. After this time in London, it was going to be so hard to return to their former strictly boss-PA relationship.

It would be hard for her, at least. She would remember all the emotional moments when her feelings for Zac had felt so much deeper and sweeter. Quite possibly, Zac would have no difficulty, though. He was pretty much an expert at keeping his business and personal life in separate compartments.

For Chloe, however, it had become increasingly clear that the sooner she got back to Brisbane and normality, the better. She was thinking about this when she asked, 'Would you like to collect Lucy this afternoon?'

'I don't think so,' Zac answered slowly, as if he was giving the matter careful thought. 'I hope this doesn't sound selfish, but I feel as if I need a little more time to adjust.'

'How much time?' Chloe asked cautiously.

'A decade?'

She must have looked shocked and Zac laughed. 'A joke, Ms Meadows. Don't worry. I'll speak to the hospital about collecting her tomorrow. In the meantime...' His eyes suddenly gleamed with unexpected merriment. 'I think we've earned ourselves a night out, don't you?'

An unhelpful fizzing raced along her veins, as if they were filled with champagne. 'I...I'm not sure,' she said. A night out sounded risky.

Zac frowned at her. 'Surely you don't want to squander this perfect chance to enjoy a Saturday night in London town?'

Even to sensible Chloe it did seem like a wasted opportunity, and she found it especially difficult to voice her very reasonable concerns when her less sensible self was jumping up and down like an excited child.

'Of course you don't,' Zac answered for her. 'We'll have a fabulous night. It's my last night of freedom and it's your duty as my employee to help me enjoy it.'

Before she could summon an effective protest, the train pulled into Oxford Circus and Zac launched to his feet, so the subject was dropped until they'd battled their way out of the crowded Underground and found themselves once more on the footpath.

By then Zac had it all planned and he was quite exuberant. Even though it was at the last minute, he was sure he could wangle a table for two at a good restaurant.

'And what about theatre tickets?' he asked Chloe now, his eyes shining with expectation. 'What sort of show do you feel like seeing? I must admit I could do with a little comedy.'

'Definitely comedy.' Clearly, there was no point in trying to argue about going out with him for the evening. 'We've had enough of real life drama.'

'Great.' Zac was almost boyish in his excitement. 'We'll go shopping this afternoon to buy clothes—for ourselves, not for the baby. We don't have to worry about sticking to carry-on luggage for the journey home. We'll have the suitcase with Lucy's things, anyway, so why not lash out? I'll pay for your new outfit, of course.'

'No,' Chloe said swiftly and firmly.

Zac stopped abruptly and a pedestrian hurrying behind them almost bumped into him. 'Don't be silly, Chloe.' He reached for her hand, but she slipped it into her coat pocket.

'Now you're being stubborn. This night out is my idea.' Zac ignored the pedestrians streaming around them. His attention was solely on Chloe. 'Let me buy you a dress and hang the expense. Think of it as a thank you gift for everything you've—'

'No,' Chloe said again, even more firmly to make sure he got the message. 'Thank you very much, Zac. It's an extremely kind offer, but I can't let you buy me clothes.'

This was one line she knew she mustn't cross. It was the difference between being his PA and a member of his chorus line of girlfriends.

'It's just a dress, Chloe.' Zac's smile was charming now. Bone-meltingly charming.

Chloe could feel her skin warming and her limbs growing languorous. It would be so easy to give in, but she had to remember that this was the special smile Zac used to conquer his countless female victims.

'Chloe, come on, loosen up. You're in London, for heaven's sake. You can't be in London without buying at least one new dress.'

He was right about that, she conceded. She would regret it later if she arrived home without some kind of memento, and what better than a chic new dress from London's famous Oxford Street?

'I was planning to buy a dress anyway,' she said.

Without dropping the smile, Zac narrowed his eyes at her. 'No, you weren't.'

'Of course I was.' She lifted her chin for emphasis and kept her expression deadpan. 'It'll be my Christmas present to myself.'

CHAPTER SIX

BY THE TIME Chloe carried her shopping bags back to her hotel room she felt quite sick. She couldn't believe she'd spent so much money. On one dress.

The expense was almost obscene. She should never have tried the dress on, but as soon as she'd entered the store she'd been seduced, and she hadn't looked at the price tag until it was far too late.

The knee-length dress with cap sleeves had looked so simple and demure on its hanger. Admittedly, it was a bold red and Chloe had never worn such a bright colour before. She usually stuck to soft pinks or browns, but it was Christmas after all, and she was in a mood to be daring. And as soon as she'd stepped into the changing room and slipped the dress on, her senses had instantly fallen under its spell.

The silk lining whispered against her skin like a lover's kiss and when she closed the underarm zip, the dress settled around her like a second skin. Then she'd turned to the mirror and experienced a true *oh-my-God* surprise.

Was that really her?

How could one dress make such a transformation? The bright red seemed to give her complexion a fresh glow and the scooped neckline enhanced the line of her collarbone and décolletage so that she looked… amazing.

As for the fit of the dress, Chloe had no idea how the designer had done it, but he'd managed to give her an hourglass figure. In a blink she'd become positively vain. She couldn't help it. She twisted this way and that, looking at herself from every angle. She'd never dreamed she could look so good and she knew there was no question. She simply *had* to have this dress. She couldn't possibly walk out of the store without it.

It was only after she'd arrived at this decision that she reached for the label and tried to read the price with the help of the mirror. At first she thought she'd made a mistake—she'd read the price upside-down, or back to front or something—so she was still feeling reasonably calm as she took the dress off, once again delighting in the cool slide of the silken lining over her skin.

With the dress back on its hanger, she looked at the price tag again. And almost had a heart attack.

Just as well there was a seat in the changing room or she might have keeled over.

Huddling on the seat in her undies, Chloe wanted to cry. She'd fallen in love with the red dress. While she was wearing it, she'd been quite certain that the designer had dreamed it up just for *her*.

But, dear Lord, the price was horrendous. Normally, she could buy six dresses for that amount and, with the current exchange rate, it would be even worse in Aussie dollars.

A small voice whispered: *That's why this dress looks ten times better on you than any of your old ones.*

And then, in the next breath, Chloe pictured the expression in Zac's eyes when he saw her in this dress, and that was probably about the time her synapses fused and she stopped thinking clearly. She simply got back into her clothes, marched to the counter and handed over her credit card.

Now, as she hung her purchase in the hotel wardrobe, she tried to ignore the sick feeling in the pit of her stomach. She consoled herself that she'd got a bargain with the black platform heels she'd bought to complete the outfit. And she told herself she'd atoned for her sins by buying a beautiful expensive silk scarf for her mother and an equally costly cashmere pullover for her dad.

And now the only sensible thing was to make sure she enjoyed this evening. Surely that couldn't be too hard?

In fact, it was impossible not to enjoy herself. Zac had bought himself a new dark grey suit which he teamed with a fine grey turtleneck instead of a traditional white shirt, which meant that his already devastating good looks now took on an extra sexy European appeal. Chloe found herself staring. And staring some more.

Of course, Zac did quite a bit of staring, too, especially when they arrived at the romantic candlelit restaurant in Piccadilly and Chloe removed her coat.

After he recovered from his initial dropped-jaw shock, he stared at her with an almost bewildered smile, as if he couldn't quite get over the surprise of seeing her all dressed up.

Illogically, Chloe wanted to cry. The look in Zac's eyes was so out of character. So unguarded and intimate…and *unsettling.*

'Ms Meadows, you've outdone yourself,' he murmured and he didn't drag his shimmering gaze from her till the waiter cleared his throat.

'Sir? If you'll come this way, I'll show you to your table...'

'Yes, yes. Thank you.' Zac sent Chloe a wink, as if to cover any embarrassment, and he touched his hand to her elbow ever so lightly to indicate that she should go ahead of him.

To her dismay, his touch set off flashes and sparks and she almost tripped as they wound their way through the tables.

It was a relief to be finally seated but, throughout the meal, Zac's eyes revealed a range of emotions as his initial shock gave way to amused delight, and finally to a more serious smouldering heat that stole Chloe's breath and set her pulses drumming.

Later, she could barely remember the meal although, of course, everything was delicious. She was too absorbed in the experience of being with Zac in such a romantic setting. Everything was so different—their vast distance from Australia, her red dress, the romantic Christmas decorations—and for one night she stopped thinking of herself as his PA. She was a woman very much enjoying the company of an exceptionally handsome and charming man.

Zac was, not surprisingly, an excellent conversationalist, and once they'd been through the typical chat about favourite books and movies, Chloe encouraged him to talk about himself. He told her how, when Liv was three, his family had lived on an island on the Great Barrier Reef for two years while his mother studied, among other things, the nesting habit of sea turtles.

His father couldn't be with them all the time, apparently, because of his work in the central Queensland coalfields, so he used to fly in and out from the island in a seaplane, which also delivered the family's provisions.

To Chloe, who'd only ever lived in the same small house in a Brisbane suburb, this life sounded wonderfully adventurous and romantic. Zac had lived in a timber cottage perched on a hill overlooking the Coral Sea, and from his bedroom he could reach out of the window to pick coconuts. His mother had taught him how to skin dive, and at night she'd built campfires on the beach and, while Liv was curled asleep in her lap, she'd taught Zac all about the stars and planets.

'It's a wonder you didn't become a scientist, too,' Chloe said.

Zac shrugged. 'I started out studying marine science but, after my parents' boat disappeared, I—' A corner of his mouth tilted in a briefly awkward smile. 'I needed to try something completely different.'

'At which you're equally brilliant,' she told him warmly.

His eyes shimmered again as he smiled at her. 'Thank you, Ms Meadows,' he said with exaggerated modesty.

But Chloe was sure that talking about his family couldn't be easy and, as they dug their spoons into a shared dessert of sinfully divine chocolate mousse, she directed the conversation to Lucy. 'Would you like her to have an adventurous childhood like yours?'

'You know, I almost want her life to be boring,' Zac said.

Chloe couldn't help herself. 'That would be such a shame.'

'But boring's safe.'

'It might be safe,' she responded, perhaps a little too vehemently. 'But it's certainly not fun.'

Now Zac regarded her thoughtfully before he helped himself to another spoonful of mousse. 'Sounds to me like you're speaking from experience.'

'I'm afraid I am.'

Of course, he wanted her to explain about this, which was how she ended up telling him about her parents—how her dad had worked in a hardware store and her mum was a teacher's aide, how they'd married late and never expected to have a family, so when baby Chloe arrived at the last moment, she had been a complete and bewildering surprise for them.

'My parents were already very set in their ways, so it was a very quiet life,' she said. 'Mum gave up work to stay at home with me and we didn't have much money, so we didn't go out very much, or entertain, and we only went on holidays every second year. Then it was always to the same place, Maroochydore. I love the beach, of course, but I was too shy to make new friends, so I used to sit under a beach umbrella with my parents and watch the other kids having fun.'

She rolled her eyes. 'I know, I know…that makes me sound like such a loser.'

'A loner, perhaps,' Zac said kindly. 'But hardly a loser.'

'It's not what you'd want for Lucy, though.'

He smiled. 'I guess I'll have to aim for some kind of middle ground.'

A picture flashed into Chloe's thoughts of Zac and Lucy with Marissa Johnson, sharing a new 'middle ground' life together. She found the thought incredibly depressing, so it was probably just as well that they'd reached the bottom of the chocolate mousse and Zac checked his phone for the time.

'We'd better get cracking,' he said. 'Our show's starting soon.'

He took Chloe's hand as they left the restaurant. She knew it was only practical to hold hands as they hurried through the crowds in Piccadilly Circus but, as they passed beneath a dazzling wonderland of Christmas lights, she was excruciatingly conscious of his strong fingers interlinked with hers. She'd almost forgotten the heart-zapping intimacy of even the smallest amount of skin contact.

Then they were in the warmth of the theatre, taking off their coats and settling into comfy velvet-upholstered seats, with all the attendant excitement of the lights being dimmed and the curtain rising…

'My sides are aching from laughing so much,' Chloe said as they stood outside afterwards, waiting for a taxi.

'Mine, too,' said Zac. 'I can't remember the last time I laughed so hard.'

'I'm so glad you picked a comedy.'

'Yeah, laughter's certainly good medicine.'

They were freezing on the footpath, but the air was crystal-clear. Above them stretched a network of lights in the shapes of stars, snowflakes and angels that made the night even more enchanting.

Chloe was still feeling relaxed and happy when they reached their hotel, which was probably why she didn't object when Zac suggested a nightcap in the bar.

'Here, allow me,' he said, stilling her hands with his as she was unbuttoning her coat.

At his touch, she froze, and her heart began thumping as she looked up at him.

The world seemed to stand still and she was trapped by his smiling silver-grey eyes.

'I've been dying to do this all night,' he said softly.

She couldn't breathe as she dropped her gaze to his hands, as she watched his long fingers slowly undo each button, as he gently slipped the coat from her shoulders and let his gaze travel deliberately over her.

'You know this dress is…magnificent.'

Chloe could feel a blush rising from her neck to her cheeks.

'I'm so glad you wouldn't let me pay for it,' Zac said.

'Why is that?'

'You would have chosen something sensible and inexpensive and not nearly as attractive as this.'

Now she couldn't help smiling. Seemed her boss knew her only too well.

'Actually, I have a better idea,' Zac said next as he looked around him at the rather crowded bar. 'Let's not have a drink here. We should go upstairs and get room service.'

And, just like that, alarm bells began clamouring in Chloe's ears—loud and clear—a reality check as effective as the clock at midnight for Cinderella.

There was no way she could share late night drinks in her playboy boss's hotel room. But, before she could insist on staying at the bar, Zac took off for the lift, still carrying her coat. She hurried after him, planning to drag him back, but the lift doors were already opening and there were other guests inside. She didn't want to make a scene so she held her tongue until they reached their floor and were out in the corridor.

'Zac, I don't need a nightcap,' she told him quietly but decisively as they arrived at the door to her room.

He tipped his head to one side with the look a parent might give to a troublesome child. 'You're not going to be a spoilsport.'

Chloe sighed. She should have guessed that this would happen and she should have had a strategy already planned. 'Look, tonight's been wonderful. I've had a fabulous time, but we both need to remember this isn't a date.'

'But it so easily could be.'

This was true and in the confined space of the hallway Chloe could smell Zac's cologne, musky and expensive and very masculine. When she looked up, she saw that his jaw was now lined by an attractive five o'clock shadow.

Help! She was still tingling and zapping from having him take off her coat. Anything more intimate would probably cause her to self-combust.

This was such a dangerous moment. She only had to give the slightest hint of acceptance and Zac Corrigan would be kissing her. And she couldn't pretend that she didn't want to be kissed. It was such a long, long time since she'd been in a man's arms…and this wasn't just any man. It was *Zac!* His lips were so close, so scrumptious, so wonderfully tempting.

The air between them was crackling and sizzling. At any moment, he was going to lean in…

Now she was struggling to remember why this was wrong. *I'll only be another of his Foolish Females.*

'Zac, we can't—'

'Shh.' He touched her arm, sending dizzying warmth

washing over her skin. 'Forget about the office for one night.'

'How can I? How can *you*?'

'Easy,' he said as his thumb rode a sensuous track over her bare arm. 'Tonight you're not my PA and I'm not your boss.'

'But we—'

'Chloe, you're an incredibly sexy woman in a gloriously sexy red dress and I'm the poor, helpless guy who's absolutely smitten by you.'

His words sent shivery heat rushing over her skin. She longed to give in. She was only human after all and Zac was a ridiculously attractive man and she'd been half in love with him for the past three years.

And in the past few days she'd learned so much more to like about him. She'd seen past the handsome façade to the vulnerable boy who'd lost his family and still longed for the safety and security of belonging.

But the yearning that filled her now had little to do with respect or friendship. It was pure and simple lust and all Chloe wanted to do was say yes… She was sinking beneath an overwhelming temptation to close her eyes and lift her face to his.

Why shouldn't she? Just about any girl in her situation would.

What the heck? they'd say. *Why not have some fun for one night? What happens in London stays in London...*

Problem was…while Chloe had been half in love with Zac for all this time, she'd also felt smugly superior to the girls who'd fallen head over heels for him. She'd watched those girls from the sidelines and she knew all too well that one blissful night could so easily lead to weeks and months of regret.

There were so many ways that love could hurt and she'd taken ages to get over Sam's death. She was terrified of risking another version of that heartbreak and pain.

It was so hard to be sensible though. So hard when Zac was a heartbeat away from kissing her… When he was looking at her with a breath-robbing intensity.

'Chloe, has anyone ever told you, you have the most amazing—'

In panic, she pressed a hand to his lips, shutting off the rest of his sentence—which was a pity because she was actually desperate to hear why he thought she was amazing. But it was time to toughen up, time to summon every ounce of her willpower. She lifted her face. 'I have one word for you, Mr Corrigan.'

Zac smiled. 'Please, let it be yes.'

She eyed him sternly. 'Marissa.'

His smile vanished as if the name had landed in his chest like a smart bomb.

'Or, if not Marissa,' Chloe went on, needing to make her message clear, 'substitute the name of whichever girl you decide to marry. *That girl* is where your focus should be.'

She felt terrible though, especially when she heard the shudder of Zac's indrawn breath.

'Good shot, Ms Meadows,' he said softly, and then, with a heavy sigh, he took a step back. From a safer distance, he regarded her with a shakily rueful smile. 'I should have remembered that I can always rely on you to be sensible.'

'That's what you pay me for,' Chloe said crisply and then she turned quickly to open her door. 'As I said, I've had a fabulous evening, so thanks again, Zac, and…and goodnight.'

Without looking back, she stepped inside and closed the door swiftly before she weakened and did something very foolish.

Safely inside, she sagged against the closed door and saw her lovely lamplit room in front of her. *Don't think!*

On the other side of the door Zac was still holding her coat, but it was too bad. She would collect it in the morning. She couldn't see him again now. Not when stupid, stupid tears were streaming down her cheeks.

That was a very close shave.

Zac was scowling as he stared at Chloe's closed door. He'd almost lost his head and broken his own golden rule.

Tonight you're not my PA and I'm not your boss.

How could he have said that?

How could he have been so crass? With Chloe, of all people? His invaluable, irreplaceable Chloe.

He knew she already had zero tolerance when it came to his love life, and now he'd just proven to her that her low opinion was justified.

Damn it. How the hell had his plans to marry someone like Marissa slipped so easily out of his head?

Of course, everything might have followed its proper course tonight if Chloe had stuck to being Chloe. But she'd morphed into a goddess in the sexiest red dress on the planet.

Sure, Zac had always known that Chloe was an attractive young woman, but she'd always been safe as his conservative, efficient PA. Beautiful, yes, but a bit distant and shy. He'd never guessed she had the confidence to dress so glamorously, to reveal herself as a truly sensual, feminine woman.

Tonight's dress had been perfect on her. The rich red had given extra glowing warmth to her complexion, enhancing the lustre of her hair and the dark beauty of her eyes.

And as for the figure-hugging lines and the beguiling scooped neckline...

Zac had been stunned. Transfixed. It was the only explanation he could summon for why he'd stepped over the boss-PA line. For a moment there, he'd allowed himself to acknowledge his secret desire for Chloe. Truth be told, his feelings had felt way deeper than the mere desire he felt for his usual girlfriends.

But Chloe had promptly broken the strange hypnotic spell that gripped him and all it had taken was one word.

In a blink he was thudding back to earth, to his real life, to his new responsibilities, to the way the world would be for him from now on and for ever after.

He supposed he should be grateful to Chloe for reminding him, and for remaining so consistent and sensible. He *was* grateful, or at least he probably would be grateful...eventually...

Now, with a sigh of frustration, Zac unlocked the door to his room and went inside, tossing his and Chloe's coats into an armchair. He let out another sigh as he stood, hands on hips, staring down at the coats as they lay in a pool of lamplight—entangled—with a sleeve of Chloe's coat looped over the shoulder of his coat. Like an embrace.

Mocking him for his foolishness.

It was back to business at breakfast in the hotel dining room next morning. Last night's flirtatious smiles and warm camaraderie were safely relegated to the past.

Chloe was pleased that Zac was cool and serious again—at least she told herself she was pleased, just as she told herself she was relieved that he made no teasing or personal remarks as she started on her melon and yoghurt, while he tucked into his full English breakfast.

Apparently, Zac had even been up early and had already made phone calls to both the airlines and the hospital.

'I've decided that we don't need to buy a car seat while we're here,' he said, getting straight down to business. 'The requirements for fitting them into vehicles are slightly different from country to country. And apparently it's easy enough to get a taxi that's set up for a baby. As for the airlines, they provide bassinets and facilities for heating bottles or whatever.'

Chloe nodded. 'Let's hope Lucy doesn't cry too much during the flight.'

'Indeed,' he agreed gravely.

It was a daunting prospect, flying to the other side of the world with a brand new baby.

Zac frowned. 'Do you think three days will be enough time for us to get used to managing her here before we fly home?'

'Three days? Does that mean you're planning to fly home on Boxing Day?'

'As long as the passport comes through in time. Thank heavens you had the forethought to contact that brilliant agency before we left Brisbane. They've broken all records in fast-tracking Lucy's passport, because of our special circumstances. So do you think Boxing Day will work?'

'It should be fine, I guess.' Chloe was quite sure they shouldn't delay their London stay for a second longer than necessary. And she knew Zac must be eager to get home. He had a great deal to organise when he arrived in Australia—including the procurement of a suitable wife. 'As Lucy's so tiny, she might do a lot of sleeping,' she suggested hopefully.

'Yes, fingers crossed.' Zac handed her a sheet of notepaper. 'I asked the hospital about bottles and formula et cetera. Apparently, we should have collected a checklist, but I've jotted down the things we'll need.'

Chloe scanned the list as she sipped her coffee. Fortunately, she was used to reading Zac's scratchy handwriting. She nodded. 'I noticed there's a pharmacy nearby, so I'll get all these things straight after breakfast.'

'Great.' Zac lifted the coffee pot. 'Like a top-up?'

'Just half a cup, thanks.'

As he concentrated on pouring, he said, 'There is one other difficulty that we haven't discussed.'

'What's that?'

He kept his gaze focused on the coffee pot as he filled his own cup. 'We need to decide where Lucy should sleep.'

'Oh, yes.' This problem had occurred to Chloe, but she'd promptly dismissed it as far too awkward. Now it had to be faced.

Obviously, while they stayed in the hotel, Lucy would be installed in either her room or Zac's. But the big question was—which room was appropriate? Zac was Lucy's official guardian and uncle, but could a bachelor be expected to cope with a newborn baby on his own? Zac had been terrified of simply holding Lucy at the hospital.

'I understand small babies wake at all hours of the night,' he said. 'I read in one of those magazines of yours that newborns sometimes need feeding every two to three hours, even at night time.'

Chloe nodded carefully, certain she could see where this was heading. 'I wouldn't mind taking care of Lucy through the night.'

'No, no,' he said, surprising her. 'I wasn't angling for that. It's asking too much of you.'

'So you think you'll be OK looking after her?'

His mouth squared as he grimaced. 'Frankly, no. I imagine I'll be pretty hopeless.'

'Then, unless you hire a nanny, we don't really have an alternative.'

Zac watched her for a long moment and the smallest hint of a smile played in his eyes. 'Actually, we do have an alternative, Chloe, but I'm afraid you're not going to like it.'

In an instant she was sitting straighter. 'You're not going to suggest we share a room.'

'But it makes sense, doesn't it?' His smile had disappeared now and Chloe could almost believe that he wasn't teasing. 'Neither of us knows much about babies. We both need moral support.'

She groaned. Of course she was remembering last night's close call when Zac had almost kissed her, when she'd almost let him...when she'd so very nearly welcomed him into her arms...and of course the memory stirred all the yearnings that she'd spent an entire night trying to forget. 'Honestly, Zac, don't you ever give up?'

'Calm down. There's no need to get all stirred up and old-maidish.'

'*I am not an old maid,*' Chloe hissed in a rush of righteous fury. Actually, she might have yelled this fact if they weren't in a refined hotel dining room filled with dignified guests.

'I stand corrected.' Straight-faced, Zac pushed his empty plate aside and rested his arms on the table as he leaned towards her. 'I certainly wasn't going to suggest that we share the same bed,' he said, lowering his voice so that she also had to lean in to hear him. 'I've actually looked into hiring a suite with two bedrooms, but the hotel's fully booked with special Christmas deals, so there's nothing like that available. And we really don't want to have to start hunting for another place at this late stage.'

Chloe had to give him credit—there wasn't a trace of a smile or a smirk.

'So what do you have in mind?' She wished her voice didn't sound so shaky.

'Well, it's easy enough to break up a king-size bed into twin singles and then our problem's solved.'

'Solved?' *So we'd be sleeping side by side?* 'What kind of a solution is that?'

'I'm only trying to think of what's best for the baby.' He actually sounded genuine. 'I swear there'll be no funny business, Ms Meadows. I'll be on my best behaviour.'

'I'm sure you have good intentions, Mr Corrigan, but I'd much rather—'

Chloe stopped. She'd been about to say that she would much rather look after Lucy on her own, but then she realised how selfish that sounded, and she would be denying Zac an important chance to get to know his baby niece and possibly to bond with her.

Maybe she *was* being a trifle prudish. After all, if Zac had really wanted to seduce her, he wouldn't have given up so easily last night. And if he could resist her in last night's red dress, he wasn't likely to pounce on her as she walked the floor at midnight with a fretful baby in her arms.

'Look, all right,' she admitted reluctantly. 'I suppose your plan makes a crazy kind of sense. I'll…I'll give it a go.'

Her boss rewarded her with one of his spectacular smiles. 'I knew I could rely on you to be unfailingly sensible. I'll organise for the beds to be changed, and for a cot to be sent up to my room. And I certainly won't let your room go. You'll need it as a bolt-hole, at least to escape to for long hot baths.'

His grey eyes shimmered and she couldn't be sure if he was teasing her again.

CHAPTER SEVEN

'SHE'S AN ABSOLUTE angel, isn't she?'

Zac stood by the cot set in a corner of his hotel room, aware that he wore a sappy smile on his face as he stared down at the sleeping baby. As far as he could tell, Lucy Corrigan was perfect.

She'd been sound asleep when he and Chloe collected her from the hospital and she'd slept all the way during the taxi ride. She hadn't even stirred when they arrived back at the hotel, where he'd rather clumsily extracted her from the car seat before the excited hotel staff rushed to make a huge fuss of them.

Now the three of them were alone. Chloe was in an armchair by the window, reading yet another magazine about mothers and babies, and Zac was pacing the floor on tenterhooks, waiting for Lucy to stir and wake for her next feed.

Standing ready in the bar fridge were a row of bottles of formula that Chloe had made up and which she was going to heat with a special travelling contraption she'd found at the pharmacy.

Zac wasn't entirely happy about this. He'd planned to ask the kitchen staff to prepare the baby's formula and he'd been quite pleased with the idea of Lucy's bottles arriving via room service. He was rather amused by the prospect of signing for a baby's bottle delivered on a covered silver tray.

But Chloe, sensible as always, had wanted to be certain about the hygiene of the bottles and about getting the temperature of the milk exactly right, so now Zac's bathroom housed a sterilising unit as well as the heating gear and a collection of baby bath gels and lotions and wipes.

Still, he liked to think of himself as tolerant—and at least Lucy was very well behaved. Not a peep out of her so far. Then again, a quiet, sleeping baby was rather boring for a guy who wasn't used to sitting around…

'Isn't she due to wake up for a feed?' he asked Chloe as he checked the time yet again. By his reckoning, Lucy had slept twenty minutes past her mealtime.

Chloe looked up from her magazine. 'I suppose she'll wake when she's ready.'

'Isn't that a bit vague? I thought there was a schedule.' Schedules were usually his PA's forte. 'Isn't it important to get a baby into a routine?'

'Zac, give her time. She's only a few days old. She'll probably wake soon.'

Disgruntled, he picked up the TV remote and pressed the 'on' button. A loud blast of music erupted and Lucy gave a start, throwing one tiny arm in the air.

'Sorry,' he muttered as Chloe glared at him while he hastily searched for the 'mute' button.

Ridiculously, his heart was pounding now. No doubt he'd terrified the baby. He held his breath, waiting for her wails of terror. But, to his amazement, she was already asleep again, lying as still as a doll. Perhaps she'd never really woken.

Zac dropped into another armchair and began to flip restlessly through the channels with the sound turned down, but there was nothing he really wanted to watch and he found his mind meandering back over the previous night…

Rather than chastising himself yet again, he allowed himself to dwell on the pleasures of the evening. And there had been many. Chloe had been such good company—so relaxing and easy to talk to at the restaurant—and at the theatre she'd laughed uproariously, even at risqué jokes that he'd feared might upset her.

As for the red dress… Zac feared he was scarred for life by that dress.

He knew that from now on, every time Chloe walked into his office, he was going to remember the tormenting way the dress had hugged her delicious curves.

Why on earth had he paid such scant attention *to* those curves before now? He was beginning to regret that he'd been so disciplined from the day Chloe first joined his staff, never allowing himself to think of her as anything but his PA.

Of course, office romances were messy and bad for business—Zac had seen several of his mates fall by that particular wayside—but, last night, it was as if he'd had laser surgery and his vision had suddenly cleared. And today, even though Chloe had changed back into a sweater and jeans that he'd seen many times before, he was aware of her body in a whole new and entirely distracting way.

He couldn't help noticing the lush swell of her breasts and the dip to her waist, or the sweet tempting curve of her butt.

Which was hardly conducive to a good working relationship, especially now that they were spending so much time together, including sleeping side by side in the same room. Clearly his brain had been out to lunch when he'd come up with *that* bright idea. He'd presumed the baby would keep them fully occupied…

With a heavy sigh, Zac switched off the TV, pushed out of the armchair and began to prowl again. If Lucy slept for too much longer he would have to take off—go for a hike—hope that the freezing winter weather outside might chill his inappropriately lustful thoughts.

'Are you quite sure we shouldn't wake her?' he demanded after yet another circuit of the room.

Chloe rose and came over to the cot. Her sweater had a V-neck that exposed the soft pale skin of her neck and a hint of the perfection of her collarbone.

'I'm not totally sure,' she said. 'Most of the information I've read is for breastfed babies.'

Zac wished she hadn't mentioned breasts. He was all too aware of the way hers swayed gently beneath the soft knit of the sweater when she walked.

He tried to concentrate on the tiny girl as they stood together, looking down at her. Lucy was lying on her side, giving them a view of her profile now—the newborn slope of her brow, her snub little nose and slightly pouting red lips.

She was so still. So quiet. So *tiny*.

A tremor of fear rippled through Zac's innards. 'I suppose she's still breathing?'

He saw his fear reflected in Chloe's dark eyes. 'Of course. Well…I—I think so.'

Zac's fear spiked to panic. 'Should we check?'

'OK.'

One of Lucy's hands was peeking out of the blanket

and his heart hammered as he reached down and touched it with his finger. 'She feels a little cold.'

'Does she?' Chloe also sounded panicked now and she gave the baby a prod with two fingers.

Lucy squirmed and made a snuffling noise.

'Oh, thank God,' Zac breathed and he nearly hugged Chloe with relief.

Then they both laughed, shaking their heads at their foolishness, but, as their smiling gazes connected, Zac's heart thudded for a very different reason.

He felt a deep rush of gratitude for this woman. In the past few days he'd experienced some of the darkest moments of his life and Chloe's presence had been like a gently glowing candle, a shining light just when he needed it. Actually, he suspected that this feeling comprised something way deeper than gratitude.

Perhaps Chloe sensed this, too. Confusion flashed in her eyes and she hastily looked down. 'Hey,' she said suddenly. 'Zac, look.'

From the cot, two small bright eyes were staring up at them.

Zac grinned. 'Well, well…hello there, Lucy Francesca Corrigan. Aren't you the cutest little thing?'

'I guess we can pick her up now,' Chloe said. 'She probably needs changing. Do you want to do the honours?'

Zac swallowed. The nurse had handed the baby to Chloe when they left the hospital, which was fine by him. He'd planned to be an observer. Then again, he'd never been one to chicken out of a challenge.

'OK,' he said bravely, peeling back the top blanket. To reassure himself, he added, 'No worries.' But he held his breath as he carefully lifted the tiny bundle.

'You can change her on the bed,' Chloe said.

'Me?'

'Why not?' Her smiling dark eyes were daring him now. 'I've spread towels for you.'

'Right, sure.'

Anyone would think he was defusing a bomb, the way he gingerly set the baby down and began to unwrap her bunny rug. Beneath this, he found that she was wearing an all-in-one affair, like a spacesuit, so his task now was to undo countless clips.

Beside him, Chloe was on standby with baby wipes and a clean disposable nappy.

'Maybe you should take over,' he suggested. 'You're probably an expert. You've done this before.'

She shook her head. 'I haven't actually, but I've watched friends change babies, and I'd say you're doing a fine job.'

Soldiering on, Zac eventually managed to free Lucy from her nappy and it was a bit of a shock to encounter her naked lower half. Her hips were minuscule, her legs thin and red as she kicked at the air.

'She's like a little frog,' he said in awe.

'She's beautiful,' reproached Chloe.

'Well, yeah. A beautiful little frog.'

Chloe handed him a wipe. 'You can put on a new nappy and dress her again while I heat her bottle.'

'Right.' Zac felt a stab of alarm as Chloe disappeared, but then he took a deep breath and manfully got on with the job and, although it was tricky getting tiny limbs back into the right sections of the garment, he was absurdly pleased with himself when he had Lucy properly dressed again by the time Chloe came back with the bottle.

'She hasn't cried at all,' Chloe commented.

'No, she's frowned and looked cross-eyed at me once or twice,' Zac said. 'But not one wail.'

'Isn't she good?'

'Amazing.' In a burst of magnanimity, he said, 'You can feed her if you like. I'm happy to watch and learn.'

But Zac soon realised this wasn't such a great idea. The picture Chloe made as she settled in the armchair with Lucy made him choke up again. This was partly because he was suddenly thinking of Liv and the fact that she should be here with her baby. But also…even though he was missing Liv, he knew that Chloe looked so damn right in this setting.

Perhaps it was something about the tilt of her head, or the way the light from outside filtered through the hotel's gauzy curtain, making the scene look soft, like a watercolour painting.

Or perhaps it was the fondness in Chloe's face as she looked down at Lucy, and the way Lucy looked straight back at her, concentrating hard, so that she almost went cross-eyed again as she sucked on the teat.

He was damn sure those two were forming a bond.

'I should put the kettle on and make you a cuppa,' he said, wishing his voice didn't sound so gruff.

Chloe flashed him a brilliant smile. 'Thanks.'

As Zac went to fill the kettle he couldn't remember the last time he'd made a cup of tea for anyone else. He knew he should be dismayed by the sudden domestic turn that his life had taken, but the craziest thing was that he actually quite liked it.

Chloe was secretly amazed that the first day with Lucy went so smoothly. After the baby was fed and burped she went straight back to sleep again and she continued to sleep while Chloe and Zac watched an entire DVD.

Now, the short winter daylight had disappeared already and the dark streets outside once again flashed with traffic lights and neon signs and Christmas decorations.

'This baby-raising is a piece of cake,' Zac declared as he poured two glasses of the Italian wine he'd ordered from room service and handed a glass to Chloe. 'How much do they pay babysitters and nannies for sitting around like this?'

'I don't really know,' Chloe said. 'But I'm quite sure they earn it.'

'I can't see how.' Zac was grinning as he lifted the cover on the cheese platter he'd ordered to accompany the wine, and Chloe guessed he wasn't really serious. Then again, it was hard to argue that their new responsibility was onerous as they clinked glasses in a toast to the sleeping baby in the corner.

Their afternoon had been surprisingly pleasant. She and Zac had established clear ground rules and he'd been on his best behaviour...and this evening promised ongoing pleasantness.

They planned to have dinner here in Zac's room and perhaps watch another movie, having discovered an unexpected mutual liking for sci-fi. It was all very agreeable. Zac was so much more at ease about caring for Lucy now and Chloe was genuinely pleased for him. He'd been through so much turmoil over the past few days and he still had to face his sister's funeral in the morning, and heaven knew what challenges awaited him when he got back to Australia.

A quiet, relaxing evening was exactly what he needed

and so they'd planned for dinner at seven-thirty, allowing plenty of time for Lucy to wake and be changed and fed and settled back to sleep again.

Chloe always felt better when she had a clear plan…

'Is that someone knocking?' Zac shot a frowning glance to the door. He couldn't really hear anything with a baby screaming in his ear. 'What's the time?'

'Seven-thirty,' said Chloe, who'd been pacing anxiously beside him.

'That'll be our dinner.' Zac, who was fast becoming an expert, deftly shifted Lucy, plus a hand towel to catch spit-up milk, to his other shoulder. 'We should have rung through and told them to hold the meal till we got her down.'

Chloe winced, knowing that normally she would have thought of this. 'I guess I'd better answer the door.'

'Wait till I take Lucy through to the bathroom. We don't want to blast the poor guy's ears off.'

Chloe's stomach was churning as she watched Zac disappear with the red-faced, yelling babe. This had been going on for over an hour now and they weren't quite sure how or why Lucy was so upset.

She'd woken from her sleep and together they'd bathed her and changed her into clean clothes from head to toe. This had taken a little longer than it probably should have and by the time they'd finished Lucy was desperately hungry and letting them know. When Zac offered her the bottle—they'd decided it was his turn—she had sucked quite greedily and the milk had disappeared in no time.

'Piece of cake, this looking after babies,' he'd said again, smiling smugly as he laid Lucy back in the cot.

Thirty seconds later, the wailing had begun. Lucy kept pulling her little knee into her stomach as if she was in pain.

'She needs burping,' Chloe decided. 'There's a diagram of what you have to do in one of the magazines.' And, following the instructions carefully, she'd sat Lucy on her lap, holding her tummy firmly with one hand while she gently rubbed her back.

It hadn't worked—and neither had walking up and down with Lucy. The hoped-for burp never occurred and after more than an hour of valiant efforts to calm her, her cries still hadn't stopped.

Despite the closed bathroom door, the yells could be heard all too clearly now as their room service dinner was wheeled in…

Chloe gave the fellow a generous tip.

'Thanks.' His eyes were wide with curiosity and he sent more than one worried glance to the closed door.

'Colicky baby,' Chloe told him with the knowledgeable tone she imagined a nursing sister might use. 'She'll settle soon.'

The fellow nodded and hurried away and Chloe hoped they weren't going to be reported for creating a disturbance.

She opened the bathroom door for Zac and he emerged looking somewhat haggard, although Lucy's howls had finally begun to quieten to whimpers.

'Do you think she's settling?'

Zac's shoulders lifted in a shrug. 'I have no idea. From now on I'll admit to total ignorance and I take back everything that I said about nannies and babysitters. Whatever they're paid, it's not enough.'

Chloe couldn't help smiling and, although this wasn't

the right moment, she also couldn't help noticing how utterly enticing a strong hunky man could look with a tiny baby in his arms. Moments like this, she could almost imagine…

But no. She reined her thoughts back. Imaginations were dangerous.

'That dinner smells amazing,' Zac said, casting a longing glance to the trolley.

'I know. My tummy's rumbling.' Zac had ordered a Greek lamb dish for both of them and Chloe doubted any meal could smell more tempting. 'I wonder when we'll get to eat it.'

At that moment, Lucy's knee jerked upwards again and she let out another heart-rending yell.

'She's definitely in pain,' Zac said. 'Maybe we should ring someone. Do you think there's a helpline?'

'I'm pretty sure she just has colic.' Chloe said this more calmly than she felt. 'Early evening is supposed to be the worst time for it.'

'Perhaps it's my fault?' A totally uncharacteristic look of guilt appeared in Zac's eyes. 'Maybe I held the bottle the wrong way.'

'Of course you didn't. Here, let me take her for a bit. You eat your meal. It's getting cold.'

'No, no. You eat first.'

Chloe shook her head. She couldn't possibly eat while Lucy was still so upset. 'Perhaps we should try changing her again…'

In the end, they ate their cooling and congealing dinner in shifts, while taking it in turns to pace the floor with the baby. Several times her crying calmed down and she began to look sleepy and their hopes soared.

Twice she nodded off and they actually placed her back in the cot, holding their breath and hoping she would stay asleep as they backed silently away on tiptoe. Both times, just when they thought all was well, Lucy suddenly threw up her hand and began to cry more lustily than ever.

She kept crying on and off until it was her feed time again. This time, when they changed her, they encountered their first dirty nappy and Zac rose another notch in Chloe's estimation when he didn't flinch, but gamely went to work with the wipes.

He insisted that Chloe be the one to feed Lucy this time. She made sure that the baby didn't guzzle and she stopped the feed halfway through for a little burping session—this time with results—and, to their infinite relief, when they tiptoed away from the cot, Lucy remained sleeping.

As the silence continued, they let out relieved sighs.

Bliss.

They shared tired smiles.

'I'm knackered,' Zac admitted with a sheepish smile. 'I was looking forward to kicking back with some more of that wine and cheese, but I'm not sure I have the strength.'

'Nor me,' agreed Chloe. 'Not if Lucy's going to wake again in three hours or so.'

She went back to her room to shower and to change into sleepwear and of course she chose the safety of a voluminous grey T-shirt and opaque black tights, but, when she came back, Zac was already in bed and he appeared to be sound asleep.

She smiled wearily. After making such an enormous fuss about the dangers of sleeping so close to Zac, the reality was going to be a non-event. All either of them wanted was the oblivion of deep sleep.

A small sound woke Chloe.

Drowsily, she rolled over without opening her eyes, then nestled back under the covers. No sound now. All was quiet again. Lovely. She didn't have to worry. The sound wasn't Lucy.

Zap!

Lucy? Shocked into wakefulness, Chloe shot up, heart thudding. The room was mostly in darkness, but there was enough light from a lamp in the corner for her to see that Zac was awake and sitting on the edge of his bed.

'I thought I heard something,' she whispered. 'Was it Lucy?'

'It's OK,' he whispered in answer. 'Go back to sleep.'

'But there was a noise. How is she?'

'She's fine. I've just fed her.'

'*You've* fed her?' Chloe stared at him in amazement. 'You mean you've done it all—changed her and fed her and burped her?'

'The whole deal.'

'So what's she doing now?'

'Sleeping again. Like a baby.'

Chloe gave a dazed shake of her head. 'Why didn't you wake me?'

'Didn't want to bother you.' Zac yawned. 'You were snoring your head off.' He yawned again. ''Night. See you in the morning.' And then he lay down with his back to her and pulled the covers high.

Chloe was too surprised to fall straight back to sleep. She was supposed to be moral support. She was sleeping in this room because Zac needed her help. Except he clearly hadn't needed her at all...and she wasn't sure how she felt about that...

She'd grown accustomed to him needing her...

Although perhaps she shouldn't be so surprised. She knew that Zac threw his whole weight into any project he undertook.

As she lay staring into the darkness, she thought again about the fuss she'd made this morning over sharing this room with him. She'd expected him to try to seduce her again. She'd imagined having to fend off his advances, even though she didn't really want to...

If she was brutally honest, she'd probably hoped he might try...

But, as Zac had promised, this was an entirely practical arrangement. He hadn't shown the slightest glimmer of sexual interest in her and now she felt a bit foolish about the way she'd made such a hue and cry.

Of course, it probably helped that she'd chosen to wear these gym clothes to bed rather than slinky pyjamas, but tonight she'd gained the impression that Zac would probably have ignored her even if she'd been wearing a transparent negligee. His focus was entirely on Lucy. And Chloe was delighted about that. She was. Really.

But she wasn't sure if she would get back to sleep.

CHAPTER EIGHT

AFTERWARDS, ZAC'S MEMORIES of Liv's funeral were fragmentary at best. He could recall the harrowing hollowness he felt on entering the small church lit with candles and Christmas brightness, and filled with a surprising number of people. But he remembered very little of the short eulogy he gave, although he did his best to give his sister's new friends a few cheering pictures of Liv's happy family life in Australia, and of the deep love he'd always felt for her.

He thanked everyone gathered there for offering his sister the welcoming warmth of their friendship and for coming today to honour Liv's memory. He thanked Father Tom…having earlier handed him an envelope with a cheque that he hoped would convey his immense gratitude.

Moving outside again was the worst moment—bidding farewell to Liv's coffin before it was driven away. Zac felt as if he couldn't breathe. His throat burned as if he'd swallowed a hot ember and his hand was shaking as he reached into his coat pocket and drew out a piece of coral, one of two pieces he'd found on a shelf in Liv's room.

Bleached white and bony, like miniature antlers, Zac had recognised them immediately as coral their mother had collected when they'd lived on the island, pieces that Liv had always kept with her.

Today he placed one slender branching cluster on her coffin.

'Bye, Liv,' he whispered. Then, blinded by tears, he wrapped his fingers around the other piece still in his pocket.

When he felt an arm slip through his, he turned to see Chloe, who offered him a markedly wobbly smile.

'You were wonderful,' she told him, and her eyes were shiny with tears as she picked up the tail of his scarf and tucked it back inside his coat, before lifting her face to press a warm kiss to his cheek.

Zac closed his eyes, more touched by the simple gesture than was possibly appropriate. He suspected that, while other memories might fade, this particular moment would stay with him for ever.

Even though it was Christmas Eve, Skye and Liv's other housemates insisted on inviting everyone back to the house. In no time the place was crammed with a huge range of young people, including Father Tom.

As mugs of mulled wine and savoury platters were passed around, Chloe was introduced to a fascinating crowd with a wide range of British accents, as well as the more distinctive voices of people who were clearly new arrivals, just as Liv had been.

She met a Brazilian man, a kitchen hand who was not only stunningly handsome but extremely polite and charming. Next, she was introduced to two Polish plumbers with shaved heads who looked fierce but were actually super-friendly. A large West Indian girl showered everyone with her beaming smile.

Of course, all of Liv's friends wanted to make a fuss of Lucy and, to Chloe's surprise, they'd even brought presents for the baby—so many gifts, in fact, that Zac was going to need another suitcase.

Zac was extremely tolerant as the baby was passed around, and Chloe guessed that he was as touched as she was to discover how supportive Liv's community of friends had been. And, fortunately, Lucy seemed to enjoy all the attention.

'That went well,' Zac said quietly as a taxi took them back to the hotel. 'I had no idea what to expect, but it couldn't have been better, really.'

But he still looked sad…terribly sad…and Chloe's heart ached for him.

Almost as soon as they got back to the hotel, Zac made his excuses. 'There are one or two matters I need to see to,' he said enigmatically before disappearing.

Chloe knew he had to collect Lucy's passport, but she was also sure he needed a little time to himself. Actually, she was more than ready for some thinking space, too… There were one or two matters she needed to chew over…including the fact that the longer she was in close proximity to Zac Corrigan the more she liked him, the more she cared about him. Deeply. Maybe even *loved* him…

In the past few days her understanding of her boss had changed massively, especially since they'd begun caring for Lucy. There were times when Zac had looked at her with an emotion that went way deeper than teasing or desire. Moments when Chloe saw a kind of tenderness that made her heart tremble and hold its breath, as if…

Her more sensible self wanted to argue with this, of course, but Chloe was tired of her internal debates…or perhaps she was just plain tired. Lucy had been colicky again in the early hours…

Curled in the armchair, she must have nodded off, and she woke with a start when Zac returned.

'Sorry.' He sent her a smile as he tiptoed across the room to peek into the cot. 'I was trying not to wake you.'

'Doesn't matter. Is Lucy still asleep?'

'Out like a light.'

Chloe's limbs were stiff as she unfurled from her cramped position and sat straighter. She rubbed at her eyes and blinked. No, she hadn't imagined it. Zac was not merely smiling; he was looking particularly pleased with himself.

She'd assumed he'd been walking around London's streets, sunk in his grief, but his smile was definitely triumphant as he tossed his coat onto the end of his bed before he sank comfortably into the other armchair. 'I've collected Lucy's passport and I've sorted out our Christmas,' he said.

'Sorted it how?' Despite the beautiful decorations and lights and the frenzy of shopping all around them, Chloe had almost stopped thinking about Christmas. 'I thought we'd have turkey and plum pudding here in the room.'

'No, Chloe, you deserve better than that.'

'I do?' she asked, frowning.

'Yes, you do, Chloe Meadows.' Zac smiled gently and she wished he wouldn't. 'You've given up your own plans for Christmas without a word of complaint and you deserve some fun.'

An edgy uncertainty launched her to her feet. What was Zac planning? That she should go off and celebrate Christmas on her own while he stayed here with Lucy? She couldn't imagine she'd enjoy that very much.

'Zac, I don't need a fancy Christmas. I've said all along that I'm happy to help with Lucy.'

'Don't worry about Lucy. I've organised a sitter.'

She stared at him in surprise. 'But you don't believe in babysitters.'

Zac frowned. 'I don't think I ever said that exactly.' Now he rose from his chair to stand beside her. 'I'm not keen on nannies, particularly if they're used as a mother substitute. But this is different. It's not fair to you to be locked up in here on Christmas Day with someone else's baby.'

His eyes sparkled. 'After all, I did promise you a flash London Christmas to make up for missing our office party.'

'So you did.' Chloe found that she was smiling too as she remembered what a big deal the office Christmas party had been for her. Only a few days ago. So much had changed since then. And now…the very fact that Zac had obviously been thinking about her, making plans in an effort to please her made her feel unexpectedly happy and glowing…

'Actually, I've also been thinking ahead,' Zac said. 'I've been thinking about when I get home. I've realised that I can't expect *any* woman to be tied to the baby around the clock. She'll have to have help.'

Any woman... He was referring to his future wife, of course, and a shiver skittered down Chloe, as if he'd dropped a cold key down the back of her shirt. How silly she'd been to imagine…to think that he might possibly…

'So,' she said stiffly as she tried to ignore the chilling slap of ridiculous, unwarranted disappointment. 'What do you have planned for tomorrow?'

'Are you all right, Chloe?'

'Yes, of course.' She was working hard now to ignore the confusion and tumult that seemed to have taken up residence in her head and her heart.

Turning away from him to the window, she stared out at the park with its huge bare trees. She saw children in woolly hats chasing each other, saw businessmen with newspapers and furled umbrellas. An elderly couple were walking their dogs. And then her vision blurred.

She certainly wasn't all right. She was very afraid that, against her better judgement, she'd fallen in love with her boss.

She was as foolish as all his other females. More foolish actually, because she'd always known that falling for Zac was dangerous.

Somehow, over the past few days, she'd been seduced by their moments of deep connectedness. She'd been charmed by those times when he'd looked at her with a true appreciation that went way deeper than the mere respect of a boss for a trusted employee.

Saturday night had been different—Chloe had found it difficult but at least possible to resist Zac when he'd so clearly set out to seduce her. After all, she knew that Zac Corrigan would try to seduce any young woman he dated. But this morning, outside the church, Zac had needed her emotional support. And her heart had never felt so full…

'Chloe, what is it? What's the matter?' Zac was standing close behind her now and at any minute he was going to discover her tears.

'I—I was just thinking about…Christmas,' she said, grasping at any excuse.

'I suppose you must be missing your parents.'

'Yes.' Across the street a young woman was running through the park. The woman wore a red coat and her blonde hair was flying behind her like a banner.

'Chloe.' She felt Zac's hand on her shoulder and she tried to keep her head averted. The girl in the park was running to meet a young man. The young man was hurrying too and at any moment they would fall into each other's arms.

'You're crying,' Zac said and he made a soft sound of despair. 'Come here.' With sure hands, he pulled her around to face him. 'Let me see you.'

Chloe shook her head, made her eyes extra wide in a desperate attempt to hold back the tears. *I'm being an idiot.*

Zac had positioned her in front of him now, a hand on each of her shoulders as he searched her face, his grey eyes mirrors of her sadness. 'Chloe, what's the matter?'

How could she tell him? She shook her head and she might have held up her hand to ward him off but, before she could, his arms were around her, drawing her against him.

'Oh, Chloe.'

Now she was clinging to him, pressing her damp face into the comforting wall of his chest, and his arms were around her, warm and strong, holding her close. She could smell a faint trace of his aftershave, could hear his ragged breathing, could feel his heart thudding against hers. Now she could feel his lips brushing a soft kiss to her brow…and that tiny intimacy was all it took.

In the next breath she was coming undone, wanted nothing more than for Zac to kiss her properly. On the lips. And if he kissed her, she would kiss him back. She would kiss him deeply, passionately, throw caution to the wind.

With him suddenly so close, her emotions were a fiercely rushing tide. Desire churned deep inside her, and she knew she had no choice but to ride the flood… rising, rising… She was gripped by a kind of desperation. It was now or never… If Zac kissed her, she would surrender. She would give herself to him completely. Nothing else mattered.

Oh, how she longed for him to kiss her.

Fortunately, he was a mind reader.

With a hand beneath her chin, he lifted her face and touched his lips to hers and everything went wild. Their kiss flared from hello to explosive in a heartbeat and Chloe wound her arms around his neck, pressing close, turning to fire.

Neither of them spoke. It was as if they both feared that words might break the spell. This coming together was all about emotion and longing and heat…as their mouths hungered and their hands turned feverish…as clothing fell silently onto white carpet…as they stumbled in a lip-locked tango to the nearest bed.

For a fleeting second, as they landed together on the mattress, Chloe's more sensible self tried to slam on the brakes. But Zac was gazing down at her and he had that look in his eyes—a look that was a mix of heartbreak and surprise and unmistakable desire. A look that melted her.

And now his hand was gliding over her skin and

flames leapt to life wherever he touched. He lowered his lips to her breast and the longing inside Chloe bucked like a wild beast fighting to be free. All hope of resistance was lost…

Afterwards…the thrashing of their heartbeats gradually subsided as they lay side by side… And the silence continued…

Chloe couldn't find the right words. What did you say to your boss when you'd just shared blazing, uninhibited, mind-blowing sex with him? She had no idea, and it seemed Zac had been struck dumb as well.

Cautiously, she turned her face towards him. With equal caution, he turned to her and his eyes reflected the same shell-shock she felt.

They both knew this wasn't supposed to happen. They'd clarified on Saturday night that there were very valid reasons why this should never happen.

But now…their lovemaking had been so spontaneous, so flaming and passionate, it had taken them both by storm.

'Are—are you OK?' Zac asked gently, his words touching her skin and reaching into her heart, just as his kisses had, mere moments ago.

'Yes,' Chloe whispered.

He let out a huff of breath and a soft sound that might have been a sigh or the merest hint of a laugh. 'At least one of us is OK then.'

What did he mean? She knew she should ask, should at least say *something,* but she certainly wasn't willing to analyse the whys and wherefores of this, and she was still struggling to find the right words when Lucy woke with a lusty yell.

Grateful for the distraction, both Chloe and Zac rolled out of opposite sides of the bed and began to drag on clothes with the speed of commandos responding to an alarm.

'You can heat the formula,' Chloe said as she pulled her shirt over her head. Zac knew how to look after the formula now and he was quite expert at testing the temperature of the milk on the inside of his wrist. He was standing by with Lucy's bottle when Chloe had changed her nappy and re-dressed her.

'Why don't you feed her?' Chloe suggested, without quite meeting his gaze. 'I'll make a cup of tea.' OK, so perhaps it was another ploy to avoid talking to him about what had just happened, but the tea making had also become part of their surprisingly domesticated routine. 'Then you can tell me what you have planned for Christmas,' she added.

'Christmas?' Zac gave a soft, self-deprecating laugh. 'Went clear out of my mind.'

'And remember, don't let her guzzle,' Chloe warned, desperately needing to remain businesslike and matter-of-fact, but her thoughts were churning as she went to fill the kettle.

Zac found it hard to concentrate on feeding the baby. He had too much to think about. He'd always believed he was reasonably knowledgeable when it came to women and seduction. He'd also thought he knew his PA quite well. He'd been wrong on both counts and to say that he was stunned was putting it mildly.

He cringed now when he recalled accusing Chloe of being an old maid. Clearly, she was far more worldly than he'd ever dreamed. He didn't want to start making comparisons, but something amazingly spontaneous and earth-shatteringly good had happened just now. Something way, *way* beyond random meaningless sex…

No doubt he'd stuffed up the very fine working relationship he had with his PA, however, and that was damn stupid. At this point, he had no idea where to take things from here, but one thing was certain—he would have to think this situation through very carefully before he made another move.

Perhaps his Christmas plans would be a useful diversion. He'd pulled off quite a coup, managing to wangle tickets for the hotel's sumptuous Christmas banquet. There was to be a six-course menu with every delicacy imaginable.

He reckoned the best news was that he'd secured a properly certified babysitter for the entire afternoon. Of course, he'd had to pay an exorbitant sum for a sitter on Christmas Day and at such late notice but, with the help of the concierge, it was all settled.

He'd been really looking forward to sharing this news with Chloe, but now…a Christmas feast paled into insignificance after what they'd just shared.

As Chloe poured boiling water over tea bags, her mind was spinning. Why hadn't she remembered that leaping into bed with Zac was simply *not* an option? Clearly her brain had snapped. She'd fallen into the oldest trap—giving in to lust and confusing it with love.

Surely she knew better than that? She was opening herself up to all kinds of pain.

Zac was never going to love her, so the outcome could only be painful. After all, she'd experienced what it was like to truly love someone and to be loved in return. And she knew Zac's attitude to love was light years away from her own. He was focused on finding a wife from a database, rather than searching his heart.

Her problem was that she'd spent too much time in his company. She'd become too caught up in his personal life and, for a short time, she'd totally lost her perspective.

Her only choice now was to accept that she'd made a very silly mistake and then to forgive herself. Forgive and forget. That was what Zac would expect her to do and, with luck, she would survive the emotional fallout.

OK. She felt marginally better now that she'd thought this through. It meant she simply had to put her feelings for her boss on ice until she got back to Australia and then she should be safe. She would come to her senses. Surely that was a workable plan?

Their lunch of toasted ham, cheese and tomato sandwiches with coffee was a strained and quiet affair.

'I guess we should talk about…you know,' Zac said as he finished his second sandwich, but he still looked extremely uncomfortable.

Chloe drew a quick breath for courage. 'If you like… but I don't expect a post-mortem.'

'What about an apology?'

Shyly, she shook her head. They both knew this had been a two-sided affair.

'That's good,' Zac said. 'Because I wouldn't want to apologise for something so—'

He left the sentence unfinished, as if words were inadequate…or too revealing…

'Maybe it was inevitable,' Chloe said without looking at him. 'A guy and a girl in constant close proximity.'

When she looked up, she saw his puzzled smile. No doubt he'd expected tears and recrimination. That would have to wait till later when she was alone.

'Chloe, for the record, I'd like you to know that—' Zac hesitated again and his throat worked. 'It's so hard to express this properly, but you must know that kind of chemistry is pretty damn rare.'

Heat flooded her face. For her, their lovemaking had been astonishing, an outpouring of passion beyond anything she'd ever experienced—even with Sam—but she mustn't think about what that signified, or she'd end up with a broken heart. 'Maybe it's best if we don't say too much right now,' she said.

Zac nodded, a cautious smile still playing at the corner of his mouth as he picked up a final sandwich. 'A cooling-off period.'

'Yes.' She was too worried that she'd let her emotions show, that she'd burst into tears and make an awkward situation a thousand times worse.

'I'm sure that's probably wise,' Zac said, but he looked thoughtful, as if he was in the middle of a puzzle he hadn't quite solved. Then his expression lightened. 'Actually, to change the subject, I was wondering if we should brave the elements this afternoon and take Lucy for a walk.'

It was a brilliant idea. Chloe nodded enthusiastically. 'I think we're all in need of fresh air. If we put a little bonnet and mittens on her and bundle her in an extra warm blanket, she should be fine.'

Seemed they were both eager to hit the streets for a final Christmas shopping spree, and Chloe hoped fervently that the bustle of crowds and the dazzle of decorations would prove a very welcome distraction from her way too sexy employer.

'I'm keen to buy something for Lucy's first Christmas,' Zac said as they headed down Oxford Street. 'Any ideas?'

'I was thinking this morning, when Skye was madly taking photos, that it would be lovely to start an album for Lucy and to include shots of London.'

'Good thinking.' He didn't add *Ms Meadows* this time, but he was smiling again, almost back to the Zac of old. 'Lucy should have a record that begins right here with her very first Christmas.'

'I took photos of Skye and her friends with my phone. I'll email them to you, if you like.'

'Great. They should certainly be part of the record.' He definitely looked pleased. 'So an album's first on our list. What else? Liv already bought Lucy her first teddy bear.'

'Maybe you could buy her a gorgeous Christmas stocking while you're here, something that will become a tradition for her every year.'

'Yep, sounds good.' Zac trapped her with a private smile. 'Am I right in guessing you're a girl who likes traditions?'

'Possibly.'

For too long, they stood in the crowded and busy store, smiling goofily at each other until they realised they were blocking an aisle.

'And I think I'd like Lucy to have a little gold bracelet,' Zac said. 'I remember Liv used to wear one when she was a kid.'

'With a heart locket?' Chloe asked.

'Yes.'

She smiled. 'I had one of those too. I loved it, but I lost it once when my neighbours took me water-skiing.'

Zac's grey eyes shimmered and Chloe gulped. She was so susceptible to that look. 'What's the matter? Do I have a smut on my face?'

'I'm trying to picture you as a little girl.'

Her heart tumbled like a snowball on a very steep slope. 'Don't talk like that,' she said, almost begging him. 'Concentrate on the shopping.'

CHAPTER NINE

At breakfast on Christmas morning, when Chloe announced that she would like to go to church, Zac surprised her by saying that he'd like to come too.

'Church two days in a row?' she queried.

'I've been reading about St Paul's Cathedral.' Apparently, Zac was fascinated by the cathedral's history. It was rebuilt after the Great Fire of London in 1666, and then later survived the Blitz in World War II when most of the surrounding buildings were flattened in bombing raids. 'It's become a symbol of resurrection and rebirth,' Zac said. 'And that seems rather fitting for Lucy's first Christmas.'

Considering the sad and miraculous circumstances of Lucy's birth such a few short days ago, Chloe had to agree.

'I don't think another outing will hurt her, do you?' he asked.

'She should be fine. She was actually better last night after all that shopping.'

While Zac checked the times of the services, Chloe rang her parents, who had almost finished their Christmas Day in Australia.

'It was wonderful,' they gushed. 'The loveliest Christmas, Chloe. The chauffeur took us to church and then brought us back here in time for lunch. And, my goodness, you should have seen the spread. We've never eaten so well. Please give our love to Zac.'

'My parents are probably your biggest fans,' she told Zac as she hung up, and she felt unexpectedly happy at the thought of going off with him and Lucy to celebrate Christmas in St Paul's.

OK, it might feel like the three of you are almost a proper family, but don't get ideas, girl.

'We've time for presents before we go,' Zac announced as they finished their simple breakfast of coffee and croissants, in lieu of the banquet to come. With a boyish grin, he crossed to the wardrobe and produced a small package.

'Hang on.' Chloe dived for the floor and rummaged under her bed. 'I have a little something for you, too.'

It was also a small gift, but the shop assistant had worked magic with a square of green and white striped paper and a bright red bow. Chloe set the gift on the table in front of Zac, rather than placing it in his hand. Probably an over-the-top precaution, but after yesterday's 'mistake', she was super-conscious of the dangers of any skin contact with this man.

Zac, however, had no qualms about kissing her cheek as he handed her his gift. 'Merry Christmas, Chloe,' he said warmly.

'Thank you.' She knew she couldn't refuse to return his kiss, but she did this so quickly she barely touched his cheek. 'And Merry Christmas to you.' She nodded towards the little green and white package.

'Thanks!' He looked so genuinely delighted that she

wondered how he normally spent his Christmases. It was possible that, without close family, he was often quite lonely. The thought stabbed at her soft heart.

'Aren't you going to open it?' Zac had already freed the red ribbon and had started ripping into the paper.

'Yes, of course.' Her parcel was wrapped in pink and silver tissue and topped by a posy of tiny silk roses. 'But it's almost too pretty to open.'

Zac grinned. 'Go on, get stuck into it. I dare you.'

Chloe laughed. She was actually far more excited than she should have been, but a hand-selected gift from Zac was quite a novelty. Back in Brisbane, it was her job to order his corporate gifts for employees and business associates, as well as sending flowers and perfume to his girlfriends.

His gift to her usually came in the form of a Christmas bonus and, generous and welcome as this was, she couldn't help being curious about what he might buy when he made the selection entirely on his own.

There was a box inside the wrapping and it looked like a jewellery box. Chloe's heart fluttered and she shot a quick glance to see if Zac had opened his gift.

He was watching her and smiling. 'You go first.'

'All right.' She knew her cheeks were pink as she lifted the lid to find, nestling inside in a bed of cream silk, a solid gold chain bracelet with a heart-shaped locket. 'Oh, Zac, it's beautiful. It's just like Lucy's.'

'Hopefully, a grown-up version.'

'Yes, a *very* grown-up version.' Unlike the delicacy of the baby's bracelet, this one was solid and shiny gold and Chloe knew it had probably cost a small fortune.

'I almost bought you a necklace,' Zac said, 'but I

knew you'd lost your bracelet when you were little.' He gave a self-conscious little smile and shrugged. 'I thought you might like a replacement.'

This was so much more than a replacement. It was a gift that mirrored the one Zac had bought for his niece. It wasn't only expensive, it was *personal*…

There was a good chance Chloe's blush deepened. 'I'll love wearing this. Thank you.' On her wrist it looked perfect. Toning beautifully with her skin, it made her feel mega glamorous.

She looked pointedly at the box in Zac's hand. 'Your turn.'

'Ah, yes…'

Chloe held her breath as he lifted the lid on the silver cufflinks she'd bought him. She watched his face, saw the flash in his grey eyes when he recognised the significance, and his face broke into a delighted grin. 'Sea turtles!' His grin broadened. 'You remembered from the other night.'

'I loved your story about living on the island and I thought these were incredibly stylish but cute,' Chloe said. 'But I also thought they might bring back happy memories.'

'They do. They will. They're wonderful.' He looked as if he might have hugged her, but perhaps he'd picked up on her caution. Perhaps he was as afraid as she was that they'd end up in bed again, ravishing each other…

'Thank you, Chloe,' he said instead, but his eyes had that look again, the one that told her he was remembering every detail of their passion, the look that made her head spin and her insides tremble.

* * *

'I feel dangerously virtuous after all that carol singing.' Zac was in high spirits as they came back into the hotel room. 'I'm certainly ready to eat, drink and be merry.'

Chloe knew what he meant. She'd felt wonderfully uplifted by the beautiful music in the magnificent cathedral and it seemed somehow perfect to follow up with her first slap-up Christmas dinner in a posh hotel.

Just the same, Zac's flippant comment about dangerous virtue sent her thoughts off once again in inappropriate directions, which was probably why she made herself busy writing notes for the babysitter, double-checking with room service for the delivery of the sitter's special Christmas dinner, and ensuring that everything Lucy might need was already laid out for her.

'At least we'll only be a few floors away, so the sitter can call us if she has any worries.'

Zac pulled a face. 'I wouldn't encourage her to call.'

'But we have to leave her a phone number, Zac.'

'Oh, if you insist.' His smile was teasing again as he walked to the cot. 'You go and get ready, while I have a quiet talk to this child. It's time I delivered her first lecture. She needs to understand that we expect nothing from her but her very best behaviour.'

For Chloe, entering the hotel's special banquet room was like walking into the dining room of a royal palace. There was so much to take in—the high ornate ceiling and stunning red walls with huge mirrors that reflected back the splendour, a tall Christmas tree covered in fairy lights in the corner, candles everywhere in glass holders, chandeliers overhead.

Down the middle of the room stretched long tables covered in red tartan and set with sparkling glassware, shining silver, starched white napkins. The guests were beautifully dressed and Chloe was more pleased than ever that she'd lashed out on her expensive red number.

With a glass of Yuletide punch in her hand, Zac's lovely bracelet on her wrist and his tall, dark and exceptionally handsome presence at her side, she'd never felt more glamorous and confident.

She had such a good time. They met a lovely Canadian couple who'd come to England to track down their family history, two genial elderly Scottish brothers who apparently spent Christmas at this hotel every year, a group of New Zealanders…

There was even a famous American author called Gloria Hart, who was accompanied by a much younger man whom she openly introduced as her lover. Chloe had read a few of her books, so meeting her was quite a fan girl moment.

Gloria made a beeline for Zac and although she kept her arm firmly linked with her young man's, she made sheep's eyes at him, and then she turned to Chloe with a coy smile. 'I do like your young man,' she said. 'I'm almost jealous.'

'Ah, but I'm taken,' Zac said gallantly as he slipped his arm around Chloe's shoulders and dropped a proprietorial kiss on her cheek.

Chloe hoped her smile held. Zac probably had no idea that his simple gesture gave her lightning bolts of both pleasure and pain.

Champagne was opened as they all took their seats and settled in for a truly sensational meal. White-coated waiters brought the most amazing dishes—Colchester rock oysters, shellfish platters, roast middle white pork with winter jelly, roast goose with Brussels sprouts and all the trimmings. These were followed by mince pies, Christmas pudding, Ayrshire cream and cider and chestnut syllabub.

Fortunately, there was plenty of time between courses, plenty of laughter and storytelling. Zac, as always, drew more than his share of feminine interest, but he got on well with the men, too, and he was attentive to Chloe throughout the afternoon.

Like Gloria Hart, everyone assumed they were a couple. Chloe almost set them straight, but then she caught Zac's eye and saw an ever so subtle warning smile, as if he was urging her to leave things be. She could almost hear him say, *What's the harm in a little pretence?*

She just wished she could feel happier about it, wished she didn't mind that it was only a charade…

Of course, when she explained that the occasional texts she sent were to their sitter, it was also assumed that she and Zac were Lucy's parents.

'You've regained your figure so quickly,' one woman commented.

Chloe smiled her thanks and this time she avoided catching Zac's eye. But she couldn't help silly thoughts that began with the fireworks of yesterday's unforgettable passion and ended with the bleak sadness of *if only...*

Give up now, Chloe. You know it's never going to happen...and you're not in love with him. You can't be. She didn't want to fall in love again, couldn't bear to risk that kind of heartbreak. And falling for Zac could bring nothing but heartbreak. She knew him too well. *Just play the game. It's only for a few more hours and tomorrow you'll be on the plane, safely winging your way home.*

In the breaks between courses, people got up and moved about, mingling and chatting with other guests, going to the tall windows at the far end of the room to look out at the views across the park. Twice, Zac went back to the room to check on Lucy, which made Chloe smile.

The second time he left was just before their coffee arrived, and when he came back he hurried to Chloe and leaned close to her ear. 'Come with me,' he whispered.

Turning, she saw unmistakable excitement in his eyes and he nodded to the windows. 'I want to show you something.'

'What is it?'

His smile was the sort that made her ache inside. 'Come and see for yourself.'

Of course she was curious, so she excused herself from her neighbour and Zac grabbed her hand, hurrying her to the far end of the room.

'Look.'

Chloe looked and gasped.

Outside, it was dark, but the street lights and the lights of the buildings caught the dazzle of dancing, snowy white flakes. *Snow!* Real, no-doubt-about-it snow was falling silently, landing on tree branches, along railings and on the roofs of parked cars.

'Wow!' she exclaimed, gripping Zac's hand in her excitement. 'I've never seen snow before. Isn't it beautiful?'

'I thought you'd like it.'

'Oh, Zac, it's amazing. It's the perfect end to a perfect day.'

'I don't know how long it will last. I vote we skip coffee and go outside to dance about in it.'

'Yes, I'd love to. But we'll need to go back for our coats and gloves.'

'All sorted. I collected them while I was up checking on Lucy.'

Lucy. 'I forgot to ask. How is she?'

'She's fine, Chloe. The lecture I gave her paid off. She's a fast learner.' Zac slipped his arm through hers and gave a tug. 'Come on. Let's go.'

They made their farewells.

'It's snowing,' Chloe explained, which caused quite a stir. 'I'm afraid I've never seen snow before, so we're going outside. I want to catch the full experience.'

'Yes, off you go, lass,' one of the Scotsmen said. 'Although I should warn you that London doesn't have real snow.'

'Zac, make sure you keep Chloe warm,' called Gloria Hart.

They were laughing as they left amidst calls of 'Goodbye, lovely to meet you' and 'Merry Christmas'.

Chloe hadn't thought it was possible for her Christmas Day to get any better, but she was floating with happiness as Zac slipped his arm around her shoulders and they walked together along the paths in the park while the snow fell softly all around them.

'I'm going to wake up soon,' she said, holding out a red-gloved hand to catch a flurry of snowflakes. 'This is so magical. It's simply too good to be true.'

'It might not stay pretty, so I wanted you to enjoy it while it's fresh.'

She looked back to the hotel, where she could see the big window of the dining room, the twinkling lights of the Christmas tree and the chandeliers, and the silhouettes of people moving about inside.

'Thanks for dragging yourself away from the party

and bringing me out here,' she said. 'I would have hated to miss this.'

'So would I,' Zac said with a mysterious shy smile.

Even though it was dark now, the park was well lit and the space rang with the excited shouts and laughter of children and adults alike, making the most of the white Christmas. Chloe was zinging with excitement as she and Zac walked on, under bare-branched trees that now gathered white coats, and she loved the way he kept his arm securely around her…

They reached the far side of the park and were turning back when Zac said, 'Actually, while I'm in your good books, Chloe, I wonder if I could put a proposal to you.'

She frowned at this. Something about Zac's careful tone took the high gloss off her happiness. Thinking fast, she tried to guess what this proposal might be about. No doubt something to do with work, or with Lucy, or possibly with Marissa Johnson. She certainly hoped it wasn't Marissa. Not now. Not today.

'What kind of proposal?' she asked cautiously.

'Actually, I was thinking of a marriage proposal.'

Chloe's reaction was inevitable. Her silly heart toppled and crashed.

'Your proposal to Marissa?' She knew her shoulders drooped. She thought Zac had more tact than to bring this up now and spoil Christmas Day.

He gave a soft groan and came to a standstill. 'No, Chloe. This has nothing to do with Marissa.' He was standing in front of her now, blocking her path, as white flecks of snow floated onto his shiny black hair. 'I want to ask you to marry me.'

Chloe struggled to breathe as she stared at him and a cyclone of emotions whirled chaotically inside her, stirring all the longing she'd ever felt for him, along with the confusion and pain, the sympathy and tenderness.

For a giddy moment she allowed herself to picture being married to Zac and of course her silly brain zapped straight back to yesterday's lovemaking and she was instantly melting at the thought of a lifetime of fabulous sex.

And she thought about Lucy. The baby was now an inevitable part of the Zac Corrigan package, and Chloe knew she would adore taking care of the little girl and stepping into the role as her mother. And then there was Zac's business which Chloe knew inside out and was almost as passionate about as he was.

For so many reasons his proposal felt right. But, oh, dear heavens, she had to be careful. She had to remember that this gorgeous, kind and generous man was also the playboy she knew all too well. As far as she could tell, Zac had no real concept of being faithful. As for love... for crying out loud, until five minutes ago, he was planning to pick his prospective wife from a spreadsheet.

Chloe shivered inside her warm coat. 'Don't play games,' she said wearily. 'Not today, Zac. Please, don't be silly.'

He gave an angry shake of his head. 'Why do you always assume I'm playing games? I'm absolutely serious. Think about it, Chloe. It makes so much sense.'

'Sense?' Her eyes stung and it wasn't from the cold.

'I thought you liked to be sensible.'

Oh, give me a break, Zac. How many girls want to be sensible about romance?

But the question wasn't worth voicing. 'So why is this so sensible?' she demanded instead. 'Because I tick most of the boxes on your checklist?'

Zac looked surprised. '*Most* of the boxes? Chloe, you tick every single one of them. Actually, I'd have to add extra boxes for you. You're an amazing girl.'

'And I'm so good with Lucy,' she added flatly.

His smile wavered. 'Well, yes,' he said as if this was obvious.

Oh, Lord. Chloe couldn't hold back a heavy, shuddering sigh. *Please, please, don't let me cry.*

Zac stood very still now, watching her with troubled eyes. He wasn't wearing his scarf and she could see the movement of his throat as he swallowed uncomfortably. 'I've stuffed this up, haven't I?' he said quietly.

Fighting tears, Chloe gave a helpless flap of her hands. 'Maybe you got carried away after the luncheon today, when everyone assumed we were married.'

Now, with his hands plunged into his coat pockets, he tipped his head back and stared up at the dark sky. He sighed, releasing his breath in a soft white cloud. 'Give me some credit, Chloe.'

She could feel the weight of the gold bracelet around her wrist, reminding her of their happiness this morning when they went to church together and opened their presents. She hated that this had happened, hated that they were so tense now, on the raw edge of a fight, at the end of this beautiful, perfect day.

'Can I ask you a difficult question, Zac?'

He looked doubtful, but he nodded.

'Are you honestly in love with me?'

'Honestly?' he repeated, looking more worried than ever.

'There's no point in lying,' she said bravely. 'I know we've been pretending to others all day, but I need brutal honesty now.'

There was a long uncomfortable silence as Zac stood staring at her, his silver-grey eyes betraying a haunted uncertainty. He seemed to try for a smile and miss, then he said, 'I told you I don't really believe in "love".' He made air quotes around the word. 'And I'm afraid that's the truth. I think it's a dangerous illusion.'

Lifting his hands, palms up, as if protesting his innocence, he smiled. 'But I really like you, Chloe. As I said before, I think you're amazing. And you can't deny we have fabulous chemistry.'

A sad little laugh escaped her. Here she was in the perfect romantic setting for a marriage proposal, and instead she received a sensible, practical, *logical* proposal without a glimmer of romance.

Zac's eyes were shiny as he watched her. 'So…I take it that's a no then?'

Oh, Zac.

She had an eerie sense of time standing still. She felt so torn. She knew this was her big chance to be reckless and brave and to grab a wonderful opportunity. She had no doubt she could give her heart to Zac and to Lucy, along with her loyalty to ZedCee Management Consultants.

But the big question was—what could she expect from Zac in return? A comfortable, entertaining, possibly exciting lifestyle…until his interest in her waned.

She was far too familiar with the pattern of Zac's love life. When it came to women, he had the attention span of a two-year-old, and if Chloe was ever going to risk love again, she needed certainty. She needed a man who could bring himself to say and mean those dreaded words: *I love you.*

'I'm sorry,' she said, fighting tears. 'I'm still an idealist. A romantic, I guess.'

'So you want an admission of true love *as well as* brutal honesty? *And* you want both from the same man?' Zac shook his head and it was clear he believed she was asking for the impossible.

Inevitably, the day ended on a low note.

There was no reassuring arm around Chloe's shoulders as they went back to the hotel, where they shook out their snowy coats and took the lift upstairs to find Lucy fast asleep and the sitter about to watch the Queen's Christmas message on TV.

So they watched the royal message with the sitter and then she left them with some reluctance, assuring them that she'd had a lovely day.

And Chloe left, too, going next door to remove her make-up and to change out of her red dress. She put the bracelet back in its box, and stowed it in her already packed suitcase. Then she added the dress, carefully folded between sheets of tissue paper.

Although she wanted to cry, she forced herself to be strong as she cleaned her teeth, creamed her face and brushed her hair.

A faint *'waa...'* from next door warned her that Lucy was awake so, although she really didn't want to face Zac again this evening, she went back to his room to help with the evening feed, which was often the most difficult and colicky time.

However, the baby settled quickly, even before Zac and Chloe had drunk their ritual cuppas, but Chloe didn't join Zac in the armchairs for a cosy chat.

'I'll get on with Lucy's packing,' she said, knowing

they would need to head for Heathrow soon after breakfast in the morning.

Taking up space in the middle of the room, Zac managed to look spectacularly manly and helpless. 'Anything I can do to help?'

'Probably better if I look after it,' Chloe muttered, ducking around him. 'I have a list.'

He smiled crookedly. 'Of course you do.'

She was so anxious and edgy and sad, she was glad of an excuse to keep busy, collecting scattered items like a baby sock from behind a cushion, a bib from beneath a pillow, and sorting out exactly what they'd need for Lucy on the journey. She packed a special carry-on bag with baby bottles, formula, nappies, wipes and several changes of clothes. Then she double-checked all their passports and travel documents.

'I've already checked those papers,' Zac said.

'Doesn't hurt to check again.'

Now that she'd rejected his marriage proposal and their final evening was ruined, she was extra keen to be on her way. If there was a hitch at the airport tomorrow—anything that meant they couldn't leave the UK—she was likely to have some kind of breakdown.

She wanted to be home. She needed to be caring for her boring sweet parents, needed to get her life back to normal as quickly as possible. Once she was safely home, she would put this London experience and everything that came with it behind her. Once again she would be nothing more than Zac Corrigan's highly efficient and more or less invisible PA. As always, she would co-ordinate his private life as well as his business affairs, while she secretly turned up her nose at his *Foolish Females*.

CHAPTER TEN

ZAC WAS BEGINNING to suspect that Lucy could pick up on their vibes. Tonight he and Chloe were both as tense as tripwires, and Lucy was fussier than ever after her next feed. It was close to midnight before she settled back to sleep.

'We're going to have a hell of a trip home if she's like this tomorrow night,' Chloe commented tiredly.

'It will help if we make sure we're relaxed.'

'Relaxed?' The word snapped from Chloe like a rifle shot and, out of the corner of his eye, Zac saw the baby flinch.

He sighed. 'Look, I apologise if I've spoiled your Christmas. I know I've upset you.'

'Of course you haven't upset me. I'm fine.' Chloe's eyes were unnaturally wide as she said this and she promptly made an about-turn and headed for the door.

'Where are you going?'

She gave an impatient shrug. 'It's probably best if I sleep in my own room.'

'You really think that's going to help?'

'Help what?' she shot back with a scowling frown.

Was she being deliberately obtuse?

'Help *us*,' Zac said patiently. 'This walking on eggshells tension.' He had visions of a twenty-two-hour flight back to Australia without resolving whatever bugged her.

At least Chloe gave a faint nod, as if she acknowledged this, then she leaned her back against the door and folded her arms over her chest and speared him with her nut-brown gaze. 'So you're saying that you need to talk about our relationship—or rather our lack of a relationship?'

'Well, from my experience, talking things over is usually what girls want.'

She smiled. Damn, even when the smile was glum, she looked incredibly lovely when she smiled. Zac had to work hard to curb his impulse to cross the room and haul her into his arms. He wanted to relight those wild flames again. Taste her lips, her skin, feel her going wild with him. Hell, how could he ever forget that blazing encounter?

How could he forget how much he'd loved having her around on a twenty-four hour basis? He'd never met a girl he felt so comfortable with. Until he'd wrecked things with his clumsy proposal, sharing his personal life with Chloe had felt so unexpectedly *right*...as if their personalities slotted magically together like one of those Chinese puzzles...

'So what do you think we need to talk about?' Chloe asked.

'To be honest, I'm not totally sure, but it sure as hell can't happen if you're on the other side of that wall.'

Now she lifted her hands in a gesture of surrender. 'OK. No big deal. I'll stay here. I'm actually very tired, though.'

'The talk's not mandatory,' he said, feeling ridiculously relieved by this small victory.

Nevertheless, after they both got into their separate beds, he could see, via the faint glow of Lucy's night light, that Chloe remained, as he was, lying on her back with her hands beneath her head, staring up at the ceiling.

It wasn't long before her voice reached him through the darkness. 'So what do you want to talk about?'

There was no mistaking the distrust in her tone.

Zac couldn't help smiling to himself. 'I thought I was supposed to ask that question.'

'But I've already told you. I don't have any issues. I'm perfectly fine.'

This was patently not true. Since they'd arrived back from the park Chloe had been tearing about like a wound-up toy on top speed.

'But I must admit I don't understand *you*,' she said next.

Zac had heard this comment before from women. Had heard it with regular monotony, if he was honest.

'I mean,' Chloe went on in that earnest way of hers, 'I don't understand why you're so convinced that falling in love is nothing but a fairy tale.'

She wasn't going to let go of this. Clearly, it was at the heart of her tension.

'Well, OK,' he said smoothly. 'Convince me otherwise. I'm assuming you have a vast experience of falling in love?'

'I don't know about vast,' she said. 'But I was certainly in love with my fiancé.'

Whack.

Zac's smugness vanished as surprise juddered through

him like a jack-hammer. How had he never known about her fiancé? More importantly, why hadn't Chloe said something about this guy when she so quickly and forcefully rejected his proposal?

Although he'd tried to make light of her rejection, her loud and clear *no* had stung. Zac had felt as if he was standing at the door of Aladdin's Cave, where the glittering riches and jewels represented a chance for a lifetime's happiness and contentment.

Heaven help him, he'd actually pictured a home with Chloe and Lucy and then, just when this dream was within his reach, the portcullis had slammed down, cutting him off from his vision of happiness.

Now, he said, 'I...I didn't realise you were engaged.'

'I'm not any more,' Chloe said softly. 'My fiancé died.'

Another shock. Despite the hotel's perfectly controlled heating, Zac was suddenly cold. 'Hell. I'm sorry. I had no idea.'

'I wouldn't expect you to know. It happened before I started working for you.'

'Right.' He swallowed uncomfortably as he absorbed this news.

Lying there in the dark beside her, it occurred to him that his assumptions about his PA had been entirely based on the image she presented at the office, but over the past few days that image had been crumbling and now it was blasted clear out of the water. 'Is it OK to ask what happened?'

After a small silence she said, 'Sam was a soldier—a Special Forces soldier. He was killed in Afghanistan.'

Zac swore and then quickly apologised. But this was almost one surprise too many. Special Forces soldiers were so damn tough and daring—the most highly skilled—which meant that Chloe had been about to marry a real life hero. 'I had no idea,' he said lamely.

'I don't like to talk about it.'

'No, I guess it must be hard.'

From the bed beside him, he heard a heavy sigh.

'I was a complete mess when it happened,' she said. 'That's why I came home to live with my parents. I didn't want to go out like other young people. I just wanted to hide away and…and grieve. I guess it wasn't exactly a healthy reaction.'

'But understandable.'

He heard the rustle of sheets as Chloe rolled to face him. 'Anyway, for what it's worth, I did love Sam. For me it was very real, an inescapable emotion. I suppose it was an attraction of opposites, but it worked for us. We were very happy and we had big plans for a family and everything.'

'That's…great…'

Zac had no idea what to say, but thinking about Chloe and her soldier made him feel inexplicably jealous… and depressed…

Inadequate, too. He understood now why Chloe had rejected him. She thought he merely wanted a mother for Lucy.

Damn it, he should have tried to express his feelings more truthfully but, chances were, anything he offered now would be a very poor second best to her true romance with her heroic soldier.

And if he tried to tell her how he really felt, how his days were always brighter when she was around, how, even at home in Brisbane, the weekends so often dragged and he couldn't wait till Monday mornings to see her again, it would sound crazy, as if he was in love…

'Are you asleep, Zac?' Chloe's voice dragged him back from his gloomy musings.

'Sorry. Were you saying something?'

'Now I've spilled my story, I was asking about you. Are you still going to insist that you've never fallen in love?'

His mind flashed to that one time in his past when he'd been young and deeply in love, with his head full of dreams and his heart full of hope. Until…

No. He never talked about that. He'd worked hard to put it all behind him and he wasn't going there now.

Chloe, however, was waiting for his answer.

'Well, yeah, sure I've been in love,' he told her with a joviality he didn't really feel. 'Hundreds of times.'

This was met by silence… It was ages before Chloe spoke and then she said quietly, 'That's exactly the answer I expected from you.'

After that she rolled away with her back to him. 'Goodnight, Zac.'

Her fed-up tone left him with the strong conviction that their conversation hadn't helped either of them and he knew he was going to have trouble getting to sleep.

Damn. The last thing he wanted was to lie awake remembering Rebecca…or what was now far worse—wrestling with regrets about Chloe…

The flight was scheduled for midday and both Chloe and Zac were nervous about how Lucy would behave during the long hours that stretched ahead of them.

To their relief, their fears were unfounded. When Lucy was awake the flight attendants seemed to love fussing over her, and when she slept the droning hum of the plane's engines seemed to soothe her into a deeper slumber.

'She's gorgeous and such a good baby,' several of the female passengers told Chloe. 'You're so lucky.' Chloe could tell from the way their eyes wandered that they considered Zac to be a major component of this luck.

Of course, Chloe thanked them and once again she didn't try to explain that she was neither Lucy's mother nor Zac's wife. But afterwards…she had to try to ignore the gnawing hollowness inside her, the annoying regret and second thoughts that had plagued her ever since she'd turned down Zac's proposal of marriage.

She knew she was going to miss Lucy terribly. In these few short days, she'd lost her heart to the baby. She'd grown to adore her, to love the feel and the smell of her, to love her bright curious eyes and hungry little mouth. When Zac wasn't looking, she'd even given Lucy little baby massages, following the instructions she'd read in one of the magazines.

As for Zac…despite the many strict lectures she'd delivered to herself, she felt desperately miserable whenever she thought about the end of this journey…when they went their separate ways. She'd grown so used to being with him twenty-four hours a day, to sharing meals with him, sharing middle of the night attempts to calm Lucy, listening to him in those quieter moments when he'd felt a need to talk a little more about Liv.

As for making love with him…Chloe's thoughts were seriously undisciplined when it came to *that* subject. She spent far too much time torturing herself by recalling every raunchy detail of going to bed with Zac…before firmly reminding herself it would never happen again.

'A penny for your thoughts.'

Chloe blushed. 'Excuse me?'

Zac leaned closer. 'You had your worried look, Ms Meadows. I wondered what was bothering you.'

She had no idea what to say. 'Um…I wasn't thinking about anything in particular.'

'Lucky you,' Zac murmured, leaning closer still.

'Why am I lucky?'

'You're not being tormented the way I am. I can't stop thinking about how much I want to kiss you.'

'Zac, don't be crazy. You can't start kissing on a plane.' Was he no longer bothered that she'd rejected his proposal?

'Why not?' he asked with that winning smile of his. 'They've dimmed the lights and no one's looking.'

So tempting…

'You want to, don't you?'

'No,' Chloe whispered, but she knew she didn't sound very convincing. No doubt because it wasn't the truth. She wanted nothing more.

When Zac leaned even closer and touched his lips to her cheek, she felt her whole body break into a smile. Instinctively, she closed her eyes and turned to him so her lips and his were almost touching. He needed no further invitation. His mouth brushed over hers in a teasing whisper-soft kiss that sent warm coils of pleasure spiralling deep. Chloe let her lips drift open and she welcomed the slide of his tongue.

'Mmm…' With a soft sound of longing, she moved as close to him as possible, kissing him harder…losing herself in the strength and the taste and the smell of him.

'I love you,' he whispered and wave after wave of happiness welled inside her. Everything was all right after all. It was OK to love Zac. There was no reason to hold back.

She slipped one hand behind his neck to anchor herself and then she nudged her leg against his, as she was seized by a hot and feverish longing to climb into his lap.

'Chloe?'

Zac's questioning voice sounded quite loudly in her ear.

Chloe blinked. Her head was on Zac's shoulder. Her hand was curled around his nape. Her knee was hooked over his thigh. When she pulled back to check his face, he was staring at her with a strangely puzzled smile.

'What happened?' she asked.

'I think you fell asleep.'

Oh, my God. Had she been dreaming?

Cheeks burning with embarrassment, Chloe whipped her hand away and swerved back into her seat. 'I…I'm so sorry. I have no idea how that happened.' With a soft moan she sank her face into her hands.

'Hey, don't worry,' she heard him say. 'I'm already wishing I didn't wake you up.'

Chloe lowered her hands from her face. 'How long was I—?'

'Climbing all over me?'

She cringed. 'Yeah.'

'Only about ten minutes or so. I'd say there were only about a dozen people who walked past.'

She stared at him in horror. 'They saw me?'

But Zac was grinning hard now and she realised he was teasing her. She gave his arm a punch. 'You're a lying rat, Zac Corrigan.'

Her embarrassment lingered, however. Even if half the people in the cabin hadn't seen her draping herself all over Zac, *he* knew all about it. She thanked her lucky stars that he hadn't pushed her for a proper explanation. But what must he be thinking?

They were finally flying over Australian soil, although it would still be several hours before they touched down in Brisbane.

Chloe had just come back from the changing room with Lucy, and Zac was waiting with the heated bottle the flight attendant had delivered.

'Do you want to do the honours?' Chloe asked him.

'Sure.' He held out his arms for the baby and Chloe's heart had a minor meltdown as she watched the tender way he smiled at his niece.

'You know,' he said, as he settled Lucy in his arms and carefully tipped the teat into her eager little mouth, 'I hate to think about trying to do this on my own when I get home. It won't be the same without your help.'

Chloe closed her eyes against the pang of dismay his comment aroused. She was going to miss this, too, more than she could possibly have imagined. When she opened her eyes again, the sight of Zac and Lucy together was beyond gorgeous.

In moments like this, the temptation to retract her rejection of Zac's proposal was huge...until she remembered that he only wanted her because she was good with Lucy...and possibly because their chemistry was undeniably hot. Was she crazy to believe these reasons weren't enough?

She thought about Sam and the way he'd made her feel and the many ways he'd showed her that he cared...just through little things like gifts or a surprise invitation, or the way he held her close. Of course, those gestures weren't all that different from Zac's behaviour, really. And the annoying thing was there were times when she felt even closer to Zac than she ever had with Sam.

Truth to tell, during the two years Chloe had known Sam, he'd spent a good proportion of the time on deployment in Afghanistan. So she was certainly better acquainted with Zac, with his good and bad habits, his strengths, hopes and fears. His belief that love was an illusion…

This thought sobered Chloe. 'You'll find some other woman to help you,' she said.

'Not straight away. That will take time to arrange.'

'Well, yes, I doubt that even you could manage to pull off a wedding inside a week, Zac. You'll need to hire a sitter or a nanny for the interim.'

'And that won't be easy in the week between Christmas and New Year.'

Chloe slid him a sideways glance. 'You'll manage.'

'So you wouldn't consider it?' he asked, trapping her once again with his clear grey gaze.

'Consider what, exactly?'

'Helping me out for a few more days?'

She should have seen this coming, should have been prepared, but she'd thought, after her rejection, that Zac would back right off.

'Chloe?'

'I don't know,' she said. 'I'm thinking.'

'I've plenty of bedrooms,' he went on, offering one of his customary coaxing smiles. 'You could have your own room and we could put Lucy in the room next door to you.'

'Where would you be?'

'Just down the hall a bit.' Now he had the cheek to

grin at her. 'Safely out of your way, but near enough to be on call to help with Lucy.'

If she thought about it rationally, without her silly emotions getting in the way, his request was probably reasonable. As long as this wasn't the thin end of the wedge…

'So what's your plan, Zac? You're still planning to… to…get married, aren't you?'

Chloe saw an unreadable flicker in his eyes, but his face was deadpan. 'I still think that's the preferable option.'

'And Marissa's the preferable candidate?'

'I guess so, yes.' His tone suggested that he still needed to give this serious thought. 'But I know I'll have important groundwork to do before I can convince her. At the moment, I don't even know if she's still available.'

'So it could take some time…'

Zac set the baby's bottle on the tray table while he gently lifted Lucy onto his shoulder to help her to bring up her wind. 'I wouldn't expect you to stay at my place for too long, Chloe. Just for a night or two, till I get my bearings.'

'My parents might—'

'Your parents are welcome to stay on at the hotel, as long as they're enjoying it.'

'Oh, they're enjoying it all right.'

'Then, would you consider it?'

The last thing Chloe needed was more time in Zac's company. What she needed was distance. Time and space to regroup and to clear herself of her tangled thoughts and emotions. But then she looked at Lucy. Zac had shifted her onto his lap and she was curled over his big hand as he gently rubbed her back. She was such a dear little thing and she looked so cute now.

'I wonder if Marissa likes babies,' she found herself saying.

Zac lifted a dark eyebrow. 'I have no idea. I guess that's one of the many things I'll have to ask her.'

Chloe had never been to Zac's penthouse apartment, perched high in an inner city tower block. He'd project-managed its construction and it was a striking piece of architecture with views up and down the Brisbane River—all very shiny and modern with high gloss timber floors, large expanses of glass and a flashy granite and stainless steel kitchen.

By the time they'd emerged from Customs it was too late to try to go shopping for baby gear, so they went straight to Zac's place and made a snug nest for Lucy by pushing two black leather lounge chairs together and then lining the space with a quilt.

'She looks impossibly tiny, doesn't she?' Lucy said as they stood looking down at her.

'Yeah.' Zac reached down and softly stroked Lucy's dark hair. 'Welcome home, tiny girl.'

The love shining in his eyes brought a lump to Chloe's throat. Then he straightened and his eyes were still shiny as he smiled at Chloe.

'There's a restaurant downstairs,' he said. 'I could send down for a takeaway meal.'

'I'm not especially hungry.' She would blame jet lag for her low mood, but from the moment she'd arrived she'd felt on the verge of tears.

'Maybe just one serving to share?' Zac suggested. 'Something light? They do great chilli prawns.'

Which was how they ended up on that first night, sitting on his balcony with a fresh breeze blowing up the river, eating chilli prawns and washing it down with a glass of white wine, while they enjoyed the city lights.

'You must love living here,' Chloe commented as she watched pretty ladders of light stretch across the smooth surface of the river.

'It's been great,' Zac admitted. 'At least it's been very handy for a bachelor.'

'Party Central?'

'At times, yes.' But Zac was frowning. 'I'm not sure I'd like to stay here with Lucy. She'll need a backyard with swings and other kids in her street to play with.'

'That safe suburban life you dream of,' Chloe suggested with a tired smile.

'Exactly.'

'Do you think you'll find it hard to adapt to that kind of life?'

'I guess that depends on who I can convince to come and live with us,' he said quietly and there was just enough light for Chloe to see the way his gaze flashed in her direction.

Without warning, her throat was choked and her eyes were stinging, spilling tears.

'Chloe.'

She threw up her hands. 'It's just jet lag. I need to hit the sack.' Already she was on her feet. 'Thanks for the prawns, Zac. They were delicious.'

'Don't get up when Lucy wakes,' he called after her. 'I'm not too tired. I'll be fine.'

'OK, thanks.' She kept her tear-stained face averted. 'See you in the morning. Goodnight.'

Of course, after that, Chloe took ages to get to sleep. She tossed and turned and agonised about Zac, but when she finally nodded off she slept deeply and soundly. She woke to find bright daylight streaming through the crack between her curtains and from below she could hear the sounds of city traffic.

Feeling guilty about spending an entire night without helping, she sprang out of bed and hurried to the lounge room, but the baby wasn't in her makeshift cot.

Chloe shot a hasty glance to the kitchen. An empty baby's bottle stood on the granite counter, but there was no other sign that Zac had been up and she couldn't hear any sounds from within the apartment. Quickly she dashed back to her room to check the time. It was only just coming up to six o'clock, much earlier than she'd expected, but of course the sun rose super-early in Brisbane in midsummer.

And where was Lucy?

She tiptoed down the hallway towards Zac's room, then stood listening for Lucy's snuffles and snorts.

Nothing.

She knew it was silly to panic, but where Lucy was concerned her imagination leapt into overdrive. Something had happened. Lucy was ill. Zac had rushed with her to a twenty-four-hour medical centre.

Having thoroughly alarmed herself, she dashed into Zac's bedroom. And came to a skidding halt.

He was sound asleep, lying on his back. And Lucy was in the bed beside him, while another empty baby's bottle stood on the bedside table.

Chloe found herself transfixed as she looked down at them—the great big man and the tiny baby girl. Zac had kicked the sheet off and he was only wearing a pair of black silk boxer shorts, which allowed her a perfect opportunity to admire his broad bare chest, his muscular arms and shoulders, the smattering of dark hair narrowing down to the waistband of his shorts.

She couldn't help reliving her amazing experience of being up close and personal with that toned and golden body.

'Morning.'

His deep voice startled her. She'd been so busy ogling him, she hadn't noticed that he'd woken.

'I…I was just checking to see where Lucy was,' she stammered.

Zac grinned sleepily. His eyes were mere silver slits, but she knew he'd caught her checking him out. Then he sat up, scrubbed a hand over his face and blinked at the baby beside him. 'I didn't mean to bring her back here, but with the jet lag and everything…' He frowned as he leaned closer to check the tiny sleeping girl. Her tummy was moving softly up and down as she breathed. 'Thank God I didn't roll on her.'

'When's she due for another feed?' Chloe was eager now to shoulder her share of the duties.

Zac squinted at the bedside clock. 'I'd say in about another hour.'

'You should go back to sleep then. If she wakes I'll deal with her.'

'Sounds great. Thanks.' He was smiling as he flopped back onto the bed.

As she left Zac's room, Chloe hoped he hadn't been keeping tabs on her recent 'lapses'. First there'd been her attempt to climb all over him in the plane, then her tears last night, and now this morning's ogling. Surely these added up to highly inappropriate behaviour from a girl who had flatly rejected him?

* * *

It was a difficult day. They had to drag themselves around while their body clocks readjusted, and between snatches of sleep they made phone calls. Chloe rang her parents and Zac rang Marissa. His phone call took ages. Chloe had no idea what transpired and her curiosity was killing her but Zac chose not to tell her, which was appropriate, of course, now that she was simply his PA again. In the afternoon they went shopping for the necessary baby gear.

They aimed for an early night and fortunately Lucy co-operated. While Chloe put through a load of washing, Zac cooked their dinner, making a fair fist of grilling steaks on the balcony barbecue. He served them with mushrooms and beans and they ate the meal outside again, enjoying the warm evening and the city lights.

'Wow,' said Chloe as she tucked in. 'This is delicious, Zac. You've put lemon and chilli on the beans, haven't you? And some kind of herb on the mushrooms?'

He ducked his head towards the attractive cluster of potted herbs on his balcony. 'I sprinkled a little thyme over them.'

'Hmm.' Chloe speared a succulent mushroom with her fork. 'I think I've uncovered a dark horse, Zachary Corrigan.'

'What makes you say that?'

'You're actually a closet chef.'

He lifted a gorgeous black eyebrow.

'You are, aren't you, Zac?'

This brought an embarrassed smile. 'Closet chef? That's a big statement to make after sampling one hasty meal.'

'Hasty or not, this meal is sensational.' Chloe sliced

off a tender corner of steak. 'But I actually have further evidence. I checked out your pantry and fridge.'

'When?'

'While I was stowing away Lucy's formula.'

'So you've been spying on me?'

'I couldn't resist a little snooping. Sorry, it's a bad habit of mine, but I have a thing about fridges and pantries. You see, they tell so much about a person—in the kitchen, at least. And, well, I noticed you keep a French brand of Parmesan and an Italian brand of risotto, and you have all these bottles of Thai and Vietnamese sauces and about three different types of olive oil...'

'So?'

'Zac, you know very well that only a serious cook would bother.'

'I like to eat.' He shrugged. 'And cooking's actually relaxing...'

Relaxing? This was such a surprise Chloe laughed. 'And here I was, imagining that you ate out every night.'

'No way. Only every second night.'

They smiled at each other across the table. It was a smile of friendship and understanding and...something far deeper...which made Chloe feel all shivery and confused again.

'Do you like to cook?' Zac asked her.

'Well, I usually cook for my parents, but they only like very plain food like shepherd's pie or—' She stopped. This conversation was becoming far too intimate. It was making her feel closer to Zac when she was supposed to be stepping away.

CHAPTER ELEVEN

CHLOE WAS GIVING Lucy her bath when Zac left, shortly after breakfast.

'See you later,' he said, ducking his head around the bathroom doorway.

Unhappily guessing that he was heading off to see Marissa, Chloe forced brightness into her voice. 'You might heighten your luck if you take her flowers and chocolate.'

Zac frowned. 'I guess…'

'Marissa likes Oriental lilies and ginger chocolate.'

'How do you know these things?' he asked, but then he gave a soft humourless laugh. 'Don't tell me. It's all on a spreadsheet.'

'Naturally.' Chloe wished him luck but, as soon as she heard the apartment's front door close behind him, her face crumpled and she was overwhelmed by the most devastating, painful loss.

Zac was gone. She'd thrown away her very last opportunity and this was the end.

She felt cold all over as she scooped the baby out of the water and wrapped her in a fluffy bath towel.

'Oh, God, Lucy,' she whispered. 'You know what I've done, don't you? I've just thrown away the chance to be your mummy. And I've lost my very last opportunity to be with Zac.'

A terrible ache bloomed in her chest as she hugged Lucy to her and breathed in the scent of her clean baby skin. 'Honestly, Luce, I was only trying to be sensible. I can't marry a man who doesn't even know if he loves me.'

But how could I have known that being sensible and letting him go would still break my heart?

Misery washed through her, as cold and bleak as when she'd lost Sam. She carried Lucy through to the spare bedroom, now designated as the baby's nursery, and laid her gently on the new changing table, part of the furniture she and Zac had bought yesterday. Carefully, she patted the baby's skin dry and sprinkled and smoothed talcum powder into her creases. She picked up one of the tiny singlets and slipped it over Lucy's head, before angling her arms through the holes.

Luckily, she'd done this many times now because the entire time she worked her mind was miles away. With Zac. She was picturing his arrival at Marissa's, making his charming apologies or doing whatever was necessary to placate her, and then inviting her out. They would probably go to the beach. Chloe could imagine them walking hand in hand along the sand at the water's edge, or having a drink at a bar overlooking the sea. Zac would be at his alluring best as he explained the sad situation that had left him with Lucy. By the time he'd finished, Marissa would be putty in his hands.

Of course she would want to marry him.

And Chloe couldn't bear it. Couldn't bear to think that Zac would marry a woman he didn't love—and who probably didn't love him, simply to provide a mother for Lucy. How could he be such a fool?

She finished dressing the baby and took her through to the kitchen to collect a bottle of formula from the fridge. As she waited for it to heat, she paced restlessly, agonising over her own foolishness. And Zac's foolishness, too.

Surely he was deceiving himself when he claimed that he didn't believe in love? For heaven's sake, she only had to think back over the past few days to see all kinds of evidence of Zac's love in action.

He'd gone above and beyond the call of mere duty for Liv and for Lucy, but he'd also gone out of his way for Chloe as well. Not just with lovely gifts like the bracelet and the Christmas banquet, although she knew these were more personal and special than the gifts Zac usually bestowed on his women—but, beyond that, he'd also been thoughtful and considerate and kind. And fun.

Both in and out of bed…

Chloe wondered now, too late, if she should have given Zac a chance to explain his vision of the marriage he'd proposed. She'd simply jumped to conclusions and assumed he would continue to play the field.

But if she thought about the past week, when she'd been with him day and night, she couldn't really fault his behaviour. Actually, if anyone had misbehaved, she had. She'd practically thrown herself into his arms on that day they'd made love.

Now, as she went back to the kitchen to collect the heated bottle, she was more depressed than ever. She couldn't believe she'd brought this pain on herself and she'd thrown everything away because she'd needed to hear three stupid words from Zac. Hadn't she known all along that words were easy? Actions carried so much more weight...and Zac's actions had said so much... but now she'd lost him and she had no one to blame but herself.

'I hope I don't weep all over you,' she told Lucy as she settled in an armchair to feed her. 'I don't want to upset you. Don't take any notice of me, will you, darling? I'll try to stop thinking about him.'

It was impossible to turn her thoughts off, of course. She figured that by now Zac would be well on his way to the Gold Coast—too far down the expressway for her to phone him with some weak excuse that would bring him back. She had tried to be sensible one time too many, and as a result she felt as bereft and as heartbroken as she had when she lost Sam.

And Lucy had already finished her bottle.

'Sorry!' Chloe felt all kinds of guilty as she set the bottle aside and lifted Lucy to her shoulder. She hadn't been paying attention and she'd let the baby feed too quickly. Now the poor darling would probably be in pain.

Chloe stood, hoping that a little walking up and down would do the trick, but she was only halfway across the lounge room when the doorbell rang.

'Who on earth could this be?' she complained, sounding scarily like her mother, and as she went to open the door she dashed a hand to her face and hoped it wasn't too obvious that she'd been crying.

A young woman stood on the doorstep—a very pretty young woman with long blonde hair and the kind of slender figure that came from living on lettuce leaves and very little else. She was wearing strong perfume, tight floral jeans and a tiny tight top that revealed a toned and tanned midriff, as well as a silver navel ring.

The girl's jaw dropped when she saw Chloe and Lucy. 'Who are you?' she demanded.

'Are you looking for Zac?' Chloe asked in response.

'Yes. What's happened to him?' The girl looked genuinely worried. 'He just took off and he's been away for the whole of Christmas.'

'There was a family emergency and he had to rush to London.' Chloe felt obliged to explain this, even though she had no idea who this girl was. She certainly wasn't one of Zac's regulars. 'Zac's sister died,' she said.

The girl frowned, clearly struggling to take this in. 'That's sad. So are you a relative then?'

'No, I'm Zac's PA and this is his little niece, Lucy.'

'His PA? I think you rang Zac last week. Yes, it was you, wasn't it? And then he went racing off.'

'Yes, it was all terribly sudden.' Chloe realised this had to be the girl who'd answered Zac's phone on that fateful Wednesday night. She'd pretended to be answering from a Chinese takeaway.

'I'm sorry to hear about his sister,' the girl said.

'It was terrible,' Chloe agreed just as Lucy pulled up her knees and began to wail loudly.

'I take it Zac's not here now?' The girl raised her voice to be heard above Lucy.

'No. I'm not sure when he'll be back.'

'I guess I'll just have to keep trying his mobile then.'

'I'm not sure that's a good idea,' Chloe responded hastily. 'Not today. He's...he's still very busy.'

The girl pouted. 'Well, can you at least tell him that Daisy called?'

'Of course I can, Daisy. I won't forget. Nice to meet you.'

Lucy was distraught as Chloe closed the door. 'Oh,

sweetheart, I'm so sorry.' She began to pace, jiggling the baby gently. 'I'm afraid I know how you feel. I want to wail along with you.'

Back in the lounge room, she tried sitting with Lucy in her lap. Zac had perfected the art of burping her this way and Chloe willed herself to forget about her own woes and to concentrate on comforting the baby. She was rewarded by a massive burp.

'Oh, wow! Good girl. Aren't you clever?' She kissed the baby's downy head and cuddled her close and she sat there for a while, enjoying the warmth and snuggling closeness. But she was close to tears again as she took Lucy back to her brand new cot and tucked her in. She set the teddy bear that Liv had bought where Lucy could see it and then she tiptoed away.

From the doorway she looked back. 'I'm going to miss you so much.'

She waited for an answering wail, but the baby remained silent. When Chloe stole back into the room to double-check, Lucy's eyes were already closed. Chloe went back to the lounge room and collected the empty bottle, took it through to the kitchen…

Now what?

Unfortunately, the answer came almost immediately. Her next task was to write her letter of resignation.

She gave an agonised groan as this thought hit home. But she had no choice. It had to be done. She couldn't continue as Zac's PA now that she'd become so intimately involved in his personal life. She cared too much about Lucy *and* about Zac and she would care too much about the personal choices Zac made in the future.

And how could she pretend that their blazing lovemaking wouldn't always be there between them? A teasing, haunting memory. How could she ever forget that amazing spontaneity and passion? Heavens, if she stayed in Zac's office, she might find herself hoping it could happen again.

For that reason alone, she had no choice but to leave. It would be untenable for her to continue working for Zac after he was married to Marissa.

She hoped he would see that, too.

She should act immediately, draft a resignation now and have it ready for when he returned. She could type it on her phone, could even email it straight to Zac. With luck, he would accept it without too much argument.

It was so hard, though… Chloe felt sick as she started to type.

She began with *Dear Mr Corrigan,* then deleted it and replaced it with *Dear Zac.* Her hands were shaking, her thumbs fumbling on the keys as she forced herself to continue.

It is with deep regret…

Again she stopped and deleted. She had to keep this businesslike.

I wish to advise that I am resigning from my position as Personal Assistant to the Managing Director of ZedCee Management Consultants.

The terms of my contract require two weeks' notice for the termination of employment from either party. I will make myself available to assist in a smooth transition for my replacement.

Chloe pressed her hand against the new ache that flared just beneath her ribs, then she continued to type…

I've enjoyed working at…

She stopped and let out another soft groan. What was the point of telling Zac that? He knew only too well how much she'd loved her job. Better to just ask him for a reference.

Did she want a reference? She supposed she should have one, but she hated the thought of having to hunt for another job…

As she began to type again she heard a noise… Once again, it was coming from the front door…

Another caller?

This time there was the unmistakable sound of a key turning in the lock…

Not another of Zac's girlfriends? Chloe wasn't sure she could face another of Zac's blonde beauties. And it seemed that this one had privileged status and her very own key.

Wincing as she set her half-written letter aside, Chloe got to her feet. Her *bare* feet.

She couldn't remember the last time she'd checked her appearance in a mirror and there was every chance she had baby dribble on her T-shirt, and if this woman had a key she was sure to be at least as glamorous as Daisy. Chloe was madly finger-combing her hair as she heard footsteps coming down the hallway. She braced herself for a vision of sexy high fashion.

She had the words ready. 'I'm sorry, but Zac isn't—'

The figure coming into the lounge room was tall and

dark and exceptionally masculine. Chloe's heart almost stopped.

'Zac?'

'Hi.' He dropped his keys into a pottery dish on the low entertainment unit, and then he set down a pot of bright red double gerberas and a box of chocolates. He looked pale, almost unwell, and deep lines furrowed his brow and the sides of his mouth.

'What happened?' Chloe had visions of a highway smash. 'Is everything all right? Did you get as far as the Gold Coast?'

'No.' Zac stood in the middle of the room with his hands on his hips. His chest expanded as he drew a deep breath.

Something had clearly gone wrong. Had Marissa refused to see him?

'Is there anything I can do? A cup of—'

A faint sad smile briefly tilted a corner of his mouth. 'All I need is for you to listen, Chloe. There's—' his Adam's apple rippled as he swallowed '—there's something I need to tell you.'

The growing knots of anxiety in Chloe's stomach tightened as Zac turned, looked around his lounge room, almost as if he was seeing it for the first time. Then he took a seat in the chair opposite her, and he leaned back against the smooth leather upholstery as if this could somehow help him to relax.

He was wearing jeans and a white shirt, unbuttoned at the collar and with the sleeves rolled back. Despite the crackling tension, Chloe couldn't help admiring the way his dark hair and bronzed skin contrasted so gorgeously with the whiteness of his shirt.

'I hope you haven't had more bad news,' she said gently.

'No, just a painful revelation.' Again, he cracked the faintest glimmer of a smile, before he dropped his gaze and traced the arm of the chair with his fingertips, as if he was testing the texture of the leather.

Chloe tried not to notice how beautiful his hands were, so long-fingered and strong, and she struggled to banish unhelpful memories of his hands touching and caressing her, driving her to rapture.

'I didn't go to the Gold Coast,' he said. 'Actually, I have a confession. Almost as soon as I dialled Marissa's number yesterday, I knew that proposing to her would be a huge mistake, but then I had to spend the next hour coming up with a crazy explanation for why I'd rung her...and then more time trying to wriggle out of seeing her again.' He gave a wry smile as he shook his head. 'It was yet another of my famous stuff-ups.'

Chloe swallowed nervously, unsure what to say.

'I'm sorry I gave you the wrong impression, Chloe. I should have set you straight this morning when you mentioned the flowers, but I wasn't ready to explain.'

'It's not really my business.'

Zac smiled at her then. 'Of course, Ms Meadows.' Then his expression was serious once more as he said, 'Truth is, I've been walking the streets, trying to clear my head and think everything through.'

Chloe nodded. This was understandable. He'd had next to no privacy in the past few days.

'You asked me in London if I've ever been in love,' he said next, somewhat abruptly.

In an instant her skin turned to goosebumps. 'Yes, I did.'

'I said I hadn't, but I lied.'

Oh. Chloe couldn't think what to say, but her heart had begun to pound so loudly now that she was sure Zac must be able to hear it.

'I was in love once, a long time ago,' he went on quietly. 'It was in my first year at university.' His shoulders lifted in a shrug. 'I guess it was first love, or puppy love, or whatever, but it certainly felt real at the time.' He looked away to the far window and its views of the sunny city skyline. 'Her name was Rebecca and I was crazy about her.'

Chloe had no idea why Zac had come back with flowers or why he was telling her this, and she certainly couldn't risk trying to guess, but she was so tense now she thought she might snap in two.

'Of course, I had all these dreams,' he went on. 'Nothing flash. Just the usual—marriage, family, happy ever after…'

The things he no longer believed in.

'Then my parents disappeared,' he said. 'And my life changed overnight. I felt I had to give up university and get a job, and take on the responsibility of looking after Liv. I needed to be home for her on the weekends and in the evenings. I didn't have time for a social life, so I put my dreams on the back burner.'

'And you broke up with Rebecca,' Chloe guessed.

'Yes.' He gave another crookedly cynical smile. 'She soon took up with another guy and within two years she married him.'

Oh, dear.

Chloe could see it all so clearly… Zac's world had been turned upside down when his parents disappeared… He'd sacrificed his dreams, only to be rewarded by heartbreak…

But as she sat there, listening and watching him and not daring to analyse why he was telling her this, she realised something so surprising that she gasped and felt quite giddy…

Surely, Zac's whole playboy persona had been a reaction to this heartbreak? After he'd lost his parents and his first girlfriend—a girl he'd genuinely loved—he'd been desperate to save his little sister. But then Liv had proved rebellious and Zac had responded with his own form of rebellion—his never-ending procession of *Foolish Females.*

Playing the field had been Zac's way of escaping, of protecting himself from ever being hurt again…

Of course it was far safer to never fall in love. Chloe knew this only too well. She'd been doing the same thing in a different way. After Sam's death, she'd avoided a social life, with its accompanying risks and pain, by hiding away and caring for her parents.

Oh, Zac. Her heart ached for him as she watched him now, as he drew another deep, nervous breath and let it out with a sigh.

She wondered if his current dilemma was her fault somehow. Had he realised that Marissa would also expect a declaration of love…and that, for him, it was still a step too far…

'So does this mean…?' she began, but then she stopped, uncertain of how to voice her thoughts diplomatically.

Zac looked across at her, not quite smiling. 'The long-winded point that I'm trying to make is that I do know what it's like to love someone and to lose her.'

'Yes, but that shouldn't—'

Chloe stopped again as the silent message in Zac's eyes made her heart thump so loudly she was sure he must hear it. She was poised on the edge of her seat now and she held her breath, not daring to say anything more, not daring to wonder, even fearfully, where exactly this revelation was heading.

Without warning, Zac launched to his feet again.

'I walked over the bridge and into the city,' he said. 'One of my mates is a real estate agent and I was going to ask him to look out for a place for Lucy and me.'

Chloe nodded miserably. Zac had decided to take responsibility for Lucy after all—without 'using' one of his women. It was an important step forward for him and she knew she should be pleased.

He forced an edgy smile, then turned and picked up the pot of red gerberas. 'I didn't get as far as my mate's office. I walked past a florist's.' The flowers trembled in Zac's hand. He was shaking and Chloe couldn't bear it.

'There were all these lilies in the window. You'd told me to get lilies for Marissa, but I suddenly knew: if I bought flowers for anyone, it had to be for you.'

She could barely hear him now over the ridiculous thundering of her heartbeats and it was almost impossible to see him through her tears.

'But I had no idea which were your favourites,' Zac said. 'I don't have a spreadsheet for you, Chloe.' He gave her another of his gorgeous crooked, sad smiles. 'But these made me think of your red dress and…and I hope you like them. Anyway, I had no choice. I had to bring them back to *you*.'

She was shaking, pressing a hand to her mouth…

'I was hoping to…to have another shot at that proposal.'

Now Chloe was on the edge of her seat, so tense she could only bite her lip as tears filled her eyes.

'I…I think I might have given you the impression last time that I only asked you to marry me because you would make a good mother for Lucy. And you would—you'd be perfect, but that's not why I need you, Chloe. That's so, so wrong.'

She swiped at her stupid, blinding tears. She wanted to see him—*needed* to see him. Oh, dear Lord, he looked so worried.

'The truth is,' Zac said, 'I reckon I've probably been in love with you since you first arrived in the office. I guess I just wouldn't let myself admit it, but I love being around you, Chloe. I love seeing you, whether you're serious or happy, or telling me off. I love hearing your voice. I love asking your advice. I even love drinking your damn cups of tea… I know it sounds crazy, but I hurry to work each day, just to see you.'

She thought of all those mornings that she'd looked forward to, too… Zac almost always arrived early, around the same time that she did and they always shared a little harmless light conversation. He would crack a joke, talk about something he'd heard on the news as he was driving to work, share a little gossip about one of their competitors. Drink the tea that she made.

Those mornings, before the rest of the staff arrived, had been her favourite time of day and now she could feel the truth of his claim filling her with light. Golden light was flooding her from the toes up, filling her chest, her arms, her head.

'No, it doesn't sound crazy,' she told him.

Zac swallowed. 'No?'

'I've felt the same about you.'

His eyes widened. 'You have?'

She felt brave enough to tell him now. 'Hopelessly in love from Day One. Probably ever since my job interview.'

For a trembling moment they stared at each other while this astonishing truth sank in. Then Zac set down the flowers and held out his arms and at last—at *last*—Chloe flew to safety.

As she hurled herself against him, his arms came around her, holding her preciously close. 'Oh, Chloe, I do love you. So, so much.'

'I know, I know.' She pressed her face against his shoulder, loving that she now had the right to be there, in his arms, leaning in to his strength.

'But I need to apologise about the way I carried on with the rubbish about romance and delusions,' Zac persisted. 'I was deluding myself. I *know* love's real. It's how I feel about you. Standing outside that florist's, I couldn't breathe when I realised I was losing you. I love you so much.'

He pulled back to look into her eyes. 'You do believe me, don't you?'

'I do, Zac.'

'Honestly?'

'You've already shown me in so many ways.'

'Oh, God, I hope so.'

There were no more tears now as she kissed his jaw, his cheek.

'Oh, Chloe.' Framing her face with his hands, Zac touched his lips to hers and his kiss was so tender and lingering and loving, Chloe thought she might actually swoon with an excess of happiness.

It was some time before their kiss ended and she nestled her head against his shoulder again. 'You were right,' she said. 'We don't need the words.'

He gave a soft laugh. 'But I want to say them now. I'm not scared of them and it feels so good. I'm going to tell you every day that I love you.' With gentle fingers, he traced the line of her cheek. 'Isn't it incredible that we've both been waiting? Why did it take us so damn long to work this out?'

'We're both sticklers for office protocol?'

This brought one of Zac's beautifully devilish grins and, a beat later, he slipped one arm around Chloe's shoulders, then a hand beneath her knees as he literally swept her off her feet. 'Stuff the protocol, Ms Meadows.'

He was already halfway to the bedroom.

EPILOGUE

AT FIRST, WHEN Chloe woke, she forgot what day it was. She lay very still with her eyes closed, enjoying the warm stream of the sunlight that filtered through the poinçiana tree outside the bedroom window.

Then she rolled towards Zac, reaching for him…only to find an empty space in the bed. Her eyes flashed open and she saw their bedroom, bright with summer sunlight, saw the little silver tree on the dressing table, the red glass tumblers holding the tea light candles that she'd lit last night. She'd had so much fun decorating the house for Christmas.

Zap. She sat up with a jolt as she remembered. This was it. Christmas morning.

How on earth could she have slept in? She'd been looking forward to this day with an almost childish excitement.

Now there was no time to waste. She had to see if Lucy was awake and she needed to know what Zac was up to.

Throwing off the sheet, she smiled at her new Christmas pyjamas—a red T-shirt teamed with cotton pants decorated with bright green holly and red bows. Although Chloe had always loved Christmas, this year she'd probably gone a trifle overboard, with decorations in every room of the house as well as extra details like special tablecloths and napkins for their Christmas dinner. She'd even bought special festive coffee mugs. Luckily, Zac didn't seem to mind.

Now, she ducked into Lucy's room. 'Merry Christmas, baby g—'

The cot was empty and Chloe felt a stab of disappointment, but she quickly squashed it as the smell of coffee wafted from downstairs…and then, as she descended, she heard the deep rumbling voice that she knew so well…

'And this is a special ornament that Mummy bought last Christmas in Selfridges in London… You were there, too, you know, pumpkin. Such a teensy little thing you were then…and it was wintertime and cold, not sweltering and hot like today… And over here under the tree are all the lovely presents… No, no, hang on. You can't rip them to pieces just yet. We can't open them till Mummy wakes up…'

At the bottom of the stairs now, Chloe caught a glimpse through to the lounge room and she stopped to admire the view of Zac and Lucy together. Zac was balancing Lucy on his hip with the practised ease of an expert and the baby was chuckling and reaching up to grab at a bright decoration. When she couldn't reach, she tried to squeeze his nose instead.

In response, Zac ducked, then playfully pretended to nibble Lucy's hand, which made her squeal with delight.

Chloe grinned. She never tired of seeing these two together. Over the past year they had formed a very special bond that boded very well for the future.

Lucy had grown into such a cute little bundle of mischief. She was a sturdy and determined one-year-old, now, and her hair was a mass of glossy dark curls, her eyes a bright, vivid blue. And she was constantly breaking into the most wonderfully happy smiles.

In Zac's strong arms, however, she still looked small and vulnerable…but safe. So wonderfully safe.

'And up here is something incredibly important,' Zac told the little girl as he pointed to a bunch of greenery in the doorway. 'This is a VIP plant that I have to show your mummy. It's called mistletoe and it's a tradition. Your mum's very fond of tradition…'

Chloe smiled again and felt a flush of pure, unfiltered joy. Soon it would all begin—the exchange of presents, the feasting, and sharing the day with her parents…

It would be quite a simple Christmas compared with last year's cathedral and banquet, but for Chloe this felt like the perfect end to a year that had been wonderful in so many ways—bringing happiness beyond her wildest dreams. At times it had seemed almost too good to be true and she'd had to pinch herself.

Of course, the three hundred and sixty-five days since their Christmas in London hadn't been a total bed of roses. In fact, the year had started off quite busily, and Chloe had spent most of January learning to balance caring for Lucy with helping a new PA to settle into her job.

Zac had been worried that Chloe might be bored with staying at home full-time and so they'd experimented with hiring a babysitter, who minded Lucy for one day a week while Chloe worked on the ZedCee files from her home office. It had worked well. Chloe loved being Lucy's mum, but she also found it rewarding to keep in touch with projects that had nothing to do with nappies or feeding schedules.

Then, in March, they'd moved out of the inner city apartment and into their contemporary two-storey home in the leafy suburb of Kenmore. They'd had a ton of fun house-hunting together, and they loved this house. With Zac's assistance, Chloe's parents were resettled two blocks away, in a lovely cottage in a retirement complex.

Chloe visited them almost every day, often walking there and taking Lucy for an outing in the pram. The little girl loved her Grammy and Gramps, and of course Hettie and Joe Meadows were utterly smitten by the baby, and they were completely shameless about their hero worship of Zac.

The wedding had been in June. Zac and Chloe had chosen a simple ceremony on the beach with a select group of friends and Chloe's misty-eyed parents. Afterwards, Zac and Chloe had flown north to Hamilton Island and, naturally, they'd taken Lucy with them. It was all quite magical.

There'd been tough days too, of course, times when Zac's grief for Liv had caught up with him, but it helped that Chloe had been through her own dark days of grief and she understood.

She'd been worried when Lucy's first birthday drew near, knowing that it coincided with a very sad anniversary. But six days ago the three of them had taken the ferry across to Stradbroke Island and there, while Lucy crawled on the sand and tried to chase tiny crabs, Chloe had watched as Zac paddled alone on a surfboard, out beyond the breakers. He'd taken a bunch of yellow roses and the small urn with Liv's ashes…

Afterwards, they'd stayed on the beach, playing with Lucy and talking quietly, remembering their journey to London…and Zac had shared one or two memories of Liv…

Eventually, Lucy had fallen asleep in Zac's arms and so they'd stayed there, sitting together on the warm sand and watching the distant horizon until the last of the daylight faded into the black of night…and the moon rose, bright and golden and full of new promise…

'I'd like to come here every year,' Zac had said. 'Liv loved this place…and…and I reckon it helps.'

'Yes, it's important,' Chloe had agreed. Somehow, the sea and the wind, the wide open sky and the reassuring crash and thump of the surf seemed to help to soothe Zac's pain. 'We should definitely make it a tradition.'

Now, Zac turned and caught sight of Chloe at the bottom of the stairs.

'Hey,' he cried, his face lighting up. 'Lucy, look who's awake!'

'Mumma!' the baby girl shouted as she held out her chubby arms.

Still holding Lucy, Zac hurried over and slipped an arm around Chloe and kissed her. 'Merry Christmas, my bright-eyed girl.'

'Merry Christmas.' Chloe couldn't resist stroking his lovely bare chest. 'I hear you've been educating Lucy about Christmas traditions.'

'Like mistletoe?'

'Uh-huh.'

His eyes shimmered with secret amusement as he smiled at her. 'If you'd been listening carefully, you would know that there are one or two other traditions I'm reserving just for you.'

Chloe grinned. It was a promise she would definitely hold him to.

* * * * *